THE CITY OF TURQUOISE AND GOLD

TALES OF CASTLE RORY

BOOK 8

R. MARSDEN

Hurogol Press

SHIELD AND MOTTO

Book Cover by Bespoke Book Covers

Published by Hurogol Press 2025.

ISBN: 978-1-917063-15-9 (Paperback Edition)

ISBN: 978-1-917063-16-6 (Ebook Edition)

Hurogol Press

To Will and Kerry, two of my favourite people.

CONTENTS

JOIN THE HOUSEHOLD!

Join The Castle Rory Household — an exclusive and free club for my newsletter subscribers!

Members of The Household will receive
Mansurah: Jonny's Tale,
an ebook *only* available to The Household.

You'll also get my newsletters, full of exciting medieval facts, quizzes, stories
and background information.

All you need to do is
click here to subscribe to my newsletter
and that's it, you're in!

If you would like to know more about Lord Rory's adventures,
please go to: www.talesofcastlerory.co.uk

ALSO BY R. MARSDEN

Tales of Castle Rory

Book 1: The Box of Death

Book 2: The Soldier of Fortune

Book 3: The Man in the Moon

Book 4: The King's Ransom

Book 5: The Paradise Garden

Book 6: The Foucois Legacy

Book 7: The Minstrel's Daughter

Book 8: The City of Turquoise and Gold

Book 9: The End of Time

All books in the series can be found at

https://mybook.to/TalesOfCastleRory

MANSURAH: JONNY'S TALE

Exclusively available to members of
The Household:
Mansurah: Jonny's Tale

Your free e-book when you join
The Household!

To join **The Household**, go to
https://talesofcastlerory.co.uk/

You will be able to download your free book immediately!

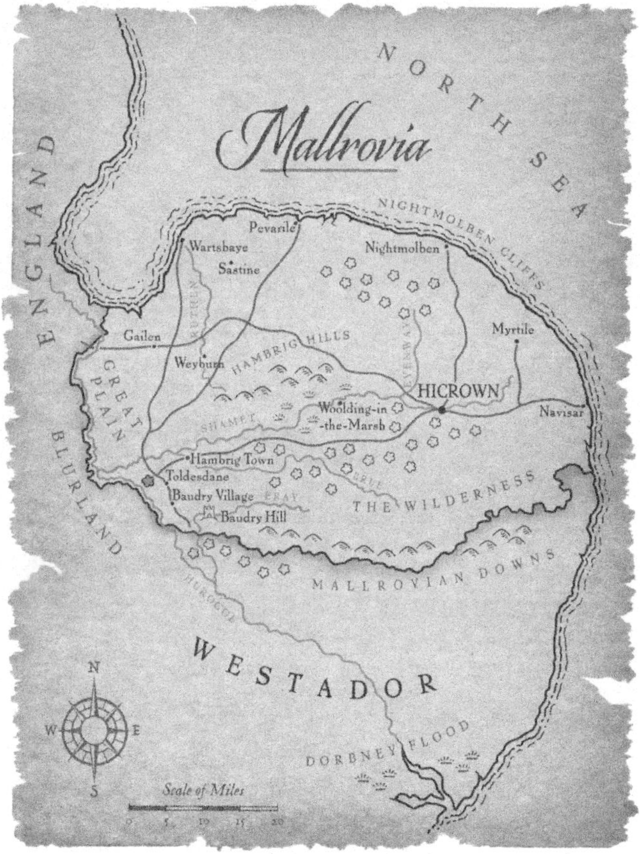
Mallrovia
NORTH SEA
ENGLAND
NIGHTMOLBEN CLIFFS
Pevarile
Wartsbaye
Sastine
Nightmolben
Gailen
HAMBRIG HILLS
Weyburn
Myrtile
HICROWN
Navisar
GREAT PLAIN
Woolding-in-the-Marsh
Hambrig Town
Toldesdane
Baudry Village
Baudry Hill
THE WILDERNESS
BLURLAND
MALLROVIAN DOWNS
WESTADOR
DORBNEY FLOOD
N
W
E
S
Scale of Miles

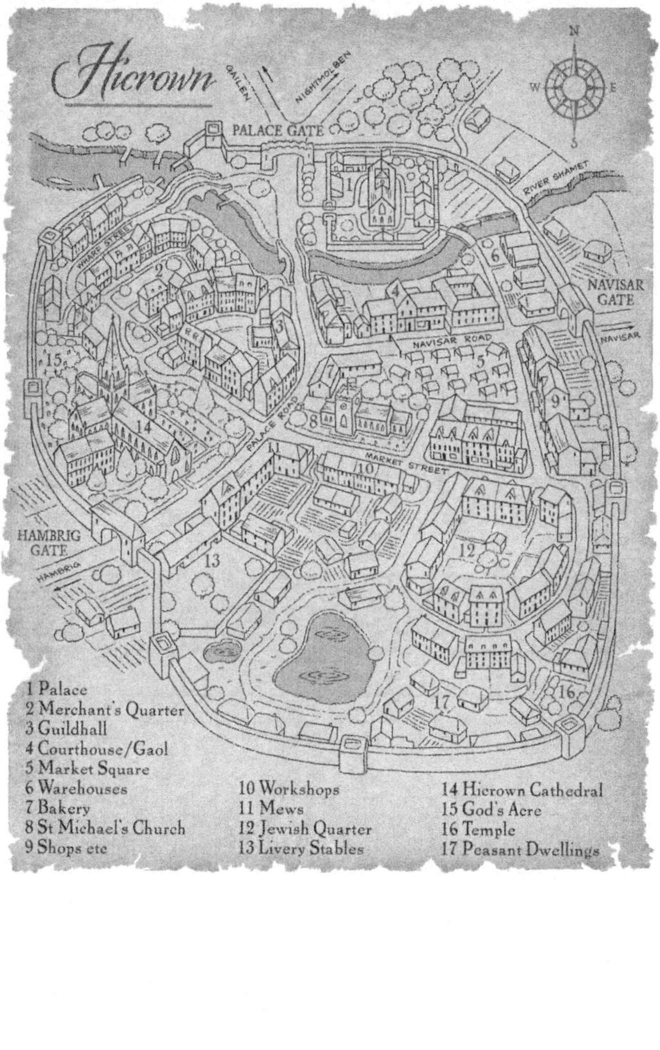
Hicrown
GAILEN
NIGHTMOLBEN
N
W
E
S
PALACE GATE
RIVER SHAMET
WHARF STREET
NAVISAR GATE
NAVISAR
NAVISAR ROAD
PALACE ROAD
MARKET STREET
HAMBRIG GATE
HAMBRIG
1 Palace
2 Merchant's Quarter
3 Guildhall
4 Courthouse/Gaol
5 Market Square
6 Warehouses
7 Bakery
8 St Michael's Church
9 Shops etc
10 Workshops
11 Mews
12 Jewish Quarter
13 Livery Stables
14 Hicrown Cathedral
15 God's Acre
16 Temple
17 Peasant Dwellings

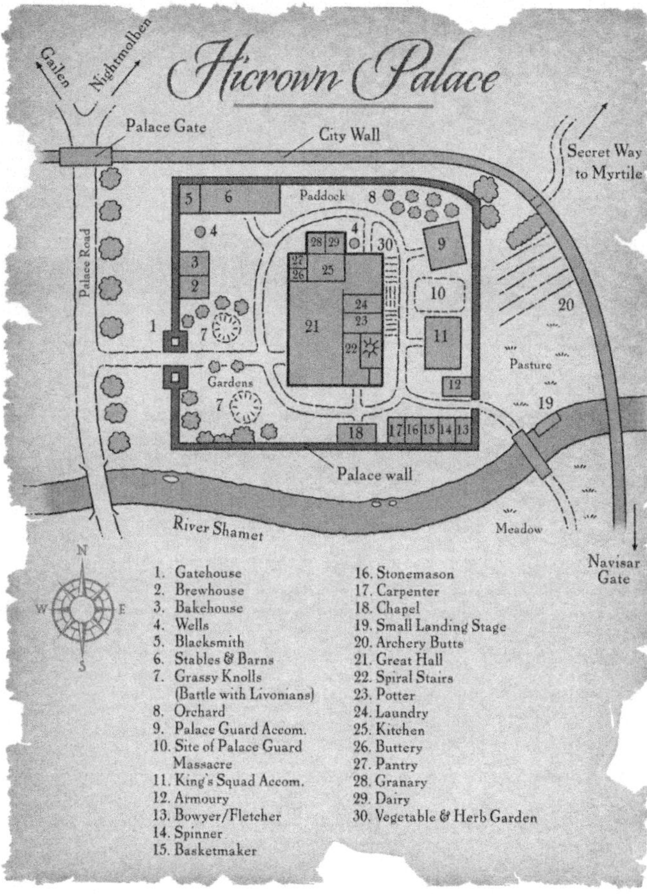
Hicrown Palace
Galen
Nightmolben
Palace Gate
City Wall
Secret Way to Myrtile
Palace Road
Paddock
Gardens
Pasture
Palace wall
River Shamet
Meadow
Navisar Gate
N
S
W
E
1. Gatehouse
2. Brewhouse
3. Bakehouse
4. Wells
5. Blacksmith
6. Stables & Barns
7. Grassy Knolls (Battle with Livonians)
8. Orchard
9. Palace Guard Accom.
10. Site of Palace Guard Massacre
11. King's Squad Accom.
12. Armoury
13. Bowyer/Fletcher
14. Spinner
15. Basketmaker
16. Stonemason
17. Carpenter
18. Chapel
19. Small Landing Stage
20. Archery Butts
21. Great Hall
22. Spiral Stairs
23. Potter
24. Laundry
25. Kitchen
26. Buttery
27. Pantry
28. Granary
29. Dairy
30. Vegetable & Herb Garden

PROLOGUE

March, AD 1215–October, AD 1229

He can't believe how rich he is. Too rich. How could anyone own this much? The coins lie gleaming inside two massive chests, and he steps mindlessly between them, staring, just staring. He thought there was just one chest, and for years he assumed it held farm implements. When he opened it he was astonished to find the money. An absolutely *enormous* amount of money. But then he discovered the *second* chest, hidden in a dark corner, and larger even than the first. He can't begin to count the wealth the two of them hold.

He looks around the old farmhouse. It has belonged to his family for generations, and they farmed the land, which is good and fertile, but not quite so good, nor quite so fertile, that it can yield such a dividend. He lets his fingers push through the coins, feeling them dribble back onto all the others, letting them flow like water from his cupped hands. He even considers taking off his clothes and dipping his whole body into this, his wholly unexpected inheritance. But he's much too sensible to do that. Instead, he thinks.

It's exactly two weeks past his seventeenth birthday, and he's known very little of life, besides his first seven years spent on this farm, and the next ten years living with his dead mother's sister in the village of Sastine. Which is where he'd hoped to stay. He has no desire to be a farmer, nor to lord it over the poor serfs who worked the land for his father. He's seen their hovels, the way they live, owning nothing. *Being* owned, rather. Even as a seven-year-old, he noticed how his father used and ill-treated them. He wants nothing to do with it, and would have been happy to stay away for ever.

Yet here he is, his father dead and buried, and now he's the owner of all these men and women, all this land and *all this money*. More money than he thought one man could ever have in a lifetime. Therefore, he has decisions to make.

Because he is that sort of person, he does not rush into deciding anything. He sleeps in the farmhouse and lets the serfs get on with their work. During the day he rides around the farm, looking at everything. When he gets home, he writes descriptions of all he has seen. In the evenings, he visits his serfs and talks to them. At first, they are suspicious. They are not used to their master 'popping in' for a chat. Then they try to take advantage of him. He's very young, after all. So they whine and wheedle and ask for all sorts of rubbish. He takes it all in good part, and diligently writes everything down, which seems to impress them.

And still nothing happens. Still he sits, and thinks, and reads his notes, and thinks again. Then he rides off to the capital city to find some people to talk to, and all the while the farm labourers are wondering what will happen and what's going on and what their fancy new young master is up to. When he returns, it's with a large number of men. It seems he's found himself an architect, some stonemasons and a group of carpenters. They are, he tells his people, the very best.

The first thing 'the very best' do is build themselves a large hut in which to work, eat and sleep. This hut has a bench, and the architect sits at the bench with his pen, his rule and his compass, together with copious supplies of parchment, and the young owner of the farm goes and stands behind him and watches and comments and slowly, slowly, the design takes shape. Meanwhile, the stonemasons cut their blocks, the carpenters saw down trees and the master builder oversees everything.

Eventually, the young master gets all the labourers together in a field and addresses them as if from a pulpit in church. He is tall anyway, but he chooses to stand on a platform which his carpenters have made especially for this announcement. And afterwards, as the young man steps down and nods slowly to his team, he knows his people are with him and the work can begin. The dingy, dirty dwellings will be demolished. The labourers, however, will still labour. There is a great deal of work to do, and it will take a long, long time. *Years*, they all tell themselves. It will literally take *years*.

It takes precisely fourteen years, three months and three weeks. Many of the older labourers never see the final result. Others do, and their children will never know anything else. For the young visionary has built a city. In this city, everyone will have a house, and everyone will have a job. In this city, no one will be hungry and no one will be poor. The young man is no longer quite so young. He is now thirty-one. After sending a great deal of money to Aunt Helena, he has worked hard on his project. He has learnt new skills, carried blocks of stone, carved timbers and built the huge bridge over the new moat.

He sees how good it all looks now it's finished, but he feels no pride. No sense of achievement. Making sure to use up every last penny in the two enormous chests, he has paid for everything. This towering, gleaming city is the result, with happy people living in it. But the money was dirty and he knows it. It took him a long time to work out how to clean it, but now that the project is almost finished, he's not convinced he succeeded. His architect designed a magnificent house for him to live in. It is beautiful, elegant and proud. Yet he does not want to live there. He feels nothing but shame, and all he wants to do is leave.

1

I HOPE HE COMES TO HAMBRIG

July, AD 1272

So far, my journal has led a charmed life. I sit at my desk, pen in hand, and think about this. Outside, the day is bright and warmish, but the summer is proving slow to arrive. We're getting wet days, cool days and windy days, but not too many warm ones. And yes, I do often record the weather.

So that you can picture it for yourself, I'll tell you that my journal consists of piles of rolled parchments, some of them rather the worse for wear. Each new one goes with me wherever I go, and I write in it when I can, sometimes in ink and sometimes with charcoal, and then the parchment gets rained on, or squashed inside my jersey, or it gets lost and has to be retrieved later... which is what I mean by a charmed life.

It's all here in my library now, a record of my life from when I was thirty-three years old – and in two months' time I'll be forty-three. A ten-year archive of life as the fourth Lord of Hambrig. Which nobody has ever read. Perhaps no one will ever read it. If so, what a waste of time, writing everything down!

Suddenly I hear footsteps in the tower, and I know someone's coming to disturb my thoughts and intrude on my private time in this room I call my library. From the footsteps themselves, I can tell that my steward will soon be entering, a worried frown on her plain, fifty-six-year-old Frisian face. And she will twist her apron strings as she talks to me, irritating me beyond measure, although I've never asked her to stop. Her request will either be for something trivial, which she should be adjudicating herself, or it will be for something serious, which requires a judgement I'm no longer capable of.

My back is to the door, and I don't turn round, even as I hear it open. In comes Inka Kaufmann, shutting the door carefully behind her. I hear a quiet clearing of the throat behind me. She's letting me know she's there, in as respectful a way as she knows how, not realising that I do, already, know, and I'm simply being the rude, boorish man I've become. More throat-clearing, and something sounding revoltingly like clucking. She thinks I still haven't heard her. I lay my pen down on the desk, and my parchment journal rolls up by itself.

'What is it, Inka?' I stood up and turned round, but Inka, though short, dumpy and female, was not intimidated.

'Lord, I wish to talk with you,' she said, squaring her shoulders in a way I'd come to recognise as a sign of her determination to say what had to be said.

'That's why you're here, I take it.' I tapped my foot impatiently on the floor. 'What's the matter?'

'There is no singing.'

'No singing?' What on earth did the woman mean?

'I'm told, lord, that there used to be singing. A bard, or a musician. Even a group of musicians, all performing at the hearth during and after dinner. Now nobody performs. Dinner is lifeless without music.'

I could hardly believe what I was hearing. How was this something I needed to deal with? I had a hundred things to do...

'Lord, I can see you think this a trivial matter,' Kaufmann went on bravely. The shoulders were pushed back even further, resulting in her enormous bosom jutting out under my irritated gaze. 'But I assure you it is not trivial. Morale is low. People are disgruntled—'

'Who is "disgruntled"?' I demanded. I was fed up with this stupid conversation. I hoped it showed.

'Everyone is unhappy, lord,' declared my steward, whose job it must surely be to ensure the happiness of my household. And if it wasn't her job, it must be somebody else's, for it sure as hell wasn't mine. Wait, though. Perhaps my household's 'happiness' was not an issue anyway. Who says people have to be happy?

'Look,' I began, trying to sound reasonable.

'There was once a bard called Amie,' Kaufmann interrupted. 'I have heard about her and her wonderful playing of the harp. Then she went away to marry someone in the north of the country, and now she has a child. After that, there was a couple called Christopher and Annis. They sang merry songs, and did magic tricks! Everybody loved their performances. And then there was Master Kit, who is really a nobleman, and him I know from crossing the ocean in a tiny boat! He plays many instruments and he can sing beautiful songs. Yet he, too, is gone.'

'What do you want me to do about it?' A feeble question. I don't ask any other kind these days.

'We must appoint another bard, another musician or juggler. Someone to entertain the household over dinner. It will lift their spirits.'

'Inka, I still haven't appointed a commander of my garrison. I think that's rather more important than a song-and-dance act, don't you?'

But she stared at me. 'If you think it's so damned important, why haven't you done it yet?'

I knew Kaufmann had no experience of being a steward in a large castle, but she should have known better than to speak to me in that way. Then again, she's not Mallrovian, and English is not her first language. I should make allowances.

Since Nicholas left for Naples, the garrison has been without a leader. The garrison? I gave a small, humourless laugh. No. I had no garrison, although Kaufmann had been kind enough not to point this out. Nicholas took our two best warriors with him when he left. The remaining soldiers continued to eat and sleep here at my expense. They became soft and flabby. Nobody trained or disciplined them. They were a rabble, a group of revolting men, blind drunk most of the time, nobody in charge. And then what happened? They deserted. The whole bloody lot, all at the same time. They left in the middle of the night two months ago, and no one even noticed them go. So, of course, we have no watchmen patrolling the wall-walk, and no one to defend us. King Philip would have been furious. My father would have despaired. And it would never have happened while either man was alive.

'I'll think about it, Inka.' She must have known I'd give it no thought whatsoever.

I caught the disappointed look on her face as she turned to leave. I called her back. 'Has anyone actually asked for music?'

'No, lord. They are too damned dejected even for that.' And then she left.

I hadn't realised how bad things were. No, that's another lie. I had realised, but I hadn't cared. Kaufmann's courage made me care. She hadn't had to come to my library. Nobody, she said, was calling for music and entertainment. But she wanted to improve things here, and she'd thought of a way to do it. Perhaps she'd spoken with Rachel, Eliza or Joan, who would all remember the old days. And perhaps they'd suggested something, but it had been Kaufmann who'd climbed the endless spiral steps in the south-west tower to talk to the grumpiest man in the castle.

I put away my pen and stuffed my journal into my breeches pocket. Slowly, I descended to the courtyard.

My wife, Rosa, is the daughter of King Alfonso X of Castile. She has his haughty manner and his dark Spanish looks. She isn't tall, yet you always feel you're looking up to her. Today, she wanted to know why I'd been closeted in my library, by myself, all morning.

'I didn't realise I'd been there all morning,' I said testily. 'It didn't seem like more than an hour or so.' But I'd heard the horn for dinner some time ago. It was now mid-afternoon, so Rosa was being generous in her chastisement. Not that I cared to be chastised, generously or otherwise.

'Let's go and see the children,' I suggested. I hoped to please her. It didn't please her.

'You only say that to distract me. The children and I had dinner in the *Egg* with Joan and Eliza. It was very pleasant.'

'Did you want me to join you?'

'That would have been even more pleasant, lord.'

'I shall go there now.' It was Joan I wanted to see. My children – well, that would be nice too.

Joan's cottage is called the *Egg*; it doesn't matter why. It was all a long time ago. As I entered, Joan jumped to her feet and gave me a wide smile. 'Rory! How lovely to see you!'

I felt ashamed. Joan's joyous and enthusiastic greeting was more effective than Kaufmann's stolid entreaties or Rosa's scornful comments.

'Where are the children, Joan?'

'Eliza has taken them to the kitchen for sweeties. Rachel will have kept some extra pudding back for them.'

It was only Baby Rory who'd want pudding, I thought. Little Maya, only eight months old, was too young to care.

'That's true,' Joan agreed, when I put this to her. 'But Baby Rory always insists she has some too! Anyway, when are we going to stop calling him "Baby Rory"? He's two and a half! Not a baby, now, surely.'

'No, I know. Call him whatever you like, Joan.'

I sat down at her table, and Joan pulled up a chair opposite me. 'Do you feel you're getting better, Rory?'

'No.'

'I thought your adventures with the Livonians and that business with William and Nightmolben Castle had brought you out of your apathy.'

Only Joan can talk to me like this. Other people might have done so once, but they're all gone now. 'I thought so too,' I said sadly. 'I really did. When we were fighting in

Nightmolben, when I was sailing the *Wolf*, I felt alive then. I had a job to do. A purpose. Now there's nothing.'

'Nothing? What about Baby – I mean, what about Rory and Maya? They need you!'

'They don't, Joan. They have you, Rosa, Eliza, Jenny and Rachel. A whole bunch of you.'

'I heard from Nicholas,' Joan said obliquely. 'He is making something of that fortress in Naples. He's garrisoned it—'

Something like a groan came from my throat.

'Find someone,' Joan said gently. 'Someone to command the garrison, someone who'll recruit good men and women. We need to find our self-respect again.'

We do. There was no point in staying to hear more from Joan, so I wandered back to my library, right at the top of the south-west tower. Rosa was waiting for me. My heart sank when I saw her.

'Something wrong?'

'I just wanted to tell you. I have written a letter, and I sent it with a messenger, so I cannot now undo the deed.'

'To whom have you written, Rosa?' It was clear I was not going to approve. She hadn't waited for approval; she'd sent the letter already. And who, I wondered, was the messenger? There's nobody we can spare, surely.

'I have written to Sir Jonny in Kettering.'

I gasped. How dare she do such a thing! I felt the blood flood into my face, my eyes clouding with the familiar, and all-too-frequent, Red Mist. I clenched my fists and clutched at my self-control. What right did this woman have to write to my oldest friend? I still think of Jonny as that, although we have not been friends for the last eight years, and in all that time, have seen each other just once.

'I knew you would not want me to,' Rosa continued,

unperturbed. 'Which is why I waited until you were not near the gatehouse.'

'Who's taken the letter?' My voice was a low, desperate growl. This wife of mine was too much, and as soon as I had all the details, I would tell her so.

'Thomas Farr has taken it. He is a good horseman, reliable and sensible.'

I could scarcely take it in. The insolence of it. The high-handedness. The manipulation of my household without my permission. But the thing could not be undone. There was just one other question to ask. 'What have you said in this bloody letter?'

'I have asked Sir Jonny to return to Hambrig, even if just for a short while. And I have mentioned that you did not ask me to write the letter, nor did you know about it at the time. He will not think this is subterfuge. He will know it is I, the daughter of the great Alfonso X of Castile, who asks this.'

'Why, Rosa?'

'Because you need help, lord. We no longer have the minstrel's daughter to guide us with her words of wisdom. Your steward is an ignorant and uneducated woman, and I cannot understand why you have promoted her. But that is your own affair. We are defenceless, with no warriors in the gatehouse and no one to watch from the walls. You have allowed all this to happen, and you have done nothing. I understand very well that you have been suffering from your "Darkness". But have you ever questioned why this is? What is the reason for this "Darkness"? I think you know already, but you will not admit it, and it is obvious that you will never reveal it to me. Not only I, but others also, are convinced it is something to do with Sir Jonny, and it is time, surely, to speak of it with him and to begin your recovery. Your household is tolerant, but even their tolerance will have its limits. We must hope Sir Jonny understands the grave nature of our situation, and that he will come to our aid. I have couched my letter in those terms.'

Rosa stood in front of me in my library. There was a high colour in her cheeks, as if she knew she had transgressed, and she was waiting for my reprimand. Perhaps even punishment.

'Rosa,' I said, and saw her chin lift in defiance. 'You should not have written without telling me first. You should not have sent Thomas without asking if I can spare him. You are always doing things you shouldn't do! And yet...'

'And yet, lord?'

'You are my wife. I hope – well, I hope he comes to Hambrig.'

2

WE MUST PROTECT THE VULNERABLE

My wife had written the letter I couldn't write. So many times I'd tried to write to Jonny. Given up. Despaired. But perhaps I just didn't try hard enough. And it was a good decision to send Thomas. Thomas Farr is our stonemason. His son, Bryce, is our odd-job boy. I was surprised – but relieved – Rosa hadn't sent Bryce as well. It should take no more than a week for Thomas to get to Kettering, and he'd be there a day or two before returning, so maximum wait time was three weeks.

In the meantime, my household was unsettled and edgy. Rosa's letter was common knowledge now. Those who'd never known Jonny questioned those who'd been here a long time, and pretty soon everyone was of the opinion that some sort of super-hero was on his way. Once arrived, the legendary Sir Jonny would quickly depose the ineffectual Lord of Hambrig, take over the castle and instantly populate the garrison with brave, strong warriors. Oh, and perhaps build a few more fortresses along our borders. He would spend his time riding valiantly between them and the palace in Hicrown, after which he would, naturally, marry Queen Phoebe and become King of Mallrovia.

I thought there was a strong possibility Jonny would ignore the letter and remain in his manor house in Kettering. Rosa disagreed.

'You do not know the exact words I wrote,' she said reproachfully. 'I have never met this man, but he will not ignore my letter, I can assure you. He was once your closest friend and your confidant. He will be here soon, escorted by your stonemason.'

I shook my head. Rosa had put into words the thing I'd never acknowledged. Which was that something went sour between Jonny and me all those years ago, and I haven't been able to unsour it, because I don't know what it is. My wife is unaware of all this. I didn't meet Rosa until after it all happened. But I said nothing, and I did nothing, and life went on while we waited the three weeks it took for the message to be delivered, read and responded to.

Until, on 9th August, there was a lot of shouting outside the gate, which nobody heard at first. With no watchmen on the wall-walk, and no soldiers in the garrison, we keep the drawbridge up at all times and we never know if anyone's approaching. If someone happens to be on the wall-walk, looking out over the hill, they would raise the alarm, but today that wasn't the case, and there was nobody near the gatehouse either. So we didn't know how long the visitors had been there, until Luke, passing the gatehouse on his way from the kitchen to the orchard, heard the commotion and came pelting into the courtyard to let us all know.

Obviously, the entire household congregated by the gate, eager to see Thomas Farr and Jonny – and to give Jonny the hero's welcome they'd been planning for days.

The drawbridge clanked into place. I stood at the front, not sure what I'd say to my old friend, but hoping I'd somehow find the right words. I could feel the breathless anticipation from the crowd at my back; it crackled in the air. Branca was holding her small son by the hand. For days she'd been telling him stories of Sir Jonny's adventures as a great warrior. Eliza had Baby Rory's hand in hers, and Joan held Maya in her arms. It would be an historic moment, this reuniting of the Lord of Hambrig with his comrade-in-arms. For that was what we'd been.

Knight-Crusaders with Louis IX of France, we'd ridden through Cyprus, Egypt and the rest of Outremer. We'd been inseparable, Jonny and I, doing everything together and looking out for each other. It's no exaggeration to say that neither of us would have made it home without the other's protection and friendship. When that all went, suddenly withdrawn by Jonny for reasons he never divulged, I was devastated. Now, standing in the gatehouse, I waited to set eyes on Jonny again, and this time I was determined to find out why he'd renounced our friendship. Soon – perhaps even today – I would know the truth.

But the gates creaked open to reveal four mounted strangers ranged on the hillside. Behind me, there was a concerted gasp. It took a few disbelieving moments for me to register that it wasn't Jonny and Thomas Farr after all. Two of the strangers were in priests' garb, and all had ridden at speed, for their horses were sweating and everyone looked exhausted. On both sides of the enormous gates, no one moved. Time, it seemed, had stood still.

'Everyone back into the hall,' called a guttural Frisian

voice. Inka Kaufmann, a short woman lost in the crowd, shouted her order twice more, and, slowly, the crowd obeyed. They were disgruntled. Disappointed it wasn't Jonny after all, and reluctant to obey Kaufmann; nonetheless, they drifted back into the courtyard. My steward, who should have been by my side, did not return.

Alone, I stood in the entrance arch and called across the drawbridge. 'Who are you?'

'We're from Hicrown,' answered one of the non-priests. 'There is serious trouble, and we need your help.'

'What sort of trouble?'

'May we enter? It will be easier to explain.'

But it could be a trick or a trap. I was painfully aware of our lack of defence capability. 'No,' I called to them. 'Explain yourselves from where you stand now.'

The four looked at each other. One, their spokesman, slid down from his horse and set foot on the drawbridge. I didn't even know if anyone was ready to raise the damn thing. *Someone* should be in the gatehouse tower, but it was nobody's particular job these days. These four could rush in and I wouldn't be able to stop them.

'Stop right there,' I said, cursing that I was unarmed. Fully expecting to see friends, I had neither buckled on my sword belt, nor fetched my dagger. But I put a hand to my belt, as if feeling for a weapon there. I closed my fist around nothing, and hoped it looked convincing.

'It's a rebellion,' the other man said, moving a pace or two forwards on the drawbridge. 'A riot. In Hicrown. We need you and your garrison. Even then, even if you mobilise right now, it may be too late.' His voice rose in pitch. If it was an act, it was a good one. And then, suddenly, he was across the bridge and right up to me. He was my height, and he looked directly into my eyes. 'Come now, we implore you.

Bring your troops and put a stop to the bloodshed. We fear for the life of Queen Phoebe. We fear for the lives of our families and our friends. Hicrown is in uproar. If Hicrown goes down, what of the rest of the country?'

I was shaken by the intensity of his plea. His eyes told me he believed what he was saying. 'Who is rioting?' I asked.

'We only just escaped. These men of God' – he pointed to the priests – 'what harm have they done? I and my companion, humble servants in the cathedral, we are also innocent! Yet they've attacked us, they've robbed us, they've made fools of us, and now they're shooting us with arrows—'

'Wait!' I held up my hand. 'Who is doing these things? Start at the beginning, for God's sake.'

But he was too distressed, and so I let them all cross the drawbridge and enter my home. Rachel brought food into the hall, where we sat at one of the trestle tables, and I learnt a great deal about these riots in Hicrown.

'I don't see we can do owt about it,' Peter declared at the meeting I held in my library, while Bart and Andrew looked after the visitors in the gatehouse accommodation. Bart is our carpenter and Andrew is our blacksmith. Both are loyal; neither is young. But this is what hospitality has come to in Castle Rory.

'Yet we must,' I said firmly. 'I know we have no warriors, and that's what these men have come for, but we must go to Phoebe's aid.'

'And Hicrown Cathedral is under attack?' Rachel said

doubtfully. 'It could be some kind of trap, lord. We should take care.'

I knew she meant the men had told an unlikely story. A story which began many years ago, with the disaffection of the city folk. It seems many people were avoiding paying taxes, and that was because those people lived on land owned by the cathedral, which was, itself, exempt from taxation. Nor did the people living on cathedral land believe themselves bound by the laws of the land. The city officers had tried to take control of the situation, but there had been quarrels, a few serious fights and even a murder or two.

'Why did King Philip never mention any o' this?' Peter asked, perplexed. 'If it's been goin' on for all this time...'

'Because he was always out of the country,' Rachel responded briskly. 'And, perhaps, now we know why.'

I looked at her. It wasn't like Rachel, our cook, to speak so bluntly, nor to be disrespectful to the King. But the King is dead. I guess that makes a difference.

'You only have that letter, though,' said Joan. 'A letter written by a traitor, telling you the King died by falling over a cliff.'

'The letter didn't say that, Joan,' I said. But the King was dead, however it happened, and his funeral had been held in Hicrown Cathedral eighteen months ago. Together with that of his son, Barney. They'd died on the same day.

'The letter din't say t' King fell over t' cliff?' Peter queried, blinking at us through the thick lenses of his spectacles. I believe those lenses have thickened over the years I've known Peter. 'I thought tha told us he did!'

I opened my desk drawer and removed the parchment that made Allan of Hicrown's treachery crystal clear to any who read it. I read it aloud to Peter, Rachel and Joan, my three most trusted companions.

Lord Rory,

King Philip and Prince Barney were pushed over the cliff at Nightmolben and they are both dead. It looks like they slipped and fell, but this is not what happened. This was murder, and the killer is still at large. Queen Julia is nowhere to be found, and the killer may have taken her. But there are evil forces here, and if you try to find out what has happened, your family will be taken as well. Your wife and son are in danger. Do not leave them alone for a single moment. Protect your own.

Sir Allan of Hicrown

'So this is why you haven't been to Hicrown since it happened?' Joan asked, staring at me in shock. As they all were, in fact.

'I have been there. This letter makes it sound like anarchy—'

'It *is* anarchy, lord!' Peter exclaimed, while Rachel, at the same time, said much the same thing. Peter pushed his chair away and stood up, clearly upset. 'This is terrible news! I wish I'd known of it sooner, like. I wish tha'd *told* us...' He took off his glasses and wiped the lenses on his tunic. I thought perhaps he was blinking back tears. Why was the man so agitated?

It was Joan who asked him, her tone gentle and concerned. 'What is the matter, Peter?'

'I cannot tell thee. I'm sorry, Joan, but I must not say owt about it.'

He left the room and clattered down the tower steps, leaving us all puzzled and dismayed.

'It's certainly very bad news about the riots,' Rachel said

uncertainly. 'And, of course, discovering now that the King and poor Prince Barney were murdered—'

'Yes, I know it's a shock,' I said, interrupting her. 'I kept the letter to myself for two reasons, and I'm sure you've both worked them out anyway. One, I didn't even know if it was true. Allan is hardly the most reliable source of information and I have never liked or trusted the man. And two, if the letter *is* accurate, I did not want to provoke any consequences to Rosa and the children.'

'But neither of those things explains Peter's reaction,' Joan said. 'Should I go after him, do you think? Or Rachel could?'

'Yes,' Rachel said. 'I'll find out what's wrong. But, lord. What are you going to do?'

'I'm going to do what I said at the start of the meeting. I'm going to Hicrown to find out for myself, but first I need to put a plan in place. We shall meet here again tomorrow after Mass and I will tell you my plan. Whatever happens, and whatever I decide to do, we must protect the vulnerable.'

3

SOME QUESTIONS WILL ALWAYS REMAIN UNANSWERED

There was nobody I could take from Castle Rory. We are now a household of middle-aged women, elderly men, very small children and those of a nervous disposition. My craftsmen and women are all getting on in years, and there was no way I could ask Peter, my alchemist, or any of the servants to face whatever dangers lay ahead. Other than that, there's the doctor, the cook and the kitchen team. All needed here, and it would be folly to remove them. Still, a plan had begun to form in my mind as soon as I dismissed Rachel and Joan from my library.

After supper, I held a further meeting with the four Hicrowners. I needed more details.

'They throw things at us, and they won't listen,' said Master Mancroft, the man who'd first spoken to me on the drawbridge.

As a complaint, it sounded trivial. But I learnt the disputes had been going on for twenty years, and I began to think Rachel was right: King Philip had travelled widely, simply to escape the problems on his doorstep. Although all kings travel... And it hardly mattered now, anyway.

I found it more difficult to get the priests to talk to me. They were affronted at the behaviour of the Hicrown citizens and took it as an insult to God. They could scarcely bring themselves to talk about it.

'Yet you've come here with Master Mancroft and Master Conesford,' I pointed out. 'Was that simply to escape? Or to help bring about peace in your city?'

They took mild offence at that, but they did see my point.

'The land belongs to the cathedral,' the older priest said in a tired voice. 'It's called "God's Acre", and it's *always* been a fief of the cathedral. Those who live there do so at our discretion and with our blessing. They are not in the city's jurisdiction.'

'Because it's your land?' I asked.

'But the city claims it isn't cathedral land,' interjected Master Mancroft, 'because it's outside the walls of the precinct.'

'Ah, I see. So there's some confusion? The land is outside the cathedral, yet it belongs to the cathedral. Why was the cathedral wall not built around this fief?'

'It just never was,' said Master Mancroft, the pitch of his voice rising again. 'This goes back decades, Lord Rory. *Decades*. In the meantime, the people of Hicrown tried to evade taxes demanded of them by the King, God rest his soul, and now Queen Phoebe has increased those very taxes.'

'Has she? I didn't know that.'

'It will not affect Hambrig, but the citizens of Hicrown are not only annoyed at this increased taxation, but doubly annoyed because those living in God's Acre are exempt, yet have access to all the facilities of the city.'

'Then they have grounds for complaint—' I began.

'Not really,' the younger priest said quickly. 'Because it's always been this way, and those who live in the cathedral fief are there at our invitation. As has always been the case.' He spoke quickly and abruptly. Not unlike a soldier.

'Only *then*,' Master Conesford put in with great emphasis, 'some of the city people put up targets – quintains – for spear-throwing practice. On God's Acre! A gross impertinence!' He sounded thoroughly affronted. 'We shot one of them.'

'You *shot* someone?'

'I didn't. One of the other cathedral servants fetched his bow and shot one of the townspeople, and then he was arrested. After that, the bishop ordered the cathedral doors closed, so now we are in a state of siege. And we don't know what to do.'

'And the palace? The Queen?'

'We do not know, lord. Mancroft and I escaped and met up secretly with the priest of St Michael's Church and his curate, and they agreed to come with us to seek Hambrig's assistance.'

'The bishop's still inside the cathedral, then?'

'He is. But many of us are trying to shoot down our attackers from behind the walls of the precinct.' He caught my look of horror, and hastily added, 'They deserve nothing less! They are like animals, attacking God's holy buildings and His representatives in Hicrown! What else can we do?'

'Do you know who began this insurrection, Master Conesford?'

'As I said, it began a good twenty years ago—'

'But something, or someone, has brought it to a head. Who? Or What?'

Mancroft looked at Conesford.

'We think it was the palace,' Conesford said abruptly. 'Not the Queen of course. Someone from inside the palace.' The man's voice was clipped, his sentences short and succinct.

Mancroft, who turned out to be the cathedral's sacristan, had mentioned the curate of St Michael's. But when I spoke directly to Pockthorpe, the curate, he flew into a rage.

'They burnt our church!' he shouted, and the older priest shushed and soothed him, attempting to wrap his arms around the furious younger man. But Conesford, who was the cathedral cantor, confirmed it was true. The rebels had burnt down St Michael's Church. No wonder Hicrown was in uproar.

After Mass the next day, I told Peter, Joan and Rachel I'd be riding to Hicrown. I would take nobody from the castle household, but would find people in Hambrig Town, and they, a rudimentary fyrd, would be ordered to come to Hicrown with me. Clearly we can't have citizens burning down churches and besieging their own cathedral! The situation is preposterous.

I know from experience that small grievances, stirred up with malicious intent, can result in terrible and life-changing consequences. Then, when you look back at what happened, you can't believe it all started with something so trivial. I explained all this, and in return I received a concerned look from Joan, a nod from Rachel and a stammered offer of help from Peter.

'Peter, I need young men with me.' It was blunt, I know, but also true. Peter, in his mid-fifties, and never a warrior, would be a hindrance.

'Aye, lord, I know,' he answered miserably. 'But I – I would like to come with thee anyroad. I'll not get in tha way, I promise thee that.'

'No, Peter, but I thank you for the offer.' And of course I know now I should have asked him why he was so desperate to come, but I was in a hurry to leave. It takes three days to ride from Castle Rory to Hicrown, but I'd need to stop for an extra day in Hambrig Town. I was anxious to make a start.

I told the priests and their servants we'd be leaving within the hour. And I asked Joan to find out what Peter's problem was. My only question now was to decide who to leave in charge while I was away. It should, of course, be my steward. But I've broken that rule on many occasions, sometimes preferring my garrison commander, while other times it's been Rachel, my cook, and Peter, my alchemist, who've carried the responsibility for – not only this household and the castle we live in – but the defence of Hambrig itself. Were they aware, at the time, of the huge burden I placed upon their shoulders? I don't think so. But they wouldn't be my choice now, and the question was, obviously, did I trust Inka Kaufmann enough? And if not, why had I agreed to make her my steward.

'You've been my steward now for nearly a year. How do you think you've done?' I hated asking her this. It was a cowardly question; it was for me to *tell* her how she was doing and to point out any deficiencies in her work. Still, I wanted her own assessment.

'I hope I please you, lord.' A deferential answer. Cautious.

'You do as I ask,' I said brusquely. 'And that's good. But it's not enough.'

Her head snapped up, her eyes widening. Because she always stands so close, she has to crane her neck to look up at me, and I stared down at her plain features, her mouth open in surprise, greying hair bundled under an unflattering snood. 'Not enough, lord? Damn! How have I failed in my duties?'

'You need to know how I think, what I'd do and how I'd react in any situation. Because I won't always be here, and when I'm not here you have to stand in for me. I'm not convinced you can do that. That's why I say it's not enough to obey orders. You have to be able to think for yourself, Inka.'

Crestfallen, she nodded, mumbled something and trailed away down the tower steps. I dashed off a set of instructions on what to do if I didn't return from Hicrown, left the parchment on my desk and descended to the courtyard, which was bathed in sunshine. At last, the summer had arrived. Travelling is always so much easier in good weather.

The four Hicrowners had their horses, refreshed after a night in our stables, cared for by Luke, our talented young stable hand. Blue, my warhorse, was saddled and ready. Rachel had prepared food for the journey, neatly wrapped in canvas and stowed in a capacious leather saddlebag. As per my instructions, someone had lashed four sharp pikes to Blue's girths.

I had my sword, my dagger and my ancient wooden shield, emblazoned in our red, blue and gold, our family's motto *Fac Fiat* scratched across the middle. I'd scratched it myself, years ago, in the Egyptian desert. The motto means 'Make It Happen', and it was my father's guiding principle. His father's too, for that matter, all the way back to my great-grandfather, the first Lord Rory of Hambrig. *Fac Fiat*, our battle cry. It's supposed to guide everything we do. Sometimes the relentless positivity of it makes me tired. As if there's no way I can live up to such drive, such unremitting momentum. But I have to, don't I? It's my destiny.

That shield, battered now, had saved my life many a time. Someone, though, had buffed up the colours. Or perhaps even repainted them. Probably Andrew, our dedicated blacksmith since God knows when.

The five of us clattered across the drawbridge and made our way down Baudry Hill in the hot August sunshine. We'd turn right onto the Wartsbaye Road and then, some miles further, right again onto the Hicrown Road.

Conesford and Mancroft were used to obeying orders. They quickly fell into line. Pockthorpe, the curate, maintained a taciturn silence, his brow permanently furrowed. The outlier was Father Wymer. He was a querulous man, possibly around forty, with a habit of questioning everything.

'Why are we stopping in Hambrig Town? We should be getting back to the riots,' he grumbled as I found and paid for lodgings.

'I've explained already, Father Wymer. I need to find people to come with us—'

'But why? We are five already. More will be a drain on our resources, and in any case, we won't be able to fight those rebels. They are determined to beat us into submission. They've even threatened to fire the cathedral! What do you think of that, Lord Rory?'

I'll admit that shocked me, but Father Wymer's nitpicking continued unabated, as he questioned my judgement on every single thing. I sent two riders to Wartsbaye with a terse message for Baron Giles. I despatched a man to commandeer one of the tumbledown cottages along the road between Hambrig Town and Hicrown. And I drafted three young fellows into my makeshift army, ordering them to borrow horses from the livery and join us on the road.

Father Wymer thought all these things a criminal waste of time. Neither could he understand why I hadn't turned out my own garrison and marched them to Hicrown.

'This is quicker,' I explained. 'Not all our warriors are mounted; they're used to defending the castle, not going to war in other territories. Foot soldiers would take too long...' It sounded less than convincing, and Father Wymer tut-tutted and turned away.

But eventually I'd done everything I needed to do, and the next day we packed our saddlebags again and set off along the road. Conesford and Mancroft had their bows with them. Neither of the clergymen was armed. Wymer persisted in grumbling as he rode, and his riding was bad too. He was clearly unused to it, and his poor horse suffered the results. Pockthorpe was an experienced horseman, controlling his mount with just one hand.

We rode about twenty-five miles towards Hicrown and located the cottage I'd requisitioned for the night. It was just outside the King's Forest, and was owned by an elderly peasant. He'd be one of Queen Phoebe's tenants, although it was clear the man hadn't heard that King Philip was dead as he still referred to him. The curate made a fire, on which he cooked a tasty dinner of lentils and onions. Then everyone settled down to sleep.

Tomorrow we'll reach Hicrown, and that's where my plan comes to an end. It all depends on what I find when I get there. My messengers will be at Wartsbaye sometime tomorrow, I hope. Baron Giles will read my letter and his troops will begin to march down to Hicrown the next day. They'll come through the Hambrig Hills, which is not easy terrain, and they'll be on foot, so I'll assume four days of marching. They should be in Hicrown five days from now, which means it'll fall to me to maintain some sort of peace in the meantime.

You may have guessed I'm writing in my journal again. This is the current one, a roll of parchment with a couple of stubs of charcoal to see me through the next week or so. I've become used to writing everything down, and this is how I work out what to do next. The act of writing down my actions, the behaviour of others, my thoughts, feelings and predictions – these things seem to help me plan my next move.

I need to work out how to break the siege while keeping the city of Hicrown happy. I need to talk to the bishop and find out why he took such drastic action, and to the city officers to learn why they set up their quintains on sacred land. It was obviously to provoke the cathedral to notice them – but it was risky and unnecessary. Finally, and most importantly, I must speak to Queen Phoebe. She, as I remember, is hard to fathom. King Philip once said Phoebe was the most placid and the most adorable of his three children. We shall soon discover if that's true.

This journal is my own personal diary, and I have shown it to no one, nor will I. It's my dream that one day, maybe a long time from now, someone will read my *Tales of Castle Rory* and understand how and why we did what we did. As for *this* Tale, hopefully by the end of it, we will know why this long-running dispute between the city and the cathedral has suddenly blown up, and how we're going to resolve it. But then again, maybe not. It's my belief that some questions will always remain unanswered.

4

INTO THE DUSKY CITY

The Hambrig Gate was closed. This gate is the only way into Hicrown from the west, and it was not only closed but barred to us. However, there seemed to be no guard on the walls and we heard no challenge. I wished to God I had warriors with me, but I unloaded the pikes I'd brought and gave one to each of the three young Hambriggers I'd recruited. I kept one pike back for myself, and explained to my three Hambriggers that we were going to use our pikes to charge the gate and force it open.

Pikes would not be the instrument of choice for this. Although long and strong, they lacked the hammerhead needed for this job. But they'd have to do, so we formed up in a line the width of the road, aimed our pikes at the gate and charged. The gates gave a little, which surprised me. I'd have thought they'd have been more resistant. But it was encouraging. Four charges later, and the gates had splintered badly. On the next assault – and still no one had come to challenge us – we broke through, and one of the gates, holed and torn, swung wide to let us in. Everyone mounted again, and we entered Hicrown, the capital city of Mallrovia.

I led the way to the palace, which is to the north. The main street was deserted, but there were people hidden in doorways, and some crouched by the wall. They looked scrawny, half-starved. All watched us, but nothing was said. We made an impressive procession, and people may have thought us the militia. Which, I suppose, is what we were, unless you called the unruly citizens that. There were eight of us, clattering noisily on horseback through the sun-dappled cobbled streets of Hicrown, our pikes in a warlike, attacking position, the shafts under our arms, blades pointing forwards over the shoulders of our horses. And in this way, we drew near to the palace.

'But why not the cathedral?' whined Father Wymer. 'We should go there first. The palace is much less important...' And he grumbled on, but I don't suppose anyone was listening.

It was at the palace that I saw the first sign of a response to the riots. A large phalanx of the King's Squad marched up and down the square in front of the building. They wore plate armour as well as mail, and they held good quality weapons. The sight of these men and women was heartening. With this group of warriors, we'd have no trouble crushing the rebellion, identifying and punishing the ringleaders, and restoring normal life to the city. I led my pikemen to the palace gatehouse. Again, there was nobody on duty. But the commander of the King's Squad, a young man I didn't know, watched my approach and stepped forward.

'I am Lord Rory of Hambrig,' I called to him. 'I bring you reinforcements, although perhaps you don't need us now?'

'Reinforcements from Hambrig?' He sounded sceptical.

'And I know who you are, but you have no authority here. This city is under my command, and the cathedral is besieged. This morning I declared an indefinite state of martial law in the city. If the bishop agrees to co-operate, this may be reversed, although that will depend on how helpful he's prepared to be.'

Early on in this pompous, swaggering speech, I realised my error. Unbelievably, the King's Squad are the rioters. Or, if not rioting themselves, they certainly support the cause. Father Wymer was right; we should have gone first to the cathedral.

'What is your name?' I asked the young captain.

'My name is Leo. I've been in the Palace Guard all my life, and in the Squad for the last year and a bit.'

'Are you in command here? Where is Sir Allan of Hicrown?'

He narrowed his eyes, his head cocked questioningly. 'I don't have to answer to you, Lord Rory of Hambrig. If you've truly come to offer your support, you and your men can dismount and fall in behind mine.'

And then he looked more closely at my 'men', and saw the clerics' headgear.

'And who have we here?' Leo asked in mock-indignation. 'Isn't that the priest from St Michael's? We burnt his church, you know. Nothing left of it now.'

Father Wymer was about to make some angry response, but Mancroft stepped in. 'Sir, we are a deputation from Hambrig. Our military appearance is merely to keep the peace on the streets of this fine city. We would be grateful for the chance to talk to you and help resolve your grievances. For resolved they must be, as I'm sure you will agree.'

Leo stared at Mancroft, who swept off his hat and

bowed, although still in the saddle. 'My name is Bartholomew Mancroft, and I am the sacristan of Hicrown Cathedral. Let us convene a meeting to discuss the plan.'

It was high-handed of Mancroft to propose a meeting, without having agreed this idea with me first. And I wasn't sure we were any kind of 'deputation from Hambrig'.

Father Wymer said, 'We should find out what is happening in the cathedral, lord. There may be no one left alive!' His voice rose.

'I can tell you what's happened in the cathedral,' Leo called to him. 'And I agree to a talk, but I'll speak only with the Lord of Hambrig and the sacristan. The rest will stay *outside* the palace.'

Father Wymer looked mutinous, Pockthorpe was enigmatic, while everyone else was simply weary. But I gestured at them to remain where they were.

Dismounting, Mancroft and I followed Leo into the palace, and we went, as I expected, to the sumptuous great hall. It was being used as a dormitory, with blankets, goblets and other detritus scattered around. I wondered why the Squad wasn't using its normal accommodation. They have a special building behind the palace, an austere and functional place, nothing like the rooms in the palace itself. Still, Leo led the way onto the dais, where parchment was spread out on the high table. Someone had drawn a rough sketch of the city, and there were several large circles marked on it. I didn't know what they meant. The gates were clearly shown, with the roads that provide access to the city. The cathedral had been blocked in too. It's around a quarter of a mile from the palace, in the south-west of the city.

Leo hastily rolled up his map. 'What do you propose?'

We all sat at the table. I wondered what Mancroft had had in mind when he suggested 'talks', but perhaps he'd just been playing for time. In any case, it was for me to start the proceedings.

So I looked at Leo and asked, 'What's your actual grievance with the cathedral?'

'You must know. The priest will have told you, and that's why you're here. Probably to stop us getting justice for the city. For far too long, the bishop and other officials have owned protected land outside the cathedral precincts, and they've settled their friends there, claiming those people don't have to pay taxes like the rest of us. Do you know how high taxation was in this city under King Philip? The greediest man God ever created.'

'And now he's dead. But you know that.'

'Of course. And after that, we all assumed the new Queen would lower the taxes. But you know what? She was worse. She collaborated with the bishop to put taxes up even higher! Father Wymer and his poxy curate supported the bishop, and everyone is suffering. High taxation, and the abuse of the land known as "God's Acre", are examples of the Queen's shameless exploitation of the people of this city. It has to stop.'

'Where is Queen Julia?' asked Mancroft.

'She's dead,' Leo informed us.

'How did she die?' I asked. 'I didn't see her body at Nightmolben.'

'She died in the forest. That's all you need to know. And Phoebe is now Queen, of course.'

'Where is she?' I asked.

'You don't need to know that,' Leo snapped. 'And if you've come to negotiate, it'll have to be with me.'

'I think we've heard enough,' I said, rising. 'Mancroft, we shall go to the cathedral with the others and find out their side of the story. And Leo, there must be no more bloodshed. This dispute isn't worth it.'

'Not to you, perhaps,' he said heatedly, but I raised my hand to calm him.

'I didn't say the dispute doesn't matter. Unfair taxation, privilege and bias are important, and we should stop this happening. To that extent, I agree with your complaints. But martial law? Fighting and killing? Burning down churches? It's not a proportionate response.'

I took the sacristan by the elbow and we stepped down off the dais. Leo stayed where he was, clearly unconvinced by my words. I had a feeling there would be a great deal more of the fighting and killing before he was satisfied.

To our horror, we found that the cathedral had also been severely damaged by fire. The roof had been burnt and completely destroyed. Parts of the walls were ruined and none of us knew how much harm had been done to the precious relics within – or even to the Holy Book. As Pockthorpe had told me, the rioters had had no concern for these things when they fired St Michael's.

But the cathedral sits in a very large precinct, and it was hard to understand why anyone felt the need for land outside the walls. There was plenty of space within them. Not that we could get in. The siege meant nobody could get in or out, and all the gates were locked.

I called out in a loud voice. Nobody responded, even when I identified myself as Lord of Hambrig.

'What shall we do?' Father Wymer asked in a quavering voice. 'How shall we attract attention?'

On my instructions, Mancroft scribbled a message on a piece of parchment and impaled it on one of the pikes. One of the young Hambriggers hurled the pike over the wall towards the main door, and it stuck in the ground, quivering and twanging. We waited. At first it looked as if our efforts were in vain, but after some time, a cleric in his long robe emerged.

'Who is that?' I asked Conesford.

'That is Master Westwyck, one of the clerics. Master Westwyck was in favour of meeting the city's demands, but the bishop was adamant there could be no compromise.'

'Will Master Westwyck deliver our letter to the bishop?'

'Indeed, I hope so.'

We waited another very long time, during which I noticed the absence of peels from the cathedral's bells. 'Is no one sounding the hours?' I twisted round to look at Wymer and Pockthorpe. They shrugged, clearly as ignorant as I was. But the more time passed, the more obvious it became that the bells would remain silent.

And then, as dusk fell over the city, we heard footsteps on the gravel, and someone unlocked the gate.

'You may enter,' called a soft voice.

But soft voices often hide unpleasant surprises, so I told my three young companions to keep hold of their pikes and remain outside the gates. I also gave very clear and detailed instructions on what they should do if morning came and no one had returned to them. Then Mancroft, Conesford, Wymer, Pockthorpe and I entered the cathedral precinct.

'Come with me,' Westwyck said. 'The bishop is very pleased you've arrived.'

He led us to a side building, where at least the roof was still on – the bishop's house. We mounted steps to a door which opened into a large hall. There was the usual dais and high table at one end, a screens passage at the other.

'Lord Rory of Hambrig!' A thin man with wispy hair moved towards me with outstretched arms, seizing me and shaking my hand in both of his. 'I am delighted to see you! Now, I hope, we can put a stop to the mayhem of the last few weeks.'

'The last few weeks?' I queried. 'I understood this dispute to date back to the 1250s.'

'Earlier than that, even,' Mancroft murmured. 'But never as violent or as wicked as now.'

'No, indeed,' agreed the bishop, and he indicated the two priests. 'These poor men have had their church fired.'

'Do the rebels have grounds for complaint?' I asked. 'Whatever their means of settling it, do you think they have some cause?'

'Certainly not!' declared the bishop. 'They are a rabble, but it's the King's own daughter who's leading this. It's her presence that has caused this business to flare up in this way.'

'Have you seen her?'

'She came here. She tried to tell us we're wrong, but she doesn't understand. And the new commander of the Squad is some young upstart. Yet this dispute goes back forty years. Many people don't know the history, the *facts*. The cathedral has owned God's Acre for a century and a half! Hence its name, Lord Rory, hence its name. People simply don't understand the historical reasons for our claim.'

'They see it as unfair. The history behind it is irrelevant to them.'

He bridled at that, but it was clearly the truth. This man Leo had done wrong in inciting rebellion and the violence that went with it, but his judgement that the situation wasn't fair or right was understandable. As for Phoebe though... All my previous impressions of her were that she had few if any meaningful thoughts or ideas in her fluffy little head. Someone was pulling Phoebe's strings.

I took Master Mancroft on one side. 'Go back to the palace and track down Queen Phoebe. See if you can find out from her what really happened to Julia, and then, if you can, bring Phoebe to the livery stables. I'll meet you there with the others tomorrow morning. But see no harm comes to the Queen.'

Mancroft looked at the bishop, who would, in normal circumstances, be in charge here. These were not normal circumstances, and the bishop simply gestured towards me. Without another word, the sacristan sped away into the dusky city.

5

I SAW THE BODIES

The self-imposed siege was mild enough. Food was brought in by servants who sneaked out of the gates at night and returned before morning, the cathedral's treasurer having given them money to bribe the market traders to put food by for collection later. Naturally, the traders charged a hefty premium for their wares, and even offered to deliver them personally – for a further fee of course. But there's never any shortage of funds in a religious house, so the bishop affected not to notice what was going on, and the treasurer continued to ensure that nobody went hungry. It was the same with firewood.

In this way, the officers and servants of the cathedral carried on pretty much as normal – apart from the fact that they were all confined to the few buildings whose roofs remained intact, there were no services to conduct, and no one came in. With St Michael's having been burnt to the ground, there was now nowhere for the people of Hicrown to seek solace and the saving of their souls.

'Why should I mind about that?' the bishop asked testily.

'They've chosen to act this way. We had no option but to close our gates.'

But I knew that men from the inside had ventured out and killed people. And there were rumours that, on at least one occasion, the bishop himself had prowled the streets after dark, a dagger hidden beneath his cassock. I didn't question him on that. Not then, anyway.

While Conesford took his usual bed in the monks' dormitory, Wymer, Pockthorpe and I slept in the lay brothers' range, which was huddled against the west wall of the precinct. Many dwellings were given over to the lay brothers, and ours was a large, two-storey house, with four bedchambers. But I awoke during the night, troubled, and I didn't know why.

I was upstairs, while Wymer and Pockthorpe had elected to sleep in the downstairs rooms. I sensed something was wrong. As I made my way down to the ground floor, I heard nothing – and it was the sort of nothing that tells you there's nobody there. I searched all the rooms, both downstairs and back up on the higher floor, but Wymer and Pockthorpe had gone from the house.

Cursing, I went back to my room and pulled on my clothes, checked my sword would glide quickly from its scabbard, and buckled on the belt. With my dagger in my hand, I ventured out into the garth, a lawned garden bordered by trees and hedges. Moonlight showed me the square was empty, so I walked quickly to the bishop's house. I had a feeling I'd find my missing churchmen up to some mischief there, but the mischief proved to be serious.

'What the hell's going on?' I cried, bursting in on the four of them, who stood in the hall with cowls raised, their faces in shadow, although lighted candles shed pools of light around the room. I'd no doubt the men would be armed, but I was in a bad mood and felt ready to take them all on if I had to. Armed they might be, but that didn't make them fighting men.

'You should have stayed in bed, Lord Rory,' Pockthorpe said, his rough voice full of menace. I'd thought of the curate only as a man in anguish at the destruction of his church. He wasn't well spoken, and he'd clearly had other, non-clerical, experiences. Although uncommunicative, he'd been willing to cook for us and to fall in with my plans. Well. My mistake. And it was soon clear I'd made another error.

As I made to block the door, still trying to discover their intentions, Pockthorpe kicked out sharply with his left foot, striking me painfully on the shin and knocking me off balance. I made to recover myself, but Pockthorpe drew a dagger and the tip darted up to my throat. The man loomed closer, his cowl tipping back slightly. Unusually for a clergyman, Pockthorpe knew how to fight.

'I was a Knight-Hospitaller,' he spat out, his dagger tip remaining perilously close to my Adam's apple. 'Out east. Where you was yourself, twenty years ago, but I was there last year and, you know, we was defeated. Do you know who ground us into the dirt?'

'Baibars,' I said.

The dagger withdrew just a little. 'Baibars,' he repeated. 'We was there to defend our fortress in Syria, but we knew it would be a disaster once we saw the extent of the Mamluk forces. De Reval, though, Guardian of the Hospitallers, which he still is, was all for negotiating. A truce. A peace deal! Which was exactly what Baibars knew he'd do, but Baibars had set a trap, just as he did in Mansurah when you was there—'

'How do you know so much about me?' I asked suddenly.

'I know a great deal about you.' Pockthorpe's voice was little more than a whisper. Conesford, Wymer and the bishop had moved back against the wall. The message was clear: they had nothing to do with Pockthorpe's attack on me. Well, that was good. Pockthorpe, who'd barely said a word on our journey to Hicrown, was emerging as a man filled with rancour. And if he'd truly experienced the heat of the Egyptian desert, the intelligent aggression of Baibars and the terror of the Mamluk horsemen, then I knew I could deal with him.

'What happened?' I asked.

'He slaughtered us. Not many survived, and fewer still escaped.'

'So you were lucky?'

'No. I was prepared. I knew about him, you see. My uncle told me.' I waited, knowing he'd say more. 'My uncle's Joel Rice. He told me all about you and your Crusade.'

I'd never heard of Joel Rice. 'In that case,' I said, 'you'll know how Baibars spoke directly to me and spared my life, though he could easily have taken it.'

Pockthorpe's eyes widened. 'Baibars spared your life? Why'd he do that?'

'He knew he didn't have to kill us. Our whole army was at his mercy, and he didn't have to bother with two lowly knights-at-arms.'

'Two? Who was the other one?'

'A friend.'

'Oh yeah. My uncle knows this friend. Your friend didn't trust you, did he. He said you was a liar. He said you was a dishonest man.'

I was bewildered. How could this man's uncle know

Jonny? How could he know about the secrets I'd kept from my best friend? The lies I'd told? It was impossible!

Pockthorpe's dark eyes were moving over my face. 'I think I've set out my credentials convincingly enough. So will you join us, Lord Rory? Uphold the law of the church?'

But I was still rocked by Pockthorpe's knowledge of Mansurah, and I couldn't think. Impatiently, the curate repeated his question.

'I will not join you,' I said at last. 'The people of this city have a point, and I will not join you in fighting them. I'm here, at your request, to resolve things peacefully.'

'That's *his* request, not mine.' Pockthorpe jerked his head towards Wymer.

'Tomorrow,' I said, 'we shall get the leaders of both sides round a table—'

'It's been tried,' Pockthorpe told me, interrupting rudely. 'Tried: failed; tried again: still useless. D'you think Sir Allan is the type of man to negotiate? I tell you now, he'd rather put an arrow in all our hearts.'

'And where is Sir Allan? Do you know?'

'Mancroft'll find him,' Pockthorpe said. 'You sent him for Queen Phoebe, and that's where Allan'll be too. If you speak to the Queen, it'll be through Allan. Nothin' happens here without his say-so. The girl's his puppet.'

I turned to the other three. 'Bishop, I am asking you to do nothing further in this dispute. We do not want anyone else to die. I will try to settle things at the palace. Father Wymer, you will remain here and do your best to help the bishop.'

I turned on my heel, put my hand firmly on Pockthorpe's shoulder and marched him outside. The sky would begin to lighten soon, as Mallrovian nights are short, even towards the end of the summer.

I turned to face Pockthorpe. 'I don't know who Joel Rice is, although he seems to know who I am. But if he's your uncle, he's likely a good deal older than you are. So we shall leave Master Rice out of things for now. You are going to help me arrive at a peaceful solution to this dispute, Pockthorpe. I want your word on that, as a former Knight-Hospitaller.

'Aren't you forgettin' this?' he said, thrusting forward with his dagger.

'Not at all,' I replied, flicking it from his hand with my own weapon. As the curate's dagger fell to the grass, his eyes blazed with anger, and I realised I couldn't leave him with the others. So I picked up his dagger, put it through my own belt and told him to follow me.

In the moonlight, we made our way on horseback to the palace, Pockthorpe, Conesford and me – and I had my three Hambriggers alongside, all armed with their pikes. Pockthorpe could see the situation well enough, and he had the good sense to go along with it. By my calculations, Baron Giles would be here in a couple of days, and I hoped his garrison, in their bright blue-and-silver blazons, would put the fear of God into everyone: cathedral, palace and citizens alike. In the meantime, I intended to do what I could.

I spoke quietly to the Hambriggers. 'Leave your pikes here, but take your daggers and search the palace. You're looking for Queen Phoebe. Check the livery stables first. Master Mancroft should have taken the Queen there by now, but if he hasn't, you must look for her yourselves. When you find her, bring her to me. If she's being well guarded, use your judgement. Don't get yourselves killed, and don't put Phoebe in danger either. If Sir Allan is with her, come back here and report to me. You can't take him on, so don't even try.'

I had no idea where Allan's allegiance lay in this dispute, but it seemed likely he agreed with Leo. After all, Allan himself must have put Leo in charge of the Squad, and clearly he'd promoted himself to be the Queen's bodyguard-cum-advisor. I couldn't disagree that she'd need both those things.

My men told me they understood. The royal palace is not a fortress. It relies on the high city walls and impregnable gates to defend Hicrown. The palace itself is a showy building with beautiful grounds and gardens. The walls surrounding it are no more than five feet high. Successive monarchs have wanted their subjects to see and admire the palace's splendour.

So the three of us dismounted, and I boosted my Hambriggers over the wall. I was left with Conesford and Pockthorpe, and I didn't trust either of them, especially the unstable Pockthorpe. The pikes were leaning against the palace wall, around eight feet away. I stationed myself on Blue in front of the other two, the sun rising behind me as the new day dawned.

Conesford looked bored. Pockthorpe reminded me of Yan, the evil priest in the church in Saintes. It gives you authority, priesthood. You can tell people whatever you like, and they'll believe you. You represent God, so you have absolute power. I stared at Pockthorpe with dislike. He was subservient to Wymer, but Wymer was an old woman, and no one would listen to him. And who was this Joel Rice who'd told Pockthorpe so much detail about my crusading years? That was still a mystery.

A couple of hours went by. Neither the King's Squad nor the Palace Guard arrived, and the Hambriggers were still absent as well. No sign of Master Mancroft, Sir Allan or Queen Phoebe. Although it was still early morning, the sun had risen into a cloudless sky, and everyone was hungry and thirsty. Pockthorpe licked dry lips every few moments, and then, alarmingly, began to sway in the saddle. I'd allowed each of them to dismount for a piss, in view of us all, and then get straight back in the saddle. But illness would be another matter. Pockthorpe suddenly cried out. He let go of his horse's reins, and his arms began to flail in the air.

'Are you ill?' I called to him.

'If I don't eat, I feel bad,' he moaned. 'Sometimes I pass out.'

'What do you know about this?' I asked Conesford, but he shook his head. He wouldn't know; he was a cantor in the cathedral and almost certainly had few dealings with St Michael's.

I spoke to Pockthorpe, who was now bent low over his horse's neck. 'What does Father Wymer do when you get like this?'

'He gives me bread. I feel better at once. Bread's what I need.' And with that, he toppled right off his horse and lay, face down and unmoving, on the path.

Conesford looked at me, but I had my dagger in my hand and I raised it so he could see. 'Don't move,' I said. 'I don't care if he's dead or dying, you don't move.'

Time dragged on and on, while Pockthorpe's inert form told me this was no trick. He couldn't have lain that still for so long.

'Conesford.' I pointed my dagger at him. 'Dismount, turn Pockthorpe over and find out if he's still alive.'

The sick man's face was grey and clammy.

'I think he's dying,' Conesford called up to me. 'We should get him to a physician.'

'We're not moving from here.'

But Conesford was a man of the church. He objected to this cavalier attitude to a dying man. Before I could stop him, Conesford had run to the palace wall and was levelling a pike at me.

I drew my sword, leant forwards and down between Blue's ears, and I dug in my heels. Blue thundered back towards the palace wall, and I used my sword to knock Conesford's pike to the side. Blue took off in a beautiful arc, clearing the wall easily. We landed in the palace garden, but galloped on, past the palace itself, then right behind it and towards the King's Squad accommodation. Which was where I saw the bodies.

6

DO EXACTLY AS I SAY

The Palace Guard has always been inferior in status to the King's Squad. The Squad are the elite in Hicrown, the best of the best, and their commander is second only to the King and his tenants-in-chief in the whole of our Mallrovian hierarchy. The Palace Guard commander ranks far below, and as I gazed at the man's body, and cudgelled my brains to try and recall his name, I thought of how King Philip loved an elite.

His Spiderboats, for example. A small fleet of hand-picked captains and crews in gleaming vessels, sent out to patrol the country's waterways and to deliver and collect messages from all corners of the kingdom. The Spiderboats had been Philip's special project. They nearly broke the treasury, but they looked so bloody good, Philip thought they were worth it. Mallrovia's taxation levels reflected this need for everything to look perfect. Philip needed to impress people. Perhaps this was something to do with being monarch of a tiny country hardly anyone has heard of, or perhaps it was just his nature.

Whatever the reason, the King's Squad, like the

Spiderboats, were an elite – but, after a while, a reciprocal view also took hold. Now, those in the Palace Guard were seen as failures, the ones who didn't make it into the Squad. Perhaps that subtle shift in thinking shouldn't have made a difference, but it did. The Palace Guard grew resentful, and the Squad became overbearing and haughty. It was an unhealthy situation, but Philip, far from stamping it out, seemed to encourage it. It was always the Squad that paraded in the main square where everyone could see them and admire them. The Guard had their duties, but they were seldom on show.

Well, the King's dead now, and so, it seemed, were the Guard. I gazed at the twenty or so men, in their Palace Guard surcoats and insignia, and I wondered how they'd come to be slaughtered in the grounds of their own palace.

Scattered among them lay others – civilians – but how they'd got themselves so deep inside the palace walls I had no way of knowing. Blue picked her way carefully through the bodies, which lay haphazardly where they'd fallen. Had there been an actual battle here, I wondered? What had caused this carnage? I saw no arrows sticking out, no daggers protruding from anyone's dead flesh.

And then I saw my Hambriggers. All three of them lay dead on the bloodstained grass, their daggers gone. I halted Blue and stood looking at those three men. They'd been obedient and loyal, and I'd barely even learnt their names. Whoever had done this to my people would pay for it.

I moved on, and came, eventually, to the Squad's accommodation block, which was, of course, separate from the Guard's inferior quarters. I dismounted and tied Blue to a spike in the wall. I'd never been inside this building before, and when I entered I was surprised to find it austere and functional. The Squad, when they parade, are always immaculately turned out in red and silver, their uniforms of the highest and most expensive quality. Yet this building reflected none of that.

I mounted a bare staircase and came to a room I instantly recognised. It was similar to the mess in our gatehouse, where our off-duty troops can relax. Or they would, if there were any. My mouth twisted at this reminder that Castle Rory has no garrison, no troops and nobody in the gatehouse. And now even I wasn't there. I could only pray no one would attack us. This must surely be the weakest point in our entire history.

But there was no one here either; the Squad had gone. I continued up another flight of steps, and here, at the top, were two doors, one each side of the top step. I listened outside each. From behind the door to my left I heard voices – a man's and a woman's. With my sword in my hand, I opened the door and entered the room.

'Lord Rory!' gasped Queen Phoebe, jumping to her feet. She didn't look at all like a queen. She was dressed in drab clothes, with a dirty wimple covering her hair. Her face was exactly as I remembered it: small and pretty, but with a vacant look in her eyes. As I stared at her, she began smoothing down her apron with her hands, over and over. I'd seen this behaviour in other women a couple of times before, and it always shows nervousness and tension. This woman would be easy to manipulate. The man beside her was Sir Allan, former commander of the King's Squad, now, presumably, elevated to some higher status. They'd been sitting at a small table, on which a couple of empty goblets rested. Allan sat there still, his legs spread wide, one arm draped over the back of the couch. He was making it quite clear that Phoebe might be Queen, but he was in charge and she would do as she was told.

'How did you get in?' he asked. It sounded as though he was merely interested.

'My horse jumped the wall.'

Phoebe gasped again and turned to look at Allan. Seeking guidance on what to say or do now.

Allan ignored her. 'Then, Lord Rory, I suggest you jump right back again. If not, your corpse will join all the others.'

'What happened to them?'

'It's not your place to ask questions—' Phoebe began petulantly, but Allan smoothly interrupted her.

'It's natural for Lord Rory to want to know how so many died here,' he said. 'You'll have heard about the fuss the cathedral is kicking up? All because a few people wanted to do some good, honest target practice with their lances?'

'So they set up their quintains in God's Acre,' I said. 'A piece of land that belongs to the cathedral. Why there?'

'Why not there?' Allan countered at once. 'It's a nice open area, perfect for the exercise.'

'It was to provoke hostilities,' I said. 'Which it did. So how did it result in the deaths of all in the Palace Guard, Allan?'

'It's "Sir Allan", if you please, Lord Rory. Unfortunately, the Palace Guard failed to recognise Queen Phoebe's authority. There was an uprising, and it had to be quelled.'

'I don't believe that. As Prince Barney also died at Nightmolben, Queen Phoebe is Philip's successor.'

'Exactly!' Allan said, smiling broadly. 'It's just a shame the Guard didn't accept Barney's death. But the lad always was impetuous—'

'You murdered him,' I broke in. 'You *murdered* the King and his son.'

Allan pursed his lips. The fiction that King Philip and his son, Barney, had slipped and fallen to their deaths on the ruined cliffs of Nightmolben, had been accepted by everyone at Castle Rory, and no doubt by everyone here in Hicrown too. But it had been Allan himself who'd written me the letter in which the word 'murder' had been used.

I wondered if Phoebe had conspired to have her father and brother killed. Or had she been so weak, she'd been easily persuaded it was for the best? And if so, what was the argument? I knew this dispute between the cathedral and the city, for all that it dated back decades, was just a front. Allan was using it for his own ends. I just needed to find out what those ends were.

'Look, Allan,' I said, sitting down on a vacant stool. Tentatively, Phoebe sat down again too. 'Why not tell me what's going on? I've no love for patronising clergy either. Arrogant bastards, all of them. What's your aim? I may be able to help.'

'I don't think so,' Allan said drily. 'Wasn't it you who sent a message telling the King I was a traitor? Telling him to hang me? I think that was you?'

'It was Reinhard von Lutterberg. King Philip had a right to know Reinhard's testimony.'

'Before the chief witness so conveniently vanished? Philip had my men out searching for that Livonian day and night for weeks. They knew they'd never find him. Once you'd decided Reinhard would "disappear", we didn't have a chance. Not that the Squad should be used for such duties, but Philip would have no one else. It must be the best, and we must find the man. Philip was beside himself. He couldn't believe he'd been duped so thoroughly and for so long.' Allan gave a short laugh. It was true the King had been duped, and by Allan himself. Allan and the von Lutterbergs had been smuggling textiles from Mallrovia to Europe for years, evading taxes and making massive profits at the King's expense. No wonder he'd been mad.

'I don't understand,' I said, doing my best to sound genuinely puzzled. 'If King Philip thought you were a traitor, why did he put you in charge of finding Reinhard after he escaped?'

'He didn't,' Allan growled. 'He promoted another man over me. I was in chains by then. And if the Squad found Reinhard, I'd be hanged as a traitor, but if they didn't, I'd be hanged for helping him to escape. Which I didn't, because that part of it was you, wasn't it?'

'Not at all.' I shook my head. 'Reinhard escaped, but at least I'd got a written confession out of him first. So what exactly happened at Nightmolben? Can *you* tell me, your Majesty?' I turned to look directly at Phoebe, who flushed and looked away.

'Your Majesty,' I repeated. 'What happened to your father and your brother at Nightmolben?'

'Enough!' Allan shouted, his fist banging down on the table. 'You don't come here and question the Queen!' He rose from his seat, a restraining hand on Phoebe's shoulder. He jerked his head towards me. 'Come with me.' Allan went out, but stood on the top step, holding the door.

I had little choice. Outside the room I watched him close – and then bolt – the door. 'Is she a prisoner?' I asked.

'For now.'

We descended to the bailey. Through the open door to the accommodation, I glimpsed again the bodies strewn around.

'Who killed them?'

'They thought to mount a defence. A stupid gesture.'

'The Squad turned on the Guard?' It was unthinkable.

Allan looked at me long and hard. 'You have no idea of

the scale of this,' he said crisply. 'You think this is a petty dispute between the cathedral officers and the disgruntled townsfolk. You could not be more wrong.'

He was turning to walk away, but I had one last question.

'What's the name of the man who was promoted over you?'

Allan shrugged. 'It hardly matters, Rory. The man's dead now, you can look at his corpse among the others if you want to. Leo is now Captain of the Squad, and he'll do a fine job. He's a good soldier and a natural leader. And I can depend on him to do exactly as I say.'

7

MASTER PETER

The Palace Guard, the former commander of the Squad, a few civilians and my three Hambriggers had all been stabbed to death, not with a dagger but with polearms. Once stabbed, the pike, halberd, bill or harpoon had been pulled free, and, no doubt, used on the next luckless person. The dead soldiers were unarmed, which told me they'd been on their way to the great hall, probably for a meal. Looking behind me, I saw the guardsmen's quarters some yards to the left of the Squad's accommodation block. If you were walking from the Guardsmen's block to the main building, you'd be in the exact line where the bodies lay. So a phalanx of the Squad had lain in wait for their fellow soldiers to walk, unsuspecting and unarmed, to the palace for their dinner. Then the cowardly attack had taken place, running the guardsmen through. Most of the wounds were in the chest and stomach, and those men would have died painful deaths. It took little time to check there was no one still alive. I guessed someone had already done so, and any survivors would have been quickly despatched. This massacre was very recent.

Allan had disappeared, so I quickly sprinted back up the steps of the Squad's block and unbolted the door at the very top.

'Your Majesty, I'm here to rescue you.' I spoke rather breathlessly, standing in the doorway.

She was sitting at the table again, idly throwing a handful of dice around. They clattered onto the table and came to rest before she looked up at me. 'Rescue me? What on earth do you mean, Lord Rory?'

'Allan had locked you in. He's keeping you prisoner. I will take you away from here. To safety.'

'You misunderstand. I am already in a place of safety, indeed, that's exactly why Sir Allan bolts the door.'

'How can that make any difference?' I exclaimed. 'He bolts it from the outside! Anyone can enter, but you can't get out!'

'Sir Allan is keeping me safe here,' Phoebe repeated as she rearranged her dice. 'He's told me it's for my own good.'

Could she really be that stupid? I tried another line. 'Do you agree with the killing of the entire Palace Guard, Phoebe?'

Her eyes widened, but whether that was because of my blunt question or my discourteous form of address I didn't know. She faltered. 'I don't know what you mean.'

'I'll show you what I mean.' I pulled her to her feet and steered her out of the door and down the steps. She tried to resist.

'I can walk by myself,' she protested, but I kept a firm hold of her arm.

We emerged from the block and I walked her right up to the spread of corpses on the ground. A nasty smell was already making itself known, and the fat August flies buzzed as they gorged. A sickening sight. Phoebe gasped, one hand shooting to her mouth. She wobbled on her feet, and I steadied her.

'I don't know who's done this or why,' I said, my face close to hers, 'but I'm going to find out. And if it's your friend Allan, he will not live much longer. And now you are coming with me.'

'No,' she screamed out suddenly, wrenching herself free. 'Sir Allan warned me someone might try to take me away, and I won't go!'

The scream alerted the Squad. Round the corner of the palace they came running, feet pounding along the path, swords drawn. I had my own sword, but there were – what? – twenty of them? Thirty? I grabbed Phoebe and ran, not to the Squad's own accommodation, but to the other building. I dodged behind it, dragging the Queen along too. It was undignified, and I had to keep a hand over her mouth so she didn't scream out where we were. The Squad hadn't gone past their own accommodation block; they wouldn't have seen us. Which didn't, of course, mean they wouldn't find us.

Phoebe's eyes implored me to let her speak, but I kept my hand clamped over her mouth. Behind the building was an area of unkempt scrub, perhaps six feet wide, and beyond that was the palace wall. This part of the wall was rough and badly maintained; hardly anyone ever saw it. The back of the palace faced east, and on the other side was a field used for archery practice, and some common grazing land. I heard the Squad pelting towards us. Selecting the lowest portion of the palace wall, I threw the girl onto the top of it and was slightly alarmed to see her disappear over and down the other side. I quickly scrambled over myself, yanked her up and looked around for the best direction to run in.

'How dare you,' Phoebe spluttered, her mouth full of grass. She'd cut her hands and grazed her knees, but there were no serious injuries. We had landed in rough pasture, and there was no point in heading for the city wall as there was no gate here. The nearest gate out of Hicrown would be the Palace Gate to the north, but we'd have to skirt the entire palace to get to it, and if Captain Leo had any sense, he'd send someone in that direction to head us off. Instead, I made for the Navisar Gate in the east wall of the city. It had the added advantage of being permanently unlocked. Or so my brother had once told me.

'We're getting out of Hicrown,' I said to Phoebe. 'There's to be no argument, and no attempt to alert your friend Allan. Keep your mouth shut, stay with me and you'll be all right. If not, I'm warning you that I have men with pikes waiting for my return. If they don't see me by nightfall, they will come looking, and I don't give much for Allan's chances then.'

It was all a bluff. Neither Conesford nor Pockthorpe would still be there, and Pockthorpe was most likely dead by now.

In the full light of day, I hurried Phoebe round the palace wall to the bridge over the River Shamet. Once over this bridge, we could run down the narrow pathway that leads through meadow pasture, past the courthouse, to the Navisar Road. I thanked God Phoebe was wearing peasants' clothing, although I'd no idea why she was dressed like that.

A shepherd saw us, but made no comment, and two merchants were heading west along the Navisar Road. But they were deep in conversation with each other and took no notice of Phoebe and me.

And so we arrived at the Navisar Gate. I was unfamiliar with this part of Hicrown and tried to recall my brother's description of it. Warehouses had been mentioned: *There are warehouses just inside the gate. I had a good look at them, and guess what? They were full of crates of stuff!* And then: *Men turned up and moved the boxes out of the warehouses. They had a wagon. The boxes were loaded on and the whole lot went out through the Navisar Gate. Which is unguarded and unlocked, by the way.*

But everything might have changed since then, once Reinhard, Carl and Allan were known to have been smuggling wool out of Mallrovia, evading their taxes and robbing the King. So perhaps the gate would be locked now, and perhaps the crates of 'stuff' would be gone. I needed to find out, and I needed to know how much Phoebe knew and why she had sided with the rebels. This was no way for our Queen to behave. I'd kept a tight hold of Phoebe's hand ever since we both landed on the other side of the palace wall, and now I dragged her into one of the warehouses.

These buildings were even more ramshackle than I'd imagined from Nicholas's description. Just beyond them stood the equally neglected Navisar Gate, an egress from our capital city to our exposed eastern shore. It should be the most heavily guarded, not the least. But I knew, from everything Reinhard had said two years ago, that it was Sir Allan, commander of the King's Squad, who had ensured the gate could be accessed at all times by the smugglers.

The warehouse was dark, and our footsteps echoed in the empty space. But there was no musty smell and I guessed the building saw frequent use. I left the door open, waiting for my eyes to adjust to the gloom. I was looking for the 'crates of stuff', when I heard a bang behind me and swung round to see the door closed.

Allan stood in front of it, a lighted lamp swinging from his hand. *Shit.* And now I didn't know where Phoebe was. I'd let go of her once we were in the warehouse. Never thought someone would already be here.

'I was waiting for you,' Allan said pleasantly.

'How did you know I'd come here?'

'Where else would you go? The Palace Gate was too obvious; the Hambrig Gate too far away. And you're curious about our operation out of Navisar. I knew you'd come straight across the meadows to these buildings. So I made sure I got here first.'

'Phoebe!' I called, swinging my arms in a wide circle, hoping to find her.

A small voice answered from right at the back of the building. 'I'm here, Lord Rory, but I'm frightened.'

'What do you want?' I asked Allan softly. 'What's the point of all this?'

'I thought Carl had told you already,' he sneered. 'When you were so pally with him in Bremen. The Swordbrothers—'

'Are Livonian,' I said, interrupting him. 'And therefore nothing to do with you.'

He laughed. 'Join it up, Rory. Everything you know about me. Everything you learnt from Carl. Put it all together – or write it down in your funny little diary. Perhaps that will reveal the truth to you.'

I ignored the insults, both explicit and implied. 'Where is Carl?'

'Busy. As you might imagine, it's quite a job running a business and taking over a country, all at the same time.'

He walked towards me. I've never liked him. He once came to my home to court martial one of my best officers, where he made a complete mess of the proceedings. Another time, he refused to turn out the King's Squad when Castle Rory was under attack and needed help. I didn't know what his 'business' was with the Livonians, but as for 'taking over a country' – that was treason, and it confirmed my opinion of Sir Allan of Hicrown.

'Tell me about this business you're running. Does it involve Mallrovian worsted, by any chance?'

'Well done. Worsted is the finest fabric, and therefore the most expensive. Worsted fibres come from particular sheep, grazing on particular grass in a particular place. No wonder all the rich people want it!'

'And how does Queen Phoebe fit into all this?' I wanted to keep the man talking.

'Queen Phoebe? I don't know who you're talking about.'

There was a whimper from behind me.

Allan made a rude gesture in the direction of the whimper. 'D'you mean Philip's brat? The spoilt little girl? She's no more queen than I am.'

'Didn't you approve of her father either? Is that why you killed him?'

Phoebe screamed, just once, then dissolved into low, desperate sobbing. I kept my eyes on Allan's face, which swung in and out of shadow as the lantern moved in his hand. His eyes were dark, but I could see the jawline outlined by a short, dark beard. The man was fifty-odd, his hair longish and greying. He raised the lantern, as if to help me scrutinise his features. His hand wasn't shaking at all, and he still stood squarely in front of the warehouse door, preventing any attempt at escape.

Allan isn't tall, but he's broad and well-muscled. Quick on his feet as well. For the first time, I spotted the dagger in his other hand. He raised that as well, then bent his knees. I knew he was about to launch himself at me. The lantern began to swing, the dagger's blade catching the light, glinting dangerously in the dark building, flaring towards me. I ran to my left and forwards, hoping to reach the door, at the same moment Allan fell on his face on the dusty floorboards.

Twisting the latch, I hurled the door open. It crashed against the warehouse wall. I could see nothing. Sunlight blinded me, and my eyes still stung from the glare of the lantern and the flashing blade. Someone caught me, wrenching my arm painfully behind my back.

'Best if you don't speak,' said Carl von Lutterberg in a low voice. 'We've been here before, Lord Rory, and you know I'm a desperate man. We know each other too well to pretend. Give me your word you'll stay silent, and I'll release your arm. A nod of the head will do.'

I nodded, and felt the blood rush agonisingly back into my arm as Carl let go. I wanted to rub my arm, but ignored the pain. I turned slowly.

The Livonian grinned at me. 'Good to see you again, Rory. We parted rather suddenly in Bremen a couple of years ago, and then you met my brothers. Didn't you?'

'Yes. One was clever but manipulative; the other, simply evil. Diederich tried to kill me. Reinhard merely escaped from my dungeon.'

'Reinhard did not escape from your dungeon, for he was never in it. He left with Captain William and is at sea with William and his family. As you very well know.'

'And Dicky?' I asked.

'I know you hanged Dicky. But I didn't know he'd tried to kill you. He may have been the eldest of us, but he was always the most stupid. Trying to kill the Lord of Hambrig was a very unwise thing to do.'

'I hope you'll bear that in mind, then, Carl.'

'Why do you think you're still alive? Honestly, Rory, I could have killed you several times over, and so could Allan. I'm guessing you tricked Allan in some way, so I shall have to find out what's happened to him. Come with me. If Allan is hurt or dead, I shall need you. And there is also Phoebe.'

Carl knew I wouldn't abandon Phoebe. We went into the warehouse, and I expected to find Allan laid out on the floor, perhaps unconscious. After all, why else hadn't he emerged from the warehouse as soon as I got the door open? But he wasn't incapacitated. He wasn't even hurt. He was crouching by the wall at the back. In his hand was a wicked-looking knife, which he was holding across Phoebe's throat.

'You are going to head straight back to Hambrig, Rory.' Allan's voice had a dangerous edge. 'And you're going to leave us alone. Carl and I have got work to do. I expect Carl told you you're safe, no one's going to kill you. But that's only true if you're sensible now. Head back to Hambrig, and you'll be all right. But if you double back, or try anything stupid like that, I'll knife you in the throat. Not only that, but Phoebe will not survive.' He pressed a little harder on the knife and Phoebe gave a strangled scream.

'All right,' I said at once. 'I'll have to get my horse from the palace grounds though. Then I'll go back to Hambrig. Can I ask just one question?' I waited, and saw Allan's impatient nod, even as he tilted Phoebe's head further back by pulling on her hair. 'Who killed the Palace Guard?'

Allan jerked his head, and tugged even harder on

Phoebe's hair. Phoebe, terrified, stared at me, her eyes imploring me to save her. 'The Palace Guard were looked after by Leo,' Alan growled. 'I told you he was good at his job.'

I glanced at Carl, who shrugged. My feeling was that Carl didn't agree with Allan, but Allan was in charge so Carl wouldn't argue. Leaving all three of them in the warehouse, I ran back up the road and round the palace wall until I was nearly at the gatehouse. Didn't want to encounter Leo or any of the King's Squad, so I pressed myself against the rough stone wall and edged closer, a little at a time. I heard no sound of orders, boots or weapons, and when I was eventually able to peer through into the garden, I saw it was empty. I hurried through the garden towards the Squad's accommodation block. The bodies hadn't been moved, and the stench was worse.

But Blue *had* been moved. She was no longer tied to the staple in the wall. I looked everywhere, hoping to find some trace of her, but there was nothing. I was beginning to feel faint, partly from hunger, partly from the heat of the day. My head hurt, but I needed to find my horse. She must, surely, have been taken to the stables. Trying to remember where these were, I retraced my steps, then followed the wall around in the other direction.

On the northern side of the palace grounds, I located the stables – an enormous block of loose boxes, with a paddock extending as far as the orchard by the eastern wall. Twice the size of my own stable block. Blue whinnied. She could sense me. Smell me. I hurried towards the sound. She was comfortable enough, and had even been given a nosebag of something, so I made my decision. I hurried across the paddock to the orchard and found bushes with ripe plums and cherries. Picking as many as I could carry, I decided

Blue could have a comfortable day in the Hicrown Palace stables, and I would stay here too, just for a while. Hot, exhausted and ferociously hungry, I was certain no one knew where I was. At the very back of Blue's loose box, I created a neat nest for myself in a pile of fresh straw. After feasting on my plunder, I curled up in the straw, pulling bundles of it over me so I'd be invisible. The straw was fragrant and soft, while the stable roof shielded me from the hot sun. I felt drowsy. Blue would let me know if anyone approached, and in the meantime we could both get some sleep.

And we did. We slept well, and would have slept longer, if I hadn't been unceremoniously woken by Master Peter.

8

THE ROAD TO NAVISAR

Peter had been desperate to get to Hicrown, but he's not a good horseman. Worried about making the journey on his own, he knew it would take three days, possibly four, and he was anxious about where he might sleep, where he'd find food and what he might encounter on his journey. He'd asked Bryce for help, and the two of them had set off on a couple of ageing palfreys from the stable.

Bryce assured me earnestly that Branca had given permission for him to go, which was just as well, for they'd met many roving bandits as they approached the capital. Peter would not have fared well on his own. I was unsurprised at the news. Many Hicrowners were taking advantage of this time of lawlessness, roaming the countryside in menacing groups looking for vulnerable travellers. Regrettable, but inevitable, and it would spread across the country in no time. Mallrovia would soon be in chaos.

Listening to Bryce, I came to understand that Branca is now in charge at Castle Rory. Perhaps Rosa had asked her to take these decisions. Or Inka hadn't understood what to do in my absence. I thought I'd made it clear to her, but Branca might simply have taken over. No matter – I would fix these things later.

'But why did you want to come?' I asked Peter. We were all crouching down in the hay at the back of Blue's stall, which, as Bryce explained, was how they'd found me, since they'd heard Blue whinnying, and Bryce had recognised her.

'It's my fault, Lord Rory,' Peter said unhappily. 'Please don't blame Bryce, he were only bein' helpful, like. I couldn't have done owt wi'out his help.'

'Why did you want to come to Hicrown?' I asked again.

'I d'nt' know how to explain to thee, lord. An' there's too much to explain, anyroad. Can I ask thee? Hast tha seen t' King's Squad? Are they here?'

'They're here.' My tone was bitter. 'And they've murdered the entire Palace Guard and the three young men I brought with me from Hambrig Town. This quarrel between the city folk and the cathedral is all tied up somehow with the King's Squad and those von Lutterberg brothers. And Queen Phoebe, too.' Peter's good at solving puzzles. Perhaps he might make sense of this one.

'Oh, that's terrible, lord, terrible!' Peter's voice cracked with emotion. 'That's why I'm here. I need to see t' Squad.'

'You need to see the Squad?' Peter had never been a soldier. Had never fought a battle. In fact, I didn't think he'd had even the mildest of punch-ups in his whole life.

'Shall I explain to Lord Rory?' Bryce asked.

'Yes, explain, Bryce,' I said.

'Master Peter's son is here. He needs to find him. Urgently, he says.'

For a few moments I thought I must have misheard. Peter doesn't have a son! He has no wife, no children...

'Lord, I were married once,' Peter said desperately. 'An' I have a son, who's in t' King's Squad, here in t' palace. I d'n't know what he's done. I need to find out, lord. I need to see him.'

I tried to make sense of this. How was it Peter had never mentioned the boy? Or the wife, for that matter?

I told Peter we'd look for his son, cutting short his mumbled thanks and almost-tearful gratitude, and we all got to our feet. Bryce and Peter mounted their palfreys, while I saddled Blue and led her out of the stables.

'Your son,' I called to Peter. 'What does he look like? And what's his name?'

'He's a strappin' lad, I suppose tha'd say. His name—' Peter stopped suddenly. Marching towards us was the Squad itself, under the command of Captain Leo. From Peter's gasp, and the sudden skittering of his horse, I knew he'd spotted his son among the soldiers, and, without him having to tell me, I felt certain it was Leo himself. The bright swords and burnished shields of the Squad were blinding in the sunlight. Their uniforms were, as always, immaculate, and they clashed to attention at their leader's command while some twelve feet away from us. Beside me, Peter was giving small moans of distress. He raised a hand and, with a shaking finger, pointed to the young commander.

I dismounted and stepped forwards to talk directly to Leo, but he stared straight past me, almost as if I weren't there. In fact, as if none of us were there, even though there were three horses standing directly in front of his men. Nor did he acknowledge his father, and I began to wonder if Peter were deluded. No wife or child had ever been mentioned to me. Peter had never, as far as I knew, made the journey to Hicrown to see his son, nor had any son shown up at Castle Rory. Perhaps the poor fellow was imagining a family he'd never had.

'Captain Leo,' I called, loudly enough for him to hear me. He swivelled round and his eyes fastened on me. He had a Mediterranean look to him. Golden-toned skin. Dark hair and eyes. Oval-shaped face with defined cheek bones. Slightly under average height. He looked nothing at all like Peter, reinforcing my doubts about the older man's claims.

But I needed information. 'Captain Leo, what is going on here? Your allegiance is to Queen Phoebe—'

'Stop right there,' he said. 'It's not for you to tell me my duties. Sir Allan of Hicrown is my general, and I obey him. Now that King Philip's dead, there is no King of Mallrovia. Sir Allan has told me to parade my men in the square, and I intend to do so. We shall then attack the rabble who have sought to undermine Sir Allan's authority in the city.'

'Sir Allan has no authority in the city,' I said at once. 'Sir Allan's authority is confined to the palace garrison, including the Palace Guard, who seem to have been massacred. Was that your doing?'

He flashed me a look of anger, clenching his jaw before saying, 'This is not your concern, Lord Rory. You were warned to stay away. You were warned to look after your own. Unguarded, undefended, what do you think is happening at Castle Rory at this very moment? Don't make the mistake of thinking Sir Allan's threats are idle ones. You have a wife and children to defend. Hicrown is not your concern.'

'Lord,' Bryce whispered, slithering down from his horse and hurrying to stand next to me. 'He's right, lord. Someone came to the castle after you'd left. He said things which frightened the women. Even Lady Rosa was upset.'

'Do you know who it was?'

But Bryce didn't know.

I looked round and saw Peter still sitting unhappily on his palfrey, while Bryce's horse and Blue waited patiently. Then I glanced at Bryce. Bryce Farr, son of my stonemason, had been odd-job boy and gardener at Castle Rory for the last ten years or so. He was now in his early twenties, I guessed, and – as Peter would say – a strapping lad. He carried a dirk through his belt, but had no armour, no shield and no other weapon. Still, he was strong and he was young. I must make the most of him. Peter would be no help whatsoever.

I drew my sword and positioned myself for attack, shield to the fore, sword raised. Bryce, without a word from me, tugged the dirk from his belt. It was a long-bladed knife, good for thrusting and close combat, but these men in the King's Squad would be wise to its limitations. So I pulled out Pockthorpe's dagger and threw it, hilt first to Bryce. Catching it deftly, he shoved it through his belt. It would serve him if the dirk became unusable.

'Follow me,' I shouted to Bryce, turning, running, and hurling myself into Blue's saddle. Leo's eyes widened in disbelief, and then, as Bryce and I charged our horses straight into the ranks of pretty red-and-silver soldiers, they scattered, flinging themselves to the side and onto the ground. Of course, Bryce's palfrey didn't like it one bit. It reared up and dumped Bryce on the ground, then galloped off and was soon out of sight. I wheeled Blue round in the middle of the path. The Squad were on their feet again, reaching for weapons, but Leo bellowed at them, and they snapped to attention instead. I had to hand it to Leo. He'd kept his head and rallied his men, preventing them from an undisciplined counter-attack, which would have been disastrous. Instead, they quickly surrounded Blue, Bryce and me.

Out of the corner of my eye, I saw Peter dismount and begin to walk towards us. I had the alarming thought he was about to do something heroically stupid and ruin everything.

'Stay where you are, Peter,' I called, emphasising his name, while looking at Leo for a reaction. But there was none.

I walked Blue towards Leo. 'Do you know that man?' I pointed to Peter. 'Do you know him, Leo? He says he's your father.'

There was a frisson of interest from the Squad, who were all staring at Peter now.

'Leo!' Peter called, holding his hands out. It seemed he was about to be pathetically stupid, rather than heroically so. 'Leo, tell Lord Rory who th'art! Who were thy mother! Why th'art here...' Peter's voice faltered and he stopped, though his hands were still held imploringly towards the man he claimed was his son.

Leo ignored him, but walked up close to Blue. I could have taken his head off with my sword, but if Peter really *was* his father...

'Sir Allan is going to ruin Mallrovia,' I said quietly.

'No, Lord Rory. Sir Allan will take Mallrovia for himself, so he has no desire to ruin it. And I'm sorry, but you can't appeal to my patriotic instincts since I'm not Mallrovian. I don't care who's king or queen here. If Sir Allan rules the land, I shall get a good job and be handsomely paid. That's an appealing idea for me. Sir Allan knows what he's doing. He has a good plan. One that's been ready and waiting for a long time. And now – now we're putting it into action.'

'Why now?'

'We just needed a spark. The cathedral owns God's Acre, land outside its precinct, and the people living there pay no taxes to the city. That has been going on for a long time, but we provided a spark by getting the citizens to set up target practice on that land. The cathedral didn't like it. As for why now – it's obvious, isn't it?'

'The King's death?'

'And that of his heir.'

'Yet he has another heir. Women inherit in Mallrovia, Leo. Or didn't Allan tell you that?'

He shrugged. 'It makes no difference now. Phoebe's no longer Queen. In fact, Phoebe's no longer in Mallrovia—'

'What do you mean, you pile of shit?' I snarled. 'Phoebe is in Mallrovia, I saw her myself yesterday.'

Men turned up and moved the boxes out of the warehouses, Nick's voice said in my head. *They had a wagon. The boxes were loaded on and the whole lot went out through the Navisar Gate.*

Phoebe was in the warehouse to be taken through the Navisar Gate and shipped out of the country. And I, myself, had delivered her to Allan. He'd been waiting. No wonder she'd been dressed in peasant clothing. No wonder she'd been so terrified. But could she have been moved on already?

'Bryce,' I said in a low voice. 'Do you know where the Navisar Gate is?'

'No, lord. But I'll find it.'

'It's in the eastern city wall. There are some buildings just inside the gate. Warehouses. Phoebe was in the first one you come to, but she may be in a different one, or they may have taken her through the gate and be on their way to Navisar. If she's not there, don't follow. Allan's a dangerous man. I'll join you at the gate as soon as I can.'

'If the Queen's there, lord, do you want me to bring her to you?'

'No. Watch what's going on. Keep an eye on everything. And ride fast, there's no time to lose.'

I looked into his eyes and saw intelligence and understanding. So I fell sideways off Blue, landing from a height on top of Leo, creating a diversion as the other soldiers all piled in to help their captain. By the time I'd managed to extricate myself, apologising for losing my balance, Bryce had gone.

But Peter was still here, and now he came rushing to stand in front of Leo.

'Leo! What art tha doin'? Lord Rory is tryin' to help thee!'

'I've nothing to say to you,' the young man rasped. 'I have a job to do, and the Lord of Hambrig, far from trying to help me, has been a hindrance all along. Move aside please.'

Poor Peter stood to one side, flustered and upset, while Leo got his troops in line again, marched them to the gatehouse and then out into the city. I listened to the tramp of their boots as they filed down the street, and when I could hear them no more, I looked over at Peter. He was staring at the ground.

'Peter. I have to go and rescue Phoebe. I hope Bryce has found her already, but I have to go and help.'

'I understand, lord,' Peter said, though he didn't look up at me. 'I had a feelin' 't would be summat like this. It's why I came, like. Had to see what he were doin'. Di'n't know it were treason. I don't know what to say, lord. He's my son, though he d'n't behave like it.'

'He didn't seem to know you, Peter,' I said gently, as I mounted Blue again. 'Perhaps there's some mistake?'

He looked up then. 'Some mistake? I know my own son,

Lord Rory. An' he knows me, an' all. He's all puffed up wi' bein' Captain o' t' Squad now. He di'n't want to know me in front o' his men, that's all it is, lord. He's ashamed o' who he really is.'

I told Peter to look after the horses in the stables and then stay put at the back of one of the stalls. With the Squad gone, and Allan gone too, the palace was likely the safest place in Hicrown. Then I dug my heels into Blue's sides and cantered out through the arched gatehouse, heading east, as I'd told Bryce to do.

He was waiting, exactly as instructed, by the warehouses.

'She's not here, lord,' he called, as I rode quickly up to him. 'I didn't see them take her away, but she's not in any of these buildings. The Squad turned up with their captain, and they didn't even look into the buildings. They marched straight through the gate and onto the road to Navisar. But they've killed the other man.'

'What other man, Bryce?'

'Master Mancroft, lord. His body's in the warehouse. It's sacrilege, isn't it?'

I went inside to look. Bartholomew Mancroft's throat had been cut. I'd sent him to find Phoebe, and he must have chased her here, only to be followed by Captain Leo. No mercy had been shown, not even to the man in charge of the cathedral's sacred vessels. Sacrilege, indeed.

Bryce and I rode through the Navisar Gate and followed on the heels of the King's Squad. It was by no means certain they were going to Navisar, as there's a spur off this road. It's just a rough, grassy track, but if you follow it for a few miles you come to the secret city of Myrtile. I call it 'secret' because it's not easy to get to, and people almost never go there. I, myself, had never been to Myrtile, but it was where Sir Patrick and his wife lived. Patrick was my steward once, and my father's steward before that. He'd been gone from Hambrig many years now, but I still missed him. He was far and away the best steward I'd had, and the most upright, honest and respectable man I'd ever known.

'Why would they go there?' Bryce asked, after I'd voiced the Myrtile option.

'I don't know that they would, but Joan told me once that the best worsted wool comes from Myrtile. Something to do with special sheep, although I don't remember exactly. And it's our worsted that's being smuggled out of Mallrovia through Navisar. Then again, if they've got Phoebe with them, perhaps they're heading straight for the beach.'

'But why, lord? Why take her to the beach?'

'To get her out of the way. Allan wants Mallrovia. This is a coup, Bryce, and it'll be a bloody successful one if we can't rescue Phoebe.'

'What are we going to do if her Majesty's already been shipped out?' Bryce sounded worried, but it was going to be far more of a challenge if she *hadn't* yet been put on a ship. I had no idea how the two of us were going to fight a troop of around twenty men in order to rescue our Queen. Whereas if the ship had sailed, there'd be little we could do to help Phoebe, and even less point in getting ourselves killed by Captain Leo.

'We will have to see, Bryce,' I said. 'How much fighting experience do you have?'

I looked over at him then, trying to see him as a comrade-in-arms, a warrior by my side. I found it hard. Bryce Farr, odd-job-boy, usually bare-chested or in shirtsleeves and breeches, felling trees for firewood, fetching water from the well or running errands. He was a menial servant, although not an unfree one, and his position in my household was low. His father, I now remembered, had been chosen by Rosa to take a message to Jonny in England. Had he done so? Would Jonny respond?

I looked again at Bryce. Through circumstances neither of us had envisaged, the young servant was going to have to fight by my side. As an equal. We would have to trust each other, and Bryce would have to show some initiative and not simply wait for orders.

'I don't have any fighting experience,' he said, which was at least honest. 'Apart from a bust-up in the tavern one time. Just used my fists. I can't use a sword. I have a bow, of course, but it's not with me. I didn't think. I'm sorry, lord.'

'You don't need to be sorry. You couldn't possibly have known of this situation, and you were just trying to help Master Peter. You'll have to use your wits, Bryce, along with that dagger and your dirk. Act on instinct, don't wait to check with me first, do what you think needs doing. I'll be doing the same. We must look out for each other. Do you understand?'

'Yes, lord. I'll do my best.'

'I know you will. Keep your eyes open and your mind alert. We're nearly at the Myrtile road. Look for signs that will tell us if they turned off towards Myrtile, or continued on to Navisar.'

It was, as it turned out, completely obvious. The track leading to Myrtile is grassy, and the grass had not been trampled. But the road wending its way towards the coast showed the boot prints of many men. Bryce and I nodded to each other, picked up our pace and continued riding down the road to Navisar.

9

HOW THE HELL DOES IT ALL FIT TOGETHER?

After several hours hard riding it was almost completely dark, and we stopped for the night. I reckoned we were about two thirds of the way there. There was a little food left in Bryce's saddle bag, including some of the plums I'd foraged and the cold meat and sourdough bread Rachel had thoughtfully packed. So Bryce and I ate our supper, then slept by the roadside, taking turns to keep watch. It was a restless, uncomfortable night for both of us.

'Another ten miles,' I called back next morning, when Bryce asked how much further.

Behind me, Bryce urged the palfrey forwards, and I felt confident we'd make it.

We didn't make it.

Barely an hour had passed before we heard noises. Once you've heard the sounds made by an army on the move, you can never mistake them for anything else. It was far too soon for the King's Squad to have reached Navisar. They must have turned round again, and perhaps Phoebe would be with them. I could only hope so.

There was no cover. We'd almost reached the dunes and were heading downhill to the sea, while the soldiers marching towards us had to climb up. They weren't yet in sight – hidden by a bend in the track – but they were coming nearer.

I motioned to Bryce to keep both still and quiet, and so we waited. Around the bend they came, and I felt my heart start to pound. I'd expected the red-and-silver battalion, headed by Captain Leo. But the army marching up the Navisar Road was twice the size of the King's Squad. They wore white surcoats blazoned with a red cross patee, and under it a red sword, pointing down. Their shields carried the same motifs. Their leader had an embellished version: both cross and sword outlined in gold. I recognised the man and I knew his organisation.

The Livonians halted with a thunder of boots on the track and a clash of swords against shields. Their bronze helmets reflected the morning sun, and they presented arms with a flourish.

'What is happening here, Carl von Lutterberg?' I called out, wanting Bryce to know the man's name.

'It is exactly as you see, Lord Rory,' Carl said sarcastically. 'We are the Livonian Swordbrothers—'

'You are no such thing,' I declared loudly, looking over his head at the warriors standing to attention behind him. 'The Swordbrothers have not existed since 1236. It was you, Carl von Lutterberg, who told me this. You are now the Livonian Order, and, though you wear the red cross pattee , the sword is no longer part of your blazon. It was taken from you after your defeat at Saule.'

I watched the men, and was surprised at their level of discipline. I'd expected growls of anger at my words, even the shaking of fists or the thrusting skywards of swords, but none of that happened. The warriors maintained their positions and did not react in any way. I'd spoken in Latin. They'd have understood me.

'And that, you see, is the problem,' Carl said smoothly. And in English. 'We wish to resume our status as Swordbrothers, and this I also told you. We had intended to capture a castle on your eastern seaboard. From there we would have launched attacks on other Mallrovian strongholds, defeating them and becoming masters of the whole country. Mallrovia is a strategic place for Livonians. Your land mass projects into the North Sea and provides a safe base from which to launch raids in the Low Countries and the Baltic. From Mallrovia, we can assert our independence, freeing ourselves from the Teutonic Knights, and establishing a new Order of the Livonian Swordbrothers.

'I'm disappointed in you, Rory. You must have known we would not give up. You must have known the plan might change, but it would still be operational. Otto and Dicky are dead, it's true. Two of the Brothers, gone. So it falls to me and to Reinhard—'

'Reinhard is at sea. He can't help you.'

'He has already helped a great deal, Rory, and will do so again. Look at the size of my forces. And by the way, I know all about your Darkness. Reinhard was very helpful with his information about you. I'm thinking it's not worth the risk for you. That Darkness – it hovers just on the horizon, doesn't it? So I don't think you can stop us. I don't think you'll even try.'

He was right, of course. Bryce and I couldn't stop this disciplined, well-armed force of men. Carl's references to my Darkness were stabs into an old wound. But I wanted to join things up. 'Where does Allan fit into this?'

'Allan is our contact in Hicrown. Reinhard told you that. Or no, as I understand it, Reinhard told Sir William, and Sir William told Reinhard he could get rich if he became a pirate. So off they went, the two of them pirates now. And when Reinhard returns, he'll be a rich man, and the campaign will have a war chest. Meanwhile, Allan and I take Mallrovia, reinforce our army, build ships, fortify the ports of Navisar and Pevarile and take over the *kontor* in Hambrig. Sounds like a plan, right?'

'And Phoebe?'

'I have other plans for Phoebe.'

The day was suddenly chill. I jerked my head to Bryce and we picked our way past the massed ranks of Livonians, then cantered as fast as we could, given the state of the Navisar Road, on towards the sea.

Another hour, and we were urging Blue and the palfrey up and over the sand dunes, then down the other side and onto Navisar beach. Which was empty.

Small waves lapped onto the sands, already smoothing over the marks left by the Livonians' boots. I dismounted and began to look for traces of activity. Bryce joined me.

'A scuffle or a fight, or anything Phoebe might have dropped, whether deliberately or accidentally. Any clues at all,' I told Bryce brusquely, allocating one half of the beach to him, the other to me. We quartered the entire area between us, our eyes rarely lifting from the sands, the marram grass and the flinty stones. When I shouted it was time, we met in the middle to compare notes.

'I didn't find anything the princess dropped,' Bryce told me. 'But I saw blood. You need to come and see, lord.'

He took me to the north end of the beach and showed me, first, footprints in the sand, and then patches of dried blood on the grass and stones that cover the dunes. The feet had been bare, you could see all the individual toes, and there were many of them. I don't mean there were many footprints, although there were, of course. I mean there were many feet. Many people.

'They're all girls, I reckon,' Bryce said. Not only had he bent down to look closely at the prints, but he'd taken off his boots and was comparing his own feet to the marks in the sand. 'Mine are huge compared to these.'

I stared at the prints. Bryce was right; the prints had been made by women or children. Perhaps both. 'How many people, do you think?' My voice sounded hoarse. *What* had been going on here?

'Dunno, lord. Half a dozen, maybe? Hard to say, though.'

'Follow them back. Find out where they came from. I shall wait here for you. Don't walk more than a mile or two inland, then return with your report.'

He bounded away, his eyes following the footprints, up into the dunes and over the top, until he disappeared from sight and I was left with my thoughts. I looked after the horses first, knowing Bryce would probably be gone a couple of hours. And then I settled down against a sandy hillock and took out my journal.

My stomach is growling with hunger again, but, more importantly, I'm angry that Carl mentioned my Darkness, and that Reinhard and Carl conspired to exploit it. In my head, I hear Carl's sarcastic voice. *I don't think you can stop us. I don't think you'll even try.* He's right. When I'm in the throes of it, I can't do anything, certainly not rally forces strong enough to repel an invasion. It weakens me, and, worse, it weakens those around me. For the first time, I'm struggling to understand. What is it exactly? This thing I call 'the Darkness'? Why does it happen and when did it start?

Even now, it's lapping at the edge of my mind in exactly the way the waves lap at the shore here in Navisar. Trickling forward, then sliding back, so I'm aware of the waves, but eventually they form a background to everything and I no longer think of them. They're there, but I don't notice them. But, just as the tide will eventually turn, and, in a few hours' time, the water will flood over the sandy beach and engulf it, so the Darkness could, at any moment, do the same to me. Little waves turning into an overwhelming force. King Canute had no luck in stopping it, so what chance would I have? Yet if I don't, my enemies will continue to manipulate me.

The magnitude of this threatens to overwhelm me. Could Mallrovia be lost through my own weakness? I believe it could, and I am shocked. I wait for my mind to tell me this is all nonsense. *The vulnerability of one man cannot destroy a nation.* I say this sentence over and over, both in my head and aloud. I even stand and shout it out to the stupid little waves, and eventually my heart stops hammering, my body stops shaking, the cold sweat dries on my skin and I can sit down and wait calmly for Bryce to return.

I try to focus on Phoebe and Julia, Philip's Queen. Leo told me Julia was dead, but I didn't see her body on the rocks with Philip's and Barney's. Leo mentioned the forest, and it's certainly possible Julia was killed there, but I'd searched in the forest as well. I'd seen no evidence of a fight, and I'd found no dead bodies. But, alive or dead, Julia has certainly disappeared. She hasn't been seen for two years, so it doesn't look hopeful.

Could some of the footprints be hers? It seems unlikely, and equally unlikely that they're Phoebe's, who must have been brought here by road. The people who'd trodden barefoot onto the beach had come from further north, and they'd come across country. They'd not walked along roads, but through woodland and over fields and ditches until they'd arrived at the dunes. They didn't come from Hicrown.

Two memories are clashing in my head, and I must quickly write them down. One is of Reinhard, as I questioned him in my great hall and he did his best to make me look a fool with his scornful, contemptuous answers. He'd mentioned a previous illegal trade. Before the wool smuggling started.

'*What was this "previous trade"*?' I demanded to know.

'*Ask the Myrtilers,*' he answered with a laugh.

The other memory is a conversation with Joan, when I wanted to know more about the worsted that was being taken out of the country. Joan deals in yarns, wools, fabrics and textures. I knew she'd know. I'd wondered why worsted was so valuable.

'*Doesn't it all come from sheep*?' I asked her.

'*Well, yes, it does,*' Joan said, '*but it's treated differently, and worsted is made with longer staples. There's also the way it's spun and the way it feels afterwards. If it's worsted that's being shipped out illegally, it'll most likely have come from Myrtile.*'

'*Why Myrtile?*'

'*Because of the sheep! Oh, the place is magnificent, or so I hear. Golden rooftops! Gilded spires! I haven't been there, though, so that may be all nonsense. Of course, it's Sir Patrick's home, and he will have spared no expense to make it as splendid as he could, and that may include the type of cloth they make there. It's surrounded by sheep farms, isn't it? I'm sure most of the worsted they're smuggling will be from the Myrtile estate.'*

And where is Myrtile? About ten miles north-west of here. But if the worsted is being brought directly from Myrtile to Navisar, what's the point of the warehouses in Hicrown? And whose small, bare feet have so recently walked over the sand to get to the sea?

I know the answer is here somewhere. Phoebe is twenty now, perhaps twenty-one. A woman, not a girl. What does that tell me? She'll have value, as a member of the Royal House of Mallrovia. She may be empty-headed, but she's young and she's pretty. I know what I'm thinking. Where this is leading. Just not sure I can bring myself to write it down, yet I think I must. The implications are too enormous to ignore.

If I'm right, Reinhard's 'previous trade' is people. Specifically, girls. Trading in people is called slavery, which means Phoebe, our rightful Queen, has been sold into slavery, right here, from this very beach where I now sit. I let the charcoal drop from my fingers, and it falls, half burying itself in the sand. I stare at the glittering sea, the far horizon, and I take in the emptiness of my surroundings. There is nobody to be seen, neither on the beach, nor out at sea. Yet I know, because logic, instinct and a ghastly gut feeling tell me, that Mallrovian women and girls, including our young Queen, are out at sea right now, probably in the stinking hold of a slave ship. Where will they end up? Are they to be sold as whores? I'm certain there were no men among the grim procession of bare-footed prisoners. They *would* have been prisoners, I'm equally sure of that. Any males among them would be children. Young boys, perhaps very young. Also destined for the sex market.

Queasiness builds inside my stomach, resulting in the inevitable need for a latrine, somewhere to empty my bowels. But before I put down my parchment and head into the dunes, I must finish this train of thought. Joan thinks the worsted comes from Myrtile. But the girls are coming from Myrtile as well. What is the connection between Myrtile, the worsted, the girls, and the Hicrown warehouses? How the hell does it all fit together?

10

SOMEONE HAS TO LIVE TO TELL THE TALE

I woke in a panic that I'd slept for several hours, but a glance at the sky showed me it couldn't have been more than half an hour. As my heart and breathing settled down again, I remembered my dream. Or perhaps it had just been my brain continuing with the thoughts I'd been scribbling in my journal. It had all been about Myrtile, that strange city in the middle of nowhere. Just one road leads into and away from Myrtile, and few people ever visit. I had never been there.

Yet it seems a great deal of activity may be taking place in Myrtile, and none of it good. My strange dream – or illusion, perhaps – was about the man in charge of Myrtile. The man who *owns* Myrtile and everything in it. And that man is Sir Patrick, once my father's steward in Castle Rory, and then mine. Eight years ago, Patrick met Deborah, a Jewess. They married, and Patrick, who'd been considering converting to Judaism, left Castle Rory and went home to Myrtile. Which had been run, in Patrick's absence, by a steward of his own.

It seemed likely that the trading, whether in slaves or in

worsted, had begun while Patrick was in Hambrig. But it hadn't stopped, had it. It was still going on, and had been going on two years ago, when I chased across to Frisia and back. Which meant that Patrick was definitely involved.

Patrick had been my greatest support for many years. He was dependable, loyal and intelligent. He always knew what was needed, often before I could tell him what to do. I hadn't realised how much I relied on him until he left, after which I appointed someone else, but Patrick was a hard act to follow.

I'd had several stewards since, and, compared with Patrick, all had fallen short. Inka Kaufmann was the latest incarnation, and perhaps an unwise choice. Joan liked her, and Joan's endorsements mean a lot to me, but, as previous stewards had failed, deserted or betrayed me, I was not taking anything for granted where Inka Kaufmann was concerned. I used to make assumptions about my household, but I have learnt not to do this. Kaufmann remains on trial, and a lot rests on how she runs the castle in my absence. I need a steward I can depend on for that. A steward like Sir Patrick of Myrtile.

So it's hard to believe Patrick is complicit in this slave trade and smuggling racket. But what if he isn't just complicit? What if he's running it? He will have set it up from a base in his estate which is, when all's said and done, in the middle of nowhere. And, as my steward far away in Hambrig, he had the perfect alibi. So I am forced to confront the idea that Patrick is shipping young Mallrovian girls out to be sold in the northern slave markets.

An even worse horror occurred to me. Was Patrick trying to sell Mallrovia to the Livonians? Did he conspire to have King Philip and Prince Barney murdered? Had he been offered so much money he would turn traitor and see Mallrovia invaded and conquered?

'Lord!' Bryce came running over the sands. 'Lord, I know where those people came from! It's Myrtile, lord! They all came from Myrtile! So Queen Phoebe couldn't have been one of them, because she came here from Hicrown.' He flopped down onto the sand and lay back, his arms outstretched, his eyes screwed up against the sun.

So I was right. Patrick was behind the whole repulsive, treacherous business. I felt sick with disgust, mortified that I'd been taken in for so many years. Bryce hadn't moved from his position of exhaustion on the sand.

'Surely you haven't run all the way to Myrtile and back?'

'Not quite, lord, but it felt like it. I followed the footprints, as you asked me to. I didn't think I'd see them once the sand became grass and other stuff, but they were easy to track because of the blood.'

'You found more blood?' I was taken aback. Slaves wouldn't be hurt; it would make them less valuable.

'It was a whole trail of blood, lord. Lots of it. That's how I was able to track the girls. Eventually I came out of some woodland and I saw the wall surrounding a city. I knew it must be Myrtile. So I think the girls are brought out of the city, or maybe from the countryside nearby, and taken through the woods and out onto the heath which then becomes the dunes. I know it must be girls, lord. And at least one of them was bleeding.'

'Did you see anything else?' I asked. 'Had any of them dropped anything, for example? Or had their hair caught in the branches of trees? Anything like that?'

'I found these, lord, but it's not much.'

He dug in his pocket and brought out some rope fibres. They were frayed at both ends, which told me they'd come from the middle of a rope, probably one that was well worn through much use.

'You're right,' I said. 'It isn't much to go on. We shall have to go to Myrtile, I think. Although my first priority has to be Queen Phoebe...' But I tailed off then, because I didn't see how I could possibly find the girl now she'd been taken out of the country. Where might the ship have gone? What would happen to her when they made landfall?

'Let's go.' I made up my mind. 'Get the horses, Bryce. We're going back to Hicrown.'

The Navisar Gate was open and unguarded as usual. The warehouses looked the same as before, and the road leading into the city centre was deserted. We trotted past ominously vacant grazing land and shuttered shops. But very soon we heard the noise, clashing and anarchic, of a rabble on the loose. We headed towards the main city square, the noises growing louder by the moment, and it was clear everyone must have gathered there. All other parts of the city had been abandoned.

Emerging into the square, where the normal market stalls had been kicked aside, broken and mangled, I saw a stand-off. To our right were the charred remains of St Michael's Church, razed to the ground. In front of us, the King's Squad were assembled in their carefully disciplined ranks of red and silver. Next to them stood Carl's Livonian Swordbrothers in their long, emblazoned surcoats, living up to their name with swords held aloft.

Opposite these, and alongside the burnt-out church, were ranged Baron Giles's troops from Wartsbaye, their blue-and-silver crests and shields catching the sun. They'd also drawn their swords, but they were looking doubtfully at their commander. I, too, looked at the Wartsbaye commander, thinking to see the portly figure of Baron Giles. But a much younger and slighter man stood there, his head held high, his body trembling a little, his sword arm hanging by his side. Gael, Giles's younger son and the only one living. Twenty-two years old, Gael had never wanted to be dubbed knight, preferring to study minstrelsy and practise his music. So what was he doing here?

Hearing our horses' hooves on the cobbles, Gael looked round, and when he saw me his face broke into a huge smile of relief. I walked Blue over to him, surprised Gael wasn't also mounted.

'Lord Rory,' the young man gasped, reaching for my stirrup strap and clinging onto it. 'I'm so, so pleased you're here! I didn't know what to do! You sent for us, so of course we came, but we didn't know why, and now—'

'Where's your father, Gael?'

'He is ill, lord. Seriously so. Amie is with him, but we don't think he has long to live. What are we doing here? What is happening?'

I registered the panic in Gael's eyes, the desperation of the questions and the anguish he felt at having to leave his critically ill father. 'This is an insurrection,' I said briefly. 'It falls to us to quash it and restore order and the rule of law. You must be prepared to fight. Is this the entire garrison?'

He shook his head. 'Father said I must take half the garrison, and leave half in case of – of trouble. And then he sent me off, as if I was a soldier. But I'm not!' Gael sounded close to tears.

'You have a sword, Gael, and I hope you know how to use it. Fall in with your troops. I will take charge here.'

He flashed me a watery smile of relief and dropped back to stand with his father's people. I motioned to Bryce to do the same, and then I turned to face the enemy.

'Captain Leo,' I called. We had the width of the square between us, fifty yards perhaps. Fifty yards of dirty, straw-covered cobbles, with a few broken carts lying on their sides, axles pointing to the sky, and some rag-tags of bunting that would, probably only yesterday, have adorned the colourful market stalls of our capital city. And yet you could still smell the burning; the smoke, ash and bitter taste of the church's torching.

Leo didn't move. Someone swirled a banner through the air in a token of defiance. The Squad on their own would be formidable opponents, but backed by the fierce-looking Livonians, they were probably unbeatable. I looked at my forces. Giles had sent only half his garrison, and I didn't hold that against him. It was a sensible precaution, given that he didn't know why I wanted his people. Giles and I trust each other, and have done since the Battle of Baudry Hill in '63. But half of Wartsbaye constituted only a small force of sixteen men and women. The King's Squad numbered twenty or so, and there were at least forty Livonians. This would not be an equal contest.

I called to Leo again, and this time he looked up. Finally, he beckoned to me, an imperious summoning. I walked Blue to the middle of the square and waited.

'We have taken Hicrown,' Leo declared, not moving. 'You should go home.'

'Where's Peter? Your father?'

He shrugged. 'My father doesn't matter now. This is about the King.'

'The dead King? Or his replacement?'

'Lord Rory,' Leo said impatiently. 'I'm talking to you out

of respect for your position in Hambrig. And also, perhaps, because you have taken good care of my father. But this isn't about you. Or him. This is about democracy and the will of the people. The people of Hicrown are fed up with high taxes, made even higher by those who have schemed to avoid paying any taxes at all. The arrogance of the cathedral and the tyranny of an inherited monarchy are coming to an end. The people of the city want an elected ruler. Someone who is answerable to them and who will put their needs first.'

'You've put it to a vote then?'

'We didn't have to. You know this undercurrent of unrest has been going on for decades. You know the people have tried to protect their boundaries, but the King wouldn't allow it. And you know the cathedral owns a massive amount of land, the so-called God's Acre. Those living on it pay no taxes at all, meaning everyone else has to pay more. Do you think this is either fair or right?'

I wasn't going to get drawn into the rights and wrongs of democracy. I had an urgent question. 'Who murdered King Philip?'

'King Philip slipped over the edge of a cliff.'

'Not according to a letter I received, Leo. A letter written, and signed, by Sir Allan of Hicrown.'

Leo breathed in sharply. 'Then it is Sir Allan you must ask. Now, if you will command your troops from Wartsbaye to turn around and go home, no one will get hurt. If you insist on a fight – well, as you see, we have the upper hand. None of you will survive.'

'And the people of Hicrown? Where are they?'

'Many have left, as I'm sure you've noticed. The remnants are either hiding in their dwellings, or have gathered together inside the palace walls. As you yourself gathered your Hambriggers once, when your demesne was under threat. You may think I know little about Hambrig, and even less about you, but I know a great deal. I'll ask you again: are you going to be sensible and withdraw?'

I looked round for Allan. Why wasn't he in charge here? I found him, eventually. He was near the back of the Squad, his hat pulled low over his face. Was he a coward? Frightened of the fight? Or were his men protecting him, so he could become the 'elected ruler' Leo had spoken of? Although there had, apparently, been no actual election. And Allan was in his fifties now, while Leo was more than twenty years younger. I guessed Leo would fight the battle, and if he were killed so be it. Allan would lurk at the back, protected and secure. Once victory was won, Allan would be declared King. Or whatever title he thought an 'elected ruler' should use.

Leo was turning on his heel. He'd had enough of the questions. 'Did you send for the Swordbrothers?' I called after him.

Leo pointed to Carl von Lutterberg. 'He's your man,' he called over his shoulder. And then, turning, said again, 'Go home, Lord Rory. Send young Gael back to Wartsbaye. His father's ill and these troops will simply get slaughtered if they stay and fight. Nobody wants that. Go home, all of you. Hicrown is in our hands now, and soon you'll hear proclamations up and down the land. Some things will change, but they'll be for the better. In many ways, though, you won't see any difference. Take my advice. Leave now.'

And, to this day, I wish we had.

I walked Blue back to our blue-and-silver lines. Sixteen soldiers, plus Gael, Bryce and me. Gael and Bryce were not fighters, so I revised my count: sixteen soldiers and me. I prayed Peter would keep well out of the way. The Livonians looked deadly. They were tall and strong, well-armed and trained to kill. The King's Squad were not often tested in battle, but they were highly disciplined troops.

I leant down to speak to Gael. 'We don't stand a chance here. We must withdraw. Philip and Barney are dead, Lillian is in Germany, and I have no idea where Julia and Phoebe are. Take your people back to Wartsbaye, Gael. Tell your father what has happened here.'

He looked appalled. 'You're going to give in? I never thought you'd do that!'

'Sometimes you have to. No point in getting everyone killed. The outcome will be the same either way.'

'We're here to fight!' he cried, pulling his sword from its scabbard.

'How many fights have you been in?' I asked him. Behind me, Leo's lot were getting restless. I could feel it.

'None yet,' Gael said, squaring his shoulders. 'But I'm not going to run from my first one! And there will be a great ballad to come out of this!' He shouldered past Blue, turning to his people and shouting, 'To me! To me! *Wartsbaye vincit! Wartsbaye vincit!*' Screaming his father's battle-cry, Gael charged into the middle of the square. His people pelted after him, their swords held at arm's length before them, helmets jammed down over their eyes. Sixteen warriors against a horde.

Bryce turned horrified eyes on me.

'Stay here, Bryce,' I told him. 'That's an order. You can't fight without a sword – and *someone* has to live to tell the tale.'

11

I'D FORGOTTEN ALL ABOUT YOU

Gael had once had an older brother. Davy had died on the battlefield, defending me, but his action had been rash and reckless. He'd saved my life, but had almost cost us everything else. William had rescued us that day, bringing his ship up the river and firing iron balls into the enemy. Nine years on, and there would be no William, no ship and no big gun to turn our fortunes round.

With a mouth dry as St Michael's ashes, I rode my warhorse straight into the Livonians. Blue was our only advantage. From her saddle, I slashed down at the Swordbrothers. Their swords were held high in self-defence, and I knew it wouldn't take a genius to think of hacking at Blue's legs, taking her out of the action and flinging me to the ground. So I circled round them, keeping Blue on her toes, moving in and out of their ranks, my blade dripping red with Livonian blood.

Gael and his Wartsbayes had engaged the Squad. Hauling Blue back for a few breathless moments, I noted what a lively fighter Leo was. He kept his head and used his weapons well, even deploying his shield to attack, as I'd once seen my brother do. It takes nerve to stand still and watch an enemy run you down.

Allan, to my surprise, fought with tenacity. Taking in the situation, he quickly repositioned himself at the front of his troops. He was aggressive and ruthless, and a long way short of elegant. Leo was volatile and unpredictable, leaping around with his cloak swirling about him. Leo scared Gael, but it was Allan who thrust his sword into the boy's chest. All this I took in in the time it might take you to blink twice.

And, as the battle spilled out of the square and became ragged street fights of two or three swordsmen, all trying to gain control and make headway through the city, I rode up to Allan and challenged him in person. In his eyes, I saw indecision. Perhaps he, like me, could scarcely believe that Wartsbaye and Hambrig were fighting the King's Squad, the elite troops of our country. This was not a struggle between competing nations or faiths; it was civil unrest, and people were dying for it. I suspected Allan also regretted that he hadn't brought his own warhorse into the square. He'd assumed we'd see how unequal our forces were, and we'd all turn around and go meekly home. Although he fought well, he hadn't prepared for any other scenario. That spoke of his lack of command experience. He might be a tough fighter, but his strategic thinking was poor.

Taking the man by surprise, I leapt down from Blue's back and thrust my sword into his side, just as he moved away. It was only a glancing blow, but he fell back, almost falling. I moved closer, raising my weapon for the kill, but something stung my arm, and I spun round to see Carl von Lutterberg, a short dagger in one hand, his sword in the other.

'Don't kill him,' Carl said, locking his gaze with mine. 'I

have hurt you only a little, though I could have slaughtered both you and your horse.'

Pulling my shirt tight around my wounded arm, I looked round the square. It was almost empty. Sounds of battle echoed through the city, but in the square, only the dead remained. And one gravely injured young man who was never meant to be a soldier.

'I must look after Gael,' I said to Carl, and ran to kneel beside my former page. I'd loved Gael, as I'd loved his brother, Davy. Both had left me, in their different ways, and now I could see Gael's time on this earth was nearly over. 'Can you hear me, Gael?' I cradled his head, the feel of the familiar curly fair hair bringing a lump to my throat. But I made sure he could see my face.

'Hello, lord,' he managed to croak. 'Did I do well? I wanted to defend you like Davy did.'

'You did extremely well, Gael,' I told him. 'And Davy would have been proud of you.'

'Will Father be proud? You will tell him, won't you, lord?'

I promised to tell Baron Giles all about his younger son's charge at the enemy. Giles would know the futility of it. Giles, an old soldier, and a courageous one too, would read between the lines. He'd know both his sons had died in vain.

Carl stood behind me. He waited for Gael's eyes to close, and for me to lay the dead boy down again. 'Such a waste,' he said, as I turned, sick at heart. 'None of this need have happened, you know. Our small provocation of the cathedral officers should not have ended this way.'

The victorious Livonian Swordbrothers were beginning to trickle back into the city square, together with their allies, the King's Squad. Some were injured, none seriously. A few didn't return at all. There was nobody from Wartsbaye. I looked round for Bryce, but did not see him.

'Let us go now, Rory,' Carl said quietly. 'It is over.'

'Where are you taking me?'

'You will be a prisoner here in the palace for a while. We shall, perhaps, ask a ransom for your release, but it will not be an unreasonable sum. Hambrig will raise the money, I'm sure.'

'And your plans? Now you've taken the city?'

'Yes, you are right. We have taken the city. The rest of Mallrovia will follow, of course. This young man has done half our job for us.' Carl pointed at Gael with his boot. 'First he told us his father is dying, and now he, too, is dead. Please don't misunderstand me, Rory. I would not have had either of them die like this. But it does make it easier for us, now we know Wartsbaye Castle is there for the taking. Nightmolben is gone, so that leaves only your own fortress on Baudry Hill. Once *that's* in our possession, I think you could say we'll have the country.'

I thought of my home. No one to defend it. No one manning the garrison. And Inka Kaufmann in charge. I almost laughed out loud. Carl von Lutterberg would have to do no more than rap on the door of Castle Rory, and it would fall neatly into his hands. At least there would be no bloodshed.

'You'll treat my people well?' I asked him, as he tied my hands and relieved me of my sword and my dagger.

'You know I will. They will come to no harm.'

'Who will be in charge in Hambrig, Carl? Will it be you?'

'Initially. But I intend to leave Leo there for a while. He will be acting on my orders though, so you have nothing to worry about. Your household will not be hurt in any way – providing they offer no resistance, of course.'

'And my villeins? My cottars and my farmers? The vassals who are my tenants? Will you treat them fairly and with respect? They've done nothing to deserve violence or theft.'

'Rory, I've promised to take care of your household. As for the rest, you're not in a position to negotiate, and certainly not to make any demands.'

He led me away then, on a roundabout route to the palace, so I was forced to look on the pathetic sight of Giles's warriors, sprawled on the ground in attitudes of death. Thankfully, there was still no sign of Bryce. I hoped and prayed he was safe and far away. I'd given him no orders, but had left him and his palfrey by the wall. I knew he was a young man with initiative. The chances were high that he'd ridden home; in which case he would soon be Carl's prisoner. Or would he deliver news of the battle, causing chaos and panic in the castle? If he spoke to Kaufmann and nobody else, there was a chance such panic might be averted. But what would Kaufmann do? What *could* she do?

Bryce was my only hope, and I thanked God Carl seemed to have forgotten about him. I was taken to a room in the palace, one I'd been in many times – it had been my chamber whenever I'd visited King Philip. It had a comfortable bed surrounded by rich curtains. There was a fireplace, a low chair and an embroidered footstool. There was a small window, but it was too narrow to climb through, and the room itself was on the second floor of the palace building. Even if I could have squeezed through the window, the drop to the ground would be fatal. Oh yes, I knew the room well.

'You will be comfortable here,' Carl said pleasantly. 'I will untie your hands, but do not try to attack me or run away. Captain Leo is waiting for me at the foot of the stairs. He will not be pleased to see *you* instead.'

Carl left the room, and the key turned in the lock. I waited until I'd heard Carl start descending the stairs, then I tried the door, just to be certain. But yes. I was definitely a prisoner. From the window, I could look down on a deserted street. If I raised my eyes, I could see fields, and, beyond those, the northern wall of the city. Nothing moved, and nobody appeared on the street.

I knew many Hicrowners had left the city. Frightened of the new lawlessness, or excited by it, they'd gone out into the countryside, where they would either fend for themselves or gang up to form terrifying groups of outlaws. The few who'd remained in the city were gathered in the palace – but they weren't in this part of it. Everything was silent, making me quite sure I was the only person in this wing. I wondered what value Carl would put on my life. How much ransom money would be demanded? I knew quite a lot could be raised, particularly if the chapel were raided for gold, silver and jewels. Or if tenants were made to sell their land, their livestock and their dwellings. I went cold at the thought of that happening. I'd rather take my chances here than have a ransom raised in such a way.

So now I'm sitting by the window, having dragged the chair across, and my journal is on my lap, a small stick of charcoal in my hand. I mustn't run out of charcoal! It's my duty to record my time in captivity; I have a feeling it may later be useful. So, for now, I've written down everything that's happened since my last entry of two days ago, although the slight wound Carl inflicted on my right arm doesn't make writing any easier. I've bandaged the cut as best I can, and no doubt it will heal itself in time.

I do wonder what would have happened if Gael hadn't suddenly lost his senses. I would have ordered the Wartsbaye men to turn round and march back to their castle in the north. Bryce and I would have ridden away too, heading for Hambrig. I suppose, at that point, the Livonians would have declared themselves victors and Hicrown would have fallen without bloodshed. Gael and all the Wartsbaye people would still be alive, and I would still have my freedom.

But then, I think, I'd have had to fight eventually. Or would I? When the Livonians arrived on Baudry Hill, I'd have surrendered there, too. Surrender. A sick-making word. But I cannot avoid it. Surrender would have been the only option, with a castle full of old men, women, babies and small children, and no garrison to defend it.

I've had nothing to eat since Friday night. Two days ago. I suddenly feel terribly sick. The knowledge I'm a prisoner, that money is going to be demanded for my release, that my castle will be attacked, invaded and taken, that Gael is dead... I jump up, my hand clamped over my mouth. My head doesn't quite fit through the window, and I vomit over the stone sill and down the wall. It smells foul, and I throw up twice more in response, yet there's nothing in my stomach, so I sick up yellow bile which tastes disgusting. My head is hurting now, and I don't think I can write much more.

For a while, I lay on the bed, trying to recover from the sickness and the ache in my head. I've flung the empty sword scabbard into a corner, and I've taken off my boots as well. I'm back to sitting in the chair now, but well away from the vomit-speckled window, although when I'm feeling stronger I'll see about cleaning up. There's a jug of water in the corner, but that may be all I have to drink for a while, so I'm not anxious to use it for cleaning.

The question is – am I going to sit here and wait for news? Or am I going to make a plan and try to escape? After a lot of thought, I've decided I can't really make a plan, as I don't know what will happen. Will someone bring food, for example? And if so, who will it be? Perhaps I'll be able to overpower them and make a run for it. I don't know where they've put Blue, and I have no weapon, but I'd certainly give it a try. So, I suppose, I do have a sort of plan.

It's starting to get dark. I shall strip off and get to bed. Nothing else to do, and I might as well rest for a few hours. My stomach hurts with hunger.

It was hard to sleep. I blamed the hunger pains, but it was all the other miserable things too. I turned over and over in the bed, my eyes open, my right arm aching from Carl's dagger cut, though that was far from serious. I may even have cried a little, I'm not sure now.

At one point, I got up and walked over to the window again. The moonlight was strong, but nothing outside had changed. The same view of nothing and no one. The same silence, too. I crept back to bed, holding my aching stomach, feeling my arm throb sickeningly, utterly dejected.

And then – I heard a sound. Scratching at the door? A cat, perhaps? I got up and tiptoed over to listen. The scratching came again. Using my fingernails, I scratched back. If it were a cat, it would do no harm. The cat, or whatever it was, stopped scratching. I pictured its ears going back, its tail swishing a little, as it wondered what was on the other side of the door. Perhaps it was used to coming in here. Maybe it was accustomed to sleeping on the bed.

A shuffling sound. Not very cat-like. And then some strange tapping noises.

'Who is it?' I whispered, my mouth pressed against the wood. 'Who's there?'

The tapping and scuffling noises became louder, and were joined by some excited-sounding breathing. 'Is that thee, lord?' came a voice I knew well. 'Is it really thee, like?'

'Peter! Oh my God! I'd forgotten all about you!'

12

I WOULD SLEEP WELL NOW

But he couldn't open the door. There was a lock on the catch, and no key to the lock.

'I *have* to get thee out!' He panted and wheezed, struggling to pull the lock away from the door catch. But it would be a strong lock. Carl was far to wily to use anything less.

'Take care,' I warned. 'Is there anywhere to hide if you hear someone coming?'

'Aye, there is. A sort o' alcove, in the wall. There's a curtain hangin' in front o' it.'

'If you hear anything, Peter, you must get behind that curtain at once. And keep absolutely quiet.'

'Aye, lord, but how am I goin' to get thee out o' there? An' canst tha tell me – is my son still alive?'

'He's alive, Peter. Very much so. As for getting me out, I doubt it's possible—'

'Wait! There's summat here!' More scratching and scuffling ensued, followed by an ominous silence.

'What have you found?' I called impatiently, then glanced at the window. The moment it began to get light,

Peter must vanish. Still dark for now, but this is the season of long days and short nights.

'Got it!' It was a low-voiced triumph. But what had he got? 'It were on a shelf in t' alcove, lord. T' key! An' I couldn't have hidden meself there, after all, since it's full o' shelvin', an' that's where—'

'Unlock the door, Peter. Please.'

Moments later, I stumbled out, almost into Peter's arms. I grabbed at him, and the two of us fled down the stairs and out onto the moonlit path. Hicrown Palace is built a little like a castle, but there's no bailey. Instead, there's a carefully designed garden with encircling pathways, and a large and impressive main building, behind which are the troops' accommodation blocks. Peter and I ran round the main building, then stumbled along the paths of the garden until we reached the gatehouse, and beyond it the stables.

I pointed to the stables. 'Is Blue in there?'

'Nay, lord, I don't think so. Me palfrey's there, though. I went there like tha said, and nobody came, so I just bided where I was.'

Grabbing Peter's arm, I ran to the stables. Once under cover, and in relative safety, I turned to him. 'How did you know where to find me, Peter?'

'I saw thee, lord. I saw the big blond man take thee, wi' thy hands tied, into the palace.'

'You followed?'

'Nay. I stayed put until it were full dark. Then I came lookin' for thee.'

'You knew to come up the stairs, though? You knew the very room?'

'Aye, lord, that bit were easy, like. I, er, I heard sobbin'. I knew t' were thee.'

'Well. That's good then,' I said brusquely. 'Get your palfrey ready to ride, Peter. We're going to Wartsbaye.'

Peter was doubtful. 'I don't think he'll take both o' us all that way, lord.'

'I don't think so either. But he's going to take both of us part of the way, so get moving.'

Of course, I helped him, and in a matter of moments the palfrey was ready. I recognised him then: it was Tortoise, the slowest animal in the Castle Rory stables.

'What on earth made you choose Tortoise?' I exclaimed.

'It were Luke give him to me, lord,' Peter said. 'He is a bit slow, like.'

As we left the palace and picked our way down the streets of Hicrown towards the Navisar Gate, I warned Peter about the corpses. They were everywhere. I saw civilians too. We marched along grimly, leading Tortoise for the time being, and it became clear this carnage had involved many of the city's ordinary folk.

Peter was upset, but he trudged along gamely with me, and I got him to hold Tortoise's leading rein, so at least he had something to do. I filled him in on what had happened, and felt him shudder when I spoke of Gael's reckless charge and his fatal wounding.

'But what do they want, lord?' he cried in distress. 'Sir Allan an' this Livonian? An' me son? What do they want here?'

'Power, Peter. It's always about power. With the King dead...' But I didn't finish the sentence. The King wouldn't *be* dead, if it weren't for Allan. Whether or not Allan had actually pushed Philip over the cliff, I didn't know, but I had no doubt the plan had been his. And to get rid of young Barney as well.

'But,' said Peter, after I'd mentioned these disturbing

thoughts, 'I still don't understand why. If Allan wanted power here, he could've killed King Philip long since. Why do it now?'

'Because of Nightmolben,' I said at once. 'Not because the cliff was destroyed, after all there are many ways to kill a man. But because the Livonian Swordbrothers wanted to seize Mallrovia, and Allan saw his chance. He was unable to do much on his own, but if he threw in his lot with the Livonians, he might actually get somewhere. You can tell the Palace Guard were loyal to the end, since they're all dead. The Squad though – they're Allan's, aren't they. They dance to his tune. He must have spoken filth to them, and they turned against the King. Sadly, your boy is one of them.'

'I'm that ashamed,' Peter mumbled. 'Ashamed of Leo. How could he do such a thing?'

By now, we were out of the city. I'd said we were going to Wartsbaye, and that was my eventual destination, but first I needed to talk to Patrick. So we struck out east, intending to turn onto the track heading north to Myrtile. I had to hope Patrick would help me, and I *had* to believe I was wrong when I thought he might be involved in this ghastly business. I must hang on to my memories of Patrick as steward of Castle Rory. Patriotic, loyal and honourable. Sir Patrick of Myrtile.

All that being so, my plan was to leave Peter in safety, borrow a fast horse and gallop across country to Wartsbaye. I didn't know if Patrick had garrisoned his city, but I knew Giles had half his troops left. Seasoned warriors were desperately needed now, but they were in short supply. I said nothing of this to Peter, who was deep in his own self-recriminations anyway. Tortoise lived up to his name, and we made slow progress. In any case, Peter had been right;

Tortoise refused to carry both of us, so we took it in turns to ride him, or we simply led him along.

Fortunately, Peter had provisions in Tortoise's saddle bag, and when I saw the bread, plums and sausages he produced, I nearly fainted with relief. We ate as we walked, while tiny tributaries of the River Shamet provided drinking water.

'It were Rachel,' Peter said, as we sat at the roadside and munched a hearty dinner. 'Rachel thought on it. She never lets anyone leave wi'out food in their baskets! She gave me all this, and she packed a load of food for Bryce, an' all. She thinks o' it all, does Rachel.'

'We'd certainly have been in trouble without her,' I agreed.

I was desperate to reach the turning for Myrtile. The route between Navisar and Hicrown was obviously the smugglers' way in and out of Mallrovia, and the Livonians were using it too. There might be traffic, and it would be hostile. Peter and I were unarmed, our horse was an aged animal with no turn of speed, and cover was sparse. If we met anyone we couldn't hold off with our bare hands, it would have to be another ignominious surrender. Again, I didn't mention any of this to Peter, but simply tried to keep both him and Tortoise moving along.

As we walked, or sat and ate our rations, it was easy to get Peter to tell me his story, and so I learnt that he'd been married in Italy at the age of twenty-two. His wife's name was Gabriella, and she was the daughter of a fabulous (according to Peter) mathematician. Peter had lived in their house in Pisa for many months, and had learnt everything he now knew from this elderly mathematical genius. Peter and Gabriella had had a son, Leo, and the plan had been to wait until Leo was fourteen and then travel around Europe, proclaiming the gospel of Hindu numbers. It was Peter who called it a 'gospel'. I always knew he was fanatical about these Hindu numbers, but I'd had no idea he looked on it as some kind of creed.

Anyway, the plan literally went up in smoke. One day, when Leo was only seven years old, Peter took him to the River Arno to look at the ships. Leo was fascinated by them, and they spent a long time walking up and down the waterfront, discussing the ships and their cargoes. When they eventually made their way home through the streets of Pisa, they were horrified to find their street burnt down. A fire had started in one of the houses and had quickly spread. By the time Peter and Leo arrived, the fire was under control. Teams of people had thrown buckets of water onto the flames, and now the street was a drenched, smoking ruin. Gabriella and her father were dead. Peter, distraught, hugged his little boy and tried to explain the incomprehensible.

A few months later, Peter brought Leo to his parents' house in Yorkshire. But Peter's parents were not interested, having grown morose and discontented. It seems Peter once had a brother, on whom his parents had doted. But Timothy had died long ago, falling from the roof of a building, and his parents had never stopped mourning him. So Peter took Leo away again, and they travelled through England, eventually making their way over the border into Mallrovia.

After a while, Peter found employment in Hicrown Palace, with Leo helping in the palace stables. One day, my father visited King Philip and exchanged a few words with Peter. So impressed was my father with Peter's understanding of mathematics and science, he offered him employment at Castle Rory, and doubled Peter's pay. Leo, tall and strong for his age, chose to stay and train in the

Palace Guard, and King Philip was pleased to have him. At the age of ten, Leo had set his sights on one day being good enough for the elite: the fabled King's Squad.

'What dost tha think has happened to me son, Lord Rory?' Peter asked tremulously, at the end of all this. 'Why is he fightin' us?'

'I think his head has been turned,' I said. 'This idea of a democracy replacing the monarchy, it's been instilled into him. It's called indoctrination.'

'Then who's indoctrinated him?'

'Allan, I imagine. Allan sees himself as ruler of Mallrovia—'

'That in't democracy then! D'n't that mean t' ruler should be elected by t' people? An' where are t' people? Roamin' wild in t' countryside, robbin' innocent travellers, or else slaughtered, an' lyin' dead on t' ground…' He looked down, emotional and upset.

The ten-mile-long unkempt, grassy track that leads north from the Navisar Road, did nothing to prepare us for our first sight of the city of Myrtile.

'Is this it, lord?' Peter asked in awe.

I was as stunned as he was. I turned to Peter, my hands spread wide. 'Why would Patrick ever have left this place? He was in Hambrig for *decades*.'

I had never seen anything like it. Not even among the golden minarets of Muslim Al-Andalus or inside the richly carpeted and jewel-encrusted house of Shajar al-Durr in Mansurah. Peter and I were gazing at a city of two shimmering colours. Towers rose in front of us, towers topped by shining spires and crosses, while the city wall gleamed in yellow ochre stone. Perhaps it was the setting sun, bathing the place in a warm golden glow, but it looked enchanted.

Like Osnabrück in Germany, where I'd spent some time two years ago, Myrtile was a moated city – and even the moat sparkled with a blue-green radiance. Tall lights gleamed on both sides of the bridge, inviting us to cross. The gate was open, and lights flickered in the windows beyond. The welcoming entrance seemed to lead straight to the main residence. Palace, castle or manor house? I wasn't sure. In the distance, a cathedral's gilded towers soared into the twilight.

'Patrick lives here?' Peter breathed, as dumbfounded as I was myself. For a moment, I wondered if I were hallucinating. But we couldn't both be imagining this paragon of a city.

'Well, we'll soon know. Let us go and find him.'

Riding across the bridge and through the city gate was exhilarating. The soft evening sky assumed the hues of the buildings, or perhaps they merely reflected it. Gold-tinged clouds lingered in a velvet turquoise firmament. *Is this what it's like to enter heaven*? I wondered. The so-called Paradise Garden in Saintes hadn't felt anything like this. I wondered also what King Philip had made of it – that's if he ever came here. He'd certainly never mentioned it to me, but perhaps it was a well-kept secret the rest of us weren't supposed to know about.

Once inside the city of Myrtile, we felt ourselves drawn to the large house directly in front of us. The door stood open, lights shining through uncovered windows, the promise of a lit fire, platters of rich food on a large table...

'Rory!' Patrick hurried forward, smiling, his arms

extended. 'How wonderful! And Master Peter as well! This is grand!' He drew us in, promising someone would take Tortoise to the stables. And so we entered the great hall of Sir Patrick of Myrtile, and I suppose the best word for it would be 'magnificent'.

We followed him to his high table, where, just as I'd imagined it, food was set out on big wooden trays. Our three-day trek had used up all of Rachel's bread, sausage and fruit, and both Peter and I were ravenous again.

Briefly, we filled Patrick in on what had happened in Hicrown. At the worst part of our tale, the death of Gael and my own capture, Patrick's wife entered. Deborah. She was gracious and pleasant, but she didn't join us at the table, and after a few moments she left the hall. The trays were eventually cleared by a white-haired elderly man with an uneven walk. Patrick's steward, presumably.

I'd been watching Patrick carefully. Did he support the rebels? Or the cathedral? Did he already know about the smuggling of wool and women – perhaps because he'd been behind it all the time? But Patrick's expression did not change. He showed neither horror nor complacency. I simply could not tell where his allegiance lay.

'Will you lend me a horse, Patrick?' I asked, leaning forward. 'I have to ride to Wartsbaye. Giles needs to know what has happened to Gael. And to his soldiers. And Giles and I must make a plan...'

But even as I said it, I thought how hopeless it was. What sort of plan would defeat the Livonians and the King's Squad? We had no warriors! It simply wasn't possible.

'There's no problem about the horse,' Patrick said. 'But I suggest you get a good night's sleep, and we can discuss things further tomorrow. It would be best if you turn up in Wartsbaye with a plan already formed, don't you think?'

I'm in a large and elegant bedroom, decorated with tapestries and wall hangings, a fire burning in the grate and a comfortable bed. I go to the window. There are a few lights, not many, twinkling in the night, but the countryside beyond is wrapped in darkness. I'm writing in my journal, hoping to figure out a plan in my head as I write. It always helps – writing things down. It clarifies your thoughts.

Giles will have another sixteen to twenty people, and I can march them to Hicrown, but we'll be killed like the others were. It'll do no good at all. And in the time it will take to ride to Wartsbaye and then march on Hicrown, Allan will have fortified the city and made it unassailable.

What if I go back to Hambrig? Raise a fyrd from the villages, settlements and farms? Again, more time is lost, and a fyrd will simply be slaughtered by the trained troops inside the well-defended city walls. My thoughts are certainly being clarified, as I note this all down, but all they're telling me is how hopeless it is.

When someone knocked on my door, I laid aside my journal. Peter entered. He had the next room, and clearly he couldn't sleep either. 'I asked Lady Deborah about Myrtile,' he said, wiping his glasses on his shirt, and I remembered that he'd spoken at length with her after supper. I put down my charcoal and waited to hear more.

'Patrick built it!' Peter continued, in a voice full of awe.

'There were once just a small village, an' Patrick were born in it, t' son of a yeoman farmer. When he grew up, he were s'pposed to take over t' farm. Instead, he built over t' top of it! He designed t' city himself. He paid masons an' carpenters an' tilers an' thatchers an' glassmakers an' all t' rest o' them, and he oversaw t' work. He wanted a city like no other, he said. I'n't it summat?'

Peter was as impressed by Myrtile as I was, but I knew all the rambling chatter was just to distract him from thoughts of Gabriella and Leo. Especially Leo. I took his arm, walked him back to his room and told him to get some rest.

Standing in the passage outside my own bedchamber, I gazed around me. Dim lamps in sconces lit the soft golden walls of the building. A vaulted ceiling soared above me. Gilded angels rested on top of carved pillars and soft rugs cushioned my feet. I've only ever had rugs under my feet once before, and that was in Mansurah, when Jonny and I stayed in the house of Shajar and Eleni.

Shajar had been the widow of the Sultan of Egypt, and Eleni was her niece. Jonny and I had never known such opulence as we found in their beautiful house. The rugs on their floors had looked very like these. I bent down and ran my hand over the pile. It felt soft, plush and silky. There was no dirt or grit among the fibres, and I almost wanted to bury my face in them.

I took a torch from its bracket on the wall and held it close to the rug. Swirls of colour glowed in the soft light. Reds, greens and golds. A midnight blue circle, surrounded by pink roses. A soft green border with a vibrant gold thread running through it. I stayed down on my haunches for a long time, examining the design and thinking how much Joan would love it. She would exclaim in delight at each tiny detail. The little birds in the corners and the tracery on the rose petals. The intricate swirling patterns that lead your eye to that central circle of deep dark blue. I drank it all in, wanting to be able to describe it to Joan later. Thoughts of the desert, of Mansurah, Shajar, Eleni and, of course, Karima, had somehow steadied me. Treading softly on the luxurious carpets, I went back to my room. I would sleep well now.

13

I COULDN'T WAIT TO TELL BARON GILES

The city was extraordinary. I'd seen that the previous night, but the full glorious extent of its beauty, elegance and grandeur was revealed in the morning sun. Having risen early, I'd taken myself on a walk around Myrtile, and I saw that it truly was a city of turquoise and gold. Every building had a bright blue-green roof, and many were crowned with blue-green spires, surmounted by golden finials and crosses. The stonework gleamed with a radiant golden light as the sun's rays poured into Myrtile. The architecture was bold and beautiful, with elaborate decoration on every building.

No matter where I looked, I saw no signs of poverty, wretchedness or neglect. Everything was clean, pure and beautiful. How much had all this cost? And why spend *so* much money? I wrestled with my thoughts on this. From my earliest childhood, I was taught our Mallrovian system of birthright. I believe it to be the same in most other countries, and I consider it both fair and workable. You may be born into a noble and wealthy family, or perhaps into yeoman stock, or else into an unfree life as a peasant working someone else's land. Yes, it's unequal, but in reality the system should work well. The nobleman looks after the peasants, and they labour for him. Yeoman farmers, merchants, lawyers and scholars keep everyone supplied or informed, and they are paid for their work, produce or services.

And so I say the system should work well, and for most of my life I thought it did. But a few years ago I realised that if anyone falls short in this equation of duty and service, the balance is lost and the structure collapses. And King Philip was certainly guilty of this. In his quest for Mallrovian recognition and acceptance across the world, he neglected his own people. His demesne was not well run, and his villeins were destitute. This isn't hearsay, I've seen it for myself. So what had Patrick done here? And why?

'I had too much money, and it was dirty money,' Patrick said shortly. 'Don't ask me any more, Rory, I beg you. I do not wish to talk about it. But I'm glad you like the turquoise and gold.'

'Why those colours?' I asked, thinking I might ask Peter to get the whole story out of Deborah. He seemed to have forged a bond with her last night.

'Turquoise is a beautiful colour. A mixture of blue and green, as you saw. It has a special significance, as do all colours. Turquoise symbolises tranquillity, protection and healing.'

I nodded slowly. I could see it for myself, for the shade was certainly peaceful. 'Is that why it's on the roofs? To protect the people who live underneath it?'

Patrick smiled. 'You could say that, yes. And don't forget the healing.' Before I could ask what healing was required in Myrtile, he went on. 'You want a horse. I have instructed my groom to bring out our best mount for you. I take it Master Peter will be remaining here?'

'If that's all right with you.'

'You know it is. He will be very welcome, and I will enjoy learning about the Hindu numbers. I believe Master Peter is quite the authority.'

And quite the bore, too. But I kept that thought to myself.

'You're aware we have no cook here? Rolf, my steward, is not a good cook, but Deborah has made you some food to take with you. It may require several days to reach Wartsbaye. It is not an easy journey.'

I thought he would rise then from the table. He'd explained his preparations for my ride to Wartsbaye, and for those I was most grateful. He'd refused to tell me more about the building of his city – and yet he sat there, as if there was more to discuss.

'This business at Hicrown,' Patrick said abruptly. 'Did you have any idea at all that revolution was in the air?'

Revolution. I shivered a little. I didn't like the thought, and the word itself was a threat. An enemy at the walls, that I could deal with. But when the enemy was *within* the walls, how could you know? How could you prepare?

'I didn't know,' I said.

'Should you have known?'

I looked at him sharply. 'What do you mean, Patrick?'

'When did you get the letter that informed you of King Philip's death?'

I thought back to that day. 'Two years ago. Or nearly. The autumn of 1270. The letter told me about Barney too.'

'It told you they'd been killed? Murdered?'

'Yes. But not who did it.'

'But you didn't go to Hicrown until August this year? Why did you leave it so long?'

At the time, it had made sense. The letter had contained a warning, which I'd thought prudent to heed. Rosa's second baby was imminent, not that that should have made any difference, but I'd wanted to build up my garrison at Castle Rory, to make sure we could defend ourselves if there was trouble. With no commander and no steward, I'd been reluctant to leave the castle in anyone else's hands. I remembered telling Dicky, that lying bastard, that I would not be riding to Hicrown. He'd asked me a lot of questions about Queen Julia and Princess Phoebe. I'd ridden, almost immediately, to Nightmolben. I'd seen the bodies of King Philip and his son, and I'd made arrangements for their transport to Hicrown. I had not, however, attended their funerals.

'Exactly,' Patrick confirmed, after I explained my reasoning. 'You told Dicky you wouldn't go to Hicrown. You told him you didn't know what had happened to the royal women. And he relayed all this to his brother, Carl—'

'No, Patrick, he couldn't have.' My eyes were blazing now. 'Because after that he attacked me in my own library and I defeated him. And then I hanged him. He had no chance to tell anyone what I'd said.'

'Well, that is a good thing.'

It was, but he'd left unsaid the fact I'd made a grave error in not going straight to Hicrown to find out who had killed my King.

The horse Patrick's groom had picked out was called Mirabel. She was young and lively, and I knew she'd be a glorious ride. Patrick also made sure I was armed with a new sword and dagger. I thanked Lady Deborah for filling the panniers with food and ale, and I took Peter to one side for a quick word.

'I want you to do something for me. Find out more about this city. Why was it built? Why is every building so rich and fine? It isn't normal. Talk to Deborah. Get all the facts, Peter.'

'Aye, lord. I wish I could go wi' thee, though.'

'I need you to stay here. Nowhere is safe now, and you may have to help Patrick defend Myrtile.'

But I was desperate to ensure it wouldn't come to that. I guessed Patrick deliberately did not maintain the track from the Navisar Road to his precious city. He'd let it become overgrown and disreputable because he didn't want people coming to Myrtile. I added an instruction to Peter to find out why.

Mirabel was as delightful as I thought she'd be. Intelligent, quick to adapt to my riding style, and with great energy whenever I needed it. I rode through woodland at first, leaving behind the strange city of turquoise and gold. On that first day I reached the Nightmolben road, which I needed to cross. On the far side of the road there was a vile, stinking ditch, which held foul memories for me. I asked Mirabel to jump this ditch, and she responded with enthusiasm. But that brought us to the edge of Nightmolben Forest. I'd have to go through the forest if I wanted the straightest route to Wartsbaye. Mirabel entered the dark thicket of trees. At once, everything seemed different. This forest always had a reputation: it was, so they said, the haunt of the devil, and everything that was evil lurked here.

And so it proved. As we went deeper into the sombre woods, I felt prickling up and down my spine. I reined Mirabel in and looked all around me. They came from nowhere. Men with axes and bill-hooks, men with daggers and knives. Around a dozen of them, all looking like brigands on the run from the law. Except – there *is* no law now in Mallrovia. We are lawless.

I drew my sword, hacked around me indiscriminately, dug my heels into Mirabel's sides and urged her forwards. We had to get through the forest as fast as we could. Mirabel picked up speed, moving fast through the gaits until we were cantering, swerving through trees, jumping low bushes, ducking under branches and lashed by trailing ivy and brambles. It was unsustainable, of course, but we'd left the brigands behind. I might have even injured one or two. But there could be more desperados. They'd be in small bands, like the one we'd met. They'd be out to steal, scavenge and kill. They'd know there was no one to apprehend them; no court of law, dungeon, prison or hangman's noose awaited them. It would be every man for himself.

We met no more bandits in Nightmolben Forest, because I decided to come out of it. It might be the straightest route to Wartsbaye, but it wasn't the fastest, and it was by far the most dangerous. So we emerged south of the treeline into open country, where at least we could see where danger might lurk. In the daylight, at any rate, but it was growing dark now. I looked for a safe place to spend the night, and there wasn't one. So I did the best I could, letting

Mirabel wander fairly freely, although tied on a long rein to a tree, while I climbed the tree and sat awkwardly in its branches.

I got no sleep, but I did rest a little, and I even shut my eyes for brief stretches. But mostly I was alert, peering through the leafy branches and watching the moonlit landscape, which looked empty enough but probably wasn't. We were lucky though: we'd exited the forest close to the head of the River Evenway, and Mirabel had plenty to drink.

The Evenway's a shortish stream, running south and joining the River Shamet somewhere between Hicrown and the Woolding marshes. Unfortunately, as I wandered down the next morning to wash in the spring, I disturbed a family of coots, who all scuttled away making their characteristic high-pitched hooting sound. I ducked down at once, convinced I'd given away my location to the next band of roving discontents.

But no one appeared, so I dried my chest and face on my shirt, returned to Mirabel, and we set off across the Evenway's floodplain, a low-lying, flower-carpeted meadowland which stretches between Nightmolben Forest and the Hambrig Hills.

I have often reflected that I'm rarely on my own. At home, there are always people who need me, whether it's to sort out a dispute, decide on spending, or review my warriors as they parade in the bailey. And if I'm not at home, I'm on some expedition somewhere, surrounded by others who'll be needed to attack an enemy or defend us from one.

Seldom do I get the chance to spend even one solitary day, let alone several in a row.

And do you know? I delighted in it! Even the odd skirmish with roving bands of outlaws, but they were cowardly men, every one of them. Mirabel and I soon put them to flight. So you might have thought I'd have relished the opportunity to write this journal every day, perhaps two or three times a day. Indeed, I thought so myself. But it turned out otherwise. I'm too accustomed to snatching odd moments, often, literally, *moments*, to scribble hastily on my parchment; or else I'll sit up at night, while others sleep, and catch up on several days of non-stop action. Somehow, the thought of endless hours in which to write my thoughts down actually discouraged me from doing so. I did try, but I quickly ran out of inspiration. There was nothing much to say, and I wanted to be on the move, not sitting in some quiet glade like a lovelorn poet.

So Mirabel and I plodded, or trotted, or cantered, and occasionally, briefly and gloriously, *galloped* through the four days it took us to reach Wartsbaye, while my nights were full of the sort of deep and reviving sleep I hadn't experienced for months. Perhaps years. I knew I carried bad news. I knew I had to make difficult decisions. I knew our country was in deep and dreadful trouble. Yet – those four days of solitude, good food and deep sleep, brought restoration and renewal. I even began to think I'd beaten the Darkness for good, as each refreshing sunny day brought solace, and a chance to tell Mirabel all my deepest thoughts and feelings. Her ears twitched as I talked to her, but, equally, she never complained if I stayed silent for hours at a time.

I'm writing this late at night in my chamber in Baron Giles's castle. I know it will seem impossible, but all the while I was worrying about telling Giles of his son's death, I never gave a thought to Amie. Once my bard, and a talented harpist, Amie had married Gael seven years ago. They have a little boy, Young Davy, now five years old.

Giles hadn't recovered from his illness, I could see that, but he received me in his great hall, looking pale, his hands shaking, even before he knew what had happened. When I gave him the news, his face changed. He's ten years older than I, and, before my eyes, he became old and crushed. Both his sons dead before him. Their mother too. And then, very softly, he'd called Amie into the hall, and gently he'd told her that Gael had died bravely, fighting those who would overthrow the kingdom. Giles made Gael seem heroic, but Amie was not fooled.

'He threw his life away, didn't he? He never thought of me and Young Davy. He thought only of glory for himself!'

There was much weeping in the hall. At a click of Giles's fingers, servants came and scooped up Young Davy, leaving his mother to her gut-wrenching sobs. Giles took me into another room, not unlike my library in its purpose, although larger, more grandly fitted out, and, sensibly, at ground level.

'She's right, isn't she?' he asked bluntly. 'The boy tried to be a hero. He'd have been making ballads in his head, even as he bled to death.'

'His last words were to say he wanted to be like Davy. To die defending his country. Which is exactly what he did. He wanted us to be proud of him, Giles.'

Giles made a choking sound and turned away for a moment or two. 'Well.' He faced me again, shoulders set like the veteran he was. 'What now? What the hell do we do now?'

'You have half your garrison left—'

'You want to take them? See them all dead in Hicrown?'

'Not that, no. But I want them to be the core of a fighting force. We will march the length of Mallrovia, recruiting to the ranks—'

'Whom will you recruit?' Giles's tone was bitter. Rougher than I'd ever heard him. 'There is nobody. You may get the odd peasant with his pitchfork, or a couple of middle-aged merchants who fancy themselves as fighting men, but they won't hold off the King's Squad! Nor these bloody Livonians, damn them to hell. It's a lost cause, Rory. Mallrovia is lost.'

'We *cannot* think like that,' I cried, my fists clenched. 'We have to *fight* them!'

'Then we shall all die. And for what? No, Rory. Let Allan take control. Let the Livonians man the forts, but I'm telling you, they won't have this one. I shall pull up the drawbridge and my soldiers will defend Wartsbaye Castle and everyone in it. At least we're prepared for the attack, thanks to you.' Again, he turned from me. Defeat is hard to bear. The loss of both his sons, the loss of the kingdom, perhaps the loss of his castle. Seriously ill until recently, Giles wouldn't survive much longer, and I think we both knew it.

I've been given the same comfortable bedchamber I had last time I was here, so now I sit cross-legged on the bed, my parchment in my lap. I've written down everything that happened since I left Myrtile. I wonder if Patrick will be able to defend Myrtile. I saw no defences. The bridge over the moat is lit with bright lamps, and the gates stand wide open all the time. Nobody comes and nobody leaves, for they are all far too comfortable in their large houses with the turquoise roofs and the gold-topped spires. Myrtile is too good to be true, and if the Livonians find it, with all its riches...

I left that last sentence unfinished, put down my journal and got into bed. I thought I'd never be able to sleep, and I could still hear Amie wailing, although that might have just been inside my mind. But I dutifully closed my eyes, and when I opened them again, it was morning, and I'd slept after all. Not only that, but I awoke with a fully formed plan in my head, and I couldn't wait to tell Baron Giles.

14

ON AND ON TO NAVISAR

Giles was dead. Was it the shock of Gael's last stand? Was it his previous illness returning, stronger and deadlier than before? Was it Amie's relentless screaming? A physician arrived this morning, and pronounced the baron dead from heart failure. Surely everyone dies from heart failure? I asked the physician for more information, but he told me he'd given Giles several infusions to drink when he first fell ill. If they hadn't worked, it wasn't his fault, was it?

Arrangements will have to be made to bury the man, here in his castle's vault, but I didn't want to get involved in that. I spoke to the garrison's commander, who, for some reason, hadn't been sent with those who'd marched to their deaths in Hicrown. A man named Titus. He looked strong and capable, and I brusquely told him to deal with everything, after which Amie, Lady of Wartsbaye, would give him his orders.

I dreaded meeting Amie this morning. If Gael's death had provoked so much emotion, what would she be like now? Strangely, though, she was composed and quiet. I went to her chamber and found her dressed and sitting by the window, gazing out.

'What is your plan, Lord Rory?' she asked, without turning to look at me. 'Your plan to save Mallrovia.'

'I'm riding to Pevarile.'

That surprised her, for she turned then. Her face was pale, her eyes puffy with crying. Frankly, she looked a mess, but at least she was a quiet one. 'Pevarile?'

'To find a ship. I would like to take the rest of the Wartsbaye garrison, including Commander Titus, and I shall recruit more people in Pevarile. Then I intend to sail down the coast to Navisar and march on Hicrown. I am determined to take back the country.'

It sounded dramatic. As if I thought it my destiny, or something pompous like that.

'Why?' Amie asked. 'I mean, why bother? Won't I be all right here in Wartsbaye? Won't you be all right in Hambrig?'

'No, Amie, neither of us will be all right if Sir Allan takes control of Mallrovia. He'll want both Wartsbaye Castle and Hambrig. He already controls Navisar and Hicrown. Once he has my castle he'll have my demesne, and with Wartsbaye as well, he'll rule the country. The Livonians with him want to put two fingers up to the Teutonic Knights, and that will mean war, I'm in no doubt about that. We will end up fighting a war with Germany. With the Holy Roman Empire itself. I need to at least try to prevent that.'

It felt odd to be talking to Amie like this. As my bard, she'd been a servant in my household, although a high-ranking one, but before that she'd been an orphan girl from the streets of Hambrig Town. Now a widow with a dead father-in-law, she was Lady of Wartsbaye. Wartsbaye will be her responsibility until Young Davy is old enough to take charge of it. Amie must make her plans, and quickly. In the meantime, I needed her permission to remove what was left of the Wartsbaye garrison – and that felt very strange indeed.

'Will you let me take the garrison to Pevarile?' I asked again. 'And then on to Hicrown?'

'You may take Titus and the remaining soldiers,' Amie said. 'But only if I come with you. There's nothing for me here, not now.'

'What about Young Davy?'

'He has a nurse. Rosalind's very good with him, and he loves her. He won't miss me, you know.'

'Amie, you must remain in Wartsbaye. Your son is here, and the servants. If I take the garrison away, who will be in charge of Wartsbaye? It needs to be you. Surely you can see that.'

'All I can see, Lord Rory, is that my world has ended. Gael is gone. Now Giles is gone. Young Davy is a child, and no use to anyone yet. Rosalind will look after him. I will be much more use fighting alongside Titus and the others.'

I stared at her, not understanding. Amie has never fought a battle in her life. She's a twenty-six-year-old woman with a child.

My thoughts must have shown in my face. 'You think I can't do it?' she said. 'That I'll be no use – or even worse, a burden and a responsibility? You're wrong, Lord Rory. I am fit and strong, and Mallrovian women have always fought alongside men. Captain Kerry used to be my hero. I always wanted to be like Captain Kerry. Now's my chance, and I won't let you down. Unless you let me join the expedition, I won't let you take the Wartsbaye garrison.' Her chin lifted and her eyes shone, but they shone with tears.

'You loved Gael so much then?' I asked. 'I didn't know. I knew he was besotted with you, but—'

'You're right,' she said, the tears spilling over and flowing down her cheeks. 'I didn't love Gael as much as he loved me. And, to me, he was always a child. Living here, with Baron Giles always in control, was like being in prison. But I'm free now. That will shock you, I expect, but it's true.'

I spoke at some length with Rosalind, making sure she understood. Young Davy seemed very happy with her, and Rosalind was not unlike Eliza, who used to be nurse to my younger brother and sister. So I was satisfied, up to a point. I didn't like leaving Wartsbaye unprotected. The servants were mostly elderly people, who'd obviously been with Baron Giles for many years. Most of them were tearful and distraught that he'd died so suddenly in his sleep. I told them their jobs and their homes were secure. They would stay here in the castle, carrying out their duties as best they could, and one day their mistress would return to them. Of course, they had no choice, so it was a formality, and one I got over with as quickly as possible.

Two days after Giles's death, we marched east along the coast road to the port of Pevarile. It took just one day to get there, and I was glad to have Titus riding by my side. He'd organised Giles's burial and left sensible instructions for the servants. Behind us tramped twenty men from the Wartsbaye Guard, as they call themselves, and there were no women among them.

'Baron Giles didn't like women in the army,' Titus explained when I asked him about this. 'He didn't think it fittin'.'

'Well I'm in charge now,' I told him. 'So if women want to join our small army, they will be welcome.'

'Baron Giles thought they'd cause trouble.' Titus sounded critical, his bushy eyebrows meeting in a disapproving frown. 'Know what I mean?'

'They won't cause trouble,' I told him. 'So make sure you don't, either.'

It was a warning.

Pevarile is a huge port, at least by Mallrovian standards. It's as big as Bremen in Germany, and bigger than Hastings in the south of England. Bigger, too, than Limassol in Cyprus, where we landed to fight the Infidel all those years ago. Ships from all over the world dock in Pevarile, and it's a gateway not just to Mallrovia, but to all the towns in the centre and east of England. The road south from Pevarile, and then west through Gailen into England, is a good one, well maintained by the merchants who travel frequently from the coast, inland to their marketplaces.

I stood and stared at the docks, the warehouses, the cranes, the ships and the many, many people, all hurrying about their business. I'm used to Hambrig Wharf, which is always busy with ships coming and going up and down the River Hurogol. We have our warehouse too, and our counting house, since the wharf is a Hanseatic *kontor*, and we enjoy tariff-free trade with many other cities. But this was on a different scale entirely.

The Wartsbaye men were not transfixed as I was. They probably come here when they're off duty. There are taverns galore, and, no doubt, whorehouses too. Even now, I could hear men discussing the merits and faults of this or that establishment. My eyes, though, were fixed on the ships. I wanted a large vessel, but not too large, since we'd have to beach her at Navisar.

Titus's deep voice broke in on my thoughts. 'What will you do with Mirabel, lord?'

'Leave her here,' I said. 'We shall do the same with your horse and with Lady Amie's.'

'That's our ship.' Titus pointed at a vessel tied up to one of the long jetties projecting into the harbour. 'She'll do for us.'

He had a good eye. He was pointing to a carrack, not unlike William's former ship, the *Senjo*. The *Senjo* had been wrecked two years ago, but this carrack was a similar size and had the same rig: three strong masts, with square sails on two of them and a triangular lateen sail on the mizzen. There'd be room on board for twice our number.

I turned to the commander. 'Well spotted, Titus. Find out if we can charter her, and send some men into the town on a recruitment drive. We need more people. Men *and* women. You'll also need to find weapons for the recruits. There'll be an armourer in the town somewhere.'

Titus gave me a strange look. 'Recruitment drive? Don't you mean a press gang? We won't get volunteers, if that's what you're thinkin'. But my men can round up a gang of able-bodied men and trot 'em back here at the double. Weapons can be requisitioned too. Lord.'

His tone was insubordinate, and he'd added the last word as an intentional afterthought, but he was right to correct me. 'Exactly as you say, Titus,' I responded, keeping my tone even. 'See to it, please. And find an inn where we can spend the night. We'll sail on the next tide.'

Titus was a good organiser. He was an effective leader of his men, too, and they responded well to his orders. When all's said and done, I didn't have to like him. Within moments, the twenty men had scampered off in all directions, and Titus headed across to the jetty to find out more about the ship we wanted. He'd get her, I had no doubt about that.'

'What do we do now, lord?' Only Amie and I were left on the dock. I looked over at her. She'd donned soldiers' breeches and tunic, and she'd tied her hair back behind her head, exchanging her feminine wimple for a woollen hat that came down over her ears. Reminding me, briefly, of Aldara. But Aldara had looked the part. Amie might do so too. In time.

The ship, named the *Wenno*, turned out to belong to Reinhard von Lutterberg, and he was here, in Pevarile. He'd wanted money, but Titus had refused to pay out, saying the fate of the kingdom rested on our using his ship.

I spoke bluntly to the Livonian. 'You went with William. Two years ago. What happened, and where's William now?'

'Somewhere on the high seas.' Reinhard gestured vaguely at the expanse of water beyond the harbour. 'Somewhere out there. As to what happened – you don't know this, but it was our plan all along. William had his ship ready and waiting for him in Dorbney. We sailed together to Bremen, and then William sailed on, but I remained in Frisia.'

Except he didn't remain in Frisia. He went back to Osnabrück, and from there he organised the kidnapping of the Duchess of Bavaria, onetime princess of Mallrovia, and now the wife of Duke Louis II of Bavaria, Count Palatine of the Rhine.

'A risky thing to do,' I commented, wondering how on earth he'd managed to spirit Lillian away from Heidelberg Castle, and if her husband was now in hot pursuit.

'I had help.'

'Where is Lillian now?'

He jerked his thumb towards his ship. Reinhard had stolen the ship as well as the duke's wife.'

'I learnt a lot from Captain William,' he said simply. 'And the tide will be right for your expedition around three hours before sunrise. That's when we'll leave.'

And I needed him to come too, because none of the Wartsbaye Guard knew how to sail a ship. But they'd found a dozen Pevarile men to join us, together with swords, axes, pikes and spears. It seemed the expedition was taking shape.

So we didn't stay at an inn after all. We sat around on the dock waiting for the tide, and then, in the darkness, we hoisted sail and crept away from the Pevarile jetty. As the *Wenno* picked up speed and foamed through the water, the Wartsbaye people hung over the side to say goodbye to their homeland, and even though they couldn't see it, they still waved like mad. As day broke over the empty sea, Reinhard and I took the ship even further out, then set an easterly course, parallel to the Mallrovian coastline.

Titus drilled the new recruits on deck, allocating weapons according to his perceptions of their skills or otherwise. Soon targets were set up, and spears were being hurled across the deck. Only when one had vanished overboard and another had twanged into the deck mere inches from Reinhard's foot, did Titus acknowledge the dangers. But by then, he was satisfied with his spearmen.

By now, I'd seen Lillian, deep in the hold of the *Wenno.* She was unrepentant.

'I am expecting a child, Lord Rory,' she told me with a gasp. '*The Empress* did her work! Thank you for sending her back to me. And Kit too, of course.'

The Empress was a small square of parchment, a 'gypsy card', which could help a woman get, and stay, pregnant. But when Lillian spoke of it, she was referring to a small child, daughter of Master Kit, my minstrel. And suddenly all became clear. 'It was Kit who helped you escape from Heidelberg, wasn't it?'

She nodded. 'I owe Kit and Aggie everything. Without them, I wouldn't be here.'

'Yet you're carrying Louis's child?' I was horrified at the plan they'd all hatched together. Lillian was supposed to be with her husband, who was desperate for a son to replace the one who'd died. And Lillian had been helped by Kit's daughter to conceive again. So what had gone wrong?

'I bore Louis another son,' Lillian explained. 'Last year in February. Louis is happy now. But this new child, growing in my womb, this is not Louis's child.'

'You're pregnant by Reinhard?' I couldn't believe this idiocy. If we were not at war with Germany through the Livonian takeover of Hicrown, we'd be at war with Bavaria through Lillian and Reinhard's obtuse actions.

It was then, and only then, I made the vital connection. Reinhard is Carl von Lutterberg's brother. Reinhard is a Livonian Swordbrother. This isn't two separate crackpot schemes. It's just my bad luck that they're happening simultaneously. This is *one* devastatingly dangerous plan, in which Reinhard steals Duke Louis's wife from under his nose and brings her to Mallrovia, while Carl and Allan secure the country from inside. The audacity of it filled me with a mixture of awe and revulsion.

But when I questioned Reinhard, he shrugged and professed to know nothing of his brother's plans. I told him of Dicky's death, and this got another shrug from Reinhard. He didn't care about Dicky. Carl, he cared about, but decided his brother could look after himself. That night, Reinhard and I sat together by the mizzen mast. The rest of the crew slept on deck, kept watch, or manned the tiller, while the *Wenno* sailed ever eastwards, before turning south, past the ruined cliffs of Nightmolben, on and on to Navisar.

15

YOU SHOULD NEVER HAVE ALLOWED IT TO HAPPEN

'Who or what is Wenno?' I asked, my head tilted back to look up at the stars. At night, you steer your ship by the stars, their patterns distinctive, each one unique and with its own immutable place in the night sky.

'Wenno von Rohrbach,' Reinhard said, 'is a legend. Our first *Herrenmeister* – although he only ruled the Swordbrothers for five years, and was killed in anger. The Swordbrothers, you should realise, are Crusaders. We fight for Christ, to bring Him to unbelievers in the Baltic states. Are you not on our side in this?'

I ignored the question. 'So Wenno von Rohrbach was the first Master of the Livonian Swordbrothers. Strange that you came across a ship with his name.'

A sidelong look from Reinhard. 'I agree, that would be strange. I changed the ship's name, Rory, as I'm sure you have realised. This ship had a different name when I found her.'

'You bought her? Or you stole her?'

'I told you, William taught me a great deal.' Reinhard

was opaque. 'But that was our bargain, after all. William's new ship is larger than the old one. More comfortable. Faster and more powerful too.'

'William's a privateer.' But I said it with a question in my voice.

'That's how he describes himself, yes.'

'Meaning?'

'Rory, William is a pirate. You must know this already. He steals, he kills, he attacks shipping and he cares nothing for the law or for life. He plays his own game and he sets his own rules. A man after my own heart. Privateer, however, sounds much more respectable, so that is William's line when he's ashore. Piracy pays well – almost as well as smuggling. Between us, we had enough wealth to buy the ship William dreamt of, and after that he dropped me in Bremen, where I looked for a ship of my own. You can't complain. You're getting the benefit.'

'I'd have found a ship in Pevarile,' I growled. 'It didn't have to be this one.'

He shrugged, as if to say he knew it wasn't true but he wasn't going to argue.

'What's the name of William's new ship?' I thought it might be useful to know this.

'He's called her the *Yakuza*. It means "Fighting Warrior" in the Senjo Battlefield Plan, and he's put another red, yellow and blue dragon at her prow.'

'And where is the *Yakuza* now?'

'I have no idea. William sails where he likes. After we went ashore in Bremen, William took a few days to find a crew. He wanted four people to help him and Kerry crew the ship, and fight if necessary. Which it certainly will be. Then they put to sea, and could be anywhere. But he'll come back to Hambrig. He talks a lot about his mother. He'll want to see her again.'

His mother! Joan thinks William is a respectable ship owner and trader. As I'd always thought, too. And now he has a small child on board, his own four-year-old daughter. Did that make any difference to his antics? Reinhard, laughing, shook his head at the very notion.

Daylight brought us to Navisar. We closed with the shore, and Reinhard proved he knew his ship well. As the sails came down and the oars were lifted high, the *Wenno*, though anchored in deep water, ran gently aground on the sand. She could be hauled off later.

We organised our people into a marching column. There were the twenty Wartsbaye men under Captain Titus, together with twelve men from Pevarile, now armed with spears, axes and pikes. Amie tagged on to the Pevariles, grasping a spear and standing as tall as she could – which brought the top of her head to the level of the shortest man's shoulder.

Seeing this, the nearest Pevarile recruit gave her a sneering look, and straightaway she spat in his face, reminding me of the dirty little urchin she'd once been. I shook my head at her. She was supposed to be Lady of Wartsbaye! Well, no matter. There were more important things to do now.

I left Lillian to Reinhard. I didn't see how a pregnant woman would manage the long march to Hicrown, but I made that Reinhard's problem, not mine. She set out bravely, lifting her gown as she scrambled through the sand dunes, then trudging along the Navisar Road, only a little way behind the column. But she got further behind. I didn't realise this for some time, as I was marching in the front rank. Each hour, though, I ordered a brief stop, and the men fell out to have a drink, eat an apple and some cheese, relieve themselves at the roadside and catch their breath.

'This is unnecessary, and a waste of time,' Reinhard had grumbled at the first stop. He'd fixed me with his gaze, and now, in the daylight, I remembered how hypnotic his eyes were. You couldn't look away, and you knew he could make you do whatever he wanted.

'It's not a waste of time, Reinhard. We have a thirty-mile march over rough terrain. When we get to Hicrown, it won't be supper and bed for these men, it'll likely be a pitched battle against highly trained troops. So they'd better be well fed and rested. There is no point in bringing the walking dead into the city.'

It was meant to be a stinging rebuke, but Reinhard simply leant forward and stared at me. The *Hochmeister* of the Teutonic Knights had once described Reinhard as 'the man with the bewitching eyes'. Reinhard had defied his own *Hochmeister* to be here. And now I defied Reinhard.

'You're under my command,' I told him, tearing my gaze from his unblinking stare. 'These men will all do as I say.'

At the third stop I noticed Lillian was no longer with us. I despatched Titus to find her, and he brought her back in his arms. She was tearful, exhausted and incapable of walking any further.

I scowled at her lover. 'You brought her here. Wasn't that rather stupid, considering she's pregnant?'

'Perhaps you're forgetting,' he snapped back, 'I hadn't intended a forced march to the city. You're the one with a battle to fight.'

'Tell me then. Why did you come to Mallrovia? You had your ship, you had your woman, you could have gone anywhere, much like William and Kerry. So why return to Mallrovia?'

He smiled briefly. 'You'll find out soon enough.' And then he turned away, and I was absurdly grateful not to have to look into those eyes.

Reinhard picked Lillian up. There were still twenty miles to go, and I doubted he could carry her the whole way, especially under this glaring summer sun. I said nothing, however. And we continued to stop every three to four miles, which gave Reinhard a chance to put Lillian down and rest his aching muscles. At least, I suppose they were aching; he never said.

And then, after a night march and in the early morning of the second day, we heard the city's noise and knew we were nearly there. I halted our troops and we settled down to check our weapons, make sure everyone knew what to do and dispense any last minute orders.

'You're sticking to the plan then?' Reinhard asked, his strange eyes glinting in the evening light.

'That's the point of a plan,' I said drily. 'Why change it now? We may need to change it later – that'll depend on what we find when we're through the city gate.'

I hadn't confided completely in Reinhard. He and Carl were brothers. Carl had thrown in his lot with Allan. That might well mean that Reinhard would desert me and go to fight alongside Carl and Allan when the time came. But he had Lillian to protect, and, in some ways, her presence would be helpful. The Wartsbaye and Pevarile men would stick with me, of course, giving me thirty or so deployable soldiers, some of whom could even be classed as warriors. Titus would certainly be a good ally. Amie was untried, and my sole hope for her was that she would survive the coming battle, if only for Young Davy's sake.

But then I thought of something that should have occurred to me long ago. I went to sit with Reinhard, who was holding a bladder to Lillian's lips, coaxing her to drink more water. She was trying, but was simply too exhausted. She needed to sleep, and probably a physician to check her over. Well, we could provide neither as yet.

'Reinhard.'

He looked up, forgetting to remove the bladder of water, and Lillian spluttered and nearly choked.

'Reinhard, are you with Carl or against him? Carl wants to put Allan on the throne of Mallrovia. Allan fancies himself as King. Is that how you see it?' I was looking down at Lillian as I spoke. I'd realised Reinhard's plan might not include Allan.

'*This* is how I see it, Rory: we should march on Hicrown and see how your tactics work out. When we've won, we can discuss Allan. If we don't win – well, there will be nothing to discuss, will there.'

A neat sidestepping of my questions. 'I need to know. Are you with Carl?'

'I am with Carl, yes. We are brothers: blood brothers and Swordbrothers. Yes, I shall fight alongside my brother. But I am not with Allan, *and neither is Carl*.' He ground out his final few words with great emphasis.

'Carl *is* with Allan, Reinhard.'

'I think you will find he is not. Not once he sees me.'

'Was this planned? Did you and Carl plan to kill King Philip and Prince Barney and then seize the throne?'

'You still don't understand, do you. It is *nothing* like that. But I shall say no more until after we have defeated the odious Sir Allan of Hicrown. With your help, and that of these soldiers. So let's go. Half a mile more and we'll be there – and then your questions will all be answered.'

But, unbelievably, King Henry III of England had arrived, and none of us had prepared for this. An enormous golden coach stood outside the gates to the palace. I'd never seen the English king's transport before, and could hardly take in the opulence of the gold decorations and the bejewelled rails and post finials. Over the top of the coach was strung a beautifully woven scarlet canopy with gold tassels hanging from it.

The coach stood exactly where I'd tried to gain entrance to the palace, two weeks ago. I remembered how Pockthorpe had fallen from his horse just here, his face an unnatural shade of grey, tremors racking his body.

Dismissing Pockthorpe from my mind, I looked through the gatehouse arch. A large chair had been brought from somewhere and placed on top of the small grassy knoll that occupied the very middle of the garden. Seated on the huge chair was the King of England, although I'd understood him to be seriously ill. Which no doubt explained the chair. Perhaps the man was weak and needed to sit down. Standing in front of the king was Sir Allan of Hicrown, in full ceremonial dress, his sword at his hip, and a cohort of the King's Squad formed up behind him, their uniforms immaculate, their bearing impeccable. I saw no sign of Captain Leo, nor Carl von Lutterberg.

King Henry was flanked by tall English knights, three on each side. They wore chain mail and their hands rested imperiously on their sword hilts. Their surcoats showed blazons I recognised: the Earls of Surrey, Warwick, Lincoln, Oxford, Hereford and Pembroke.

Behind the king stood a young lady with an extremely tall headdress. I didn't know her, but she also wore an emblazoned surcoat, and I recognised the arms: Azure, four bars Or. Salisbury. But impaled with those of Lincoln. So the woman, as well as being Countess of Salisbury, was the Earl of Lincoln's wife. My mind was spinning at the thought of so much haughty English nobility in Hicrown. As for why they were here – that wasn't so hard to work out.

They all heard us arrive, clashing to attention outside the palace wall. Reinhard put Lillian down, and she subsided to the ground. Amie stared, open-mouthed, at the English earls. Throwing Reinhard an order to stay exactly where he was, I squeezed past the chariot and entered the palace garden.

Everyone had turned to look, and now King Henry blinked at me, no spark of recognition in his eyes. He wouldn't know me, but he should have recognised my own blazon. It is, after all, one of only three in Mallrovia.

'Your Majesty,' Allan said, hurriedly, 'this is Lord Rory of Hambrig. He is partly responsible for the civil unrest in Hicrown.'

Well, that was news to me. I stepped forward and bowed low to the King of England, who extended his hand for me to kiss.

'How is he "partly responsible"?' asked King Henry, looking not at Allan but directly at me. He didn't have Reinhard's bewitching magic, but his gaze was penetrating, nonetheless.

'This man fought against your Majesty at Lewes. Although not an Englishman, he joined with the traitor, de Montfort, in attempting to overthrow the English monarchy.

The repercussions are felt in Mallrovia, even now, and our own problems are a direct consequence of the actions taken by those rebellious English barons, and the foreigners who supported them. Men like Rory of Hambrig.'

Allan's contemptuous tone and dishonest account made my blood boil. 'I did not fight against your Majesty at Lewes,' I said. 'I was there only to rescue my brother, which I did. I made no cause with the barons.'

Allan was about to protest, but Henry held up his hand. 'I have heard enough, and this garden does not please me. Escort me to the palace, and bring wine for everyone.'

His knights had to help him to his feet and support him as he tottered down the grassy mound and along the gravelled path. The woman followed them, and I walked with her. Allan was left to bring up the rear.

'Where is Hambrig?' asked the Countess of Salisbury.

'It is west of here, lady,' I said, but thought that too bald a reply. 'It is the largest shire in Mallrovia.'

'How many shires are there in your country?'

'Only three. The other two are Hicrownshire, where we are now, and Wartsbaye, which is to the north. But there are also wild areas, not part of any shire, such as the Wilderness, the Dunes and the Hambrig Hills.'

'My husband's presence was required,' she said, clearly following her own train of thought rather than my helpful description of Mallrovia's political landscape. 'His presence was required by the king, and my presence was required by my husband. So we are both here. And yet, I know little of what has happened or why we have come. Henry does not tell me much.'

I was startled, and she noticed. 'I didn't mean the king,' she said, laughing, and suddenly she sounded much more girlish. 'My husband's also called Henry. Henry de Lacy, Earl of Lincoln. He has very little time for me, but will seldom leave me to my own devices.'

'Many English women are chaperoned,' I said, struggling to know how to respond. King Henry was walking so slowly along the path, his unhurried progress punctuated with lengthy stops for him to lean more heavily on the sturdy knights at his sides, that the countess and I had plenty of time for conversation.

From under the tall headdress, which I believe is known as a 'hennin', she looked up at me and smiled. 'I'm not sure you understood me, Lord Rory. It's true that women are chaperoned when necessary and for their own safety, but I am talking of the irrational obsession my husband has with my chastity. Perhaps because I have not yet born him any children, though I was betrothed to him at the age of three. He will not even allow me to stay in my own home when he is not there. So I have had to come on this long and boring journey, and it has not even been instructive. I have no idea what everyone is arguing about. And I *don't* like that man.' With her head, she indicated the man walking behind us. Sir Allan of Hicrown.

'He wants to become King of Mallrovia,' I told her.

'He doesn't look like a king,' she said at once. 'And he neither speaks nor acts like one. Surely your dead monarch has an heir?'

'He had three children. One is dead, one has disappeared, and the third waits outside the palace walls.'

'King Philip's heir is here?' she exclaimed, and I heard Allan's footsteps falter behind me. 'Then produce this person! The argument will be over, that awful man can go away again and my husband can take me home!'

'It is not so simple, lady.'

I might have said more, but by now we had at last

reached the great hall, and all sorts of arrangements were being made with the servants, who hurried to fetch the wine Henry had asked for, and there was talk of dinner as well. Henry, having been almost lifted onto the dais, was now ensconced at the high table, taking Philip's normal place at the centre.

'Now.' Whatever Henry's physical weakness, his voice was clear and strong. 'Now, Sir Allan. Lord Rory. We understand Hicrown Cathedral has been destroyed by a rebel army made up of Hicrown's citizens. We are here to put an end to this, and to install a new ruler in the country of Mallrovia. We have heard Sir Allan's claims already, and the measures he has taken to subdue the rebels and restore order here in Hicrown. If you have anything to add, Lord Rory, we would like to hear it. And after that, we will make our own judgement, and you will all abide by it.'

I stood in front of the high table and hoped I didn't look too dusty and dishevelled after our thirty-mile march from the coast. 'I do have something to add, sire. I believe it was Sir Allan who began the insurrection in the first place. I don't know if he's told you, but there are foreign soldiers here as well, brought by ship, to incite further civil disobedience and violence. Which they will then subdue with even more violence, and more buildings will be destroyed. This is what Sir Allan wants: anarchy and chaos, so that he can appear to quell it, having begun it in the first place.'

'This is a blatant lie.' Allan, standing next to me, broke royal etiquette by speaking out of turn, and in a raised voice, too.

The English king turned a frosty gaze on him.

'Rory probably wants the kingdom for himself, sire.' Allan lowered the volume of his voice. 'He's the unstable lord of an unsettled shire. He has a reputation for being unpredictable, and even for being of unsound mind. I live in Hicrown, your Majesty. I know the city and its people. If you will proclaim me King, I can quickly and efficiently resolve this situation.'

King Henry turned to me. 'Who are the people you brought with you, and why have you not allowed them to enter?'

'They are soldiers, sire. I brought them to fight for control of Hicrown. When I saw that you and your knights had arrived, I realised the situation had changed. I told my cohort of men to wait outside. I'm not one for barging in and creating even more trouble.'

The king nodded. 'I shall talk to others, in particular the priests and the bishop who run the cathedral. A sad thing to see that beautiful building in ruins.' He turned suddenly to Allan. 'You should never have allowed it to happen.'

16

THE VULTURES WERE CIRCLING

We smuggled Lillian in. I didn't want anyone to know who she was, so we laid her on a pallet, covered her up completely with a blanket, and anyone who asked questions was told we had a seriously sick soldier. As we hurried her to the Palace Guard's accommodation block, I reflected that all traces of the fighting in Hicrown had been removed from the city, and here too, the bodies had been taken away.

In the streets of Hicrown, as in the palace gardens, there were now no corpses, no blood on the grass, no smell of death, no cries of the wounded. All gone, as if neither massacre nor battle had ever happened. One good thing about English Henry's arrival was that no one was likely to lock me up again. I'd seen no sign of Carl von Lutterberg.

We put Lillian in a small side room just inside the main door. Our men will also sleep in this block, in bunkrooms or on the floor. But Lillian must be on her own. Naturally, someone suggested sending for a physician, and before I knew it, a monk was putting his head round the door.

'You got someone sick here?' he asked, holding his nose. Did he think it was the plague? If so, we'd hardly all be squashed into the room next to the patient. When I say 'all', I mean Reinhard, Amie and me. Amie had already pulled the blanket back to let Lillian breathe, so the monk saw at once it was a woman who lay on the pallet. He drew in his breath sharply and released his nose.

'Who's that?' he hissed.

'None of your business,' Reinhard growled.

'Are you a doctor?' I asked.

He shook his head, still standing in the doorway and goggling at Lillian. 'I'm a herbalist. I worked in the cathedral. When there *was* a cathedral. May I ask what is wrong with the lady?'

'She's expecting,' Amie said quickly. 'And she's been sick a few times. I think she needs to drink more, but it's been difficult as we've had a long journey on foot.'

Amie had not needed to say quite so much. The monk, however, nodded jerkily. 'I know nothing at all about pregnancy,' he said. 'I will see if I can find a physician for you. And I will not mention this to anyone, you have my word as a man of God.'

He scuttled away.

'Man of God,' Reinhard said scathingly. 'He was almost pissing himself with fright, bobbing up and down in the doorway! And he'll likely blab to the first person he meets.'

He glared at Amie, but she simply shrugged and said, 'There's no point in hiding it. Her condition doesn't show yet, but it will soon. And we can't hide *her* for long, either.'

I had a horrible feeling I'd been here before. When Branca was seriously ill while she was pregnant with Rom, but I hadn't known. Our physician had been angry, not just with me, but with men in general. I looked at Reinhard. He should have known better. Lillian deserved better. I turned on my heel and walked out.

It's very late, and I'm sitting on the edge of the dais in the great hall as I write in my journal. It's imperative that I set down my thoughts and fears. I don't know how long Henry will be in Mallrovia. Normally, a state visit would be planned and advertised. This isn't a state visit. Our King is dead, our Queen sold into slavery abroad. We have no ruling monarch. Lillian herself warned me that England would swallow Mallrovia up one day. Henry isn't making those noises, but perhaps it's just a matter of time.

Philip had two tenants-in-chief, two men on whom he could rely for their loyalty, their advice and their honesty. I was one of them, and Baron Giles was the other. It has always been so; the Lord of Hambrig and the Baron of Wartsbaye are tenants-in-chief to the King, second only to him, his right-hand men in times of trouble. They are also his stand-ins for when he's abroad or too sick to rule. Or, I suppose, dead. Which he now is.

And yes, I saw his body. I made the journey to Nightmolben specifically for that purpose, after it occurred to me that Allan's letter might be completely false, and in reality the King was a hostage somewhere. But I saw his corpse, and that of his son, Barney. And now Giles, Philip's other tenant-in-chief, is also dead. Julia, our widowed Queen, has disappeared. Although Leo told me she'd also been killed, I haven't been able to verify that. It does seem likely, though.

Phoebe, the younger princess, became Queen on the

death of her father. For two years she ruled Mallrovia, Queen in name, but controlled by others. I suppose I knew this, having received Allan's letter after King Philip's murder, but I'd done nothing.

Cocooned from reality in my library, blaming the 'Darkness' for my lassitude and inactivity, I'd allowed two entire years to drift by, weakening my country and leading, inexorably, to this present situation. All that time, Phoebe had been kept quietly in the palace, amusing herself with childish games, while Allan had run Mallrovia: a simmering pot, waiting for the final leap of the flame that would make it boil over.

That leap of flame was the riots in Hicrown, carefully engineered by Allan at the exact time the Livonians were on manoeuvres. I saw how cleverly the situation had been manipulated. If I'd been more alert, more *involved*, I'd have seen it long ago. And now that Allan had achieved anarchy, he'd simply removed Phoebe from the scene.

Then there's Lillian. Philip's elder daughter. Married to a Bavarian and in love with a Livonian. She has returned to Mallrovia, but nobody knows she's here. For many reasons, her status is extremely precarious. Her adultery has undermined her moral and political position, and her child by Reinhard will not be recognised as a legitimate heir. Lillian could be forced to renounce her rights, while the Bavarian court may decide her marriage to Duke Louis is annulled. With such a messy situation, English Henry would probably regard Lillian's claim to the throne as unstable and contentious. At that point, he would surely make his move.

And so now – and here comes the point of this rambling scribble – there is only me. I am not running or ruling

Mallrovia. I have no craving for power. But it falls to me to get us out of this terrible predicament.

Yet I don't know what to do. I don't trust anyone here. Not even the King of England, who ordered a sumptuous feast to be prepared this evening, which we were all commanded to attend. The knights were there, of course, every one of them with more land, money and power than I have. And the extremely young Countess of Salisbury, who was friendly with me as we walked through the palace gardens, but who's just as formidable as the male earls either side of her.

The king himself was courteous and affable during supper, exchanging several pleasant words with me. His illness meant he retired early, and some of the knights proceeded to get drunk on Philip's wine stores, but others stayed sober, and they were the ones with the glint in their eyes. Cornwall and Lincoln, in particular. My guess is that both of them fancy adding Mallrovia to their lands. Lincoln would benefit the most, as the south-east corner of his shire has a border with my country. And Cornwall would like it because then he'd straddle both east and west in a kind of pincer action.

I feel agitated. Nervous and worried. And I fear the return of the Darkness, which cannot and *must* not happen. If the Darkness threatens again, Mallrovia will be lost, I know this now. And it makes me wonder. Do any of the English knights know of it? Would they provoke its recurrence, so as to weaken me and make it easy to invade, conquer and subdue our little kingdom?

My hand is shaking now as I write these words. The Livonians want to take my country. The English want it too. I have no professional garrison at Castle Rory. I am defenceless. Baron Giles is dead, as are both his sons. Amie cannot defend Wartsbaye, and I have removed the entire garrison there. What if the English move north while I have the Wartsbaye Guard here in Hicrown? It would be a calamity. This is, perhaps, Mallrovia's darkest hour. And mine too. What am I to do? What on *earth* am I to do?

In the morning, I asked Reinhard where Carl and the Livonian warriors are hiding. My dagger was drawn, and I meant business.

'You want to speak to Carl?' he asked. His eyes, normally so fascinating, were red and watery. He'd been sitting with Lillian all night. But Amie had been right, and Lillian had simply needed to drink a few gallons of water. Now, she slept peacefully, while her lover fretted at her side. I'd had very little sleep myself, and I wasn't sympathetic.

'Just fucking tell me where he is.'

'They left Hicrown during the night. Carl doesn't want to meet Henry.'

'I bet he doesn't. Where's Carl gone, Reinhard? Tell me, or I slit your throat.'

'Don't threaten me, Lord Rory of Hambrig. I am on your side. Carl is too. They're hiding in the woods south of the city. They'll wait it out there while Henry's here.'

'And you'll get a message to Carl when it's safe to return? Is that it?'

He nodded, wearily.

'I think you must have misunderstood me completely,' I said bluntly to Reinhard. 'You and Carl are *not* on my side.

You want Livonia to take over my country. I know you're angry with von Sangershausen and the Teutonic Knights. You want your autonomy again. You ache to be the 'Swordbrothers', as you used to be. Not the emasculated 'Livonian Order', controlled by the Teutonic Knights. I understand the aim, but I don't like the method. Don't try to recover your independence by subjugating others. Find a different way to do it.'

I thought about the woods south of Hicrown. They are extensive, and on the other side of them is the Wilderness, a dangerous tract of land stretching from the summit of Baudry Hill down to the sea. I could send men into those woods and never find them again. Especially if the wolves found them first.

King Henry was writing. He sat at the high table in the great hall, parchment, quills and ink set all around, his knights, as always, in close attendance. Seated at his side was the Countess of Salisbury. She seemed to be advising him on what to set down. There was no sign of Sir Allan, and I was glad of that.

As I entered, the king looked up. 'Good, I'm pleased to see you, Lord Rory. I am writing my instructions, and you will ensure they are carried out. Indeed, you will swear an oath to me, here and now, that my orders will be followed to the letter.'

What would I be swearing to, I wondered? Shouldn't I see the damned orders first, before I agreed to pin my honour to them?

Henry saw the look on my face. 'I am demanding fines be paid,' he said patiently. 'You must surely have guessed this would be the case. The rebuilding of a cathedral is a costly business, as Margaret Longsword, here, can attest. Although Salisbury was finished before she was born, eh, my little duckling?' He patted her arm affectionately.

But my mind was reeling.

Margaret Longsword?

Longsword?

I had not heard that name for twenty years, but it was like yesterday to me. William Longsword, Fourth Earl of Salisbury. Haughty and patronising. Calling me 'Hambrigger' and disparaging my every opinion. He'd been Jonny's sponsor and mentor on Crusade. Without Longsword, I'd never have met Jonny. Both of us had looked up to Longsword, but he'd been cut down in Mansurah in the Egyptian desert. He'd never returned to Salisbury. Neither had Jonny.

Henry looked disapproving. He was waiting for my response.

'I'm sorry, your Majesty,' I said hastily. 'What did you say?'

The English knights stared sternly at me, but the Countess of Salisbury smiled. 'His Majesty is imposing fines on the people of Hicrown. They have ruined their cathedral and it must be rebuilt to God's eternal glory. There has been, I believe, some talk of excommunication.'

'That is so,' agreed the king. 'The pope is very displeased with Mallrovia. However, I believe excommunication can be avoided if the cathedral is swiftly rebuilt and reconsecrated. I shall ensure this happens, Lord Rory. These fines I am levying will pay for English construction workers to come here.'

'Your Majesty, there are many excellent Mallrovian craftspeople, stonemasons and builders! There's no need for the English to be involved—'

Someone, it may have been Warwick, shot me a warning look. It sounded very much as if I were chastising King Henry. I withdrew my words at once. 'I apologise, your Majesty. I merely wished to reassure you that Mallrovia can handle the rebuilding. And, if you deem it a good idea, I can send an envoy to his Holiness.'

'An envoy would be an excellent idea,' said the king, tapping his quill on the table. 'I am not, as you may know, a well man. My son is on Crusade, far from home. It is my bounden and God-given duty to leave my country in a fit state. To improve the lot of my people. To manage my affairs well. There is wealth in Mallrovia. In particular, your wool trade...'

'We are a sovereign state, sire.' I tried to keep my tone neutral. I didn't want to antagonise these English knights, and certainly not their king.

Mallrovia has always had good relations with England. But Mallrovia is tiny. And our small size had never been more apparent to me than it was now. A century ago, the neighbouring land of Westador had been annexed to England, and was now a principality. Westador is a similar size to Mallrovia. How had we avoided the same fate? Through the strong leadership of our King, of course – many kings, including Philip, our most recent monarch. All our rulers had cultivated a strong and friendly relationship with England, with the result that the English left us alone. Was this all to be reversed, here and now, by this sickly man? If he truly wanted Mallrovia, I didn't see how any of us could stop him taking it.

'A sovereign state, with no sovereign?' Henry's tone was

also neutral, but when he glanced up from his documents, there was no warm smile. 'As you know, Lord Rory, there is no such thing.'

The earls, standing around him, looked as severe as their king. Mallrovia was a collapsed state, and the vultures were circling.

17

THE MEADOWS BEYOND

'We have to have Julia, Phoebe or Lillian on the throne,' I told Reinhard, Lillian and Amie that afternoon. We sat together in the small room in the Palace Guard's accommodation. No physician had arrived, but Amie's simple cure of plenty of water to drink had done the trick and Lillian felt much better now. 'We don't know where Julia is, or even if she's still alive. The same goes for Phoebe. If Phoebe's alive, she's still Queen, but in name only—'

'It can't be Lady Lillian,' Amie said, interrupting me. 'She is married to Duke Louis and has been stolen from him. Her whole life must now be lived in hiding.'

'Henry won't care who it is,' I said. 'If there's no sovereign, we are a collapsed state. That means anyone can move in and take us over.' I was looking at the two women. Mallrovians like me. Reinhard wouldn't care.

Lillian had turned pale at my words 'collapsed state'. She is a king's daughter, after all, growing up here in the palace and steeped in the history of the Kings and Queens of Mallrovia. Amie looked shocked. 'Collapsed state' sounded terrible. And final.

'I think you may be forgetting Sir Allan,' Reinhard said. The compelling glint was back in his eyes. 'Sir Allan has no intention of allowing Mallrovia to become a collapsed state. It is certain that the English will swallow Mallrovia up if that happens. I hear the Lord Edward is a greedy man, and he will soon succeed to the English throne. Sir Allan's plan is to save you from this.'

'And hand the country over to the Livonian Swordbrothers.'

This was as much Philip's own fault as anyone else's, and perhaps it had always been inevitable that one day Mallrovia would be left helpless and vulnerable. The Toosanik, that tribe-that-wasn't-a-tribe, had been deprived of their homeland through the abdication of their leader, and now Mallrovia would go the same way.

Are you going to let this happen, boy? my father asks, and my head jerks up in surprise, as I haven't seen his ghost for a long time now. In the Darkness, he stayed away. Even after the Darkness had receded a little, Father barely spoke to me. And when he did, he seemed diminished. His colours were muted, and he spoke only in a whisper. Now I see him standing in the doorway of the small room, as tall and commanding as he was in life. Feeling suddenly sick, I push past him and emerge in the palace courtyard. My head and hands feel clammy, and I wonder what's wrong with me.

Keep up your strength, Father advises uselessly. *You're going to have to fight King Henry!*

Don't be ridiculous, I grind out. *I can't fight the King of England. I've no warriors and, far more important, I've no case to make. Everything is lost, Father. Surely even you can see that?*

Well, you've certainly lost your backbone, he answers waspishly. *Here's the thing, boy. You have the Wartsbaye men and the Pevarile men. Send them out. Rouse the country! Shout it from the rooftops that the future of the kingdom is at stake! Proclaim it in the marketplaces, the farmsteads, the smallholdings and on the village greens. Send riders to the four corners of Mallrovia with orders to pick up support from our people. Those who care will flock to your banner. Those who don't will slink away, but there will be far more of the former, I can tell you. Then take them to Wartsbaye Castle and to Castle Rory and man the garrisons.*

And these Livonians? I ask him dully. His rabble-rousing rhetoric is exhausting. *What of the Livonians? They will invade through Navisar. They want Mallrovia as much as England does. Maybe more.*

Find a way, boy, Father says, more gently now. *You'll find a way. What matters is getting someone on the Mallrovian throne. Just make sure it's not that self-satisfied traitor who deprived your king of so much. First chance you get, you should hang him.*

Allan. I don't know him well, and have met him only a few times, every one of them a negative and unpleasant experience. He tried to court-martial one of my best officers. He refused to come to our aid when we were attacked by a group of insurgents calling themselves 'Dorian Liberation'. He's a traitor to our country, smuggling costly goods out to the Baltic to receive huge sums of money, tax-free: money which should have gone into the treasury coffers, but which he's creamed off for himself. I know nothing about him, nor why Philip thought fit to appoint him commander of the elite King's Squad. What did Allan do to deserve such an honour? And then, having received it, why turn against his King? I went to find him.

He was drilling his men at the butts out beyond the palace. You who are reading this may not know what Hicrown Palace is like. It's an exuberant, lavish red-and-silver edifice, sitting towards the north of the city, just beyond the main square and on the road that leads north to the Palace Gate. If you continue up that road, you'll find that beyond the Palace Gate the road forks. You have to choose your path. You can go due north to Nightmolben, which is now just a ruin, or north-west to Gailen, and the crossing into England.

Although the main entrance to the palace is on Palace Road, the surrounding wall is punctuated with smaller gates. I know them all from my time here as page to King David, and even though that was over thirty years ago, I remember the games we all played: running out through one gate and back in through another; chasing each other up and down the paths with yells of glee; scrambling over the walls, getting as dirty as only small boys can; and generally having a wild time. The gate in the north-eastern wall leads to a meadow in which, many years ago, some long-forgotten commander set up butts for archery practice. They're still here, and I had all my early training at them, a shortened, lightweight bow in my hands, a quiver of arrows at my belt, and some member of the Palace Guard patiently instructing me. Or, sometimes, not so patiently – but always constructively.

Well, here they were now: another group of soldiers practising their aim, and Sir Allan was neither patient nor constructive. He barked and bawled his orders, and his men, who knew what they were doing anyway, merely continued to loose their arrows, after which they retrieved them, stepped back to the chalked line in the grass, and did it all over again. I stood and watched for a short while, then walked purposefully over to Sir Allan. I disliked him intensely, but I was determined to find out more. Had he murdered Philip and Barney? Did he intend to sit on the throne of Mallrovia? Drilling the King's Squad implied patriotism and an understanding of the need to defend our country – but was he really a traitor? He'd certainly killed Mallrovians, including young Gael, but he'd let Leo lead the charge.

Father said I should hang him. But I had no proof, nor even circumstantial evidence against him. He'd written to me, the letter speaking of regicide. Would he have written it if he, himself, had carried out the crime? I thought not. He'd fought against me in the market square, but we had attacked first, and you could argue he was merely defending himself and his troops. He'd locked Phoebe up, the woman who was supposed to be our Queen, but he'd told her it was for her own safety, and she believed him. He'd sided with the Livonians, who had attacked Nightmolben in the hope of taking it for themselves, but Reinhard had told me the Livonians were on my side. Nothing quite added up.

I continued to watch Allan drilling his men. They were bloody good already, and I doubted the Wartsbaye Guard could match them for distance or accuracy. I hoped to God we wouldn't have to fight each other. But there was a repetitive monotony to the drill, and my attention wandered. My gaze roamed over the grassy archery field and out to the meadows beyond.

18

MAKING LOVE UNDER THE STARS

Vaguely, I remembered running along some sort of track that led through the meadowland and out of the city itself. We'd had a wager, hadn't we? I was one of three pages, aged about eight or nine, and we'd had a wager to see how far along the track we could go. We thought no one knew about it except us, and we decided to call it 'the Secret Way'. One boy was of the opinion that the Secret Way would lead to the coast. I remembered him saying it, and in my mind's eye I could see him too, but damned if I could remember his name. The second boy – Oliver? – disagreed at once, mostly because he always disagreed with whatever the last person had said. My own view was that it wasn't a proper track at all, and would just fizzle out after a few yards. I told them there was only one way to find out, and whoever was right would get to sleep by himself in our bed, while the other two had to sleep on the floor. As having a bed to yourself was the height of luxury, we were all up for it.

We'd set off as soon as our morning's training was finished. The well-trodden track took us through a narrow fissure in the city wall, and we walked for what seemed like miles in a north-easterly direction. As the sun began to set behind us, we got scared. We didn't know where we were, and we were hungry and thirsty too. In silent mutual agreement we turned back, and the three of us shared the bed again that night. I don't think any of us ever mentioned the track again. And I'd forgotten all about it until now.

I searched the ground beyond where the archers were standing, but in late summer the grass was high and I could see no sign of the path. Forgetting about Allan, I wandered into the field, my eyes searching the ground. And I found it. Someone had scythed the grass here, but they'd done it in such a way that, from the palace, you couldn't see it. It was only once you were past the butts that the path revealed itself. Those butts – lumpy, earthy mounds covered with grass – targeted time and again by archers skilled and unskilled, were in the direct line of sight from the palace to the path. Was that deliberate, I wondered? Was the path concealed intentionally? If so, why?

Idly, I wondered where the path would take me. How tantalising would it be, thirty-three years later, to resolve that wager? I knelt down at the start of the track, planting my palms in the cool meadow, feeling the flatness of the walkway under my hands and knees. I looked down, as if examining each blade of grass. In reality, though, I saw nothing. Kneeling in the grass, the burden of Mallrovia's fate almost crushed me, and I couldn't move. I didn't want this burden. This immense responsibility. What would happen to my country's people if I got it wrong? If I let others take over? Or would that be best anyway? If it meant the return of stability and the rule of law, perhaps it didn't matter who was on the throne. I could not resolve this by myself, yet there was no one to share it with.

Walking this ancient track would take me out of it. It would be, as Rosa always tells me, a distraction. The memory of my carefree childhood in the royal court had ripped away the façade I present to the world. Underneath was a core of guilt and dark self-doubt. In an agony of morbid thought, and still on my hands and knees, I began to crawl along the path.

Dimly, I hoped Father would come to me now and lift me out of this despair. He didn't. My logical mind knew I couldn't crawl for ever. It also knew I had problems to solve and a whole fucking country to save. But the rest of my mind was unsound. It could neither think nor reason. All it wanted to do was crawl away from decisions and choices, from responsibility and accountability. Perhaps it wanted to die.

I lay on my back. Above me, stars shone in the night sky. I blinked, wondering where I was, then propped myself up on an elbow and tried to see. Grasses waved around me, and hard pebbles dug painfully into my shoulders and thighs. Memory returned. I was on the path out of Hicrown, the one no one knew about. *The Secret Way*. Who had won the wager? Was it me, Oliver or Danny? Yes! The third boy's name was Danny! But no, there was no wager, because thirty-three years had somehow passed without my realising it, and we never knew who would have won, because we hadn't gone far enough. Perhaps only as far as I was now.

I stood up, fighting back dizziness and nausea. In the dark, I couldn't see the palace at all. My hands and knees were filthy from crawling. Running grimy hands through my hair, I wondered what on earth I'd been thinking of. I'd allowed the Darkness to creep up on me. My resistance had been low. I'd nearly given in to it.

Drearily, I headed back towards the palace, almost stumbling into the butts. Deserted now of course. Straight ahead, I saw the shadowy outline of the soldiers' accommodation blocks, and beyond them would be the palace. I would check on Lillian in her little room I decided. Reinhard would be there. They'd be in bed together, probably fast asleep. Rather unsteadily, I made my way into the building, opened the door of the small room and peered inside.

You can always sense when a room is empty. I'd expected two sleeping people, but knew at once nobody was there. Still, I checked, stumbling through the doorway and almost falling onto the bed. Definitely no one there. I looked in the main accommodation areas and saw our Wartsbaye and Pevarile people all sleeping soundly. So what had happened to Lillian and Reinhard?

In a daze, and unable to think straight, I climbed onto the unused bed.

Someone was tapping on my door, and when I forced my eyes open I found it was now broad daylight. I groaned, turned over, and realised I'd been sleeping in my clothes. The knees of my breeches were caked in mud. There was dirt under my fingernails, and all the creases in my palms were black.

'Who is it?' I called.

'It's Amie, lord.'

'Amie! Come in.'

'Are you all right, lord? Should I fetch anything for you?'

'I'll be all right once I'm out of these stinking clothes. I'll go to the well and have a proper wash.'

'We'll have to find you something else to wear,' she said doubtfully, staring at me.

I waved that away. 'Why did you come? Has something happened?'

'Something *has* happened, lord. Last night, nobody could find you. Everyone was looking, and Sir Allan said he'd seen you at the archery butts, but that had been hours ago. King Henry had all his knights out searching for you. I was watching, and I overheard two of them saying that if they came across you they were going to kill you. They didn't find you, and I don't think anyone but me knows you're back in the palace, lord.'

'How did you know I was here?'

'I saw mud on the steps. It wasn't there last night. I guessed you'd been out all night but had returned. I've – well, I've washed the mud away, lord. I didn't think those knights should see it.'

'That was good thinking, Amie. Do you know which two knights were talking of killing me? And did they say why they wanted to?'

She looked down, shaking her head. 'As Lady of Wartsbaye, I should know everyone's colours. But I didn't grow up with that, and I don't know them. I can tell you what they said though. They were whispering that you were a danger, lord. Something about making sure you didn't have enough time.'

'Time for what?'

'I don't know, lord.'

She flushed, and I realised I was staring at her. When

Gael first told me he wanted to marry this orphan girl who'd become my bard, I'd thought only of how his father would take it. Gael married way below his station, but Baron Giles had accepted the match because I'd sanctioned it, and events in the past had left him feeling indebted to me. He hadn't needed to feel like that, for the debt had been paid. But he'd allowed his only surviving son to marry a girl who had no family and no honourable background. She could play the harp, and Gael loved her. That shouldn't have been enough, but I'd deemed it so and Giles, reluctantly, accepted it. Neither of us had ever considered the consequences for Amie herself.

Expected to play the lady, to run a household, to know everything a noblewoman would know, she'd floundered. Probably Giles and Gael had helped her at the start. Now she was on her own. I saw how vulnerable she was, but it was more than that. Last night I'd almost slipped back into the Darkness. It could so easily have happened. Now Amie was slipping as well, slipping back into her peasant status. The lovely gown she wore looked ill on her, but it wasn't the gown's fault. It was her drooping shoulders and her expression of defeat.

The Countess of Salisbury was ten years younger than Amie, but she had more authority and more knowledge than Amie ever would. I pictured the countess in my mind: her choice of that impressively tall hennin, giving her extra height and extra power; her position at the right hand of the King of England; her inclusion among the trusted knights of the realm. Margaret, Countess of Salisbury. Margaret Longsword. The contrast with Amie couldn't be more stark.

'Amie.'

'Lord?'

'Find out more. You may not know who those knights

were, but you can find them again. Make eyes at them if you have to. Pretend you dislike me. Get them to confide in you.'

'They won't confide in me, lord,' she said, her eyes cast down again. 'I'm – I'm not one of them.'

So she knew it too.

'When you go home,' I said slowly, 'Young Davy will be Baron of Wartsbaye. Until he is old enough to understand and carry out his duties, you will act in his place. You may not officially be a baroness, but that is your role for the next ten years. You can start by letting those knights know who you are. Wartsbaye is a large shire. It includes an international seaport which the English use all the time. It's in your power to close that port to English ships, though you don't want to do that, of course. It's in your power to make life difficult for the Earl of Lincoln, the southern tip of whose land touches the north-western corner of yours. Again, naturally, you don't want to cause trouble for anyone. If you use your words well, you'll make your meaning clear without issuing any explicit threats.' I got off the bed and moved closer to her. 'I know you think you haven't the skill to do this, Amie. But you created the Battle Morning Song. Remember it? The song that helped us defeat the Nahvitch on Baudry Hill. I know you're going to remind me it was William's gunfire that did that, and you're right, but without your song in all our hearts, William would have arrived too late. It was your song that kept us going. Your song that inspired us to fight! Remember it, Amie? I do. "We are Hambrig, hearts are damn big! Stick it to them, then pursue them! Boom! Boom!" You did that. You can do this, too. Stick it to them, Amie.'

Her eyes had filled with tears, and she was biting her lip. Thinking how long ago that was, perhaps? How Gael had been with her when she wrote it, all twelve years old of him, but *he* was the son of a baron, while she was an abused and damaged waif, rescued from the streets of Hambrig Town.

'Shall I go now, lord?' she asked.

I dismissed her. Yes, we were back to our old roles of lord and servant. It was a dispiriting discovery. As for Lillian and Reinhard – it was no wonder I hadn't found them. They'd been making love under the stars.

19

I'D NEVER SPOKEN OF IT

The opportunity to talk, on my own, with Margaret Longsword came on the second-to-last day of August – the day after I'd spoken to Amie. The palace laundress had washed and mended my clothes and I was now presentable again. Oddly, I found the Countess of Salisbury watching archery practice, much as I had done two days before, at the gate in the palace wall.

'Do you think they're good?' she asked, as I came to stand beside her. She wasn't wearing the hennin this morning, just a simple but elegant silken fillet in emerald green, with a band of white gold over the top of it. Her gown was scarlet and gold, almost mirroring my heraldic colours. The mid-morning sunlight sparkled from the white gold, dazzling me as I looked down at her. The urge to touch her hair was strong, for a faint breeze was lifting the golden curls in the most enchanting way.

'They are very good indeed, my lady,' I said.

She smiled. 'I hoped you'd say that.'

'Meaning, you wondered if I'd tell the truth?'

'If you were honest, yes. You could have told me how bad

they were, knowing that, as a woman, I'd simply believe you.'

'That is not my opinion of women,' I told her. 'Here in Mallrovia, women serve in our armies. Women can shoot with a bow every bit as accurately as men, and often more so.'

'And do women inherit property and titles, here in Mallrovia?' She was laughing at me, but it was in a delightful way.

'They do, but unfortunately only if there is no male heir. In that, it's the same as in England.'

I waited for the obvious response from her.

'As you'll know then, Lord Rory, I am a countess only because the Earl of Salisbury had no male heir.'

'You're his daughter?'

'Yes. My father died when I was two years old and I was his only child.'

I tried to work out the dates, but I didn't know her exact age. 'Would that have been in 1250?' I asked.

She laughed out loud. 'You do me a discourtesy, my lord. Had that been the case, I must have been born in '48, which would make me twenty-four years old, but I'm only eighteen! No, my father died in '56.'

I frowned. Perhaps there wasn't a connection then. Yet, there must be! Salisbury. Longsword. It couldn't be coincidence.

'I knew a William Longsword,' I said, watching for her reaction.

'William Longsword was my father. And also my grandfather and my great-grandfather.'

I caught my breath. 'Do you happen to know when – and how – your grandfather died, my lady?'

'I do, for my mother spoke of him often. My father,

grandfather and great-grandfather were all named William Longsword. My mother is Welsh, and very proud of it. As I told you, my father died when I was two years old, and my grandfather died six years before that, in 1250, the very year you mentioned. He was with King Louis of France, somewhere in Egypt—'

'It was at Mansurah,' I interrupted thickly, almost as if the desert sands had clagged in my throat, as they did for so many years in the Holy Land. 'In the heat, the flies and the dust of Mansurah, where we were lured by Baibars, the Panther, and where almost all of us were killed. Your grandfather, my lady, was cut down by the Saracens, and the bodies were piled high in the streets of Mansurah. Very few escaped the carnage.'

Perhaps I should have spared her the details. But, as I'd told her, in my country women fight and they kill and are killed. There were no women in the Battle of Mansurah, but that didn't mean she shouldn't know what had happened to her ancestor.

'Thank you,' she said quietly. 'I knew about the Crusade. I knew he'd been killed. I didn't know where or how. Was it truly terrible?'

'I was in the first wave with the Templars. Your grandfather entered the city after we did, and by then the Saracens were in full flow. They stood on the rooftops and hurled missiles down on us. Lumps of rock and chunks of metal. Arrows and spears. All rained down out of the sky, and in those narrow Egyptian streets you couldn't move or turn. Crusaders were still pouring in, so how could those already there retreat? They couldn't. They lay down in the streets, battered or bleeding to death.'

'But not you?'

'And one other. As I told you, we were among the first to

enter, and a group of us managed to take control of a house near the city gates. We – well, we thought of it as *our house.* But the fighting continued, and most of the group were killed. Afterwards, my friend and I took refuge in the cellar. Later, we re-joined our group, but Baibars and his men circled around and attacked us constantly. My friend injured his leg. He couldn't retreat with the others—'

'There was a retreat?' Margaret had her hand to her mouth. Retreat, as everyone knows, is a dreadful thing. But Louis had had no choice. It was retreat or be massacred, while at the same time the Crusaders were being decimated by dysentery and disease. Louis knew – we *all* knew – one more week and there'd be no one left alive in the Crusader camp. Withdraw, regroup and wait for reinforcements. That was Louis's plan, but it didn't happen because they were routed at Fariskur. I tried to explain this, but Margaret wanted to know more about how I and my friend had managed to escape.

'We weren't at Fariskur,' I explained. 'My friend was injured, and we didn't get out in time. We went back to *our house* and stayed there for a long time. And then some Saracen women helped us escape. After that, we made our way back to Louis and we stayed for another four years, fighting the Saracens so we could take back Jerusalem for Christ.'

'And did you? Take back Jerusalem?'

'No, we did not.' Remembering the men I knew who'd died for nothing made me sick at heart. It still does. Longsword was one of them, but there were many others.

'The friend I was with,' I said, watching her again for a reaction, 'his name was Jonny. Sir Jonny of Salisbury.'

Her eyes widened. 'Salisbury? Well, I should know of him, but I don't think I do. Is he still there?'

'No, my lady. He never returned to Salisbury. Indeed, he came with me to Mallrovia and became commander of the garrison in my own castle, but he has moved on again. He lives in England now, in a place called Kettering.'

'Ah yes. We may have come through Kettering on our way into Mallrovia.' She put her head on one side, frowning slightly, dark eyes looking up at me. 'I still think I would know of this Sir Jonny of Salisbury. Is "Jonny" short for something?'

'I think it was,' I said. 'But I can't remember what his other name was. He left Salisbury in '48, my lady, well before you were born, and has never been back. So perhaps – wait, though! I know something else about him. His father was a highly regarded blacksmith who was working on the construction of Salisbury Cathedral. It'll be finished now, I suppose.'

'Finished long ago, my lord,' said Margaret Longsword. 'But this blacksmith. I *did* know him! He was injured and could no longer work. He lived on our estate and we supported him. My mother did, I should say. She has a kind heart and would never throw someone out just because they can't work through no fault of their own.'

'It must be the same man,' I said, 'but...'

'But he wouldn't have a son called Sir Jonny. Or Sir anything,' said the countess. 'The man's name was Master Rice. He was a most respected master of his craft, but not a nobleman.'

'Joel Rice?' I asked, suddenly remembering Pockthorpe's uncle. And there was something more. 'It was Longsword – I mean, your grandfather – who knighted my friend. I think it was done so he could go on Crusade. Yes, I'm sure it was. Did your Master Rice ever mention having a son?'

'I don't think I'd know,' the countess said. 'I barely saw

him or talked to him. But I don't think his name was Joel. I think it may have been Adam. His expenses were taken from our coffers, but I never saw him. Unfortunately, he died earlier this year.'

So the man's dead, and perhaps I'll never know if he was Jonny's father.

Amie reported back, somewhat breathlessly.

'I found one of the knights, lord. He's the Earl of Surrey and his name is John. I got him to talk to me. He didn't tell me who the other knight is, but they suspect you're going to try and stop Mallrovia being – is it ceded? – to the English. I think that was the word he used, lord, but I hadn't heard it before.'

'"Ceded" is the word, all right,' I confirmed grimly. 'What else did he say?'

'Just that he needs to stop you, because Henry wants Mallrovia, and if he gets it, that's another three or four castles he can give as presents to the knights who please him. One's going to be for his son, the Lord Edward.'

'He can't count. There are only two castles in Mallrovia now.'

'They want to rebuild Nightmolben, put another castle on the coast somewhere, and he was counting this palace as well. Did I do well, lord?'

'You did well. How did you get him to talk to you?'

'I slept with him.'

'Amie, you've only just been widowed. What were you thinking of?'

'Yes, lord, I'm a widow. But I'm an attractive twenty-six-year-old woman. He liked me.'

'He's married. You'll only ever be his mistress. What provision is there for the Wartsbaye estate, Amie?'

'Young Davy is lord now that Baron Giles is dead. And Giles made sure he put someone in place to guide Young Davy. I'm nothing now.'

'So who's actually in charge?' I asked.

She made a face. 'Titus. The commander of the garrison. The baron was never going to allow me to run Wartsbaye. I expect you approved of his choice, lord. You pulled me out of the gutter after I'd been assaulted and raped by a gang of ruffians. I was eleven years old. I became a servant in your household. I learnt to play the harp and you made me your bard. I loved being your bard, but I hoped for even better. I set my sights too high, I know that now. Gael fell in love with me, and I thought that was my way out. I married Gael, and instantly I became someone important. The Lady of Wartsbaye! Now I'm back in the gutter. You needed information, lord, and you told me to flirt with the Earl of Surrey. I did that, but he wanted more.'

Don't they always?

She was right, though. Marrying Gael had catapulted her into a position of power and influence. Gael had been born to it; Amie had not. Giles had known that, and he'd made arrangements, in the event that both he and Gael died before Young Davy reached his majority. I didn't blame Giles for doing that; it showed forethought and good sense, although he must have thought it an unlikely thing to happen.

I thanked Amie for the information, but I knew it wasn't the whole story. Henry could take Mallrovia whenever he wanted. He didn't have to kill me first. And the Earl of

Surrey would know that, and so would the other man, whoever he was. Someone was hiding something. That was obvious.

'Should I try to find out more, lord?' Amie asked.

'No. Don't sleep with him again, Amie. He's a dangerous man.'

But I couldn't get Jonny out of my head. And Adam Rice, who'd been the master blacksmith, doing the job Jonny had told me his father did. Could Master Rice have been Jonny's father? And if he's dead, shouldn't Jonny know?

Long ago Jonny told me he had no family other than his father. If that was Adam Rice, he must have wondered what had become of his boy. Jonny had gone to war, as I had, in '48. After twenty-four years of no communication, Rice would have thought him dead. Killed on Crusade, like so many were. But Jonny had survived, and now there would be documents to look at, and possessions, however few, to be rehomed or sold. Would Jonny want any of it? He'd certainly have to deal with it, one way or another. Seven weeks ago, Rosa had sent a letter to Jonny. There'd been no response.

I yearned to ride west. To tell Jonny what had happened in Salisbury – and what had happened in Hicrown. But could I tell him about Mansurah? About Karima? Could I admit to the secrecy and the deceit? I wanted to clasp Jonny's hand in mine, as I'd done twenty years ago, but it would not work unless I told him the truth.

It's the Darkness, Father says.

What do you mean? I ask.

It's why you get ill. The lies you told Jonny are making you ill.

That can't be right, Father. I didn't have the Darkness until a few years ago. It doesn't come from my crusading days.

Oh yes it does, boy. It's the same as the fight for Hicrown, isn't it? You were told a spark was needed to ignite the trouble that had been brewing for decades. Well, your spark was all that business with Foucois, your brother and that Persian alchemist you liked so much. If he hadn't killed himself, then resurrected himself and then killed himself again; if you hadn't had to lie to Joan about it and help her make sense of the ridiculous Paradise Garden... Father stops talking. He's become emotional. I know he's right. Everything he's just told me is right. The Darkness is Karima's fault.

I hear Father's voice very faintly, as if from a great distance. *That's not what I meant, and I have no idea who or what Karima is. No, boy, the problem is partly your fault, because you were not honest. But it's also Jonny's fault, because he expected too much. He was too unyielding, too uncompromising. He cut you no slack in the desert. Can you mend this? I don't know.*

Father's voice faded away completely. I was on my own again, and the one thing I could be thankful for was that

Father knew nothing about Karima. I was feeling very strange though, and wondering if Father could possibly be right. Did the problems between Jonny and me begin in Mansurah in 1250, and not in Hambrig as I'd always thought? If Father *was* right then I'd have to rethink everything.

It meant that for the last twenty-two years, my Darkness had been growing inside me, perhaps fed by other events, like the accusations made against me in '64, the death of poor Begoña, and the marriage that was forced on me by Alfonso X of Castile. If Father was right, then it was no wonder Jonny didn't trust me.

I closed my eyes. Did I have the courage now, after all these years, to tell Jonny the truth? Perhaps it was time for me to acknowledge what really happened in the Egyptian desert and, more importantly, why I'd never spoken of it.

20

THE NAVISAR GATE

King Henry had finished his accounts. He'd written down what he wanted from the citizens of Hicrown, and it was a large amount. I looked at the figures and caught my breath in dismay.

'This is a lot for the people to raise, sire.'

'There is a great deal of work to be done, Lord Rory,' the king countered. 'The damage to the cathedral is extensive. The damage to Mallrovia's reputation, even more so. Have I told you the pope wishes to excommunicate the entire city? Can you imagine what that will mean? The loss of your monastery, your clergy, the loss of income and financial support, and the closure of schools and other institutions. This would just be Hicrown, initially, but it will reach into other parts of the country. I have no doubt the effects will be felt in Hambrig too.'

He was staring at me. I recognised the risk, and the way Henry was using the pope and threats of excommunication to get what he wanted. The English king was known to be exceedingly devout.

'How do you suggest they raise the money?' I asked.

'That is for you to organise,' Henry said smoothly. 'I have noticed that many of the shops and houses in this city are empty. Mallrovia is in chaos, Lord Rory, with Hicrowners now roaming the countryside, robbing and thieving for themselves. Where is the rule of law? Those who are left here comprise the old, the very young and the infirm. There is little food, and no protection for these poor souls. You will rebuild the city, pay the fines, arrest wrongdoers, find the rebels and punish them.'

I didn't ask why these things were suddenly my job.

Henry swept up his parchments and gave them to William de Beauchamp, the Earl of Warwick. Then he turned again to me. 'Tomorrow, I shall return to Westminster, where my life's work is nearly complete. However, I shall leave Surrey, Warwick and the countess here. My earls will provide you with whatever you need. One other thing: it would be good to know exactly which cargoes leave the country through your unofficial harbour on the east coast. And who is responsible, of course.'

Henry gathered his cloak around him and stepped down from the dais, his little group of knights following dutifully. I knew Henry wasn't a fighter. He was a peacemaker. He always travelled with a bodyguard of trusted knights and courtiers, but it was his lack of judgement that had led to the barons' revolt eight years ago. I wasn't surprised he'd survived it, but I was astonished he was still king. The death of Simon de Montfort at Evesham had a lot to do with that, I suspected. But I thought I had the answer to one of my many questions: if Warwick and Surrey were to remain behind, it seemed likely that Warwick was the other would-be assassin.

Next morning, I looked again for Reinhard, and ran him to earth eventually, in the innocuous pursuit of dice games with the other Livonians.

'Reinhard,' I said. 'Stop chucking dice around. I want to know where Carl is, his exact location in the woods.'

He stood up and pushed his face towards me. I'm resistant to most forms of intimidation and I'm not easily frightened, but that man's eyes compel you into submission. It's almost impossible to look away. Reinhard's gaze strips you naked. His eyes seem to know your very thoughts, and you feel you want to tell him everything. As I stood there, held by his gaze, I felt my self-control slipping, as it had on the road to Osnabrück.

'Your brother, Carl,' I forced myself to say. 'He was here, fighting alongside Allan. He's not in the palace now, so where is he?' It had got easier as I continued.

But Reinhard's gaze never wavered. He didn't even blink. Nor did he speak. Behind him, though, the Livonians were getting restless at the interruption to their game. It was the Livonians who'd killed Gael, who'd fought me and my men. They were in no doubt whose side they were on, and it had long been clear that the strained peace between us all only existed because the English king was here. Which he very soon wouldn't be. And, as if in anticipation of that fact, three of the Livonians suddenly rose to their feet and upended their table. As dice hit the floor and rolled around the room, pandemonium descended. All the warriors were on their feet now, and soon I was surrounded. They were off duty and unarmed, while I had my sword and my dagger with me; I'm rarely separated from either these days. But the Livonians were too close for any kind of sword work. My dagger might take one of them out, but the others would soon finish me.

'What do you want us to do, captain?'

Captain? That surprised me, until I suddenly understood. I swung round. 'You lot! You're the Osnabrück garrison, aren't you?' And I remembered them in the Osnabrück gatehouse, playing dice with Kit, my minstrel, while he waited for me to return from my meeting with Lillian. Seemed these fellows were partial to a bit of gambling.

'I'll make you a bet,' I called out loudly. 'It's worth ten marks.' A lot of money to a common soldier. I had their attention. Reinhard stopped trying to control me with his eyes and looked at his men. He began to say something, but I held up my hand. 'Wait, captain. I want your brave warriors to have a chance to double their money!'

There was a buzz of excitement. Was I actually offering *twenty* marks, then? A year and a half's wages? There was a clamour to know what the bet was. Reinhard stood back, observing. He was an intelligent man, as I already knew. He would wait to see what my exit strategy was.

'I'll wager none of you can roll two pairs of sixes at the same time, one pair in each hand. You must all take a turn. The first to do it, fair and square, wins the wager. You go in seniority order, and your captain will confirm this for me.'

There was a laugh. 'That's not worth ten marks! It's not even worth one! You're just going to make a run for it, soon as we're all looking at the dice. We don't take your bet.'

'I won't make a run for it,' I said. 'I'll be watching. I want to make sure the winner, if there is one, wins by fair play. If nobody rolls two pairs of sixes in the way I described, I keep my money. But first, you have to tell me where your captain's brother is hiding.'

There was a growl of anger.

'I stand to lose a lot of money. I need something in return.' I put it to them as a reasonable request. But Reinhard was watching. Would they defy him?

One of them, older and more grizzled than the rest, spoke up. 'We don't know where he is, Hambrigger. But we know he's not hiding. Livonians hide from no one.'

'Give me a clue then.' I held out my hands. Just playing a game, after all. The sort of game where you give each other clues. 'Without something to go on, I'll have to withdraw my offer. Ten marks is a *lot* of money.'

'All right,' said the grey-haired fellow. 'I'll give you a clue. And then we'll take your wager – before we kill you, eh, lads? Here it is: Carl von Lutterberg is in Hicrown. But only just.'

A laugh went up, although Reinhard was frowning. I nodded. 'Ready to play?'

They all looked at each other. The odds of success were very poor. And yet – it *could* happen. Slowly, they gathered around the table, and a couple of them righted it and hunted for the dice. Four dice were set on the table.

'Captain Reinhard,' I called. 'Please make sure your men queue up in order of rank, with the most senior man going first. As soon as we have a winner, the game's over and the bet's off.'

His men looked to him, and he nodded, sending me an ironic half-smile as he did so. So much for the 'woods south of the city', I thought. Reinhard had been lying about Carl.

The soldiers jostled into line, and the grizzled one sat down first. He took the dice in his huge fists, gave the things a shake in the air, and with a roar he scattered them onto the table. No pairs at all. Angrily, he got up and went over to Reinhard. As the next man sat down, I watched the grey-haired Livonian whispering with his captain. I didn't have to watch the dice throwing. The other warriors would make sure nobody cheated. All wanted a chance, and if anybody won, nobody else would get to try.

One by one, they sat down and rolled, only to rise again, disappointed. It took a long time, and I took very little notice. My gaze was fastened on Reinhard and his lieutenant, or whatever the man was. They were still whispering, and I had no doubt a plan was being hatched.

A few pairs had been rolled by now, even a few pairs of sixes. But nobody had managed *two* pairs of sixes. I had a feeling my money was safe. The last man rolled and sighed in frustration. They all looked at me. An accusing, hostile look.

'Perhaps that was too hard,' I said. 'Two pairs of sixes?' I shrugged. 'Unrealistic. I'll change the wager. You still roll two pairs of dice, but this time you only need *one* pair of sixes to win.'

'What are you offering?' they asked, shoving each other towards the table again.

'The same,' I said laconically. 'Same reward, twice the chance. But you go in the same order as before.'

They nodded, and looked to their grey-headed companion. He broke off from his conversation with Reinhard and hurried to try again. This time, they all knew, there was a good chance one of them would win. After all, several of them had thrown a double six already. Everyone held their breath, and the old soldier rolled the four dice. Ah! Shame! No pairs at all. But when the fourth man rolled to no avail, he stood up and faced me, his face blotchy with emotion.

'I rolled a pair of sixes the first time,' he said. 'I should win the bet.'

His companions shouted that the first time didn't count. Others had rolled a pair of sixes too—

'But I was the first! I rolled them first! And if this *kvailas niekšas* had got it right in the first place, I'd have won then!'

He was youngish, blond and getting redder by the moment.

'I'm sorry I'm a *kvailas niekšas*,' I called to him, 'and though I don't speak Livonian, I can kind of guess what you're calling me. Your friends are right though. The previous wager was for two pairs, not one. So your throw then doesn't count now, I'm afraid. Time for the next man to have his turn.'

As the fifth Livonian tried to sit at the table and gather the dice, the one who felt he'd been cheated shot out his fist. The other crumpled to the floor, and so the fight began, everyone taking sides with one viewpoint or the other. Reinhard and his lieutenant were trapped behind the sprawling, scrapping bodies. The table had gone over again, and the small room was full of angry Livonians, their pent-up urge to fight finding its outlet.

I escaped down the steps. I still wasn't sure where Carl was, but the 'only just' comment had told me a lot. I didn't have much time, though. I ran through the palace grounds, only to find King Henry and his entourage mustered at the gate, the coaches and horses all blocking the way out. I tried to dodge round them, but it wasn't possible, and Henry had seen me.

'Lord Rory. We've been looking for you. We are taking our leave, and your presence is required. Remember, Warwick and Surrey will support you as you raise the funds you need. And they will make sure the money reaches me intact.'

I didn't doubt that. For an English monarch to impose fines on the residents of a Mallrovian city was a shameful business. For English knights, no more senior than I was, to take charge of Mallrovian coinage, would be an unbearable insult. But I bowed to Henry and watched his splendid carriage rattle out of the gate, with four mounted English earls following. I'd slunk round to the other side, keeping the English noblemen between me and any Livonians who might be giving chase. And as they all moved off, I moved too, jogging alongside until I was well clear of the palace.

Then I let them go, and I took off in the direction of the bridge over the Shamet. At the city bakery I turned left. Surely the 'only just' meant just inside the city walls. That could be anywhere, but my guess was one of the gates out of the city, and the mostly likely gate was the one in the eastern wall. The Navisar Gate.

21

USEFUL TO BOTH OF US

I'm lying in Margaret Longsword's arms, and I've just told her all about Mansurah. The heat. The sand. The flies. The bodies. Her grandfather's sordid and unnecessary death. Baibars grinning down at us from the rooftops, flourishing his bloodied sword and screaming Allah's name.

'Why was it unnecessary?' she asks me drowsily, her bright hair draped over my arm.

'Because we should never have charged,' I say, and my lips brush her cheek. 'Artois ordered the charge, the Templars went for it, and Jonny and I followed. We had to. Everyone was so certain we'd take the city, and it looked deserted, Margaret. We *had* to take it, you see. Mansurah stood between us and Cairo, and we had to get to Cairo. But Louis hadn't ordered the attack, and he wouldn't have done so. Artois scented victory, but he should have waited for his brother.'

'Artois was Louis's brother?'

'One of them. Another was Charles of Anjou, and he was a good commander. An intelligent man. After Artois died, Jonny and I stuck with Anjou. Until Jonny got injured and they all left us behind.'

'What did you do then?'

I tell her about *our house* in Mansurah, living like beggars in the basement. I tell her about Shajar al-Durr and her daughter, Eleni, two Mamluk women who looked after us in their own grand and opulent house. I tell Margaret that we didn't know it at the time, but Shajar had just been made Sultana of Egypt.

'Surely she told you?' Margaret cries in astonishment, moving slightly away from my embrace.

I pull her close, my lips seeking the soft fullness of her breasts, my body responding and wanting more. 'She never told us,' I murmur. 'But she and Eleni got us out of Mansurah. They thought they owed us a debt.'

'Because you rescued Eleni,' Margaret says, remembering the story.

'That's how they saw it. And it's true, I did rescue Eleni from rape and murder. But Jonny and I saw it as vengeance for our friends. Longsword. Artois. Vichiers. The Templars. All of them.'

I haven't told her about Karima. I've never told anyone about Karima, not even Jonny. But now, of course, I'm thinking about Karima, and I'm lying in a sweat-filled hollow of the mattress in my room in Hicrown Palace, and I'm completely alone.

I stared at the ceiling, aware that I'd dreamt of making love to Margaret Longsword, and that, only two days ago, Karima had entered my thoughts for the first time in nearly twenty years. The dream had been so vivid, and reliving Mansurah had been – what had it been? Good, I decided. It had felt good. It had felt good to talk about it.

Even now, I could hear the cries of the wounded and the triumphant shouts of the Saracens. As Jonny and I cowered in the basement of *our house*, we'd heard our friends die in the streets above us. There'd been little actual fighting. Our men had not had the chance to defend themselves.

Karima had understood. Had told me it wasn't my fault. Of course we had to hide – what good what it have done to add two more corpses to the pile? At the time, I thought she'd convinced me. I'd found solace with Karima, but it was both short-lived and temporary. Her biggest gift was breathing space, and a chance to organise an escape route for Jonny and me. It had been a postponement of grief, shame and despair; a delay only, nothing more.

I got up. At the well in the courtyard, I threw bucketfuls of ice-cold water over my body, cleaning it of sweat and other fluids, but there was no cleansing of my soul. I pulled on my clothes and went to find Reinhard.

'I know she's still in Mallrovia,' I said. 'I found the evidence in the warehouse you use for your "stuff". The worsted you smuggle out of my country. Now. Where's the princess, Reinhard?'

'What evidence?' he said, leaning back against the wall, his long legs stretched out. He was the picture of relaxed amusement. 'Did you find Carl? I am sure you did not.'

He was right, I had not seen Carl. But I'd seen many other things, which tallied with information my brother had given me two years ago, straight after bringing Reinhard to Hambrig, in fact. The Livonian wouldn't tell me where Phoebe was, perhaps because he didn't know, but I was positive he knew Carl's whereabouts. I was formulating a question in my mind when Lillian entered.

Lillian had made a good recovery from the gruelling march to Hicrown, and she no longer had to stay in bed, but she kept clear of the rest of the palace. Even with Henry gone, his two remaining knights were on the prowl, and if they knew Lillian, wife of the Duke of Bavaria, was here and expecting another man's child, there'd be hell to pay. So during the day, Lillian stayed mostly in her quarters on the ground floor of the Palace Guard accommodation. During the night she could take short walks on Reinhard's arm, always going towards the palace walls, avoiding other people at all costs. Not even the Wartsbaye Guard knew who she was, even though we all sailed together from Pevarile.

So it was a surprise to see her appear in the room at the top of the building, and in broad daylight.

'What's happened?' Reinhard barked, leaping to his feet.

'Titus knows who I am.'

'How?'

She shook her head. 'I'm not sure. Dominykas brought my food this morning. He said Titus spoke to him and asked sarcastically about the elder princess of Mallrovia. He even used my name. I'm frightened, Reinhard.'

'Was it Dominykas who told Titus about you?'

'He says it was one of the others. Perhaps Giedrius?'

'Did Dominykas mention Giedrius, or is it your idea it could be him?'

Reinhard was staring down at Lillian, his glittering eyes holding her, as only they can.

'Reinhard, I didn't mention Giedrius. Dominykas said—'

'Enough. You must return to your room, Lillian. Do not come out of your room until I tell you it's safe. I will arrange for food to be delivered by someone else. You won't see Dominykas again. Go now.'

He'd sounded angry at first, and Lillian had flinched, but his final few words were said more softly and with affection. He kissed her on the forehead and gave her a gentle push.

'It's hardly surprising Titus knew her name,' I observed, as we listened to her stepping carefully down the stairs. 'Titus is Mallrovian. He knows who our royal family are. Who is Giedrius? Why are you spooked by him?'

'I don't trust anyone, Rory,' said Reinhard, picking up his sword belt and buckling it round his waist. 'Especially you. And you heard what Lillian said. Perhaps, if you hadn't been here, I would not have been "spooked", as you call it. Perhaps I would just have reassured my lady and let it go at that. But now you know two of my men's names, and you know that someone has blabbed to Titus. Or, more likely, someone's tongue was loosened by drink, or by threats, or both. Makes no difference.'

'So both Dominykas and Giedrius are dead men?'

He smiled, and I averted my eyes. I did not want to be fixed by that gaze. 'Possibly. Are you going to talk to Titus?'

'I'll do a deal. You bring Carl to me, or me to him. Then I won't mention Lillian to Titus.'

'You like your wagers and your deals, don't you,' Reinhard said. He thrust his dagger through his belt and straightened up. 'My men certainly fell for your little trick yesterday. They don't like you much now, I'm sorry to say. They don't like being cheated.'

'The only cheat was the man who claimed to have won before I changed the wager. Even your men knew he was trying it on. But back to our deal. If I speak to Titus, I shall tell him to go to the English earls. Once they find Lillian here, pregnant by you, what do you think they'll do?'

'I think you know the answer,' Reinhard said smoothly. 'If England tells Bavaria where the missing duchess is hiding, and with whom, you'll have more than a desecrated cathedral to deal with, won't you. Can you risk war with the Holy Roman Empire, Rory?'

His steely eyes found mine, and I gasped. Too late to look away. In any case, he was right. My threat held more danger for me than for him. Once it was known in Bavaria that Louis had been made a fool of, there would be even less hope of Mallrovia's survival than there was now.

And then Reinhard laughed. 'But – I owe you, don't I. You let me sail away from certain execution, and now I have my own ship. You showed me mercy, and for that I am grateful. So I will take you to Carl. But after that, I shall no longer feel any debt towards you. After that – we will not be friends.'

I followed him down the stairs and out into the garden. As we headed towards the archery butts, Reinhard turned his head and threw a remark over his shoulder.

'I know you told that pretty Mallrovian wench to sleep with the Earl of Surrey. What did she find out? Now he's tasted her, he'll want her again, you know. Henry doesn't allow his knights much time to play, so these two will be making the most of their time away from the king.'

'She won't be sleeping with Surrey again,' I said, catching up with him.

'If you say so.'

Sure enough, we headed out along the Secret Way beyond the butts. Through the grazing meadows and out of Hicrown itself. The flattened grass and clear pathway told me this route was very much in use. But who uses it and why?

We walked for the entire morning, a cool and overcast one, as it happened, breaking the lengthy spell of hot, sunny weather.

Reinhard broke in on my thoughts. 'How far do you think we need to go?'

'I have no idea,' I answered shortly. 'I don't where we're going or where this track leads.'

His eyes opened wide. 'You don't know? Well, that's a surprise! I'm a Livonian, but I know this path well. Still, we are not going all the way. In fact, we shall stop right here.'

We did, and I looked behind me. Hicrown was no longer in sight. In the other direction, all I could see were waving grasses, a copse of trees to my left and land sloping down towards the marshy valley of the River Shamet to my right. Reinhard turned off to our left, leaving the track and making his way to the small woodland.

Inside the copse, the closely clustered trees made everything look dark. The woodland floor was bare of vegetation, although with summer giving way to autumn, twigs, chestnuts and acorns lay underfoot. Reinhard and I crunched through them into the middle of the wood, a sombre place on this cloudy afternoon. There was a rough building, not visible from the path. It was almost the same as the so-called 'Liberty Hut', which someone else had built on the River Shamet near Hambrig Town. I didn't know if the Liberty Hut was still there, but this rough shack looked remarkably similar.

'Welcome to Halfway House,' Reinhard said with a laugh and a friendly slap on my back. 'It's what we call it, anyway. And now I will show you around!'

He plunged through the few trees that stood between us

and the building, then knocked on the door. It must have been a special signal, as it had a memorable rhythm. The door opened, and Carl von Lutterberg emerged. He looked first at his brother, and then, in some astonishment, at me.

'I locked you up and you escaped.' Carl's tone was friendly. 'I don't know how you did it, but it was good timing, Rory. Once the King of England decided to take an interest, we Livonians had to melt away. We can conquer Mallrovia, but we cannot fight England. So why are you here?'

'I had to bring him,' Reinhard explained without apology. 'He has information he shouldn't have. He traded it for a meeting with you.'

I called to mind the order of the von Lutterberg brothers. Dicky had been the eldest, but he was dead, executed by me. Then came Otto, also dead, but honourably and in battle. Then it was Carl, I thought, and Reinhard was the youngest. But there were only a couple of years between these last two von Lutterbergs. They had little to lose and everything to play for.

'Wait outside,' I said to Reinhard. 'I want to speak to Carl on my own.'

To my surprise, Reinhard remained where he was, and I entered the hovel. A small and inefficient oil lamp swung from a hook jammed into one of the rafters. I waited for my eyes to become used to the gloom.

'What happens here?' I asked.

'Nothing,' Carl said. 'You know about the worsted. We sometimes store it here before moving it on.'

'Why are you here now? There's no worsted.'

I saw no bales, crates or boxes of stuff, but there was a small table in one corner of the building and coils of rope lay on the floor. No sign of Phoebe, but I hadn't expected that. Phoebe had been held in the warehouse near the

Navisar Gate. I'd seen just one thing there that had been proof of that, but nothing to tell me where she'd been taken since.

'You know,' Carl said softly, 'English Henry may have delayed our conquest of Mallrovia. But he didn't stay in Hicrown for long. He's not well, and he wants to get back to his beloved Westminster Abbey. Now that he's gone, the Swordbrothers will move in again. It isn't really for you to be questioning me, Rory.'

Carl knew me. We shared some adventures. We'd sailed the little *Wolf* together, over the North Sea to Bremen. We helped each other, and then we tried to kill each other. I knew I wouldn't be able to fool him, but perhaps I didn't need to.

'Look, Carl. If your intention is to take the whole country—'

'Hicrown is lost,' he said, shaking his head at me. 'You must realise it. Hicrown is lost, and you can't govern as a sovereign state with no sovereign. King Henry of England doesn't really want Mallrovia, he just needs a stable country on his eastern flank. If it comes to it, Henry's army is bigger and stronger than the Livonian Swordbrothers, but *we are already there*. We control everything now. There's nothing you can do about it, so you might as well accept it. Life will be much easier for you if you do.'

'Is Phoebe still alive?'

'Yes, she is.'

'Then she is our Queen, and we do have a sovereign.'

He laughed. 'Ah yes. Queen Phoebe of Mallrovia. And what about King Carl of Mallrovia? Do you like the sound of that, Rory?'

I stared at him. 'You have no claim to kingship.'

'Oh, but I do. Reinhard!'

Reinhard put his head around the door.

'Fetch my wife, please.'

Reinhard's head disappeared again. My heart was banging in my chest. I knew exactly what I was going to see, and, sure enough, when the cabin's door opened again, Reinhard entered. He was holding Phoebe's hand.

'We were married yesterday,' Carl said pleasantly, holding out his own hand to Phoebe. 'You will want to congratulate us, I'm sure.'

As Phoebe was handed from Reinhard to Carl, almost as if she were being given away for a second time, I tried to understand what I'd just been told. Married? How could they be?

'Tell me about your wedding,' I said, looking from Carl to Phoebe. I hadn't bothered to keep the sarcasm from my tone. 'Was it a grand affair? As befits a princess?'

Her hand shot forward, and she slapped my face, squealing, 'Don't make fun of me, Lord Rory! My father would have been proud of this match. Carl is one of the famous Swordbrothers! And I'm creating an alliance, as my sister did with Louis of Bavaria. You're jealous, I think.'

Carl shushed her. 'No, no, my love. Rory isn't jealous; after all, he's made a prestigious alliance of his own. We mustn't begrudge him his connection to Don Alfonso of Castile. Of course, he will pay homage to us in good time. He's had a bit of a shock, that's all. But he's a good leader in Hambrig, and I'm sure we can count on his loyalty to you and me from now on.' He squeezed her hand, and she simpered up at him.

'You still haven't told me about the wedding,' I said.

'We were married yesterday,' Carl said brusquely, releasing Phoebe. Reinhard took her arm again and ushered her outside. 'In the church in Myrtile. It's all legal.'

'In Myrtile?' I hadn't expected that.

'It's a magnificent church,' Carl said dreamily. 'Very ornate, very beautiful. Father Clarence was most efficient, so it was quickly done.'

'Were there many to see you wed the Queen of Mallrovia?'

'Not many, sadly. But I assured Phoebe we will have a magnificent double coronation to make up for it.'

'Why choose Myrtile for this "wedding", Carl?' I didn't believe a word he was telling me.

'Well,' he snapped back, 'it's not as if Hicrown Cathedral is fit for use, is it. And now that you've seen what you came to see, you can go back to Hicrown, raise the money English Henry wants for his already overstuffed coffers and begin the work of rebuilding the capital city. It's my country now, Rory. I'm the new King of Mallrovia, and you'll be bowing the knee to me from now on. Soon, Phoebe and I will make a grand entrance into Hicrown. Reinhard's organising everything. He knows to lay on the full works: the King's Squad, the Swordbrothers – and that ragtag lot from Wartsbaye you brought with you. They can all turn out to cheer and pay us homage. My brother will have you licked into shape in no time.' He turned and flung out his arm, indicating the pathetic little cabin we were standing in. 'Did Reinhard tell you this place is called Halfway House? I named it myself! It's temporary, you see. I'm a wealthy man, Rory. I've made my fortune selling Mallrovian wool to dealers in the Baltic states, and now I'm reaping my rewards. Phoebe was easily persuaded. She's hopelessly in love with me, but, as you know, everyone has their price. Already I'm wondering about yours, but I'll soon know it. Now go along, there's a good boy.'

I left him to his fantasy. King of Mallrovia? Over my

dead body. Reinhard was waiting in the trees. There was no sign of Phoebe.

'Where is she?' I asked.

'Safe. And well out of the way. Did Carl tell you his plans?'

'Oh yes. He's convinced he'll be King of Mallrovia. You, apparently, are organising a grand entrance into the city.'

'I am, indeed,' Reinhard said with a smile. 'But will it be Carl's grand entrance? Or Reinhard's? And now you should go back. It's a longish walk, as you know. And get that little whore to find out more from the English. I'm thinking she will be very useful to both of us.'

22

THE SECRET WAY TO MYRTILE

I'd assumed that as long as I was keeping a lid on things in Hicrown, there'd be no danger to Hambrig, my own demesne. Bryce had told me of someone's arrival there, though. Someone who'd frightened 'even Lady Rosa'. I ached to get back. I needed to reassure myself that, in Patrick's words, 'All is well.'

That thought reminded me of the city of Myrtile. I'd left Peter there, with instructions to find out more about it. When I first saw it, I'd assumed King Philip had authorised the building of it, and I'd felt angry at such wanton use of taxpayers' money. But Patrick had financed and built the city himself – a city in the middle of nowhere, with no transport links and no discernible trade. I'd long known my erstwhile steward was 'Sir Patrick of Myrtile', but I'd always thought Myrtile was a small demesne of agricultural land with, I supposed, a medium-sized manor house somewhere on it. Not a sumptuous city of lustrous gold and calming turquoise, surrounded by sheep farms producing top-grade wool. Why did it exist, and how was it connected to the abduction of young women? Bryce's explorations had shown us there *was* a connection.

As I tramped back to Hicrown along the narrow green lane, I tried to think where it would lead if you continued beyond Halfway House. After all, the ridiculously named little shack must be halfway to *somewhere*. Projecting it forwards in my mind, I concluded you'd get to Myrtile, and, if it went further still, you'd arrive at the coast, somewhere between Nightmolben and Navisar.

But my guess was that Myrtile and Hicrown were directly linked by this overgrown and little-known path. And Halfway House is exactly where its name would suggest. But why connect Myrtile and Hicrown in this way? A proper road would make a lot more sense. Unless you didn't want anyone to know of it. Unless what you really wanted was a secret route between the capital and Patrick's mysterious city. The 'Secret Way', as we three small boys had called it all those years ago.

Patrick is an intelligent and clear-sighted man. I'd already wondered if he could possibly be behind this takeover of Mallrovia. Having examined this idea from all angles, I'd decided it was easily possible he was working directly with the Livonians. It was also extremely likely that he was behind what must be a slave trade, despatching young women from Myrtile and its surroundings to be sold into slavery and prostitution abroad. I'd never have believed it of Patrick, but there seemed no other explanation. And Carl, the self-styled King of Mallrovia, had married poor, brainless Phoebe in Patrick's opulent church. Yes, Patrick was involved, one way or another.

As I made my way past the archery butts and through the gate into the garden, I saw Bryce talking with Amie. It was the first time I'd seen Bryce since the fighting in the market square, over two weeks ago, when Gael had been killed and Carl had locked me up. Intermittently, I'd wondered where he'd gone. And if or when he'd be back.

He looked up, and I saw shock in his eyes. 'I've come back, Lord Rory. But you need to know my father's dead. I found his body.'

'Your father? What happened, Bryce?' But even as I said it, I remembered. Rosa had sent the stonemason to Kettering with a letter for Jonny. There had been no response.

'He's dead, lord. When you told me that someone must live to tell the tale, I left Hicrown through the Palace Gate and rode west towards Gailen. I knew not to go home, what with no soldiers there to come to our aid. I thought I'd go to Gailen and then head north to Wartsbaye. Get the other soldiers from there. But when I got to Gailen I found the manor house in ruins. There was a room that looked like it was part of a garden. It had a tree growing through the roof. My father's body lay in that room. He'd been robbed and murdered, but it must have been weeks ago. His body was – not nice. And it must have been a whole gang of people, lord, because my father was strong and he'd been armed, too. I found his weapon lying next to him.'

'What did you do?'

'I left him there, lord. Then I rode to Hambrig to tell my mother. I hope that was all right, but I thought she should know. I stayed with her in Hambrig for a day or two, and then I came back to Hicrown. I'm not surprised my father was attacked. I was just telling Amie how awful it is out on the road. There are outlaws round every corner, and robbers in the trees and behind bushes, just waiting to jump out on you and knife you in the ribs. My mother didn't want me to come back here, but of course, I knew I must.'

Amie's eyes were full of tears, and she had her arm around Bryce's waist. It would have been a gang who'd attacked Thomas, Bryce was right about that. The country was full of them now. Brigands, robbers and murderers. I nodded my sympathy, but I had questions too. 'Bryce. You said someone came to the castle, but you didn't know who it was. Can you describe him?'

'A big man with a loud voice. He was asking for you, but Master Peter told us to say nowt. I mean, nothing. So nobody answered his questions.'

'How old was he? What was he wearing? Did he speak with an accent? Come on, man, tell me everything you can remember!'

'He was about your age, I'd say, lord. Sounded English, not Mallrovian. He was well dressed, but maybe like a soldier? I'm not sure about that. And – oh yes!'

'Oh yes, what?'

'He mentioned someone called Jonah Rice. But we never heard of anyone called that, so we still said nothing. Luke and me stood at the gate as if we were the Watch, because, as you know, there's no Watch at the moment, but he didn't know the difference, and we didn't let him in.'

'Did the man mention anywhere in England? Salisbury, for example?'

'Don't think so, lord. When he realised we weren't going to let him in, he cantered off down the hill.'

'Which way did he turn on the Wartsbaye Road?'

'He turned right, lord. Heading back to England, I reckon.'

'All right, Bryce. You've done well.'

I took Amie's arm and walked her away, leaving Bryce standing by himself, staring sadly after us.

'Has Surrey told you anything more?' I asked.

'Lord, you told me not to go with him again!'

'You can talk to him, though. And to Warwick. I want to know more about Margaret, the Countess of Salisbury, and her husband, the Earl of Lincoln. And, in particular, a former blacksmith who used to work for the countess. He was employed in the building of Salisbury Cathedral, and his name is Rice. Possibly Joel Rice, or maybe Adam Rice. Find out everything you can, Amie. It's important.'

She looked at me, biting her lip. 'Am I a spy, now, lord?'

I gave her a faint smile. 'It looks that way, Amie. Do you know what's at stake here? Mallrovia's future. Find a nicer gown to wear and do something pretty with your hair. It'll help.'

She nodded, but her mouth was turned down and she trailed away, feet dragging. Reinhard had said I should use her. And so I would, but not to further his ends.

The name 'Jonah' had sparked a memory, but one I couldn't get hold of. I told Bryce to go back to Castle Rory. He was very shaken, and I wanted him to see everyone was all right, and even – I know this sounds crazy – to make sure my castle was still standing. I've been away from it for far longer in the past, but the peril is not only the greatest it's ever been, but also the closest. Perhaps we were in more danger when the Dorians threatened us back in '65, but at least I was there. *And* we had a full garrison, under Jonny's command.

I knew only too well how badly defended we were now, and how easily an enemy could take my castle and my demesne. I desperately wanted to see it for myself, but I couldn't leave Hicrown. Not yet. So Bryce rode away, taking a letter from me to Rachel and Joan. He'd be back with their reply in a couple of weeks. In the meantime, I'd half a mind to ride to Myrtile and confront Patrick.

Reinhard turned up at supper in the great hall. He was smiling, but he hadn't turned on the glint in his eyes. I could look at him without feeling my soul draining away. I wondered how he did it. And if he knew how he did it.

'Where's Queen Phoebe?' I asked. We'd been served some kind of mutton broth, and I was determined to have at least two helpings, having missed dinner altogether. The mutton reminded me of the wool smuggling, and I needed to make sure that wasn't happening anymore. But Phoebe's whereabouts came first.

'With Carl, of course. You do know she's besotted with him?'

'And he with her, naturally,' I said with great sarcasm. Carl was besotted only with himself.

'Well, perhaps not so much,' Reinhard conceded. 'But Carl is not a selfish man. We only want the best for our country—'

'That shouldn't mean the conquest of someone else's country.' My tone was icy, but a piece of chewy mutton caught in my throat. I was overcome by a coughing fit, my eyes streaming as I hacked and hawked in an attempt to draw breath.

Reinhard watched me impassively. 'A nasty attack,' he observed.

I wiped my face and tried to regain some composure. 'Well?'

'Well, what?' He shrugged the question away. 'You talk of conquest. Yet Carl wants your own princess to sit on the throne. This is not conquest, but a partnership. A joining of our two great nations, Lord Rory! You should welcome it!'

Neither Mallrovia nor Livonia is a 'great nation', but there might be value in an alliance for that very reason.

'Go on,' I said cautiously.

'Let's say there is a Mallrovian princess on the throne. She is married to a Livonian Swordbrother. She is guided by him, and he is loyal to her. Mallrovia and Livonia trade with each other—'

'Fairly? For fair prices?'

'Yes, of course. Did you know that Livonia is famous for its linen? We do not export our linen to Mallrovia, not yet. But a trade agreement between us, involving Livonian linen and Mallrovian worsted would benefit all our people.'

'We couldn't do that,' I said at once. 'Hambrig is part of the Hanseatic League. There's an exclusivity clause, Reinhard.'

'Yes, yes, but we're not talking about Hambrig. Perhaps I should have been clearer. Livonian linen and worsted from Hicrown. And the surrounding area.'

'The surrounding area being Myrtile?'

He shot me a flinty-eyed look. 'Myrtile. Yes. It is close by, and it is the sheep from Myrtile whose fleeces make the best worsted.'

Joan had said that too. But Hambrig can't be separated, it's part of Mallrovia. In that, we are unlike the city states of the Holy Roman Empire. There can be no trade agreement unless our whole country is involved, and that's impossible because of the Hansa.

Reinhard just laughed. He slapped me on the back and told me not to worry. There would be a way around these things, and the lawyers would get rich and fat working it all out.

I'm in my chamber waiting for the dark, for I've decided to explore the Secret Way tonight. It must, surely, be the way the smugglers come and go, and I want to find out if I'm right about it leading to Myrtile. I plan to ignore Halfway House in its little stand of trees. The sky has cleared and there will be a moon, so I'll be able to see my way. While I'm waiting, I'm scribbling my notes in my journal, so I'll be up to date before I leave. Night is falling earlier every evening now, and at home the harvest will have been got in and, hopefully, some sort of feast will have been held. Normally, I help with the harvest, with Kit on hand to sing songs and encourage everyone with his music and good cheer.

But Kit is with Louis in Bavaria, and he was instrumental in Lillian's escape from her husband. Well, Lillian is no longer important. Married to Louis but pregnant by Reinhard, she can have no claim to the Mallrovian throne. Phoebe is Queen, and Carl von Lutterberg claims to have made a lucrative and powerful marriage to her. And though I hate the idea of a foreigner on the throne, our one hope of remaining a sovereign state is to have a sovereign. Perhaps Phoebe, with Carl attached, is the only way we can do that. Reinhard had insisted Carl was on my side. I'd disputed that, but this trade agreement, this *partnership*, may be what he meant. And perhaps it's the only way forward.

I wonder if it's possible to have a Queen Phoebe with no King Carl? How would that be achieved? Would the *Carta Juris Mallrovica* have a solution somewhere within its many articles? Hardly anyone ever reads that ancient charter now, and I had only the haziest memory of its contents, but it was probably created for just this kind of eventuality. There must be a copy of it somewhere in the palace, but I will not look for it yet. First, I want to come up with a plan of my own.

I find I've dug my charcoal so hard into the animal skin, I've scored a line through my previous sentence. Stupid of me. I rewrite the sentence and sit there in the dusk, desperately trying to think of a way to put Phoebe on the throne without Carl. And I come up with the obvious solution: I'll have to kill Carl. Now that the decision's been made, I feel more at ease. Carl will die, I'll get Phoebe reinstated as Queen – with a lavish second coronation to ram the point home – and Henry of England can go to hell.

Not only that, there will be just one Swordbrother left. Reinhard and Carl are working together, though, so Reinhard needs to die too. The Wartsbaye men will deal with the remaining leaderless Livonians. I'll need to brief Titus.

I stowed my journal safely away, pulled on my boots and was about to set off to see Titus and his Wartsbaye troops when I heard a footstep on the stairs and there was a knock on my door. At my invitation, Amie entered.

'Are you all right, lord?' she asked anxiously. 'Only, you disappeared after supper and I didn't know where you were.'

'Have you got information for me, Amie? You've spoken with Surrey or Warwick?'

'No, not yet, lord. I will, though. I promise!'

I stood up and took her by the shoulders. 'Then why are

you here? You should report to me when you have something to say.'

'I just wondered – perhaps you're lonely? Away from Lady Rosa—'

I shook my head in exasperation. 'Your husband hasn't been dead long, Amie, and you should remember I was once your lord. Your behaviour is unsuitable.'

But she looked unabashed. 'I'm here if you need me, lord. Whatever I do, it doesn't matter to Gael. Not now. And Lady Rosa won't know either. I just want you to know I'm available and I'm willing. And in case you're wondering, I'm good, too.' She flitted out of the room before I could respond to any of that. I buckled on my sword, found shield and dagger, and went to talk to Titus.

'You're puttin' me in charge?'

I hadn't said so. I'd merely told him I was leaving the palace to find out more and would be back in a couple of days, perhaps three. I'd told him to keep the troops on alert, to take no nonsense from the Livonians, and to prepare to report fully to me on my return.

I considered his question. 'Yes, Titus. And you're in charge of the bloody Livonians, too. If Reinhard makes trouble, arrest him.'

'The men you ordered me to recruit in Pevarile have been restless. They understood there'd be a short battle in Hicrown and then they could go home. They've been here a week now, and nothin' has happened. They're bored and they wanna leave. Go back to their families.'

I wasn't surprised. The expedition had been sold to

them as a quick and profitable campaign. 'Have you paid them?' I asked. Titus had instructions to pay each man fourpence a day.

'Payin' 'em don't make 'em less homesick,' Titus said in his boorish way. He's shortish, broad and stocky. A typical fighter; not necessarily a thinker.

'Perhaps not,' I answered. 'But I am paying them to be here, and to remain here in case they're needed. Have any deserted?'

'Not yet. They will. In time.'

'It's your responsibility to prevent desertion. Threaten punishment—'

'Such threats have already been made. I know my job. Lord.'

I tried not to be riled by him. 'As I've just said, I'm putting you in charge. I want you to use your judgement in all situations. Decide for yourself what's best.'

By the time I was back outside, it was fully night. The moon lit the way, as I'd planned. I decided to leave my shield behind after all, so I leant it carefully against the wall and made my way past the archery butts. Soon I was walking along what I was now sure was the secret way to Myrtile.

23

I'VE BUSINESS TO CONDUCT WITH YOUR SON

I wondered why Amie wanted me to sleep with her. I had no desire to do so. Amie's pretty, but a long time ago I made a vow that I would never sleep with any of my servants or my garrison. Apart from once, when I was unable to make coherent decisions, I've kept that promise. Margaret Longsword, though – that would be different. Several times now I've dreamt of making love to Margaret. In my dreams, she consents readily. But my dreams are not about the sex. When I wake, what I remember most are the conversations we have afterwards.

Lying in each other's arms, hands still roaming over each other's naked bodies, I ask about her grandfather, her father and her knowledge of the mysterious, and unfortunately deceased, blacksmith. Master Adam Rice. Who was he? How was he related to Jonny? Jonny always implied that his only family was his father. Yet there was also a Joel Rice somewhere in the picture.

Jonny, I was beginning to realise, had hidden much of his past from me. While I had been an open book, snivelling the misery of my lost love into his shoulder, telling stories of my father's iron-fisted control over his demesne, or articulating the pain of my guilt at being away from home when my mother died, Jonny had given only a few snippets of information on his former life. His father had been a blacksmith and had been hired to work on Salisbury Cathedral, which was a great honour. Jonny had no wish to be a blacksmith, and so Jonny had persuaded William Longsword (or Longsword had offered – I couldn't remember which way round it had been) to dub him knight and take him on Crusade.

Had I tried to get Jonny to tell me more? Probably not. And by the time we returned from the Holy Land, and Jonny had agreed to come with me to Hambrig, it hardly mattered anyway. I remember asking Jonny if his father would be expecting him to return to Salisbury. Jonny had shrugged the question away, and it had never been referred to again.

After a couple of hours, I came to the copse in which Halfway House was hidden. *If it lives up to its name,* I thought, *there's the same distance to go before I get to Myrtile.* And it was at that point that I remembered there was another secret way to Myrtile. Bryce had discovered it when we were on the beach at Navisar. And there'd been blood on the ground. *A trail of blood,* he'd called it.

I'd said Myrtile had no transport links, but I'd been wrong. There were quite a few, only they were all secret, used only by those in the know. You couldn't bring merchandise, carts or even cohorts of soldiers to or from Myrtile. But then – how did the smugglers get the worsted through? Making my moonlit way along the grassy track, I concluded that pack ponies would manage, and that must be the answer. As for the other despicable trade, the selling of Mallrovian girls to slave traders, that part was easy.

Simply march them down to the beach and load them into a ship.

Could Patrick really be behind such a vile business? The Patrick I knew couldn't be. And yet, even if he's not the organiser, he must *know* about it. If the worsted and the girls are coming from Myrtile, how can he not know?

Ahead of me, I saw lights gleaming in the night. Grimly, I acknowledged I'd been right. I was approaching the city of Myrtile, and Patrick would have to be confronted. Peter would, I hoped, have gained intelligence on the city itself. I was fairly sure I knew the answer to one of my questions, though. Patrick's wealth came from the slave trade. Such was my revulsion at this thought, I almost forgot the peril the entire country was in.

'What do you know of the selling of women and girls into slavery?'

Patrick and I sat in his comfortable hall, which was unlike any great hall I'd ever been in. Instead of a high table and a long, empty space below it, the whole room, square rather than rectangular, was filled with couches and chairs, all equipped with plump, soft cushions in colourful and vibrant colours. I sat on one couch and Patrick sat opposite me. I'd had Rolf, his steward, get him out of bed, taking no nonsense from the man about his master being elderly and needing a full night's sleep. Yes, Patrick is now seventy-four. But as I looked across at him, by the light of the many ensconced torches, I saw a quick-witted and perceptive man, with the ability to grasp a situation quickly.

'I know it happened,' he said. A cagey response.

'And is still happening.'

'I do not believe so, although I have sometimes wondered.'

'What has made you wonder, Patrick?'

'Small things, nothing you can put your finger on. It had been stamped out, Rory. I mean, *properly* stamped out. But, perhaps, the horrible business has been revived. I am looking into it.'

'Why have you never mentioned this before?' My voice was calm and measured; the first stage of fury for me. It's followed by uncontrollable rage, when the Red Mist descends and turns me into a wild beast. Sometimes I try to control it. I'm not always successful. And I don't always try.

'Rory, I have not mentioned it before because it wasn't relevant. I wiped it out long before I knew you. It was in 1230 – perhaps before you were even born?'

'I was born in 1229.'

'Then you'll understand why I didn't mention it. And after 1230, it no longer happened. The revival of this foul operation, if there's actually been one, must be very recent, and it is being investigated. If I find it is taking place again, I will act. But first I need evidence. Do you have evidence you can share with me?'

Patrick's voice was calm and measured too. But then, it always is. Patrick doesn't suffer from the Red Mist. I have never seen him lose his temper. However, I was stunned by the timescale. This foul trading had gone on under my father's lordship? I found that hard to believe.

Patrick continued, 'I discovered this horrible business had been going on when my father died. I was seventeen. The year was 1215. There was no slavery happening, but there was a history. Fifteen years later, the business restarted. I was informed, and then I put a stop to it. By that time, Myrtile was nearly complete.'

'You built this city using money from the slave trade?'

'What else could I do, Rory? The money was there. Collected and hoarded by my father. It took a long, long time to build Myrtile, and I got my entire demesne involved. Now, you see, no one needs to work for a living, for there is enough money for all to live on. I do expect certain things, as the city has to be kept working. There are jobs people do. And we need to buy things from time to time. All of it comes out of my father's coffers. Deborah knows. And Master Peter knows as well, since Deborah reported to me that she was being closely questioned by the Yorkshireman.

'I took him on one side and told him the whole story, and now you know it too. I never spoke of it before, and I'm sure you can understand the shame I felt when I uncovered my father's hidden riches and discovered how he acquired so much money. If girls are once more being shipped out, it's not from Myrtile. And, I can tell you this with certainty, wherever it's from, it can only just have started up again. But you may be mistaken, and I hope you are.'

'I'm not mistaken. There is blood on the track between Myrtile and Navisar. There are women's naked footprints in the sand on the dunes and on the beach.

'I will redouble my efforts,' Patrick said with a sigh.

The danger of the Red Mist had gone, although I was still not sure if I believed Patrick. I told him what had happened at Hicrown. He knew some of it, as he has news brought to him from time to time. He knew about English Henry's interest, but not about the Livonians. He knew about Lillian's abduction from the Bavarian court, but not that she was with Reinhard and expecting his baby.

After I'd filled him in, we both sat and looked at the

dawn breaking in the eastern sky. The large windows themselves were significant. Mostly, people have small windows. Large ones let out all the heat. In a castle, they would weaken defence capabilities. Patrick's windows were large and filled with glass panes. An extravagance, but no more so than the rest of this impossible city.

'Why did you build it like this?' I asked suddenly, swinging round to look at him. 'Why all this opulent glass, the lights on the bridge, the turquoise roofs and the lack of defences? What is Myrtile meant to *be*?'

'I've told you. It's a penance. It's also a refuge. It symbolises defiance.'

'Defiance, Patrick?'

'I wanted Myrtile to be different. It's a welcoming place, yet nobody knows we're here. I wanted Myrtile to scream defiance at slavery, since all here are equal. I have no servants, apart from Rolf, and even he is only here because he wants to be. He has quite a severe limp, meaning he couldn't do many types of work, even as a young man. I pay him well. I pay *everyone* well. You used to smile at my saying "All is well" when a situation was resolved, but, you see, it's permanent here. Myrtile is the place where "all is well", all the time.'

That sounded way too complacent to me. Surely even Patrick can't believe that something, or somewhere, never has any problems.

With the sun fully up, Rolf knocked and entered, and I saw what Patrick meant: the steward, who was roughly Patrick's age, walked with a pronounced limp. He seemed an educated man though, gentle and respectful. Not so different from Patrick himself. 'There is food available, Sir Patrick, if you and your guest would like to follow me. Lady Deborah and Master Peter are already in the dining room.'

The dining room? Intrigued, I followed Patrick and Rolf and found that a room on the other side of the house had been set aside for dining. A large table filled the space, with benches on each side. The walls were lined with extra chairs. Deborah and Peter were sitting waiting, and platters of meats, cheeses and fruit already stood on the table. Patrick greeted his wife with a kiss on the cheek, and Peter half stood, stammering something. Patrick waved him back to his seat, and soon we were all enjoying a very good breakfast indeed.

'Well,' I observed, 'it was worth the walk from Hicrown.'

I watched Patrick's face as I said it. 'That is the old smugglers' way,' he confirmed calmly. 'A little overgrown now, I expect.'

'And do you know of Halfway House?' I asked, watching him closely again.

'I know of it, yes. Is it still there?'

'Patrick, you bloody know it's still there!' I'd lost my patience with this to-and-fro-getting-nowhere conversation. 'It's still there, it's being used by the smugglers, and when I was taken to it, Queen Phoebe was inside Halfway House, and so was her fucking husband!'

I explained Carl von Lutterberg, which earned me a frown from Patrick and an enigmatic glance from Rolf, who ate at the table with us. Deborah helped fetch dishes from the kitchen and removed empty platters as well, presumably to save the steward having to do too much walking. I gave Rolf a questioning look, but he turned away, busying himself with straightening candlesticks, for which there was absolutely no need, as sunshine poured through the oversized windows.

'How would you know if people smuggling was still happening?' I asked Patrick.

'I'd be told,' he said simply. 'People all knew about it—'

'They'd scarcely be the same people. You claim to have stopped it a long time ago. People living here now may know nothing of what went on in their parents' or their grandparents' time. You need to have a more accurate system.'

'Rory, I've said I'll find out. I'm afraid you must be content with that.'

'And you knew nothing of the Livonians?'

Rolf jerked his head. If I'd thought I'd imagined the previous odd look he gave me, this time it was unmistakeable.

Patrick turned to his steward. 'You are from those parts yourself, aren't you, Rolf? I remember your telling me something about a military order similar to the Knights Templar?'

I jumped in before the man could answer. 'You're from Livonia, Rolf?'

'No, Lord Rory. I am from Bremen, a free city-state in the Holy Roman Empire.' He said it as if meeting a challenge.

'And this military order? Did you join it? Was it the Teutonic Knights, by any chance?'

'Yes, he did, and no, it wasn't,' Patrick answered. 'I remember exactly now. It was when I first caught you, Rolf. You proudly told me you were a member of the Livonian Brothers of the Sword.'

Rolf's eyes flashed. 'I was a Swordbrother, yes. But the Swordbrothers no longer exist, Sir Patrick. They were assimilated into the Teutonic Order six years after I came to Myrtile.'

I could hardly believe what I was hearing. Rolf was from Bremen and had been a Swordbrother? He neither acted nor talked like a foreigner. I would never have known.

But Patrick was speaking again. His voice remained completely neutral, yet I'm sure he knew how vital this information was. 'Ah, I see. So the Brothers of the Sword are no more. But there was another, wasn't there? The man who escaped?'

'Hang on,' I said. 'What are we talking about? You said you "caught" Rolf, Patrick. What do you mean by that? And this man who escaped – escaped from what?'

'I thought this was to be kept absolutely between us,' Rolf said, staring at Patrick. 'You promised me. Surely you will not break your oath, Sir Patrick?'

'You're right, of course,' Patrick said with a sigh. 'I gave you my word. Well, then. Let us help Deborah clear up, and then Lord Rory can decide what he wants to do next.'

'You will not betray me?' Rolf asked again. 'Sir Patrick, please tell me you will not speak of this to anyone, even when I am out of earshot. Please assure me you will not break your oath.'

'I have already said so,' Patrick said. 'I will not speak of it, Rolf, whether you are listening or not.'

We sat on the bridge, Patrick and I. It is a most glorious bridge with many arches, spanning the glittering moat that surrounds the city of Myrtile.

'You're going to tell me, aren't you?' I said. 'Rolf's secret may hold the key to the kingdom.'

'I will not break my oath. I will not speak of it, not to you nor to anyone.'

I was about to protest in the strongest terms, but he felt inside his tunic and pulled out some parchment. 'I've written it all down. I realise this is breaking the spirit of my promise, but, in the circumstances, I consider it justified. I can at least know I have not spoken the words myself. I have decided that this is the best compromise I can make, since I agree with you. It's important that you have this information. However, I would ask you to ride away from Myrtile before you read it, and then to keep going. Come back only once the kingdom is in safe hands. I will send Master Peter with you. He is getting your horses ready as we speak. And there is one further thing you should know. A couple of weeks ago, Deborah, Master Peter and I held a brief but important meeting. Based on the little we knew then, I decided to send a messenger to Kettering. I have asked Sir Jonny to bring troops to Hicrown. From the way I worded the message, I feel certain he will come.'

He handed me the parchment, and I stuffed it into my jersey. The sound of horses' hooves heralded Peter's arrival with Tortoise and Blue.

I stared at my warhorse in astonishment.

'She was found on the road a week or so ago,' Patrick informed me calmly. 'I did offer one of our palfreys to Master Peter, but he tells me he prefers to ride this stately fellow. I am happy to reunite you with your favourite steed, Rory.'

Peter and I mounted, said 'Farewell' to Patrick and rode across the bridge.

'Are we goin' to Hicrown, lord?' Peter asked. 'Or to Hambrig?'

It was a good question. While I ached to be back in Hambrig, finding out what had happened there, Hicrown had more pressing needs. I'd left in the middle of the night, telling no one where I was going. Perhaps the Livonians had slaughtered my Pevariles and Wartsbayes by now. Or maybe

Allan and Leo had used the King's Squad to fight back. It was equally possible that the remaining citizens had ransacked the cathedral again. I had no idea what we might find there.

'To Hicrown, Peter. I've business to conduct with your son.'

24

WHAT CHOICE DID I HAVE?

The bishop of the cathedral was waiting for me at the palace. Well into his sixties, he was looking particularly dour today. In fact, he looked like he was spoiling for a fight. Fortunately, having finally slept and eaten, I was up to dealing with him.

We'd taken our time returning from Myrtile, partly because of Tortoise's notoriously slow ambling, but mostly because I'd needed to catch up on sleep. So Peter and I had spent an exhausted night at the roadside, and the next morning I'd read Patrick's letter.

It was disappointing, revealing little I hadn't already learnt while at Myrtile. It was Patrick's 'considered opinion' that no more slavery had taken place after 20th September 1230, when his loyal Myrtilers had received a tip-off that they needed to fetch their spears and descend to Navisar beach in the middle of the night. Rolf had received a leg wound, a group of five girls had been saved from a terrible fate, and the spearmen had wrecked the slave boat. Patrick further declared he had 'put a complete and permanent stop to slavery out of Myrtile'. The fact that one of the slave dealers had 'escaped through the dunes to freedom' didn't seem significant to him. It was, he stated, 'extremely unlikely that one foreigner, without a boat or any insider help, could get home and restart this ghastly business'. But I thought differently, and I wondered who that man was and what had happened to him.

In the palace garden, the bishop's robe flapped in the afternoon breeze, while his thinning wispy hair threatened to detach itself from his head altogether. The man was clearly agitated, and I took him into the great hall, seating him at the high table and calling for food and wine.

'We need to defend the cathedral, Lord Rory.' The bishop spoke the instant his skinny backside touched the bench.

'As far as I can make out,' I said bluntly, 'it was the cathedral that began all this trouble.'

The bishop shot me a malevolent look. 'Oh no. It was the citizens of the city! They set up their quintains and began practising with lances on cathedral land! It was an outrage!'

'Because you were evading your taxes, and that meant a greater financial burden on them. Come on, bishop! Look at it in the round. You own a lot of land in the city, and your tenants, who no doubt pay you considerable amounts in rent, are exempt from general taxation, meaning everyone else pays more. How do you think that looks to them?'

'It doesn't matter how it looks to them, it is not their decision. This is an historical situation, Lord Rory. It has been this way for many decades—'

'And that's the problem, isn't it. People see it as unfair, and it's been unfair for many decades. I'm not saying they're right or wrong, but I understand how it looks. They're making their feelings known.'

'By burning down the cathedral? By destroying sacred vestments and treasures?' His voice rose in outrage.

'Because you shot them! I heard that one of your servants shot an arrow at a man and killed him. And that you roamed the streets of Hicrown, holding a dagger concealed in your cassock. You are as responsible for the rapid escalation of this dispute as they are.'

He looked pained. 'I'm not here to make a complaint, Lord Rory. I've come to inform you that a company of men-at-arms is on its way to Hicrown. They have been seen by one of my laymen, who hurried back with the news. I came at once to tell you.'

I questioned him. The company was riding east along the Hicrown Road, and must have come through Hambrig. It could only be the English. I knew Henry had travelled south from here, heading for an English town called St Edmund's Bury. He'd told me he'd give us a chance. Pay the fines, rebuild the cathedral and the city, and both he and the pope would leave us alone. Perhaps he'd had second thoughts, and sought to subdue us completely instead.

'How many men-at-arms?' I asked the bishop.

'My man says twenty to thirty, all horsed and in armour. We think they are English knights.'

'I agree. And you're right, bishop, we must mount a defence. You must return to what's left of your cathedral and make it as secure as you can. And then get on your knees and pray that Hicrown – and Mallrovia – survive.'

He strode away, clutching at his robe as gusts of wind blew it between his legs. I watched him go. Peter had taken Blue and Tortoise to the stables, and I stood in thought for a few moments. It was clear Hicrown had not been raided again. There had been no pitched battles and no bloodshed.

But the atmosphere felt strained. As if something could erupt at any moment.

I went to find Titus.

'I want the women, the servants and anyone over the age of fifty to muster in the big barn by the stables. They must be told to stay there, no matter what happens, until you or I come to release them. And I want everyone else in the great hall. Everyone. Livonians, Wartsbaye men, Pevarile men, the King's Squad, the two English knights, and all citizens under the age of fifty. And make sure Sir Allan and Captain Leo are there as well. Get this organised, Titus. You have one hour.'

An hour later, I stood on the dais with Titus on one side of me and Allan on the other. The hush in the hall was extraordinary. At home, when I make an announcement, there's always a buzz of chatter from below. People wondering what I'm going to say. Making guesses. Sometimes even betting on a hunch; money changing hands; smiling or grimacing at the outcome. But not here, and not now. Had the word gone round that we might soon be under attack? That the English were coming with swords, spears and lances? I looked sideways at the thickset Titus, but he was staring straight ahead. I'd briefed him earlier – Allan, too. And I'd made the situation very clear. The King's Squad had killed Gael and his men from Wartsbaye, but now they must stand with us. No matter what. The English are our common enemy now.

But there were few Pevariles left, and I knew many had simply taken themselves off home. The Wartsbaye men were inexperienced, the King's Squad under Leo and Allan had previously fought against me, while the Livonians were not in the hall at all. Nor was Captain Leo. Titus had done his best, but it had led to a stand-off. The Livonians would not move without their commander.

'Where is Reinhard?' Titus had growled to me. 'Apparently, they'll answer to nobody but him.'

'Last seen at Halfway House, seven or eight miles from here.'

'And not comin' back?'

'Oh, I'm sure he's coming back. But he didn't enlighten me as to when.'

I didn't bother to try to persuade the Livonians myself. We all knew that when the English arrived, the Livonians would line up alongside them. We would be heavily outnumbered, and the English, on horseback, would have the advantage. It was my job, now, to explain all this and to set out my defensive strategy.

'Warriors!' I called to the silent people. 'You are all warriors! Today or tomorrow we will be attacked by a cohort of English knights. I have no doubt that the Livonians, currently within these walls, will side with them against us. It's our duty now to defend this palace and this city. Already I have closed the city gates. We are protecting Hicrown as best we can.'

'The palace has no defences,' someone called out. 'We've always relied on Hambrig to protect us. Did Hambrig not put up a fight?'

'I don't know,' I said, feeling my stomach contract as I allowed myself to wonder again about my own people. What had happened when the English crossed the River Hurogol and rode south down the Wartsbaye Road to Hambrig? Had there been resistance? A battle? 'We don't know what happened in Hambrig,' I said firmly. 'But if Hicrown falls, all Mallrovia is lost, including your freedom, your homes and families, your farms and pastures. The English will control everything. We *must* defend ourselves!'

I outlined my plan of stationing people at strategic points along the palace walls. Townspeople were asked to volunteer for duties within the city: relaying messages, bringing food, watching for the enemy and reporting back to the palace. I put Allan and the King's Squad in charge of that. I waited while Allan briefed his people. Six of the King's Squad were despatched, together with a cobbler, a spice merchant, a weaver, two members of the guild and a middle-aged man who mumbled that he was somebody's servant. Each of the townspeople was paired with a trained soldier. The civilian would return with any news, leaving the soldier to hold the city against the invaders. They were all armed and ready, and they knew what to do.

'We'll put a ring of steel around Hicrown,' Allan called out to the King's Squad, and they cheered. 'We won't let the English have our city!'

A ring of steel. I liked the idea, although we had too few people to make it a reality. Still, the men were grinning at each other, and one or two waved their fists triumphantly in the air. I wished them good luck, and the twelve of them left the hall to go to their posts in the city.

I looked down at what was left of our forces. 'Commander Titus will now split the rest of you into groups,' I told them. 'Some of you will go up to the roof, while others will stay by the palace wall. And two groups will remain here as back-up for anyone who needs it. Four people will be chosen as runners to take messages between the groups.' I nodded to Titus, who immediately began a roll call, his deep voice rolling round the hall, and everyone gathered round him, waiting to hear which group they were assigned to.

Allan confronted me rudely. 'You think you're in charge here?'

'I am in charge here, Allan. As you can see. And now it's a waiting game. We'll know they're coming long before the English get to the city wall. Your men will see them on the road from Hambrig and they will warn the palace. Once that happens, we put the plan into action. Meanwhile, we should check everything is battened down, locked away and as secure as can be. The bishop will be doing the same in the cathedral. Now let's go.'

We jumped down off the dais, checked our armament and shields, and opened the door into the palace garden.

My hand is shaking as I write this. Indeed, I can barely write at all. My apologies; you will no doubt be finding it very hard to read – that's if you can make out even a single word. But I should tell you, I am doing my best. I'm sitting on my own by the shady palace wall. Behind the wall, the sun is slowly sinking, and the shadows flowing over the grass grow longer by the moment. My leg hurts like hell, and I need to write down this most infamous thing that has happened. You will want to know how it was that we lost so many people so soon, before the English even got here.

When Allan, Titus and I opened the door and stepped out into the garden, we were blinded by the low sun in the west, straight ahead of us. And that strong sunshine was reflected in flashes of dazzling light off the polished steel of forty Livonian swords, spearheads and axes.

Too late, we saw the dead bodies of the six citizens and the six Squaddies, strewn on the ground where they'd been cut down as soon as they came outside. Too late, we took in the Livonians, who'd arranged themselves in a semicircle around the door, and who'd waited in deadly silence while I'd explained my plan to our forces gathered indoors. A plan that is now in tatters. Too late, I realised Reinhard was behind this, briefing his men, fixing them with his hypnotic gaze and swearing them to blind obedience.

It was also too late for Leo, whose sword was already red to the hilt with Mallrovian blood. But when Allan opened the door and stood for that heart-stopping moment on the steps to the hall, Leo was transfixed. Bright sunshine glinted off Allan's armour, his helm and his drawn sword. For an instant, the man could truly have been the Archangel Michael, the Warrior of God. And *in* that instant, Leo switched sides. With a bellow that was half-roar, half-sob, he bounded over to Allan, turning on the Livonians and savaging them.

There was no sign of the English, other than the Earl of Warwick, who fought valiantly alongside Allan, Leo, the rest of the Squad and me. The Earl of Surrey had taken one disbelieving look at the carnage and had whirled away, leaping onto his horse and charging furiously out through the gate. Here in the palace garden, we were vastly outnumbered, there being thirteen of us against forty-odd Livonians, and so defeat was, once again, inevitable.

I took down four before I was disabled by a Livonian axe chopping into my leg. I'd fallen to the ground during a frenzied bout of hand-to-hand fighting. I watched my adversary raise his axe and charge towards me. In desperation, I swung my shield to the side and tried to drag myself away. But my shoulder was screaming in pain from an enemy dagger thrust, and the axeman was running at me. My shield deflected the blow, but the axe skimmed my leg, making me cry out in pain. Somehow, I crawled across to the palace wall on the south side. So now here I am. I'm unobserved, but I can see what's happening.

Leo is down, a spear in his chest. I can't see Allan anywhere, while Warwick is lunging valiantly with his sword, but he can't hold the enemy off much longer. Titus fought like a madman, before someone clobbered him over the head. I don't know if he's dead, dying or just unconscious, but he's lying very still, so it doesn't look good.

I've used a strip torn from my hose to staunch the blood running down my leg, in the hope that I can be of some help in a few moments. Looking across the garden, I see roughly equal numbers of Mallrovian and Livonian dead and injured. But the English earl is almost beaten. His back is against the door to the great hall, and he's being assailed by three Livonians at once. He does have a height advantage, as he's standing on the highest step and slashing downwards at the enemy, but he can't last. Others will flock to attack, and he will be overcome.

But where is the invading force of English knights? Twenty to thirty men-at-arms, horsed and in armour, the bishop's informant had said. Perhaps they'll arrive later. Or tomorrow. Either way, they'll be able to walk into Hicrown unopposed.

Shakily, I stood up, testing my leg carefully. It bore my weight. My shoulder felt on fire, but I was used to that. It's an old wound, and it hadn't enjoyed being prodded with the sharp tip of someone's dagger. Allan, I now saw, was in the thick of it, and I watched with a sense of awe as he held off four Livonians at once. I'd always thought him pretty useless, never having seen him fight or shared battle honours with him. It's certainly true that the King's Squad were only ever for show, parading with immaculate precision in their fine colours. They'd never fought anyone until now – but Allan himself must have done. Watching him, I saw years of experience in the way he handled his weapons. He didn't fight like a knight, but as a pikeman would. Brutally. Inelegantly. With lethal efficiency.

Seizing my sword in one hand and grasping my shield in the other, I threw myself back into the fray. We'd all perish – that was a certainty – but what choice did I have?

25

WE WILL ALL WAIT FOR YOU

As dusk fell, someone saw the English men-at-arms and the shout went up. The Livonians cheered, surging towards the gatehouse. Half a dozen of the Pevariles ran hell for leather to the far wall, leaping over it and escaping while they could. The Earl of Warwick was saved by the arrival of his countrymen, as the Livonians immediately lost interest in him. Wounded, he stood quietly by the palace building, his intelligent eyes watching to see what would happen next.

The Squad and the Wartsbayes fell back, waiting, in dread, for the inevitable. I motioned them to form up behind me, shields and weapons ready. Slaughter could not now be averted, but we had no wish to greet the conquerors. In the distance I saw waving English flags, their colours glowing in the setting sun. The horses were cantering fast through Hicrown, hooves sounding loud in the empty cobbled streets. Past deserted and ruined shops and houses they must come, no doubt gleeful at the thought of such an easy victory. Where was the resistance? It had fled. Where would the battle be? There would be none. Only annihilation.

And then they were here, jostling at the gatehouse, while the Livonians ranged themselves on either side to allow the heroes through.

'*We are Hambrig, Boom! Boom!*''

A voice I knew, and a war cry I recognised! *Jonny*. His voice filled my ears, so that, ignoring my fiery shoulder, I lifted my sword high, charged forward to the gate and swung it into the skulls of two Livonians. They crumpled to the ground, while Allan, appearing beside me, despatched a third with a lethal upward thrust of his dagger into the man's groin. The fighting broke out again, our few against the Livonian masses. And where *was* Jonny? I was so sure I'd heard him... but that was before I felt a blow to the back of my neck, and my world turned black.

'Rory.'

I opened my eyes.

'Rory, you're safe. The Livonians are dead or imprisoned. We've taken Hicrown back.'

'Who are you?' I whispered.

'You don't know me? It's Jonny. With a cottar called Tom. Patrick sent a message.'

'He told you I was in trouble?'

'He told me Mallrovia was in trouble. I came at once.'

Jonny and Tom helped me to stand. The sun had vanished, and it was almost dark. The after-battle smell was strong, as it always is at night: the blood, the corpses, the open wounds, faeces and vomit, and the churned mud of what had once been a beautiful garden.

Well, you could no longer call it a garden. It had been a battlefield. The pretty flowers and elegant paths were destroyed. The grassy circles and the knoll were no longer there. The delightful gravel tracks, meandering between rose beds and under bowers of ivy, honeysuckle and jasmine – all gone. The dead lay everywhere. Livonian, Mallrovian and English corpses.

Standing to one side were the dozen or so English survivors. I knew now that these English were not Henry's men. They had come to rescue us, not to beat us. We had not needed to prepare an elaborate defence. We had not needed to send twelve men to hideous deaths on the sun-dappled lawn. The bishop's man had seen English men-at-arms riding towards Hicrown, and I'd instantly assumed they were the enemy. Briefly, I closed my eyes again, my bowels churning, queasiness building. I should have checked. I should have assumed nothing. I should not have sent men into that silent, deadly ambush. *I* had killed them, not the Livonians.

I opened my eyes and spoke to Jonny. 'Are these your men?'

'A scratch militia, with little to no fighting experience.'

'Then – how did you win? How did you beat Reinhard of the Osnabrück Guard?'

'There's no one called Reinhard here. His men were calling for him all the time, looking round with panicked expressions, but he never showed himself. Who is he, and where is he?'

I explained Reinhard, after which Jonny brusquely told me he'd raised his militia from the people who worked on his Kettering estate, leaving his steward, Clive, in charge there. Patrick, he said, had made the situation sound extremely urgent and dangerous. And he hadn't, I discovered, mentioned me at all.

As for the Wartsbaye and Pevarile contingents, those who hadn't run had mostly not survived the Livonian onslaught. The few remnants stood about in dazed bewilderment. We had, ostensibly, won – but it was not a victory to be proud of. I looked at the carnage, and the heat of shame flooded my face. Bile rose in my throat and I vomited into the mud. Jonny looked away.

The barn where the non-combatants had been kept safe was now full. Most of the wounded had been taken there already, and there were many men lying on straw bales, or propping themselves against the wall. Lanterns had been lit and placed strategically, so there was enough light for people to see where they were. Amie ran over to me straight away. She made a fuss of my leg wound, but I refused to let her do anything other than bandage it.

'It needs stitching, though!' she wailed. 'I've watched Doctor Bethan, lord, I know what to do!'

'You don't know what to do, Amie,' I said firmly. 'Just make sure it's bandaged with something clean. It'll heal itself after that.' Something I learnt long ago from Sir Stephen, an English physician and a man who, like Jonny, used to be my friend.

'Is he still alive, lord?' Peter's face loomed into view, leaning over Amie as she wound a length of cotton tightly around my leg.

'Get out of Amie's light, Peter,' I said crossly. 'And if you mean Leo, I don't know. He was brought down by a spear, and I don't know if he survived.'

'Where are the rest of the Hicrowners?' Jonny asked.

'Fled or dead.'

Within an hour, all the survivors from the battle were in or near the big barn and the stables. Even Captain Leo was there. I'd assumed he'd been killed by the spear that had sent him sprawling, but Peter told me his plate armour had saved him. I looked for Margaret Longsword, and found her bandaging wounded men. Thank God.

I knew we must regroup and decide what to do next, for nothing was resolved. We may have beaten the Osnabrück Guard, but there were plenty of other so-called Swordbrothers out there, to say nothing of the von Lutterbergs themselves...

I was deep in thought, when I heard a concerted gasp from everyone. Two people suddenly appeared in the barn's doorway. Everyone surged back to the far wall. I stayed where I was, facing the door. For there, visible in the flickering torchlight, stood Reinhard, with a knife across Phoebe's throat.

'You've done well, so far, Lord Rory,' he called out. 'In fact, you've done exactly as I planned. Now you are all in here, and that is very helpful! As it happens, that wasn't part of my plan, but it will do very nicely. As you see, I have your Queen, and she has co-operated fully, which is good, as otherwise she would also be dead. But I have warned her: I will slit her throat if I don't get co-operation from you, Rory, as well.'

'What do you want?'

'First, lay your dagger on the ground in front of me, and then step back to where you are now. Any false move and the girl dies.'

I stepped forward and put my dagger on the ground in front of him. Then back again. 'Now what?'

'Now you are going to attend a coronation,' Reinhard said.

Fascinated, I noticed his strange, glinting eyes had no effect in the gloomy barn. There wasn't enough light for them to reflect back. 'Whose coronation?'

'Mine and Lillian's, of course. You're not that stupid. You know Lillian is King Philip's eldest surviving child. When she is Queen, I'll be King.'

'I don't think so, Reinhard. You and Lillian are not married. Nor can you be, since she is married already.'

'That marriage can be easily dissolved. The pope wants Mallrovia to come back under control. I will convince him I'm the man to achieve that. With the pope's blessing I will marry Lillian. I don't much care for this squealing child though.' He looked down at Phoebe, who was giving small moans of distress.

I wanted to keep Reinhard talking. The mass of people behind me were deathly quiet. I wondered if Jonny were planning something. If so, it had better be good.

It wasn't Jonny who made a move, though. It was Allan.

'Reinhard, you are not going to be King of Mallrovia. That honour will be mine. I am Mallrovian, you are not. And Lillian is my prisoner, so she's unlikely to marry you any time soon.'

'Prove it,' Reinhard said, and a small bead of blood ran down Phoebe's neck. 'Oh, sorry, sweetheart,' Reinhard said to her mockingly. 'Did I hurt you?'

Allan called out again. 'Don't believe me? Go and check where you left her. She's not there, and you won't see her until you let Phoebe go.'

Allan, observed by me from my withdrawal position by

the palace wall, had flitted in and out of the fight with the Livonians. I wondered where he'd taken Lillian. And now I hoped Jonny would do nothing. A confrontation between Reinhard and Allan was exactly what I needed. It was clear Reinhard didn't know whether to believe Allan or not. Allan stood his ground, in that tensed-up way he has, while Reinhard frowned and postured. Suddenly, Reinhard swung Phoebe round, while simultaneously moving to the side. Picking up one of the lanterns, he held it close to his face and turned his irresistible gaze on Allan.

'Bring Lillian here now,' Reinhard said, ominously. Swinging his lantern, he looked around the barn, eyes glinting dangerously. Another drop of blood chased the first one down Phoebe's milk-white throat. The girl had closed her eyes, her hands clasped to her breasts. Reinhard grinned, enjoying his moment. 'Go, Allan. Fetch Lillian now. We will all wait for you.'

26

THERE CAN BE NO RESISTANCE

Allan sidled past the terrified Phoebe and disappeared into the night. I thought it doubtful he'd fetch Lillian. I also knew King Henry of England would not allow Lillian to sit on the Mallrovian throne, not while she was married to the Duke of Bavaria but pregnant by a Livonian renegade.

As for Reinhard's claim that he could obtain an annulment – that was never going to happen. The duke himself would have to instigate such a thing, and none of us knew how the duke had reacted to his wife's disappearance. In any case, Phoebe had been crowned Queen of Mallrovia nearly two years ago, although English Henry didn't seem to recognise her, her authority was weak to non-existent and the country was too unstable for her to wield any kind of power.

Reinhard knew all this. He stepped further into the barn, dragging his captive with him.

'You will all lay down your arms,' he said. 'And when you've done so, you will sit on the ground with your hands clasped behind your heads. And we shall await the arrival of the Queen of Mallrovia!' He laughed, and cut Phoebe yet again.

As people began to comply with his demands, piling their weapons by the door and going to sit by the back wall, hands clasped as instructed, I managed to catch Jonny's eye. Jonny had put down his sword, but he was not yet sitting on the floor. Surely, my glance said, *surely* we can do something? All of us, against this one man?

Almost imperceptibly, Jonny shook his head. He was thinking of Phoebe. If we rushed Reinhard, we'd be sacrificing Phoebe. And we must not do that. Jonny fiddled around with his belt, as if making sure he'd surrendered all his weapons. As he did so, he began to edge closer to me. I waited for Reinhard to glance the other way, then began to move towards Jonny. Eventually, and apparently without Reinhard noticing, Jonny and I were sitting together on the floor, our hands dutifully positioned behind our heads. Reinhard looked round at his prisoners, and I wondered if he'd planned beyond this moment. There were a lot of us in the barn, although most were either wounded, or the older men and women I'd sent here in the first place. Even unarmed, there were enough of us to overpower the Livonian. His only protection was our concern for the girl he held in front of him. If we decided we no longer cared about Phoebe, Reinhard's life would be worth nothing, and he knew it. His problem was, he'd marked her as already unworthy of concern. If Lillian were to be Queen, Phoebe hardly mattered.

'Do you have a plan?' Jonny whispered.

'Not yet. I don't think Allan's coming back, though.'

'He will come back, Rory, but he'll bring men with him,

not Lillian. There are men in the city and in the cathedral. He can rouse them, get them to arm themselves and bring them here for vengeance.'

'Then Phoebe's a corpse already.'

Jonny nodded. 'She was never going to survive this coup. What was Kit's expression? That time Molly was killed on Baudry Hill?'

'He said her death was "collateral damage".'

'Phoebe will be collateral damage, then.'

I wrestled with my conscience. Sacrifice Phoebe for the good of the kingdom? I might countenance it, if I thought the kingdom would definitely be saved. Still whispering, I tried to ask Jonny what he thought, but just then Reinhard loomed in front of us. He kicked out, sending Jonny sprawling and causing me to yell in pain, as his boot smashed into the wound in my leg.

'Well, Lord Rory,' Reinhard said, sarcastically. 'What do you think of your fairy princess, now? I believe she may have wet herself, the little doxy. Not quite the behaviour we expect from the reigning monarch, is it?'

'And she *is* the monarch,' I said angrily. 'English Henry won't agree to Lillian being Queen instead of Phoebe. He'll send his army in. The Livonians will be wiped out.'

'He'll agree,' Reinhard said, and then bending down, he hissed directly in my face. 'Henry's a sick old man, Rory. And his son, the Lord Edward, is away crusading. It's not just the Mallrovian throne that's at risk. Most people don't think Henry will last the year. In addition to that, and just to make absolutely sure, I've paid the Earl of Surrey a hefty amount of money. He's easily bought, that one. When he reports to his king, it'll be in my favour. Lillian will be crowned Queen, all right. And once I'm her husband, I'll be your King! You will swear allegiance to me. You'll be my tenant! I'll own your land, and if I choose to take away your demesne, there will be absolutely nothing you can do to stop me. Did you think I was just going to toddle off to Russia like von Sangershausen said? After he'd made a complete fool of me? I think being King of Mallrovia will be a rather better outcome. And I get the very attractive Lillian thrown in! Not bad, is it!'

'We *have* to stop him,' I said desperately to Jonny, once Reinhard and his hideously grinning face had moved on.

'We do,' Jonny agreed quietly. 'Wait for Allan though. I can't stand the man, but we'll have to work with him.'

'Jonny,' I said urgently. 'Would you have come to Hicrown if Patrick had told you I needed you here? You said he didn't mention me – but what if he had?'

'Are you that needy?' Jonny asked.

Reinhard was getting impatient. He'd started growling to himself. He was tired of holding Phoebe as well, we could all see that. He'd been holding a knife to her throat for over an hour now. Not only was his right arm feeling the strain, but he was bored with it. Reinhard was a man of action. Much like the late King Philip, he couldn't play the waiting game. Reinhard couldn't leave us though. There was that great pile of swords, knives, daggers, spears and lances. We couldn't use them, but neither could he. As Reinhard realised Allan had gone, he was left with a dilemma and he had no idea what to do next.

I decided to offer him a way out. 'Reinhard. Let Phoebe

go. She's no use to you. We can talk in the great hall and find a way to make this work. You'll have to trust me, but I'll have to trust you too.'

'Aren't you scared of my magic eyes?' he asked, his lip curling.

'No.'

'You should be. I've looked into your soul before. You haven't forgotten that, I know. I'll do it again.'

'Let the girl go,' I repeated. 'We can't stay in this barn forever, and Lillian, who hasn't been fetched here by Allan, in case you haven't noticed, needs someone to bring her food and see to her needs. She's pregnant, she hasn't been well, and she must be wondering what's happened. Let's talk, Reinhard. We can come to a solution if we both try hard enough.'

'Just you and me?'

'Just you and me.'

'Then I want your word of honour that no one here will touch the weapons, nor disturb us in the hall. You'll have to make them all swear to that.'

'I'll put Sir Jonny in charge. Sir Jonny is an Englishman of impeccable integrity. He will stand by the door and make sure nobody leaves the barn, and nobody takes back their weapons. If you like, the Earl of Warwick can stand here too.'

While Reinhard still held Phoebe at knifepoint, Jonny stood up and moved carefully across to the doorway. He took up his position next to Reinhard. Jonny is a big, muscular man. If it came to a physical fight between Jonny and Reinhard, my money was on Jonny. But I hadn't taken Reinhard's eyes into account. As Reinhard swivelled his head I saw Jonny's face turn white, his mouth working. Had Reinhard seen into Jonny's soul? I shivered at the thought.

The Earl of Warwick limped over to the door and stood beside Jonny.

As I approached the doorway, Warwick put his hand on my arm. 'This is an unacceptable situation,' he said softly. 'The King of England will not allow an unstable group of insurgents on his border. Bad enough when it was your own people rebelling, but far worse if these Livonians make Mallrovia their own. In the last century, and with less provocation, England annexed Westador, making it a principality. Essentially, part of England. This will happen to Mallrovia if you allow these foreigners to take control. England will not tolerate this, Lord Rory.'

Reaching Reinhard's side, I grabbed Phoebe, taking the Livonian by surprise. He roared in anger, but by then I'd hurled the girl into the darkness of the barn, where someone would be bound to look after her. Then I grasped Reinhard by the elbow and walked him outside.

'Jonny, remember the pact we've made with Reinhard,' I called back over my shoulder. 'No one touches the weapons and no one leaves the barn.' It was for Reinhard's benefit, not Jonny's, and I marched the Livonian up to the palace itself, through the great doors and into the hall, Warwick's last sentence ringing in my ears.

An hour later, however, we were no nearer a solution. By now it was midnight, and I could see this could take all night to sort out. I insisted Reinhard's plan wouldn't work, and the Earl of Warwick would back me up. Henry wouldn't accept Lillian. Even if Henry died while Edward was abroad, noblemen in the English court would take over and carry out Henry's wishes. Reinhard thought it all depended on the monarch; it didn't, and it was my job to convince him of that.

'The knights were here,' I said, for what felt like the hundredth time. 'The Earls of Oxford, Lincoln, Pembroke and Hereford. They were all here, they all saw the situation, and they could, each one of them, raise an army of hundreds. If they decide Mallrovia's situation is untenable, they'll band together. Between them, they would have several *thousand* warriors. If they bring such an army to Hicrown, they'll destroy it, or they'll annex the country. The Earl of Warwick just said as much, and you must have heard him yourself. You Livonian Swordbrothers, who were taken over yourselves after Saule, must know how it works. The larger and stronger power takes over the smaller one.'

'Why hasn't this happened before, then?' Reinhard demanded.

'Because we've had strong kings. King Philip, for all his faults, was bold and tough. His father, King David, was also a forceful man. They kept Mallrovia on an even keel and traded profitably with England and Europe. It is *you* who have ruined this. With the worsted smuggling, you've undermined our trade and our financial independence; and by murdering the King—'

'You're saying I did that?' Reinhard stood suddenly. 'You're accusing me of murder?'

'I don't know who did it. But I'm going to make it my business to find out.'

'Rory, you need to know that Carl will be here by morning. He will expect to find the city has been taken by the Swordbrothers. He will expect you and your ragtag army to have been soundly defeated. He will assume you are either dead, or in chains and ready to be ransomed. He will know I'm claiming Mallrovia for myself and Lillian – and then he will fight me for it. He has married Phoebe, and his position is stronger than mine. All I have is the claim that Lillian is older than Phoebe, and the rightful heir, but Carl will play the same card you did. Lillian, he will say, is already bound to Bavaria, while Phoebe, now Carl's wife, is the true ruler of the Kingdom of Mallrovia. And he will have himself crowned King. This is what Carl wants, so there will be a fight between the Swordbrothers, a fight which only one of us can win.'

Someone emerged from the shadows by the door. 'There is a third player in this game,' Allan said quietly. 'I will not let either of you take the Mallrovian crown. It is mine by rights. I was the commander of the garrison here for many years. As I told you in the barn, I'm Mallrovian. My claim trumps yours and your brother's. Mallrovia belongs to me, now.'

He stepped calmly up onto the dais, a large dagger in his hand, and, from across the other side of the table, he thrust it towards Reinhard's chest, intending, no doubt, to pierce the man's heart. But Reinhard moved just in time. The dagger ripped his sleeve, but that was all. Full of rage, Allan darted round the table, intent on stabbing Reinhard, furious not to have succeeded already.

Unarmed, I kept out of the way. Let them kill each other, I thought. Fine by me. I stepped down off the dais and hurried out of the hall. Running as fast as my injury would allow, I went to the Palace Guard accommodation block, where Lillian would, I hoped, be lying in her room. But, of course, she wasn't there, and the entire building was empty. Allan said he'd taken Lillian prisoner, and, realistically, there was only one place he could have taken her.

The city's streets were dark and deserted, and the wind swirled the leaves around, unchecked and unrestrained, as if the city had been abandoned by every single inhabitant. Once or twice, even at this late hour, I heard voices behind the closed shutters of shops. Everyone was scared, as they had good reason to be.

The Navisar Gate stood wide open, but it was the warehouses I made for, expecting to find Lillian tied up inside one of them.

'Well done,' Carl said, as I entered the first warehouse. 'You worked it out. Are you going to kill me?'

'I think Reinhard's hoping to do that,' I said. My eyes searched the gloom, but here there were no lanterns, and it was too dark to know if Lillian were there.

'Reinhard thinks he only has to look at you, and you'll collapse at his feet in terror,' Carl observed. 'That's a dangerous assumption.'

'He calls his eyes "magical".'

'I know. But I grew up with Reinhard, and I'm immune to the magic. Reinhard, with or without his eyes, is all bluster. We worked on this plan together, and then he double-crossed me. Snatching Lillian away from her Bavarian duke was a crass thing to do.'

'Will Louis come after her?' I asked.

'I doubt he'll come himself. He'll send someone. And the girl will be whipped and humiliated. It is fortunate she gave Louis another son, though. That will tell in her favour.'

'Will it tell in her favour that she's now pregnant with Reinhard's child?'

'It will not,' Carl said shortly. 'Where is Phoebe? Has Reinhard killed her yet?'

'No, she's alive and safe.'

'Good. My men are on their way, Rory. If you thought of mounting some kind of defence, you should think again. I know my brother has already had a few skirmishes with you in the palace yard, and perhaps you've slaughtered the Osnabrück lot, but a hundred of my Livonians are arriving. They will be here by dawn. We intend to take Mallrovia. Phoebe is your Queen. There's no point in fighting it. You must accept the situation. There can be no resistance.'

27

THEY CHARGED TOWARDS THE FIREWALL

I'd thought the Livonian Swordbrothers had already arrived, had been housed and fed at our expense and now lay slain in the palace garden. No more Livonians, I'd naively thought. But that had just been 'the Osnabrück lot'. The real troops, some one hundred of them according to Carl, were now pounding their boots along the moonlit Navisar Road, and in all likelihood there would be cavalry too.

This was a disaster, and Reinhard would find it so as much as I did. Jonny's militia, men from his estate, hurriedly armed, equipped and mounted so as to make the fastest possible journey from Kettering to Hicrown, were reduced to half their number, and their experience and skills were limited. We were an assortment of remnants, rebels and raw recruits. We would not be able to defend Hicrown against a hundred Baltic warriors.

My intention had been to kill Carl and get rid of the threat. But the threat had arrived, and if Carl didn't command them, someone else would. These Livonians had been organised by somebody, gathered, armed and transported to Mallrovia by somebody, and now that same somebody was marching them towards Hicrown. Carl's death would only inflame tensions. I revised my plan.

'All right,' I said to Carl, although my eyes were on the road, and my ears strained to hear the invading army. 'We won't fight you. The English might, though.'

'Why would they? Henry wants Mallrovia to be stable and secure. It isn't, not while Phoebe is so weak and so challenged. Not while there's lawlessness and anarchy on the streets and in the countryside. Once I'm in charge, with Phoebe by my side, Henry will withdraw. He'll see order has been restored and Mallrovia is stable again. He doesn't want unnecessary battles.'

This was almost certainly true. But was it really that clear-cut? 'Aren't you forgetting your brother?'

'I told you. I can deal with Reinhard. And Lillian, once she's whelped his brat, will be sent back to Louis. We both know what he'll do with her.'

'He'll have her executed. You'd send her to her death?'

Carl gave me a twisted smile, and at that very moment, the sound of boots crunching on the pebbly track came to my ears. Horses' hooves too, and someone shouting orders.

'That's Walther von Nortecken,' said Carl. 'The Master of the Livonian Order, as we are now termed. Walther took over after my brother, Otto, was killed at Karuse.'

'Why not one of the other Swordbrothers?' I asked curiously. 'Why not you, for instance?'

Again, the twisted smile. 'A very good question,' he said softly. 'There's nothing wrong with von Nortecken. He's a good fighter. Von Sangershausen chose him. But we shall break free from von Sangershausen and all the Teutonic Order. With Mallrovia as our country and Hicrown as our base, we shall once more be the Brothers of the Sword!'

I listened for a few more moments, finding it hard to believe that an invading army could really be marching, unchallenged, from the coast to our capital city, with nothing we could do to stop them taking Hicrown and proclaiming their lordship of the whole country. Mallrovia is a tiny nation, and, right now, a hundred or so disciplined warriors could easily hold it. Wartsbaye in the north has been left undefended. Hambrig, to the south-west, has had no garrison for months. The Palace Guard is dead. The King's Squad, what's left of them, are of uncertain allegiance. There is absolutely nothing we can do – Carl was right about that.

With a heavy heart, I made my way back to the city centre. I knew the Livonians wouldn't move until dawn, perhaps four hours away now. That time must be spent hunting for Lillian. If she wasn't in the warehouses, where was she? After all, it was Allan who'd taken her, not Carl. Perhaps he'd known Carl would be waiting at the Navisar Gate, so he'd put Lillian somewhere else... I spent some time racking my brain for the hiding place he might have used. And, of course, hoping that somehow, Allan and Reinhard had each put the other out of action.

It was a fruitless quest, and I realised I'd been a fool, because there was more than one warehouse by the gate. I'd found Carl lurking in the first one and hadn't searched the others. Well, too late now. The sky was lightening in the east and birds could be heard greeting the new day. The Livonians would not wait much longer, and neither must I.

The bishop hadn't been in his cathedral, where, of course, he absolutely should have been, especially as the cathedral was supposed to be under siege. I'd seen little sign of that.

But I needed to find the man. I looked into many empty buildings, tore down the shutters of shops and stalls, kicked open flimsy doors, and generally turned the city over. The ruins of the burnt-out church of St Michael's squatted forlornly in the corner between Market Street and Palace Road, a monument to the futility of the feud between the city and the cathedral.

With the sky lightening by the moment, I ran the bishop to earth in what had once been a bakery on Navisar Road. Stone-walled and floored, the bakery was now one of the few undamaged buildings in the city. The bishop sat on a stool in a corner, and next to him stood Master Conesford and Father Wymer, two of the four clergymen who'd first alerted me to the troubles here. There was also a man I didn't recognise, but he was keeping to the shadows. The bakery was chilly inside, its whitewashed walls cold to the touch.

'What's going on here?'

A moment's silence; then Conesford was the first to speak. 'There has been much violence and fighting as you know, and the monks were unable to protect the cathedral from further harm. Indeed, many monks have lost their lives or been grievously wounded. So much damage has been done to the building, we have been forced to leave.' He took a deep breath. 'As you see, the bishop is not a young man, and until recently we were trying to save Master Pockthorpe, curate at the ruined church of St Michael's. Sadly, poor Pockthorpe died two weeks ago, while you were attacking the King's Squad in the market square. We could hear the battle's noise from the infirmary. You lost that battle, and, in our opinion, should never have fought it. Nothing was gained and much was lost. It was most regrettable. Not only that, Lord Rory, but you witnessed Master Pockthorpe's collapse and fall from his horse – yet you did *nothing* to help him.' Another pause. 'On my own,' Conesford said slowly, 'on my own, I took him to the infirmary, but by then he'd gone blind, and a few hours later he became unconscious. He died the next day. It's quite possible that if you'd helped him when he first became ill, he'd still be alive.'

'Highly probable, in fact,' murmured Father Wymer.

'He needed bread,' the bishop said sourly. 'Father Wymer always used to give him bread.'

Pockthorpe, though, had been yet more 'collateral damage'. I doubted he could have been saved.

'I'll ask you all again. What are you doing here?'

'The bishop has a plan.' Conesford's tone was brusque again. 'He wants to share it with you.'

I looked at the bishop. Another old man. Was Mallrovia to be defended by such as these? No wonder the Livonians felt so confident. Despairing, I subsided onto a vacant bench in the opposite corner. The baker's oven was cold, and I guessed no bread had been baked here for weeks; the Hicrowners all looked emaciated. Pockthorpe's death from lack of bread was unsurprising. *This*, then, was the siege. Supplies had been stopped – or perhaps the yeoman farmers were too frightened to approach a city in turmoil. The Livonians wouldn't have to do much; the people here were slowly starving to death.

The bishop began to speak, looking directly at me, and

we all drew closer, as if taking part in a treasonable conspiracy. 'My lord, my name is Roger Scarning, and I am originally from Hambrig, your own demesne. I trained for the priesthood in Hambrig Abbey, and was a contemporary of your chaplain, Laurence. But our paths diverged, and I became a monk, while your father took Laurence on as chaplain to his household. After a while, I was appointed Prior of Hicrown, but the complaints about the cathedral land had started a few years before, and I became embroiled in it from the first. We kept a lid on things for a long time, because King Philip spoke sternly to the people and they did not dare oppose him. I was consecrated bishop six years ago. There were a few flare-ups of trouble from time to time, but nothing we couldn't deal with. Then our King was killed, and it is my view that the Hicrowners have taken advantage of this for their own ends. They fear the taxes King Henry of England will impose on them, and they are determined to get their own way in regard to God's Acre, land the church has owned for centuries. It is despicable that they should exploit the King's death in this way!'

'I agree,' I said. 'But we have less than an hour to put this plan into action, so can you please explain it to me, bishop?'

'Less than an hour?' Father Wymer exclaimed.

'Considerably less,' I confirmed grimly. 'The Livonian army is at the Navisar Gate. They are getting ready to strike at dawn. We don't have the manpower or resources to defend ourselves, so we can all die trying, or we simply surrender to them. Does your plan offer us a third option, bishop?'

'I believe it does,' he said. 'But it's not strictly my plan. We all devised it, and it hinges entirely on one person knowing what to do.'

The man in the shadows stepped forward. He was of

average height. A thin face, darkened by the stubble of many days. Short, dark hair. Strong, capable hands. He made a brief bow in my direction.

'This is Master Billinge,' Scarning said. 'And these are his premises. Master Billinge is a baker, one of two in Hicrown. He knows how to set fires.'

I began to get an inkling of the plan. 'Where would you set the fires, Master Billinge?'

'I believe we need to change the plan, but it will be an improvement, lord.' Master Billinge had a gruff, resonant voice. Better than that, though, he sounded confident. 'We'd thought we were fending off the English, you see,' he continued. 'And the English would enter either through the Hambrig Gate or through the Palace Gate. But if the enemy's coming along Navisar Road—'

'They're here already, and they have less than half a mile to walk before they'll be at the palace. We do not have long. I can't impress this on you enough.'

'Very well, lord. What I was trying to say was, the wind direction is better for a blockage of the way in from Navisar.'

'This is what we plan to do.' Roger Scarning took over, speaking quickly. 'We'll build a blockade of timber across the road. Master Billinge will set a fire. The blockade will create a firewall, which will stop the enemy getting any further—'

'Do it,' I said, preventing further explanation. 'Get to work on this blockade, and start the fire. Master Conesford, fetch as many as you can, both from the cathedral and the city. Everyone must help. After the fire has started, we shall need to feed it. Father Wymer, get help and collect as much timber and firewood as you can find. Master Billinge, you're in charge. Direct the work parties however you like, but get this firewall going and stop the Livonian invasion!'

My ears were on stalks, listening for the thunder of Livonian boots on the cobbled streets of Hicrown. Reinhard might have killed Phoebe by now, which would earn him the wrath of both Allan and Carl. The three of them were vying to be Mallrovia's ruler, a situation which should be advantageous to me, since surely I could play them off against each other. Titus was unhurt, and Leo was recovering in the barn – where Jonny was too, and a great many weapons. My promise to Reinhard counted for nothing now. Jonny would realise this.

Meanwhile, the work parties were busy, and I'd seldom seen activity as frenetic as it was here, outside this bakery in Hicrown. There was just one way to the cathedral, the market or the palace from the Navisar Gate, and that was along Navisar Road. Once on Palace Road, the Livonians could turn right for the palace or left to reach the market square and the cathedral, but I knew they'd want to secure the palace first. The bakery was at the western end of the shops, but the barricade would have to be both wide and deep to do any good. And even as it was still being strengthened, people taking the doors and shutters from their shops and houses to pile onto the bonfire, I heard the sound I'd been dreading.

Scarning heard it too. 'They're on their way.'

Billinge hadn't yet lit the fire. I knew he planned to start it in the middle and fan it out in both directions. His team had pushed handfuls of dried hay from the recent harvest into holes and cracks in the firewall. The hay, dried and warmed in the sun, would take light instantly, and the old timbers from the city would catch quickly. Most of Hicrown's timber buildings had been sacrificed. Thatch from rooftops had been plundered too, and those famous Mallrovian reeds from the shores of the Shamet would burn brightly. But did we have time?

'Lord,' the bishop said urgently, his hand on my arm. 'Master Billinge needs to hear you say the word.'

'And he shall.' My heart was racing and my skin was clammy, but it wasn't the invasion that was making me queasy. It was the thought of fire. Raging and out of control. The Saracens and their lethal Greek Fire outside the fortress city of Mansurah; and the fireball that had ripped through me in Sir Bernard's house in Hambrig Town. The fire in the brothel that had killed Clare of Gailen and so many others; and the fire portrayed on the gypsy card that was supposed to represent me. The card was called 'Strength', but it had revealed only my weaknesses. Finally, the fire in the glass – a jewel of such beauty, many had either died for it or killed for it. One day, I thought, as I waited for Billinge to signal he was ready, one day fire will consume me completely. My body will burn to ash, and there will be nothing left. This will be my fate, one day. Perhaps even today.

So I removed my journal from inside my jersey and gave it to Roger Scarning. 'This is a precious and private document,' I told him. 'Guard it for me. If I survive, I will take it back. If I do not, please give it to my son. Can I trust you to do that, bishop?'

'You can trust me,' Scarning said, his hand resting on my life's work. I swallowed hard. I had never, ever, entrusted my journal to anyone before. But it must survive. *It must.*

Billinge stood on top of the huge pile of wooden trestles, tables, doors, shutters, planks, fencing and God knows what else. He waved his hat in the air. The barricade was a triumph. Billinge had shown good sense in the way he'd directed the building of it, making sure everything was secured in place, while keeping an airflow around and between the structures. Our secondary objective, of course, had been to preserve as much of the city as possible. No point in saving Hicrown from the Livonians if the entire place burnt down around us. Billinge looked as confident as he'd sounded though, and we could only hope and pray it would be enough.

The sounds of marching were louder. The Livonians were closing on us. As they drew level with the courthouse, I saw their leader, Walther von Nortecken, on his proud chestnut charger, Carl von Lutterberg marching at his side. Behind them came column after column of swordsmen, pikemen and archers, all wearing white surcoats with a red cross pattee and a red sword, point down, in pale.

'Master Billinge!' I shouted from the bakery doorway. 'Fire the barricade!'

Billinge jumped down from his tower. I hadn't seen it before, but he was already holding a lit taper. He touched the taper to various points along the bottom of the edifice. Licks of flame grew bigger and stronger, the fire eagerly seeking fuel, finding it, devouring it, moving onwards, upwards and sideways along the firewall. Behind the wall stood citizens with more timber. Billinge would tell them when and where it was needed.

I climbed onto the roof of the bakery. Von Nortecken's horse didn't like the flames. He stamped and threw his head. Von Nortecken tried to get him under control. Carl von Lutterberg's face showed his rage. He raised his fist. There was no way his columns could march through the furnace that spanned the road.

'Wait!' he roared. 'We'll wait it out! You can't keep a fire going for ever!' I didn't hear the words over the roar of the flames, but I saw his lips move and I could guess the rest. The columns of men had halted, unsure of what their officers wanted them to do. But there was a commotion behind as well as in front. I turned, and saw people pouring down the Palace Road towards the market square. I recognised the Wartsbaye soldiers and those Pevarile men who'd survived. I saw Titus, Jonny, Peter and Amie – even Leo. They spotted me standing tall on the bakery roof, and broke into raucous cheering. Brandishing weapons, they charged towards the firewall.

28

MASTER BILLINGE

I stayed on the roof of the bakery until I saw an archer nock an arrow to his bow and point it skywards. Hastily, I clambered down, ignoring the twinges in my wounded left leg. Roger Scarning had found an axe from somewhere; despite his age he had no difficulty lifting it. Wymer was armed with the baker's tongs, though what good he thought they'd do I couldn't imagine. As for Master Billinge himself, he was having the time of his life, scurrying up and down on our side of the firewall, checking the flames were burning strongly, yet under control, directing his teams on where to fill up the gaps, or open them further so as to fan the flames into greater heights.

I was impressed that nothing else was burning. The fire had taken a good hold of the barricade, but the buildings at the side of the road were not aflame. To the north, there was only open scrub, land belonging to the courthouse where the stocks and the gibbet were positioned. I didn't think anyone would care too much if they were fired. But to the south stood the shops and stalls of Hicrown Market. They might have been stripped of their doors and shutters – and, in many cases, their roofs too – but they could be repaired, and would be needed later. Whichever king or queen was on the throne, Hicrown Market would need to function. Billinge had placed wet, green timbers on the south side of his barricade. There was a considerable amount of dirty black smoke, but the market still stood.

The enemy still stood as well. Bewildered and angry, Carl von Lutterberg and Walther von Nortecken were having an argument that blazed almost as fiercely as the fire that had stopped their victory march to the palace. I couldn't hear anything of what they said, but there were a good many furious gestures by both men.

Watching them intently, willing them to retreat, I failed to notice the sudden silence behind me. It was Wymer who plucked at my sleeve and made me turn around. The Hicrowners, who'd charged so jubilantly into action, were huddled now on both sides of the road, as Reinhard, dressed for battle, dragged his still-living hostage towards us. Down the middle of the road he came, swaggering as if he owned it. Phoebe, her gown so ragged now she was barely decent, cringed away, but couldn't escape. Reinhard's grasp was too strong, and his pace was fast. She couldn't keep up. Literally, the poor girl was hauled down the road as if she were a sack of turnips, her shoes rasping over the cobbles, her arms nearly torn from their sockets.

'I am going to show her to her husband!' Reinhard shouted. 'Yes, her husband! My elder brother, Carl! But perhaps he won't want her now – look at her, Rory! Look at your Queen! I've ruined her, haven't I! And I've made her mine! I think Carl might revoke this hasty marriage when he knows what I've done—'

'And what *have* you done, you piece of shit?' I shouted back, moving towards him. I knew, of course. But as I approached, I realised the man was blind drunk. Perhaps it was all just bluster after all.

He pulled out his sword and flourished it at me. 'Don't come any closer, Rory. If you do, you're a dead man.'

'Did you find Lillian?' I called to him. I was sure Reinhard genuinely loved Lillian.

'Lillian is dead,' he spat back at me. 'Dead! With our child inside her.'

'How? How did she die?'

'That moron killed her. If he's with you, bring him out. I'm going to disembowel him while he still lives!'

'He means Sir Allan,' said a clipped voice by my side. Conesford. 'And I suggest we go no closer to this man. He's heartbroken at the loss of his woman. He has imbibed too much of the palace wine. He is no longer in control of himself.'

But I had no choice. Reinhard was striding towards me now, his sword arm outstretched, his other hand wrapped around Phoebe's wrists. She wasn't crying; she was beyond that. Her eyes stared wildly, her face drained of all colour, her expression tormented. There was blood on her shift, which lent credence to Reinhard's boast. As you may know, despair makes some men lustful. The von Lutterberg Swordbrothers, reduced from four to two, had become arch enemies, even to the extent of defiling and killing each other's women.

I held out my hand. 'Stop there, Reinhard. Look at the firewall.'

Scarcely believable, I know – but he seemed not to have noticed the inferno that raged the width of the road, just a hundred yards from where he stood. Instead, with a face black as the night sky, Reinhard swung his sword in a drunken arc, then lunged at the people lining the edges of the road. There were shrieks and gasps at this, but then Reinhard released Phoebe, who flopped onto the road, inert.

Grasping his sword with both hands, the Livonian whirled it around his head, before flinging himself forward and attacking me directly. By now I'd drawn my dagger, but I'd left my sword in the pile of weapons by the barn door. Probably someone in the crowd was holding it now. I ducked out of the way, but Reinhard was in a frenzy. And when one of the Wartsbaye warriors stepped forward, his sword raised to parry Reinhard's, the Livonian simply turned and sliced into the warrior's neck, decapitating him instantly.

Reinhard was uncaring of his own life. Others surged towards him now, and he was soon brought down, sliding in the blood of the dead Wartsbaye soldier, but inflicting wounds on our people to the last. Nobody cared about Reinhard's magical eyes anymore, for those eyes were dimmed and dying. Someone was carrying Phoebe into the bakery. Others were crying out that all the Livonians would go the same way as this one. It wouldn't be so easy, of course. But the fire still raged and Carl's men were on the other side of the barricade. He'd have heard the noise from our side, but he wouldn't know his brother and Lillian were dead. I thought Phoebe's survival also hung by a thread.

According to Conesford, all this was Allan's doing. So where *was* Allan?

I turned to the cantor, who was still standing by my side. His face showed no revulsion at the lynching of Reinhard. 'Go back to the palace,' I said to him. I must have interrupted some deep thinking, because his head jerked round in surprise. 'To the palace,' I repeated impatiently. 'Find Allan and bring him here. And find out what happened to Lillian as well.'

'The fire's nearly out,' someone shouted. Master Billinge. He was back on the ground, and running towards me. The barricade had burnt itself out. Through gaping holes and spaces, we could all see Walther von Nortecken and Carl von Lutterberg. Their men were no longer in neat columns, but had been allowed to fall out and rest at the roadside. I saw someone coming out of the courthouse and wondered what evil he'd been up to inside.

'What next, lord? We've delayed them for hours, but they can climb over the rubble and ash now.'

Jonny's men were in place, while the remnants of the Wartsbaye Guard and Pevarile conscripts, and the King's Squad under Captain Leo, were ranged on the other side of the burnt-out barricade, their weapons raised. It seemed it would be a pitched battle after all. I went into the bakery.

'She will live,' said Margaret Longsword. I was shocked. I hadn't known she was there, in such danger. Phoebe lay on the bakery floor, and a blanket had been found to cover her. Margaret knelt beside her, sponging her face and lips. Phoebe's eyes were closed, but I could see she was breathing regularly. 'The poor girl has had a terrible time, but she'll survive.' Margaret rose to her feet.

'You should have kept well back,' I said, wiping a charcoaled hand over my face. 'Where's Warwick?'

'The Earl of Warwick is helping Sir Jonny outside. He knows what he's doing, Lord Rory. He will make sure these foreigners do not take over your country.'

'He's a foreigner too,' I said bitterly, sitting down suddenly. My legs ached, even the one that had not been injured. 'And so are you, lady. This is Mallrovia, not England, and certainly not Livonia. We don't want to be annexed by anyone.'

'We know that,' she said gently. 'The Earl of Warwick

knows it too. But you cannot be an independent state with no sovereign and no government. Someone needs to take over—'

'You said Phoebe will live. She's our sovereign. Mallrovia will recover.'

'Perhaps.' It was said soothingly, as if to a truculent child. And then, 'What I don't understand, Lord Rory, is why you're here, in this bakery, leaving Sir Jonny and the Earl of Warwick to defend your country. You say you don't need the English, but it seems you do. Sir Jonny himself is English!'

Jonny is indeed English, and that has never been a problem. In fact, for the ten or so years he commanded my garrison in Castle Rory, I never gave any thought to the fact he was born in Salisbury and grew up there. He has never been back. Margaret was staring at me, even as she stroked Phoebe's hair. But I didn't move. Baron Giles was dead; Nightmolben was gone; Sir William was at sea; the King and his two closest heirs were dead; our defence was in the hands of two Englishmen, and on our doorstep was a hostile Livonian army, outnumbering us ten to one. Was Mallrovia even *worth* saving? It seemed to me we were finished.

It was nearly noon, and the sky was still black with smoke. Outside the bakery, Livonians were taking their lives in their hands, trampling into the smouldering firewall in an attempt to clear the rubble; while the King's Squad had advanced right up to it and were discharging volleys of arrows into the enemy's ranks. At the top of a teetering and highly unstable pile of ash and partly burnt timbers, stood Leo, his legs planted wide, his sword slashing downwards and toppling the Livonians. Could this really be Peter's son? Perhaps Peter had been like this once – a thought that would never have occurred to me in Leo's absence. Peter had been in his early thirties when I first met him. Twenty years ago, that was. In all that time, Peter had never mentioned a wife or a son.

Leo turned and yelled to his men, who'd clearly been expecting this. They swarmed over the barricade and hurled themselves into the Livonians. My heart was in my mouth; there were a hundred Livonians and only a couple of dozen of our troops. I saw Wartsbayes, Pevariles, Kettering men and the Squad, fighting shoulder to shoulder, bravely pushing back against the invaders. Titus and Jonny, both big bulls of men, swung their swords as if they were featherweights, knocking down the enemy like ninepins.

But Walther von Nortecken, mounted on his proud black stallion, was incensed at their impudence. He allowed the horse to rear up and bring his front hooves down hard into Leo's people. Cries of terror and pain filled the air. Leo, unhurt, whirled round, a look of horror on his face. As the horse crashed down for a second time, Carl von Lutterberg brought the rest of the Livonians into the attack, their swords scything into the helpless bodies of those the stallion had felled. It was a bloodbath. Titus fell to his knees, hunched over a wound I couldn't see.

Leo yelled some profanity, and I watched him leap towards von Nortecken. Leo's dagger, held low, was thrusting upwards, aiming to stab into the horse's belly. Disable the horse; kill the rider. He needed back-up, but there was nobody helping. I looked for Jonny, and saw he was engaged in hand-to-hand fighting with von Lutterberg.

'Aren't you going to help them?' I hadn't noticed Margaret coming to stand beside me. 'They need you, Rory.'

The first time she hadn't used my title.

'There's nothing I can do. They're all going to die, whether I'm there or not.'

'You know, from everything I've heard about you, I thought you'd be at the front, leading the attack. Not skulking behind our line.'

I looked round. I was the only uninjured warrior left on this side of the barricade. The madness of the battle raged over and beyond the obstruction which had been our firewall, but we would be overcome. We didn't have the numbers, and we didn't have cavalry. Beside me stood a young Englishwoman, and in the bakery lay the injured and terrified girl who was our only hope of survival. Dead and dying littered the road; among them, Reinhard von Lutterberg.

'Wait there,' I shouted to Margaret, running to Reinhard's body. I stripped him of his surcoat with the bright red cross pattee and I pulled it on over my jersey. I crammed his helm on my head, making sure the aventail covered my face, then I grabbed his sword and yanked my dagger from my belt.

'Whatever happens,' I gasped to Margaret, 'don't let Allan take the Mallrovian crown. Please, Margaret. Proclaim Phoebe as Queen of my country. She was crowned, once. It still counts. Phoebe must be Queen, do you hear me?'

Margaret saw I wouldn't go without her assurance. 'I'll do as you ask.'

I ran for the barricade. It was another Forlorn Hope, and I'd as likely be killed by my own side as anyone else. But Leo and his people weren't looking in my direction, and the Livonians, who were, cheered. Reinhard von Lutterberg had finally joined the fray. Jubilantly, they yelled his name, although Carl, Reinhard's brother, took no notice. I marched up to them, knocking a few men of both sides out of my way as I did so. Reaching the duellers, I pushed Jonny's shoulder with the hilt of my sword, sending him lurching to his right.

'Reinhard!' Carl exclaimed, lowering his weapon. 'Thank God! I thought you were dead!'

'I am,' I said. 'And so are you.'

But he wasn't. At the last moment, he ducked. Perhaps my voice had alerted him to the disguise, or something had seemed wrong. As Carl darted away and was lost from sight, I hacked into several astonished Livonians – before they realised I wasn't on their side after all.

Tearing off the Livonian surcoat, I raced towards the barricade, where von Nortecken's horse was under attack from Leo and several Wartsbayes. Titus had recovered, and was back in the fight, stabbing and hacking wherever he could. But it was the Earl of Warwick who triumphed. Swinging a lance into von Nortecken, he dumped him on the ground, where Jonny quickly finished him off, while Leo leapt into the black stallion's saddle and expertly turned the horse round.

Leo deployed the same tactic von Nortecken had used, and the Livonians fell back. They had no commander now, but there were still a lot of them. And there were fewer of us than there had been. Leo began to chase the Livonians down. I thought this rash. They could easily respond in exactly the way we had, and once the horse was disabled, Leo would be a dead man.

There were many brave fighters that day, and Leo was one of the bravest, but the real hero was Master Billinge. One man on a horse, however big and proud, could not contain fifty warriors for long. But Master Billinge could and did. On his own initiative, he opened the gaol. The gaol was attached to the courthouse, just as it is in Hambrig Town. I found out later that he set fire to the door and simply burnt it away. He dowsed the fire quickly, and out traipsed a few wretched prisoners, clawing their way through the blackened hole into a road they may not have seen for years. Most of them simply stood there, dazed and bewildered, but one man, his face hooded, weaved his way into the Livonian ranks.

'Save me,' he croaked, holding out his hands in supplication. 'Save me, I beg you. For the love of God!'

He was a leper.

There was instant pandemonium.

Both sides surged back, as far from the leper as they could get. The Livonians, with no leader to rally round, and no war cry to pull them together, scurried back down the road towards the Navisar Gate, while our own people hurried to put the barricade between them and the leper. Where, only a few moments past, there had been a battlefield full of skirmishing men, now only the dead lay there. The other released prisoners had melted away, as criminals always do, leaving the solitary leper surrounded only by corpses.

'Are you going to find out who he is?' Jonny asked me.

'Eventually. Not sure I want to get too close, though.'

Jonny laughed. 'He's not sick, Rory. They don't put lepers in gaol. They put them in the leper hospital.'

'Take down your hood,' I shouted to the leper.

He did, and it was Master Billinge.

29

THE CROWN OF MALLROVIA

Jonny called to Leo, Titus and all the victorious warriors. Whooping in triumph, they chased the Livonians down the Navisar Road towards the gate. Would someone think of closing the gate? Its hinges would protest; they'd not been asked to do any work for years. Guards should be mounted, too. This gate must never again be an open invitation to the world's criminal gangs or those seeking to control Mallrovia.

Once the gate had been closed and barred, there'd be no need to continue the chase. The routed Livonians could slow down and tramp the thirty miserable miles back to the beach. I thought of Reinhard's proud new ship. The *Wenno*, named after Wenno von Rohrbach, the first *Herrenmeister* of the Swordbrothers. The Livonians would take her out to sea, no doubt with Carl in charge.

I stayed by the barricade, and was still there when everyone returned, although a contingent of Wartsbayes remained at the gate, securing and guarding it. Jonny was walking with Leo, the two of them laughing about something.

I smiled at them. 'Well done, both of you. Leo, your father will be pleased you survived this. And he'll be proud of you, too.'

'Will he?' Leo said, his voice stilted. 'I didn't fight the Livonians for you, Lord Rory. Nor for my father. Not even for Mallrovia, since I'm not Mallrovian. I fought for my general, Sir Allan of Hicrown. And now I need to report back to him.' Leo turned on his heel and strode away towards the palace. Without a word, the King's Squad survivors formed up and marched smartly behind him.

'He doesn't like you,' Jonny observed.

'I have to find a way through this mess.' I gazed at the chaos of the burnt-out firewall, the bodies in the road, the groaning wounded and the debris scattered everywhere. But I didn't just mean the physical mess, and Jonny knew it.

'Because you're in charge now?' Jonny asked. I caught the sarcasm in his tone.

'It's not just Leo who doesn't like me, is it. Why, Jonny? I thought we'd made amends years ago, after Jabir healed you with the *takwin*. I thought we were friends again.'

But Jonny avoided the subject. 'I asked if you're now going to take charge of Mallrovia?'

'Of course not. I'm not of royal blood. Phoebe must be paraded as Queen, and now that the Livonians have been sent packing—'

'Why do you *always* see everything in black and white?' Jonny snarled. 'You always think there's some easy fix! "Phoebe must be paraded as Queen!" Have you forgotten Allan? Leo's supporting him with the Squad. Will you send *them* packing too?'

'Allan can't be King any more than I can,' I retorted. 'Phoebe was legitimately crowned two years ago—'

Once again, though, Jonny interrupted me.

'Legitimately! Who cares about that? Allan fucking won't. I remember him in Captain Kerry's court martial: puffed up, full of his own importance, unable to see what a farce the whole thing was. He sees himself ruling the country, Rory. And you won't be able to stop him, not if he has the Squad. Who do you have? Where's *your* army?'

'Will you help, Jonny?'

'I've been helping. I brought armed men from Kettering. I wasted no time; as soon as Patrick's message arrived, I mobilised a strong force and brought them here.'

'Thank you for that. We couldn't have defended Hicrown without you.'

I pictured Patrick, sitting in his office, composing a carefully worded letter to Jonny, in which neither I nor Hambrig were mentioned. Patrick probably spoke of King Philip and Prince Barney. He may have mentioned the Livonians and their destruction of Nightmolben. Perhaps he'd emphasised Allan's treachery, or the uncertain survival of the kingdom.

The survival of the kingdom was still uncertain, but at least today we had averted disaster. I heard a shout, and looked along the bloodstained, body-strewn road. Conesford was running towards me, screaming something and clutching his arm. 'He tried to kill me!' the wretched cantor shrieked. 'Sir Allan is wild with fury! He has hacked into my arm!'

Conesford fell, some ten yards from Jonny and me. With an oath, I ran to him, knelt down and saw his arm had been viciously slashed.

'You go,' Jonny said. 'If you want Allan, you'll have to get him yourself. I'll stay with this man and get someone to bandage his wound.'

I hesitated. Leo would be with Allan. The Squad would

be behind them both. When I'd sent Conesford, I'd thought Allan would be unsupported and Leo was on our side. Not only that, but I'd had no sleep since Thursday night. I doubted I could take even one of them on in my present state.

But sometimes you have to find reserves you didn't know you had. I seized a discarded sword. Before going to the palace, I entered the bakery again. Phoebe was awake. She looked pale. Margaret had lit two oil lamps and was sitting with the girl. She looked up, but lowered her eyes again almost immediately. Father Wymer and the bishop sat nearby, and, in silence, I reclaimed my journal. In the corner, Master Billinge had lit his oven.

'Baking some bread, Lord Rory,' he said cheerfully. 'I reckon the princess needs feeding up. Sorry, I mean the Queen!'

My mouth watered at the thought. Not only sleep-deprived, I was ravenously hungry as well. Food and sleep would have to wait, but congratulating the baker could not. 'Master Billinge, that leper disguise was a stroke of genius. As was releasing the prisoners from the gaol. What made you think of it?'

'I don't know, lord, not really. It just came to me. I just thought, I know what'll make these buggers retreat – the threat of disease. And no one ever goes near a leper, do they?'

'It was a brilliant idea,' I said. 'Brilliant, because it worked.'

I left him to his bread-making. Margaret didn't glance up as I passed her this time, and Phoebe looked vacantly into the distance, saying nothing. Wymer and Scarning barely glanced at me. As I walked up to the Palace Road, I knew why Margaret hadn't looked at me. I knew why only Billinge had spoken to me. I knew why the bishop had been anxious to rid himself of my journal. Was Mallrovia truly finished? Or was that me?

Entering the palace through its gatehouse, at first you'd have thought nothing untoward had happened. The royal standard flew from the gatehouse tower, and you'd have thought it a perfectly ordinary day, apart from the fact that no guardsman came hurrying up to ask you your business. But as you walked through the gatehouse arch and emerged in the garden, you'd have caught your breath at the sight of the churned mud, the trampled plants and the many bodies still lying where they'd fallen.

Yet it was like looking at a wall painting. Nobody moved, and there was no sound. You could stand and stare, taking in the details, examining each small part of the scene and trying to make sense of it, much as you would with a painting. I moved slowly through the garden, noticing there was an equal number of dead on both sides. The artist would have arranged it so, making it unclear who the victor was. I was also unclear on that score. We'd certainly vanquished the Livonians, and the Wartsbaye sentries would make sure nobody returned through the Navisar Gate. But who, now, was the enemy?

I searched the buildings and found no one. The palace was deserted – by the living, anyway. So where were they all? I went back through the gatehouse arch and stared up and down Palace Road. To my right, empty of traffic, it stretched to the Palace Gate in the city wall. To my left, the road crossed the River Shamet, then wound gently round to the Hambrig Gate in the south-west wall. If you followed it that far, you'd pass Hicrown Cathedral, the precinct of which occupies a vast area between the city walls and the Merchants' Quarter.

I realised, as I walked towards the cathedral, that anyone travelling this road a few hours ago wouldn't have been able to see the firewall, even when standing on the bridge. The bridge over the Shamet gives you extra height, but the large courthouse obstructs any kind of view down the Navisar Road.

They'd surely have *heard* the fighting though. It wasn't worthy of being called a 'battle', but skirmishing can be pretty noisy, and the roar of the flames *must* have been heard. There'd have been smoke drifting through the air as well. So if Allan had sauntered out of the palace and had walked down the road towards the Hambrig Gate, he'd have been aware *something* was going on. Something involving Captain Leo and the King's Squad, most likely. Why didn't he come to find out? And where had he been heading?

He could have gone north and left Hicrown altogether. Beyond the Palace Gate, there are two roads, one leading west to Gailen, the other, north-east towards Nightmolben. I could see no reason for him to go to either place. And then – I paused. What about the Secret Way? The path across the fields to Myrtile? Had Allan hurried towards the city of turquoise and gold, while his men fought for their lives in the streets of his home? Or even just to Halfway House, where he could rest and wait it out. But Allan was no coward, as I'd seen for myself. He'd been well favoured by King Philip, and Philip hadn't lacked courage either. So, I decided, unless there was a very good reason for it, Allan hadn't sneaked away.

Eventually I came to Wharf Street, and beyond it was

the cathedral itself, its blackened roof, damaged stonework and burnt-down outbuildings looking miserable against the afternoon sky. The bishop was right; further damage had been done to the building, and it was now unusable as a place of worship, and even for general habitation. English Henry had visited it, and it had made him angry. The sacrilege of a group of citizens choosing to set light to a church or a cathedral had appalled him.

Two years ago, Lillian warned me about this, saying, *My father will fight till his dying day, we both know that, but in the end, someone will take Mallrovia.* Well, her father's dying day had come sooner than any of us had expected. And, just as she'd predicted, the predators were circling – the Livonians or the English, perhaps the Flemish from across the North Sea, or the Bavarians, now that their duchess had been stolen from them. One way or another, *someone* was getting ready for the kill.

I made my way to the cathedral arch, but it had been blocked. I walked round the outside, going partway up Wharf Street, and there I found a small, unlocked postern. I let myself through into the cloisters. I hadn't been in Hicrown Cathedral many times, and now, after the arson attack, things looked very strange. Even so, it was easy to find the main building and to walk the length of the nave to where, positioned next to and facing the High Altar, Sir Allan of Hicrown sat on the Coronation Chair. On his right stood Roger Scarning, Bishop of Hicrown. He must have gone straight to the cathedral while I was searching the palace. A monk stood next to Scarning, and in his hands was a velvet cushion. Resting on that cushion was a stunningly beautiful band of gold, with eight jewel-encrusted cruciform palisades mounted on it. A sacred diadem. The crown of Mallrovia.

30

PHOEBE SLEPT BLISSFULLY ON

Breaking into a run, I crashed through the roofless choir and presbytery. Several chairs went flying and I ripped my breeches on a protruding nail in one of them. I leapt onto the dais, but fell, my foot kicking against the High Altar, arms stretched high, hands reaching for the monk who held the velvet cushion. I grabbed his black Benedictine habit, and, when he resisted the tug, I pulled harder, using my grip on the rough woollen cloth to haul myself up, push hard, and bring him crashing to the floor.

'This is an outrage!' shrieked Bishop Scarning, whirling round in fury.

Allan was on his feet. 'What the hell do you think you're doing?'

Only then did I notice his polished leather boots, his best braided tunic and the extravagant silken hose. The man was dressed for the occasion.

'Stopping this travesty of a coronation,' I growled at him. And drew my dagger.

There was a gasp from everyone. To draw one's blade in a church? Even a ruined one? It was against every law made by God or man. I didn't care. I pressed the tip of my dagger to Allan's throat. He stumbled backwards, falling onto the throne.

I'd never seen a coronation before, Philip having been crowned King while I was on Crusade, while Phoebe's ceremony had taken place during the darkest days of my Darkness. I had not attended. I'd assumed a king's throne would be solid gold, but this one was made of oak. Its high back was shaped into a pointed spire, and the entire piece was gilded and decorated with ornate carvings. Allan pressed himself into the chair. His eyes stared scornfully into mine.

'Think you can stop this, do you?' His lip curled in hatred. 'You can't. Go back to Hambrig and hide away in your little den, just like you did after that business with the Orsinis. Everyone knows you're a snivelling little coward.'

I wondered how he knew about the Darkness; I've told so few people about it. But my hand stayed steady, and I ignored his taunts. 'What's your claim to kingship, Allan?'

'King Philip's Will. Not that you've read it.'

'Tell me about it, then.'

'Oh, get out of the way!' He tried to push my dagger arm to the side, and I suppose he thought I'd just capitulate. He got a shock, as I whipped the dagger hard across his face and back again, opening up scarlet lines from one cheek to the other, lacerating his forehead and slashing his nose almost in two. Blood streamed out, the wounds instantly opening to create a gruesome parody of a face. Allan screamed, and his hands flew up.

'This is an outrage,' Roger Scarning repeated behind me, the same words in the same tone. Meaningless drivel.

'The outrage, bishop,' I said, not turning round, 'is that you were prepared to place the Mallrovian crown on the head of this imposter. Queen Phoebe will be crowned again in this place, by you, as soon as she is well enough. A reaffirming of her coronation vows.'

'I was told all the royal children had died.'

'Then you should have made sure of your facts. I don't know if Princess Lillian is alive or dead, but in any case, she is now Duchess of Bavaria. Queen Phoebe is very much alive, and is being cared for by the English noblewoman, Margaret Longsword, Countess of Salisbury.'

'You told me she was dead,' Scarning said to Allan, who still hid behind his hands. Blood poured between his fingers. The throne itself was turning red.

We heard the injured man gasp, 'Get me a doctor.' Blood filled his mouth, and his voice was thick. His fingers were turning blue, and it was clear he'd soon lapse into unconsciousness.

Roger Scarning told the monk to fetch the infirmarer, and the man scuttled off, but someone else arrived at the same moment. Scarning drew in his breath at the sound of boots coming down the nave, although I neither looked up nor removed my dagger from Allan's throat. Even through the pain of multiple slashes to his face, I knew he could feel the dagger's point tickling his Adam's apple, and it kept him anchored in his place. But the boots I could hear didn't belong to any monk.

'Thank God,' breathed Roger Scarning, which told me it wasn't good news. The footsteps came nearer and mounted the dais.

'Well, well, well,' said the voice of Captain Leo. 'This is some sort of treachery, I take it? The Lord of Hambrig has assaulted the commander of the King's Squad? I believe I shall have to place you under arrest, Lord Rory.'

'How old are you, Leo?' I asked. The point of my dagger

crept forward slightly, and Allan gave a strangled gasp. Fresh blood oozed from his throat, even as the face wounds were crusting over.

Leo gasped. It was as if he hadn't taken in the full extent of Allan's injuries before. 'My age is irrelevant—'

'Your age is what gives you away. You're about twenty-five years old?'

'I'm twenty-nine.'

'Older than I thought. And your battle experience? Have you any?'

He hesitated. 'Again, irrelevant—'

'Hardly. For a soldier, especially one who's been made Captain of the Guard. That's it, isn't it, Leo? You were never in the Squad, were you? You were in the Palace Guard, but you didn't make the Squad. Perhaps you might have done, if you'd had any experience of combat, but you have none. So King Philip refused you the honour of promoting you to the elite. The King's Squad, which you set your heart on joining when you were just a child.'

'It is scarcely his fault there have been no wars in Mallrovia,' the bishop protested.

'Why have you assaulted Sir Allan?' Leo cried suddenly. 'An unwarranted and unprovoked attack!' There was a break in the man's voice, but he made no attempt to disarm me.

I thought it quite possible Allan would die seated on the Coronation Chair. That, I decided, must not happen. I needed Allan alive. He had questions to answer.

In addition, Phoebe's re-coronation must be swiftly arranged. 'Bishop, you will organise the second coronation of the Queen according to the law. There is a precedent; I believe Henry III of England was crowned twice, the second time being after the Barons' War. The situation here is very similar. Make your preparations. As for you, Leo, I would like to understand why you first sided with the Livonians, and then fought alongside my men. You changed your allegiance in the blink of an eye. Why was that?'

At that moment, though, the infirmarer came hurrying down the nave. He brought a couple of other monks to assist him, and I left them all to it. I hoped the traitor would survive, but it seemed unlikely.

Jonny had organised a tidy-up of the Navisar Road. The bakery was still central to operations, and Jonny had based himself there, with Margaret and her patient at the bread oven end and Jonny at a table in the doorway. People were coming and going, reporting to him and being sent on the next mission. Jonny had written a long list of jobs to be done and various work parties were busy dismantling the firewall, clearing the bodies, stretchering the wounded back to the palace and patching up the courthouse. Sensibly, Jonny had put Master Billinge in charge of the former barricade, and had told his soldiers to pay heed to Billinge's instructions. It was unlike Jonny to involve a civilian in military affairs, but Jonny is older and wiser than when he first made his ruling on that, and Billinge had already shown intelligence and initiative. He was the right man for the job.

I leant against the doorframe. 'Good work, Jonny.'

He looked up, frowning. 'Yes.'

'See the woman who's looking after Phoebe?'

He glanced into the darker end of the bakery. 'What of her? She's doing a good job and keeping out of my way. That's all I need.'

'Do you know who she is?'

'Just get to the point, Rory. I've tons to do here.'

'Margaret Longsword.'

Jonny's reaction was extreme. He half-rose, then sank back onto the bench. His face went a blotchy purple colour, while his knuckles turned white as he gripped the edge of the table. 'Longsword? Longsword?'

'She's the Countess of Salisbury.' I leant forward and spoke slowly. 'Jonny. She knew the blacksmith who worked on the cathedral in Salisbury. She called him "Master Rice".'

There was a long silence, during which I waved away the various people who approached the bakery for further instructions. 'Use your initiative,' I barked at them. I picked up Jonny's list and thrust it at one of the open-mouthed idiots standing in front of me. 'Give this to Master Billinge and tell him he's in charge for a while. Everyone reports to Master Billinge from now on. Have you got that?' The man nodded, grabbed the list and ran.

Jonny's head was in his hands. 'I wasn't expecting to hear that name again. You took me by surprise.'

'Who's Master Rice, Jonny?' I asked. 'Is it your father?'

'His name is Adam Rice, and yes, he's my father.'

'Jonny – Margaret says he died earlier this year. I'm sorry.'

Jonny looked up, his face now as white as his knuckles. 'Died? Are you sure? He's not that old...'

'So your name is Rice?' I'd never before asked Jonny his story, perhaps because I'd spent all my time on Crusade telling him *my* story. Jonny had comforted and soothed me, and told me I'd recover, but it would take time, and meanwhile why not enjoy this great and glorious thing we were doing? Which had turned out to be neither great nor glorious, but we didn't know that then.

'My name is Jonah Rice,' Jonny said quietly. 'I haven't

used the name since '48, when I embarked for Cyprus. Twenty-four years ago. You must have heard Longsword calling me "Jonah", for I never persuaded him to say "Jonny". Not that it matters now. Is Margaret his daughter?'

'Granddaughter. She never knew him. But she told me about your father. He was injured and fell on hard times. Margaret's family looked after him and gave him a house on their estate.'

'We already lived on their estate. The Longswords were always higher than us; we were always in debt to them. My father was an honourable man. Hard working, too. He never put a foot wrong, you know that? He was courteous to the Longswords, always did as he was told, but all along I knew it would end like this. An injury. No money. Beholden to Longsword just to exist, just to eat your next meal...'

'He looked after you, though, didn't he? William Longsword? He brought you on Crusade. Made a man of you.'

Jonny's head jerked up. 'Yes, and I was grateful. Grateful, most of all, that he knighted me, giving me freedom and opportunity. A master blacksmith is far from being a servant – but I never wanted my father's life. Longsword told my father he saw something in me.'

'Will you go to Salisbury?'

'I think I'll have to. There will be things to sort out. He won't have left much, not if he was reduced to living off the Longswords' goodwill. He'll have sold everything first. Even so...'

Yes. Even so. I left Jonny to his thoughts and went to see how things were going. Billinge was doing a good job, much as I expected. We were slowly acquiring a usable road again. The barricade, what was left of it, had gone. All the bodies had been cleared and the wounded moved, but there were bloodstains as far as the eye could see.

In Navisar, Bryce had spoken of a *trail of blood*, the bloodied footprints of girls marched down to the beach against their will. And now we had a trail of blood in Hicrown. I'd fought battles on grass, in woodland and in the desert sands. Afterwards, there was always blood, and a great deal of it, but I'd never fought on a road before. The Hicrown roads are well surfaced and well maintained. This one looked a mess.

'Where have you sent the wounded?' I asked Billinge. 'Is there someone at the palace to take care of them?'

'There wasn't,' he said, 'but there's a wise woman in the city, and she's been sent for. She'll be able to help some of them, at any rate.'

'When you've dealt with everything on Sir Jonny's list, come and find me. I'll be in the palace. And I want two people with a stretcher right now.'

I took them to the bakery and instructed them to bring Phoebe to the palace. Margaret and I walked alongside the stretcher, and I told her Jonny now knew about his father.

'He was the man in the doorway?' she asked. 'That was Adam Rice's son?'

'His real name is Jonah, but I've always known him as Jonny. He's going to have to go to Salisbury and deal with things there.'

'There's not much to deal with,' she said doubtfully. 'Master Rice had very little when he died, and what he had was sold to pay the undertaker. We could find no evidence of any family: no wife, no children, no relatives at all.'

'He was upset when Jonny left. I doubt he'd have mentioned him.'

The palace was no longer a scene from a wall painting. Now swarming with people, all of whom had been detailed by either Jonny or Master Billinge, it was, like the Navisar Road, gradually being brought back to normal. We shepherded the stretcher with its royal patient past all those working in the grounds and entered the palace itself. Margaret had given me some of Billinge's bread – the first food to pass my lips since dinner yesterday. That bread was manna from heaven, and I suddenly felt a lot better. Billinge had proved to be a hero in more ways than one.

The great hall was also a hive of activity; someone had had the same idea as our own physician, Doctor Bethan, who always turns the hall at Castle Rory into a hospital when one is needed. The same had been done here. Trestle tables had been set out in rows, and on them lay the wounded.

Up on the dais, large platters of food had been set out on the high table, and people could help themselves. There were jugs of ale and wine too. The kitchen servants were kept busy bringing out more, and I was satisfied that people would not now go hungry. But it provided further proof of the dissatisfaction in Hicrown; while the citizens went hungry through lack of supplies, the palace had more than enough. I was learning more about King Philip now he was dead than I'd ever known while he lived.

I spotted the wise woman and some of her minions, weaving between the tables. Pots of herbs were placed, seemingly at random, on the floor, but people appeared to know what they were doing, so we moved through the hall to the steep stairs that led to the chambers above.

'You want us to take the stretcher up there?' asked one of the bearers dubiously.

'No. I'll carry her.' I lifted Phoebe off the stretcher and she lay in my arms. She was awake, so I got her to wrap her arms around my neck. She'd feel safer like that. We dismissed the stretcher bearers, telling them to report back to Billinge, and Margaret and I climbed up to the chamber I've always used when staying here. A small sanctuary amid the chaos. I laid Phoebe down carefully and tucked a rug around her. She rolled onto her side and went instantly to sleep. I looked at Margaret, who was sitting on the large chest.

'I think I'd better stay with her,' she said.

'Do you want someone with you?' As I said it, I realised she might think I was offering. 'I mean, I could find one of the women to come up here.'

'Perhaps in a while,' she said. 'Would you sit with me first? I'd like that.'

I thought of Jonny. Allan. Leo. The Wartsbayes and the Pevariles. All people I should find and check up on. Peter as well, of course. And I should hunt for Lillian, or at least for her body. The jobs you need to do after a battle, even such a brief one, seem endless. But I didn't want to do them. I wanted to stay in this quiet, peaceful room with Margaret Longsword, while Phoebe slept until she was recovered enough to be crowned Queen of Mallrovia again.

'Of course I'll stay for a bit,' I said, and at the time that was what I meant. There was room for both of us on the chest, but it was neither deep nor padded, and it soon became uncomfortable. Margaret dropped to the floor, where there was a carpet of sweet-smelling rushes. I joined her there, and so, in the aftermath of saving my country from the Livonians, I took Margaret Longsword in my arms. After she'd undone the lacing on her bodice, I kissed her breasts. And after she'd undone the lacing on my breeches, we made love, and I discovered she was a virgin.

'But you're married,' I exclaimed.

'We were married as children,' she murmured. 'And neither of us had any say in the matter. If Henry had been given the choice, he wouldn't have chosen me at all. He isn't interested in me, Rory.'

'All the same,' I said, for it was odd not to consummate a marriage.

'I don't think you understand. This isn't about which woman Henry might have chosen. Henry has no interest in women at all.'

'You're living dangerously,' I told her, but it was too late to change that. 'When Henry does want you – and he will, for it's his duty to provide an heir to the Lincoln estate – he'll know you've been unfaithful.'

'I don't care,' said Margaret Longsword. And nor, at that moment, did I.

We lay in each other's arms for an hour, and then we made love again. Soon after that, the need for sleep overcame me. Whatever else was going on outside, Margaret and I were oblivious to it, while Phoebe slept blissfully on.

31

TELL ME YOUR NAME!

In my journal I've written down the five potential crises for my country, four of which are existential, but all of which constitute considerable jeopardy.

The first is the expulsion of Mallrovia from the Hanseatic League. We would survive this, although it would be a massive blow to trade and to our financial position. It would also undermine our status in Europe, but I'm sure we can find ways to overcome these problems. It was King Philip who negotiated Hambrig's entry to the League; the force of his personality convinced the other city states to accept us. With Philip gone, and no one of the same standing to replace him, our membership may well be revoked.

The second source of jeopardy is invasion and conquest by the Livonian Order. I believe we have seen off this threat, and three of the von Lutterbergs are now dead. But there are many more Livonians overseas, and the Swordbrothers, as they used to be known, are determined to regain their independence from the Teutonic Knights. Will they have given up on using Mallrovia as a base for their challenge? I'm not sure, but I don't think we can assume anything. Walther von Nortecken is dead, but Carl von Lutterberg lives, and I wonder what his plan is now.

The third potential jeopardy comes from England, and the fourth is from Bavaria. English Henry has already shown his hand, and he left the Earls of Surrey and Warwick to keep an eye on us. Surrey departed early on, and Margaret told me he's always been fickle in his allegiance, something which Amie also discovered. My hope is that King Henry has lost interest. Rumour has it that he's now very unwell and has little time left. His son, the Lord Edward, is away crusading in the Holy Land, so for now, at least, I believe we are safe from the English.

The Bavarians, though, are another matter. Reinhard kidnapped their duchess, and no one has seen her for days. Reinhard was distraught because Allan told him he'd killed Lillian. If she *is* dead, we are in serious trouble. If alive, perhaps even more so, for she's pregnant by Reinhard. Bavaria can mobilise the entire Holy Roman Empire, should Louis become irate enough for that. I do have one card to play, though. Kit and his daughter, Aggie, are in the Bavarian court, and this may well be why we've heard nothing from Louis as yet. Kit is a diplomat. And Aggie, so Duke Louis believes, is the cure for every ill. So we may be saved from extinction by my curly-headed minstrel and his nine-year-old daughter.

Finally, we are in the critical situation of having no sovereign. As you will know, as soon as one monarch dies, another takes over. There is no intervening time in which the state is without a ruling king or queen. When Philip and Barney both fell over the ruined cliff at Nightmolben,

Phoebe instantly became Queen of Mallrovia. In my view that is still the case. Phoebe is our Queen. I don't like the idea because I believe Phoebe to be a spoilt and vacuous child, but at least she is one of Philip's children and his legitimate heir. Without Phoebe, we are a collapsed state with no future. But to assert her authority as monarch, Phoebe needs to be re-crowned – properly, legally, and in the eyes of God – and if someone else is crowned in her stead, where does that leave us? I believe this last source of jeopardy to be the most dangerous, because it threatens us now, not in the future, and it threatens us from within.

As I write down my thoughts on the dangers facing Mallrovia, I begin to see a way through. Allan must be confronted. Leo must be dealt with, little upstart that he is, and Roger Scarning, Bishop of Hicrown, must once more place the shimmering, spangled crown of Mallrovia on Phoebe's doltish head.

It was Titus who found Lillian. Not killed, as we'd been told, but tied up and abandoned in one of the warehouses by the Navisar Gate, but not the one Carl had been hiding out in. I'd suspected as much, and the Wartsbayes, left on duty at the gate, had made their investigations. Titus and I seem to find it hard to get along, but I acknowledge he's a thorough and effective garrison commander.

Like my brother two years ago, Titus also found evidence of other people having been imprisoned there. People had scratched their names on the walls, and every name was female. Small items lay abandoned in the dust and the dirt, items which Titus picked up and brought back to the palace.

This morning, Jonny laid the sorry little collection out on the high table, and I looked down on a bedraggled barbette, the sort young girls wear around their heads, two tawdry rings made of cheap metal, a few sharpened pieces of bone, probably used in the girls' hair, and some tatty ribbons.

'Girls,' Jonny said softly. 'Young girls, and from poor or unfree families I should think.'

I fingered the ribbons, wondering if they'd been left on the warehouse floor on purpose. As a clue, perhaps, in case someone came looking for the girl who'd worn them? Or had their captors torn all the adornments off the girls' hair and bodies: rings, ribbons, everything? Dropped them into the dirt and trampled on them.

Jonny thought either or both were possible. Lillian has been taken to a room at the top of the palace building, and is being examined by the wise woman Billinge had found, but I've sent for Doctor Bethan from Hambrig. She will soon take charge of our sick and our wounded.

'Do you think the Livonians are stealing our women?' Jonny asked.

I made no mention of it, but I noticed his use of 'our'.

'It looks like it. Stealing our wool, stealing our women... fucking Swordbrothers.'

'Well, they're dead now,' Jonny said. 'Reinhard and the other two, whoever they were.'

'Carl's alive,' I said. 'And the Swordbrothers are a military order, Jonny. They're no longer allowed to use that name, and they have to obey the Teutonic Knights, but they want their autonomy back. That's what this was all about.

They need money. A war chest. Then they can claim independence from Anno von Sangershausen.'

Jonny looked blank.

'He's the *Hochmeister* of the Teutonic Knights. I met him in Bremen. Huge man, built like a bear. Very much in control.'

'So this was to create enough wealth for their war chest? Mallrovian girls? Sold into slavery and prostitution, I suppose. Do you think they were going to sell Lillian too?'

'I'm sure of it. They had their ship ready at Navisar, and think how much money a genuine Mallrovian princess would fetch! I think Allan wanted to sell Phoebe too—'

'You're saying Sir Allan's involved in this? He's Mallrovian! Not only that, he fought against the Livonians in the palace grounds. Or have you forgotten that?'

'It was Allan who ensured the worsted cloth was brought to Hicrown and stored in the warehouses by the gate. And he made sure the gate was kept unlocked and unguarded and that hardly anyone ever used it. Allan was the Livonians' contact here in Hicrown, and his position as commander of the King's Squad gave him the licence to do anything he wanted. But it was Reinhard von Lutterberg who informed on him. There's no love lost between Allan and the Livonians. So yes, he fought against the Livonians when they ambushed us. He wasn't prepared for that, any more than I was. Allan was nearly crowned King, Jonny. I was only just in time to stop that happening. All three of them, Allan, Carl and Reinhard, were apparently operating as a team, but in reality each had his own agenda.'

'And King Philip was completely unaware of the girls being taken out of the country?'

'I'm beginning to realise exactly how much King Philip didn't know,' I said. 'I always thought... well, it doesn't matter now. What I'm wondering is how these girls simply disappeared and no one realised. What about their families? How could girls just vanish?' Still in my mind was the theory that Patrick was behind it all.

Girls from Myrtile. Worsted from Myrtile. A rich and prosperous city, whose owner had so much money to throw around, his people didn't even need to work for a living. This is not normal. It must mean something. Almost certainly, it means crime. It was as hard to accept Patrick's deceit, greed and wickedness as it was to acknowledge that despite Jonny's return to Mallrovia, he was still hostile to me. Ten years ago, these two had been my most trusted companions. How had it all gone wrong?

'Where's Gael's body?' Amie wanted to know. I had no idea what had been done with those who'd fallen in the first attack. It seemed so long ago, and so much had happened since then. Bryce probably knew, but Bryce was back in Hambrig. I sent him with messages a week ago, far too soon for him to have returned. I was desperate for both Lillian and Phoebe to survive, and I was putting my faith in Bethan to make that happen. The sooner she got here, the better.

Margaret Longsword had come into the great hall to find me. Hearing the question, her eyes widened. 'Is it your husband you seek?' Margaret asked Amie.

Amie explained how Gael had died; that he'd been her husband and the father of her son.

'We shall find him,' Margaret said with certainty, and Amie smiled. And from that moment, Amie followed Margaret everywhere. The taller of the two, and some five years younger, Margaret seemed not to mind – and what's more, she *did* find Gael. She spoke to the Earl of Warwick, who knew where the bodies had been taken.

Allan was not in the great hall with the other wounded. I didn't want him spreading sedition among the common people, so, on my instructions, he'd been removed from the ruined cathedral infirmary to a small, white-walled room which was part of the King's solar, his private suite of rooms. When I went up there, I found the wise woman with him. She was burning some acrid smelling herb in a small iron pot and wafting the fumes over Allan, who had a cloth tied round his head, covering his face. When he heard my voice, his hands clenched on the arms of his chair.

'What do you want?' he growled, and the cloth sucked in and out of his mouth as he spoke.

'To talk to you.'

'You wish me to leave, sir?' the wise woman asked, swirling more smoky fumes through the air. I began to cough. The woman came close to me. She had green eyes. I backed away, but she followed.

'You're in trouble, sir,' she said. Her teeth were crooked and yellow, but at least she had some. Most women her age are totally toothless.

I attempted to ignore her, but my coughing was getting worse. 'Take that pot away! Stop burning whatever's in it,' I gasped, almost choking now. I was doubled over, and a pain had started in my chest. 'Get away from me, you evil hag!'

I knew she'd retreated because the horrible caustic smell became weaker. Gradually, the pain in my chest subsided too. I tried straightening up, my hands pushing on my knees, but my head protested that it wanted me to lie down. At long last, I was standing again. I hadn't known my eyes were closed, but now I opened them. And got a terrible shock.

'Where is he?' I jerked out. 'Where's Allan?'

'He's exactly where you left him, sir.'

'What the hell? I didn't leave him—'

'You did, sir. You backed through the door and into a different room, which is where we are now.'

I looked at the door. It was closed. Between me and it was the wise woman, her little iron cauldron in one hand and a smouldering taper in the other. She made to touch the taper to the inside of the bowl, and I put my hands out.

'No! Don't light the stuff again.'

'It is effective, though, sir.'

'Yes, effective at putting me out of action. What is it?'

'It is human hair, sir.'

I thought I was going to be sick. The bile rose into my throat and I had to swallow hard for several moments, while odious questions tumbled through my mind. Where had she acquired the hair? Was she a witch? What spell had she been casting, first on Allan and now on me? Would I ever escape from this room alive? Would she, as many witches did, turn the hair into poisonous snakes?

I managed to chase the bile back down my throat and calm my tumultuous insides. I looked over at the woman. She was laughing. I'd thought her a witch, so her laugh should have been an evil cackle. But it wasn't. Her laugh was genuine, bubbly and infectious. And weirdly familiar. She set the small iron pot down on the floor, held out her hands to show a lack of guile, and walked towards me. I made myself stand my ground, but it wasn't easy.

'You have nothing to fear from me, sir,' she said softly. 'Not from me. But you should, nonetheless, be fearful.'

'Are you a witch?' I whispered.

'No. I am a wise woman, which is very different. How are women like me wise, you may be wondering? We are wise in the ways of the earth, the ways of the people who inhabit it, the trees and plants that flourish in it and the stars that smile down upon it. We are wise, in other words, in wisdom itself.'

'Why are you burning hair? And – whose is it?'

'Burning the hair allows healing to take place, sir. The man whom you injured needed to unblock his airways. The smell of the burning has done so. And now he sleeps.'

'How do you know?'

'That he sleeps? Because that is the next stage of the healing. Let us find out if I am right.'

She stepped back to the door and opened it a chink. I peered through and saw Allan slumped in his chair, his head back, snoring gently.

I turned to the woman in astonishment. 'What's your name?'

'Do you really need to know it? Isn't it enough that I'm the "wise woman"? It's what everyone calls me.'

'I want to know your name. I still believe you to be a witch. Or a sorceress. This is some sort of magic...' Even as I said the words, I remembered Kit telling me that all magic is an illusion. I'd seen it for myself, too. There is, we'd agreed, no such thing as magic. So what was I saying now? How did I reconcile that long-ago conversation with what I'd just seen?

'You're thinking, perhaps, about some other magic?' the woman said. Her iron pot still rested on the floor. 'Some other magic that turned out to be a deception?'

'How did you know?'

'Your face reveals your thoughts, sir.'

'Yes, I've been told that before. Now tell me your name.'

'You will wish you hadn't asked.'

The riddles and the stupid secrecy made me lose my temper. I seized her by her shoulders. 'For fuck's sake, woman! Tell me your name!'

32

YOU HAVE LEFT US WITH NO DEFENCES

Something in her expression made me not only let go of her, but apologise for my temper. Silently, she took my hand. Leading me out of the room and through the white-walled chamber where Allan remained sleeping awkwardly in his chair, the linen cloth still covering his face, we entered the solar. The King's own quarters. The solar was empty, and the wise woman pointed to the bed.

'You can sit there.'

'I do not need to sit.'

'Please sit, sir. You will find you do need to, when I reveal my name.'

Slowly, I lowered myself onto the bed and gazed at the woman whose name would, apparently, shock me.

'My name is Karima.'

When the room had stopped spinning, and my heart had settled to a more normal rhythm, I asked her to repeat the word.

'Karima. I am Karima. And this is how I know you.'

It had to be a trick. This was not the Karima I'd known

in Mansurah. This was no Egyptian girl, younger than I by five years. The woman standing in front of me was Mallrovian through and through. And I put her in her late fifties. The green eyes were not the beautiful dark, flame-flecked orbs of my Karima.

But she'd made the claim, so I would test it. 'Where do you know me from? When did we first meet?'

'Ah, I see you do not believe me. But I am not a felon, to be charged, interrogated, convicted and sentenced. So I will not, at this stage, answer your questions. But I will tell you two things, sir. The first is the form of address I use for you. I well know you are a lord, and I should use your title. Yet you will recall that I called you only "sir" when we first met. I never asked your name. You told me little about yourself. You were "sir" and I was "Karima", and we needed nothing else.'

I shivered, because everything she'd said was true. I had not revealed my identity to Karima in the desert. I could not risk betraying Jonny, who was injured and unable to move or defend himself, down in the cellar of *our house*. He must not be discovered. I was careful when I left the building. Careful when I entered it. Making sure no one saw me, and bringing vital provisions so that Jonny could build up his strength.

I looked at the wise woman. 'What's the other thing you're going to tell me?'

'When you and your friend met Sultan Baibars, he could have killed you but he chose not to. And one day, I will tell you why.'

Baibars hadn't been sultan then, not in 1250. He'd commanded the Mamluk forces, a big man with a reputation for bold leadership, enormous courage and murderous cruelty. There had been seven Mamluk warriors, and the Panther, as he was known, stood at their head. Having wandered away from our camp, only Jonny and I faced them. Two of us to their seven. I'd drawn my sword, prepared to die that day. Jonny had drawn his too, although he hadn't wanted to, but Baibars had laughed and led his men away. Jonny and I weren't important. We weren't worth the bother. I'd been furious, Jonny had been philosophical, and, still in sight of the contemptuous Mamluks, we'd had our first bitter argument.

The wise woman was watching me, and no doubt the whole incident had played itself out across my features. 'So. Let us go down to the great hall. I think you would like me to examine Princess Lillian and Queen Phoebe.'

I didn't tell her I'd sent for Bethan. But it would do no harm for this strange woman to look at Lillian and Phoebe. 'Only no burning of hair,' I warned.

She smiled. Was there something in that smile that jogged a memory? Confused, I shoved it away.

At dinner time, I told Jonny about the near-coronation of Allan of Hicrown, and how I'd slashed his face with my dagger. The rest of the wounded had been taken to the big barn where Reinhard had held us all hostage, and as soon as the green-eyed woman left to go there, I despatched two of Jonny's people to secure Allan and bring him down from the white-walled room.

Jonny's men had ripped the cloth from Allan's face. In doing so, they'd torn away the delicate scar tissue that had begun to form. His face was a mess, the wounds bleeding again, ugly weals running from cheek to cheek across the bridge of his nose, while his forehead and hairline were criss-crossed with knife gashes.

One eye was partly closed, although I didn't think my dagger tip had passed that close to his eyes. The other eye stared angrily around, but he was twitching and jerking, and I guessed he was in a lot of pain. The guards had tied his hands, as they'd been ordered to do, and they'd hobbled his knees together for good measure.

They pushed Allan roughly towards the dais, and he stood before it, the guards holding him up. The damaged eye now shut completely, and I saw close-to the heavy bruising on its lid, and the ghastly contusions all over his face and neck. My dagger had done most of the damage, but the bruising must have occurred when he fell. It was clear he wouldn't be able to stand on his own. I had a stool brought for him and he collapsed onto it, his head lolling.

Jonny's guards went to stand near the wall, on hand if we needed them. Now that Allan was seated, it would have been ridiculous to talk to him from the dais, so Jonny and I jumped down and sat on the platform facing our prisoner.

'Can you speak?' Jonny asked.

The prisoner raised his head and nodded.

'What is your claim to the crown?'

Jonny and I had not agreed that he would interrogate Allan. But I sat by Jonny's side and waited. If Jonny could get the information we needed, I'd be happy. Not so much if he messed up.

Allan's tone was bitter, although his words were indistinct. One of my gashes had slashed his lips. 'The King's letter. He wrote a letter. If he dies without an heir, I'm in charge. You have no right to treat me like this, and as for him attacking me with his dagger...' He jerked his head towards me. 'When I'm king, I'll have you executed for treason, Rory.'

'Let's see this letter,' Jonny said. Good. The questioning was going as I wanted it to.

'The bishop has it. His Majesty gave it to him.'

'You said the letter would be used if his Majesty died without an heir,' I said. 'But he did not die without an heir, Allan. King Philip's two daughters are alive, and Queen Phoebe, when she's recovered, will be on the throne.'

I thought I saw relief flood his ruined face. 'Phoebe's alive? Reinhard didn't kill her?'

'They are both alive,' I confirmed. 'Although you tried to deport Princess Lillian, didn't you. She was found by the Navisar Gate, frightened and alone. I think if anyone's guilty of treason, it's you.'

'Reinhard,' he began.

'Reinhard's dead. And Carl has gone. Reinhard tried to kill Phoebe, but she survived and survives still. Phoebe will shortly be re-crowned Queen of Mallrovia.'

Jonny said. 'We must get hold of that letter. If it even exists.'

'The letter's irrelevant,' I said dismissively. 'It's probably a forgery anyway, but it no longer matters. Phoebe is our Queen! She has been Queen since the moment the King died.'

Allan was drooping. His hands were still tied behind him, and there was no back to the stool he was sitting on. As he slumped over, he lost his balance, couldn't use his hands to save himself, and crumpled onto the floor.

'He needs water,' Jonny exclaimed, and his soldier ran off towards the kitchen. He returned with a pan of water drawn from the well.

'Help him drink,' Jonny ordered.

I couldn't stay to watch Allan's pathetic attempts to lap water out of a bowl like a kitten. His wounds still looked livid, and his clothes were dirty and smelt rank. Nobody could look less like a king.

I stood up, needing fresh air and a chance to speak to Margaret. It was hard to believe that my dreams had become a reality last night. Even thinking about it made me want her again, the sort of wanting I hadn't felt since – since Karima, I realised in shock. Making love to Rosa wasn't like this; it was freighted with Rosa's desire for babies, her obsession with pregnancy, her monthly cycle and *The Empress*. Sex with Rosa required my unquestioning obedience, and was carried out to order, strictly according to the calendar. Afterwards, my performance would be assessed and frequently condemned. Rosa never cared what I thought about either the act or the judgement. Between Karima and Rosa there had of course been others. Those women had been fun while I'd known them – an intense but short-lived enjoyment which I could barely remember – and none of their names came to mind.

But Jonny called me back. 'You can't go now, Rory.'

'Why not? I'm going to check on Phoebe.' Much more noble than my real reason. And after all, Margaret would be with Phoebe. It made sense.

'Phoebe will be fine. She's being cared for by the wise woman.'

'There is no wise woman,' Allan spluttered from the water bowl. 'She tried to make me sick with her hair-burning. Where did you get her from? We have no wise woman in Hicrown.'

'I thought she was trying to help you,' I said, watching Jonny's soldier smear water over Allan's wounds. They were still oozing. Horrible, stinking, yellow gunk dripped onto his neck and tunic. How could that soldier be so close? They must be made of stern stuff in Kettering.

'She said she would help me,' Allan wheezed. 'But she made me sick. And now I've just pissed myself.'

'That's obvious from the smell,' I told him. And then, despite Jonny's protestations, I left the hall.

The smell was just as bad in the barn. Patients lay in the straw, mostly unattended, some of them vomiting, all of them in need of attention. There weren't enough nurses.

I ran through the garden to the two bleak accommodation blocks beyond the palace building. Shouting into each doorway I bellowed for soldiers. Wartsbayes, Pevariles, Ketterings, King's Squaddies, it didn't matter. After several moments, a smattering of men and women presented themselves.

'Go to the barn by the stables. Report to the green-eyed wise woman. Tell her you'll nurse the wounded and follow her instructions.'

After an initial look of horror, they scrambled to obey.

I'm in my chamber with my journal, trying to catch up with everything that's happened. It's three days since I met the wise woman, and Doctor Bethan has just arrived from Hambrig. Most of the injured have either died or are well on their way to recovery now, so I'm not sure I needed to send for Bethan after all.

Worryingly, Lillian is still in shock. She won't speak to anyone. Even the wise woman can't get her to talk. I've been avoiding the wise woman, not wanting to find out who she really is. I know she isn't Karima, but I'm wary of her for even knowing the name. Her uncanny knowledge of the time Jonny and I met Baibars face to face scares me.

I can't speak about it to Jonny, because I'd have to mention Karima, and I can't do that. In Mansurah, he repeatedly asked where I was going when I left *our house*. Of course, I told him I was bringing food, and that was true, but he guessed there was more to it than that. And suddenly, I'm wondering if, somehow, all these years later, *this* is the cause of our feud. I don't see how it can be, though. Jonny was my garrison commander for ten years before we fell out. During those ten years, there was no inkling of any quarrel between us.

I sit here thinking for a while. About Baibars. About Jonny and me. About Margaret. About the King, and his mysterious fall down the cliff. And, finally and reluctantly, about Karima. I don't want to remember the time I spent with her, but as I relive the exotic desert encounters, I hear myself groan. My journal slides off my lap, and the charcoal stick rolls onto the floor. My hands feel clammy. My heart is beating much faster than it should. My hair sticks to my scalp. My thoughts fragment and scatter. I'm in the desert, and Karima writhes beneath me.

There was a knock on the door, and Bethan entered. 'What on earth is wrong?' she cried.

'Nothing,' I said, hastily retrieving my possessions and

running a hand over my face. 'Nothing's wrong, Doctor Bethan. I was writing in my journal, that's all.'

'So I see,' she said drily. 'It must be a racy tale you're telling in that private diary of yours. I came to tell you one of my own, actually. Queen Phoebe claims she has been sexually abused. Do you know anything about that?'

I stood up. I knew exactly what she was asking me. What she was thinking. 'It was a Livonian Swordbrother. Reinhard von Lutterberg. He raped her and half killed her.'

'That's what she told me,' Bethan said brusquely. 'She mentioned this Reinhard, and told me he married her sister. She says he dragged her down the street. But I've examined her, and she has not been penetrated. The Queen is a virgin. Why would she lie?'

I shrugged. 'You'll have to talk to her again. I don't know what happened before Reinhard tried to use her to protect himself. And he's dead now.'

'Is it true this Reinhard married Princess Lillian? I'd thought her already the wife of the Duke of Bavaria.'

'And the mother of his son. It's a bit of a mess, Bethan. Have you examined Lillian? How is she?'

'Pregnant. By this man Reinhard von Lutterberg, I'm told.'

'She loved him.' Then I thought of something strange: I hadn't seen Bryce at all. 'Didn't Bryce return here with you?'

'He did not. Someone spotted a ship sailing up the River Hurogol towards Hambrig Wharf, and Rachel asked Bryce to stay. Just in case.'

'How are things at home?' I was desperate to know. Desperate to get back, too.

'We must hope this ship does not mean trouble, Rory. You have left us with no defences.'

33

THE ASSASSINATION OF MY QUEEN

Bethan's words, *you have left us with no defences*, rang through my head for hours after she left the chamber. I'd watched her go, thinking she looked considerably older than when I last saw her. She shouldn't look old, not yet.

Unrolling the parchment, I looked at the last entry I'd made in my journal. It was about Jonny and his refusal to patch up our quarrel, which seemed to have begun eight years ago, when I was falsely accused of murder. I'd been acquitted of the crime, and the real culprit had been found. At that point, Jonny and I should have clasped each other's hands and smiled in sheer relief that we could reclaim our friendship. It had never been reclaimed.

In my journal, I'd written questions, questions to which I had no answers. Did the quarrel *actually* start, not eight years ago, but twenty? And was it anything to do with Karima? What if I'd been honest with Jonny in Mansurah, and told him what I was doing? He was always so upright, so passionate about 'the Cause', as he called it. Jonny had joined the Crusade because he'd wanted to. He'd been ardent about fighting for Christ. I had gone because my father had hastily packed me off to war so as to avoid a scandal at home. I hadn't been nearly so zealous, and Jonny knew it. He would not have approved of Karima. But nor did he like dishonesty.

A couple of hours ago, I summoned the bishop to the palace. Two things I wanted from him: first, the King's letter, if there even was one; and second, a coronation.

'My lord,' the bishop panted, having obviously run the mile or so up Palace Road. 'I was told I was needed urgently! Has someone died?'

'Not yet, bishop. Sir Allan says you have a letter written by the King, in which he states what should happen if he dies with no heirs. However, there is, as you know, a constitution in this country, so if there were no direct line of succession, both Baron Giles and I, as tenants-in-chief to the monarch, would make a decision.'

'Baron Giles is not here, my lord,' said Roger Scarning. He'd recovered his composure. Sardonically, I thought it fairly clear the bishop had been hoping someone *had* died. And that the someone was me.

'He is not,' I agreed. 'So I'd be obliged if you'd hand over the letter.'

'It names Sir Allan as his heir, Lord Rory. You don't have to see the letter itself, you have my word on the matter.'

'Nonetheless, I will see it. Give it to me, if you please.' I held out my hand. I knew he'd have the damned thing with him; it wasn't the sort of thing you'd leave lying around.

Scarning was frowning. He might be an old man, but he

was also a hard one. He'd persisted with the no-taxes-for-my-tenants policy even when the citizens made their displeasure very clear, and discontent was brewing up in the city. A more sensible – and more sensitive – man would have negotiated some sort of deal. Scarning would not have entertained that idea though. He was a man who had to have his own way. But I could be as hard as he was, and he'd seen me lose my temper and slash a man's face to ribbons with my dagger. I saw him shoot a glance at that same dagger. Then he reached into his black Benedictine robe and pulled out a document. The seal had been broken.

'Who broke the seal?' I asked. Breaking the royal seal was a serious matter.

'I did, of course. If you look, you'll see the letter is addressed to me.'

It was. Together with an instruction that it should be opened only after the King's death. I unrolled the parchment, and saw that the writing was in Philip's hand.

To the Bishop of Hicrown.

This letter is to confirm that Prince Barney succeeds to the throne after I am dead. If Barney dies before me, then Princess Lillian is next in line, and if that inheritance fails, then Princess Phoebe becomes Queen of Mallrovia.

Should I die with no heirs, then the country will be jointly governed by my two tenants-in-chief, until a legitimate member of my family can be tracked down. My two tenants will decide between claimants to the throne, if there be more than one. If no suitable claimant can be found, then my tenants-in-chief will choose a suitable high-ranking member of the nobility to wear the Mallrovian crown, and his or her descendants will form the next line of succession. These instructions make specific, and in no way contradict, the guidelines stated in the Carta Juris Mallrovica, which was drawn up by King George I of Mallrovia and his tenants-in-chief in the Year of our Lord 1101.

'I see no mention of Sir Allan in this letter,' I said, handing the scroll back to Scarning. 'He's neither a descendant of the King, nor one of his tenants-in-chief. What claim does he have?'

'I believe Queen Phoebe still lives,' Scarning said. 'When Sir Allan is married to the girl, he will have an unshakeable claim. Even you cannot disagree with that.'

'Has she agreed to marry him?'

'You know very well that she has not. But she will.'

'Why?'

He didn't answer, but his disdainful smile told me he knew that I knew Phoebe would most certainly agree. Phoebe, with her head full of fluff, would think it wonderful that her father's highly-thought-of general wanted to wed her. To be married to the commander of the King's Squad! She would see it as a high honour, not a power grab on Allan's part.

'And if you are thinking you might warn her off such a match,' the bishop said softly, 'be aware that it is now too late. You may have ruined Allan's looks, but you cannot touch his status. He is far wealthier than you, and he can buy his way into or out of any situation. He will have Phoebe, be in no doubt. Sir Allan will rule Mallrovia, and his children, assuming the little featherhead isn't barren, will succeed after him. There's nothing you can do about it, my lord, so I advise you to accept it graciously. If you do, there's at least a passable chance Allan may keep you as tenant-in-chief. Incidentally, although you were not intending to tell me, I do know that Baron Giles is dead. And now I shall return to my lodgings. There will, of course, be no need to pay fines to English Henry. Sir Allan's money will more than cover the cost of repairs to the cathedral.'

He pushed past me and left the hall. Allan was now permanently under guard, so there was no way he was going to ask Phoebe to marry him. Phoebe herself was doing well, and by now I'd visited her in her chamber and spoken to her most days. I'd made it clear to her she was still Queen, but I wasn't sure she understood what that entailed. She never had understood. It was now imperative that she did.

'There are responsibilities,' I'd tried to explain. 'You'll have advisors, of course, but—'

'Do you think my hair looks better twisted over my head or behind it?' she'd asked, interrupting me and making it clear she'd not been listening anyway.

I became impatient and irritated by these useless exchanges, and had asked Jonny to try to get through to her.

'Perhaps she *ought* to marry that oaf,' Jonny had said after one such fruitless meeting. 'At least Allan would actually think about the kingdom, and not just the latest fashion, hairstyle or gilded carriage.'

'Allan will never be King of Mallrovia,' I said fiercely, although I understood Jonny's point. 'Is there anyone else we can marry her off to?'

He didn't answer. I stared at him, and there, standing before me, was the Jonny who'd once presented himself to King Philip, expecting to be told he was now Lord of Nightmolben. The King, though, had not appointed Jonny to that position, and I was not about to sanction his marrying Phoebe. 'No, Jonny,' I said quietly. 'I'm sorry.'

He turned on his heel and walked away. Exactly as he'd done that day in Castle Rory. Later, though, he'd admitted that the King had chosen well in appointing Kerry as Lady of Nightmolben. I just needed to do something similar now, but I had no idea who would make a good husband for Phoebe and a good King of Mallrovia. I could think of nobody, and the more I thought about it, the worse it seemed. I needed to discuss it with someone, and there was one obvious person for that.

Up in Lillian's room the next morning, Margaret was holding the girl's hand, while Lillian stared wide-eyed at the rafters, her face registering nothing. I asked Margaret if she could spare me a few moments, and she rose at once. Amie, seated by her side, also got to her feet.

'No, Amie,' I said impatiently. 'I need to see the Countess of Salisbury in private. You can take over here. Look after Princess Lillian.'

'Princess Lillian won't even know I'm there,' Amie said petulantly. 'And I'm Baron Giles's only family now. Shouldn't I help?'

Furious, I started to remind Amie of her origins as the child of a prostitute. Born in a gutter, she'd been raised to become a whore herself, but I had saved her after I'd found her on the roadside: a rape victim, silenced, as Lillian now was, by the devastation of what had happened to her.

Margaret saw my anger and spoke out quickly. 'Amie, Lord Rory will call on you when he needs you. Please sit with Lillian. We cannot know what she's been through, but it has damaged her mind, and she should not be on her own. Perhaps you can understand?'

'In a way, Amie was right,' I said to Margaret as we sat in the great hall. 'She is Baron Giles's only family, I believe, and Giles was the only other person who could decide what to do now.'

'So what, exactly, is the dilemma?' asked Margaret Longsword.

I told her about the letter.

'What is the *Carta Juris Mallrovica*? I heard King Henry speak of it when we were travelling here.'

'It's the Mallrovian constitution. Getting on for two hundred years ago, King George I of Mallrovia wrote down his vision for the country: the rights, responsibilities, freedoms and limitations of the monarch and his tenants-in-chief. He called it the *Carta Juris Mallrovica*, the Mallrovian Charter of Rights. Similar to the English *Magna Carta*.'

'Tell me more about tenants-in-chief.'

'Almost all the country is owned by the reigning monarch. Some areas aren't owned by anyone, such as the Hambrig Hills and the Wilderness, but most of the land belongs to the king or queen. The land is divided into fiefs, and those fiefs are rented by tenants. The monarch himself has only two tenants, and they're called tenants-in-chief.

'Ever since King George I, the tenants-in-chief have been Hambrig and Wartsbaye. Wartsbaye has always been a barony, but Hambrig never was. Even so, the tenant of the Hambrig fief owed allegiance directly to the King. There were other fiefs, such as Nightmolben, but that was always part of Hicrownshire, the parcel owned directly by the monarch. Navisar is part of Hicrownshire too, although Myrtile isn't. I've never really understood how Myrtile fits in.

'Anyway, each tenant-in-chief has several tenants of his own, and smaller fiefs are rented to those people who pay their fees to the overlord. I have six such tenants, and Giles has – had – several too. The *Carta Juris Mallrovica* sets all this out, together with the duties and responsibilities of the monarch and the tenants-in-chief. One of those duties is to secure the succession, no matter what happens.'

'Is this the first time there has been only one tenant-in-chief, then?'

'As far as I know. But I do wonder if Amie will qualify as the other one now. Until her son grows up, anyway.'

'Didn't Baron Giles have any brothers or sisters? Other children? Cousins?'

I shook my head. 'He had another son, older than Gael, but Davy died in battle. Giles's wife died long ago, and I know of no other family. But, Margaret – I can't work with Amie. She isn't...' I wasn't sure how I wanted that sentence to finish.

'She isn't a noblewoman?' Margaret suggested.

'It isn't really that. I think I'm trying to say that she isn't *independent*. Look how she's clinging on to you. She was the same with Gael when they both lived with me. She needs someone to lean on. That's no good to me now. I need someone who can think for themselves, and whose opinions I'll respect.'

'How about Sir Jonny, then?'

'Sir Jonny isn't a tenant-in-chief and never could be. He's English, for one thing, and he no longer lives in Mallrovia.'

'And you don't get on with him.'

'I *want* to get on with him, Margaret. I don't know what the barrier between us is. He's never explained it.'

'Have you asked him to?'

'Many times.'

We sat in silence for a while. I didn't know what Margaret was thinking, but I was back to wondering if Jonny somehow knew about Karima. I wanted to scribble my thoughts in my journal, but didn't do so. Margaret was still so close I could smell her perfume and see the rise and fall of her breasts.

'You're looking at me like a starving man looks at a haunch of venison,' Margaret laughed, cutting into my dreaming.

'I want you, Margaret.'

'And I, you. Tonight, perhaps.'

So Margaret and I resolved nothing, but spent that night together, and the two after that as well. And on Wednesday 14th September, I took Phoebe to Hicrown Cathedral, to which the entire city had also been summoned, and, for the second time, Roger Scarning crowned her Queen of Mallrovia.

The silly girl smiled and simpered at everyone, wriggling her immature bottom on the Coronation Chair, which she scarcely filled half of, and enjoyed every moment that she was the centre of attention. And even if I overheard more than a few people referring to her as 'Queen Feeble', at least we had legally and formally reaffirmed that we had a crowned Queen, and perhaps English Henry would now keep his nose out of Mallrovian affairs.

But the very next day, Scarning told me with a smirk that he'd bribed the guard and had married Phoebe to Sir Allan in the middle of the night, and there was nothing I could do about it; they were wed, and Allan was King of Mallrovia.

Scarning was wrong in one respect. There *was* something I could do about it, but it was not a pleasant something. All through the next night, I sat up in bed with candles alight and Margaret sleeping beside me, and I read and re-read the *Carta Juris Mallrovica*. I'd been made to study it while I was page to King David, and had been tested on it too, but that was a long time ago.

First, I discovered that Allan was not King, but Prince Consort. That would be bad enough though, giving him power he should not have. So I looked for ways to depose Allan, and I found just one. If Phoebe dies, Allan loses his title. I saw now why Phoebe had to be kept alive, while Lillian could be sacrificed. But if something were to happen to Phoebe...

Would she even be missed, I wondered? She was highly unlikely to do any good. 'Queen Feeble' was pretty accurate; the girl could barely muster a thought in that silly head of hers, and she'd be no sort of ambassador for our country. Her father had been a tireless and effective advocate for Mallrovia. Phoebe would be useless.

So – and I put down the *Carta Juris Mallrovica* and snuffed out the candles – what was I thinking? Was I really contemplating the assassination of my Queen?

34

CAN MALLROVIA SURVIVE?

When a black stallion thundered into the palace garden, with Bryce clinging on for dear life, everyone who was physically able to do so tumbled out of the palace, the accommodation blocks, the barns, stables and workshops, to find out what terrible thing had happened now. I stood on the palace steps and waited for the tumult to calm down and Bryce to be given water to drink and a helping hand as he fell from the saddle. A stable lad led the stallion to the water trough and was heard promising him hay, oats and a calming rub-down.

Meanwhile, Jonny marched forward and stood in front of the crowd, his stance reeking of authority. He quelled the noise instantly. Over the heads of the crowd, I watched Jonny do his thing. As he dispersed the gathering with practised ease, I walked across to Bryce, who was recovering by sitting on a stone bench with a flagon of ale in his hand.

When he saw me, he jumped up to stand to attention, but I waved him back down and sat next to him.

'Lord, I had to come as fast as I could, because they'll be here soon! Very, very soon!'

'Who will?'

'Duke Louis and the Bavarians! They came by ship and docked at the wharf, then they came up the hill to the castle, and when they heard you were here, they went back down again and hurried back to their ship to collect things they needed, and while they did that, Branca got Trojan ready, and I galloped here without stopping.'

An announcement which was also made without stopping. Bryce looked like a man who'd galloped fifty-five miles without a break. The sweat still glistened on his face and neck. Whether Trojan would ever recover was another matter. Trojan was Branca's own horse, her pride and joy.

'Are you sure it was Duke Louis? The man himself?'

'Yes, lord. It was definitely him. They won't do the journey in one go like I did though. You may have a day or two to prepare.' He was calming down a little, now he'd got the whole thing off his chest.

'How did he seem? Angry? Impatient? Calm and collected?'

'I don't know, lord. He spoke to Branca, and then she hurried to get Trojan ready and told me to ride like the devil to Hicrown. Oh, and she gave me this.'

It was the reply to my letter to Rachel and Joan – and thank God, for I read that Castle Rory was in good hands, and Inka Kaufmann was exerting some authority at last. Rachel and Branca had made arrangements to fetch Thomas Farr's body back from Gailen, and both women had found time to comfort poor Bryce while he was there. Joan informed me that Lady Rosa was in good health, although saddened at the thought she'd sent our stonemason to his death. Maya and Baby Rory were thriving, but all the adults were worried about the revolution in Hicrown, especially given Bryce's lurid reports of fighting and violence.

There was sadness in the castle at the news of Gael's death, since many of my household remembered him. He'd been my page for many years, and he'd been a vulnerable and homesick child until he met Amie. It was strange to read of the daily life of my household, carrying on in my absence, but it lifted my spirits. And it was clear the women were in charge: Inka, Rachel, Branca, Joan and Rosa. A Frisian peasant woman, the cook, the marshal, a textiles worker and my Spanish wife. Well, why not? If it worked, it worked. And I could think of no one who would do a better job.

I read the letter several times, drinking in the details, all the little reminders of home. Then I stuffed it into my shirt and made ready to receive Duke Louis II of Bavaria, Count Palatine of the Rhine. I'd met him once before, when Kit and I travelled first to Bremen and then to Osnabrück for an audience with the duke. Osnabrück was also where I first met Reinhard von Lutterberg, and I would have to let Louis know of the man's death. But he'll shed no tears over Reinhard.

So we swept the hall and the chambers, we warmed the solar with roaring fires, we tidied the gardens as best we could and cleaned the blood off the cobbles. I say 'we' because I worked as hard as the lowliest servant; indeed, we all did. Even Margaret Longsword helped, and Amie tagged along after her of course. The pair of them did a splendid job of bringing the barn back to its normal use and appearance. The injured no longer needed us; they've recovered or they haven't, as is the way of things.

The one exception to this, and the source of considerable worry, is Lillian, Duchess of Bavaria, Louis's wife, and also, somehow, Reinhard's widow. Still silent, she lies listlessly in a small chamber Margaret found for her. It's at the top of the palace, up four spiral stairways, and you wouldn't go there if you didn't have to. And perhaps Duke Louis doesn't have to. That's my hope. Does he know Lillian is here? We won't know until he arrives, but I've told everyone who needs to know that we don't give any information away until we've found out why he's made the long and tiring journey from Heidelberg to Hicrown.

'What if he asks for her?' Amie said nervously on the third day after Bryce's arrival. 'We'll *have* to tell him where she is, won't we, lord?'

'Leave it to me, Amie,' I told her, and it wasn't the first time either. 'You won't need to speak to his Grace at all.'

She flushed at the rebuke. Amie is not sure who she is now, and I can't help her, since I don't know either. If she had not been a tortured and abused urchin, I'd have welcomed her as Giles's daughter-in-law and the next tenant-in-chief. I'd willingly have shared the burden of responsibility with her. But I can't get away from her past; it's all too obvious in the way she speaks and behaves. Amie knows Margaret sleeps with me, and that's dangerous knowledge. At some point, Henry de Lacy, Earl of Lincoln, will return for his wife. I need to make sure Amie is nowhere nearby when that happens.

I've stationed lookouts at the Hambrig Gate, and all along the Palace Road. When Louis's retinue is sighted, the word will be passed quickly. Long before his gilded carriage draws up in the palace grounds, we'll have tweaked everything in need of tweaking, and we'll have a guard of honour stationed either side of the path, applauding and saluting him. Louis must be made to feel welcome, respected and honoured. Whatever this visit means, it's going to be important.

Allan has been released. He has not been crowned, but seems content to wait for a ceremony to be announced. He is not, however, content with the domestic arrangements. Allan and Phoebe do not share sleeping quarters, and Phoebe refuses even to see Allan, on account of his injuries and the hideous scarring across his face. He'd never been a good-looking man, and his injuries refuse to heal up. The scars ooze and suppurate constantly. His appearance is grotesque and he's thirty years older than his bride. She may be empty-headed, but she certainly has an opinion on her husband's looks.

'Rory. You have to speak to Phoebe,' Allan said as soon as I entered the great chamber this morning. 'She refuses to sleep with me. It's intolerable. I can demand my rights, of course...'

'And have you so demanded?' I asked.

'Yes, and it made not a whit of difference. I got Scarning to marry us in secret so that you couldn't do any more damage than you've already done. Much good it's done me; what's the point of being King if I'm not crowned, I have no power and I'm not allowed to fuck my wife?'

'Will you be receiving Duke Louis of Bavaria?' I'd never have had to ask King Philip such a stupid question. Obviously one head of state would receive another. Allan wasn't stupid, but he lived life on his own terms. He had no innate knowledge of kingship.

'Are you joking? Looking like this? You've made me a monster, and I should have you hanged!'

'Is that a threat, Allan?'

'Don't use my name. Call me "sire". Or "your Highness". Fuck you, Rory!'

'Of course, your Highness. But if you're going to hang me, I suggest you do it soon. Before Louis gets here. I don't think a gibbet is the friendliest of welcomes for a foreign head of state, do you?'

'Head of state?'

Well, if Allan didn't even know the duke's status, we had a long way to go. Patiently, I explained exactly who Duke Louis was, together with the extent of his power and influence, while Allan scowled and the hideous injuries became lurid with anger. When I'd finished my explanation, Allan ground out that he would not be meeting Louis. Queen Phoebe could do so, and I must organise everything.

I didn't bother telling him that the organising had been done days ago. Allan was way out of his depth and he knew it. My parting shot was a promise to speak to Phoebe about her marital duties. And then I left. Closing the door, I thought I heard his fists pounding against the wall. For one brief moment, I felt sorry for Allan. But the feeling didn't last.

Louis arrived at twelve noon on Wednesday 21st September exactly as Bryce had described and I had imagined. Fortunately it was a bright, dry day, even if clouds sometimes hid the sun. An ornately gilded carriage bore him and his closest advisors up the Palace Road. The messaging system had worked as it was meant to, and we were spotlessly and gorgeously ready. The women's outfits sparkled and shimmered in the sunshine, while swords glittered in a ceremonial arch created by the immaculately turned-out King's Squad. No matter that there were so few of them; they looked perfect.

Remembering his bravery on the barricade, I'd allowed Leo to retain his rank, and to parade the Squad for the Bavarian duke. And so Captain Leo excelled himself, deploying his depleted forces with intelligence and flair, and he'd pressed the Wartsbayes and Ketterings into service as well. There were smart outriders to the sides of the sword-arch, while a small column of cavalry brought up the rear. When the jangling of the highly polished bits and harness had finally given way to silence, and when the carriage wheels had stopped turning, I saw the Squad's standard bearer raise up the bendy lozengy blue-and-white flag of Bavaria. A masterstroke of diplomacy on Leo's part.

I stepped forward and nodded to Captain Leo to bring his troops to attention. The carriage doors swung open, and two footmen stepped down to hold them wide and lend a hand to the duke, should it be needed. But Duke Louis is my age, and he had no difficulty making a dignified exit from the carriage.

Captain Leo's squad beat their sword hilts against their shields in the classic salute to a visiting monarch. Duke Louis graciously acknowledged the salute, and then Leo and I led him to the great hall, where a feast had been prepared and Queen Phoebe sat in pride of place in the centre. A tall chair beside her was intended for our distinguished visitor, and I would take the place on his other side. Captain Leo, Commander Titus of Wartsbaye and Sir Jonny of Kettering also took their places at the high table.

Trestle tables had been set out below the dais, and I had meticulously worked out who would sit where, and which less-favoured folk would eat their dinner elsewhere. This was to be a banquet. I'd checked that supplies could now get through to Hicrown, and I'd made my requirements clear to the cook and her team, for this would also be a delicate diplomatic event. It was important that nothing should go wrong.

Unfortunately, it went wrong from the very start. Having handed his sword to one of his footmen before entering the hall, Duke Louis approached the table. But before he could mount the dais, he stopped, and we who were walking with him had to stop too.

'Is everything all right, your Grace?' I murmured.

'Where is my wife?'

I had not prepared for this. I knew that at some point we would discuss Lady Lillian, but I'd assumed it would be later because I hadn't realised Louis knew Lillian was here. He'd certainly have known she'd been abducted by Reinhard, commander of the garrison at Osnabrück at the time, but there was no reason at all for him to link Reinhard with Mallrovia. Yes, Lillian was Mallrovian, but it would be folly for Reinhard to bring her here, and Louis would know that. A far better plan would have been for Reinhard to bear his prize away to Livonia, his own country, where Lillian would be unknown and Reinhard would be safe.

'Your wife, your Grace?' I hedged.

He turned to face me. 'Lord Rory. We do not need to play this game. I know very well that my wife is here in Hicrown, although I do not know why. That Livonian scoundrel seized her, and I have come here to dispense justice to him and to claim my rights as Lillian's husband.'

'Your Grace, may I suggest we proceed to the table where

a banquet will be served? We can discuss this while we eat, and I will answer all your questions.'

He agreed to this, although I was desperately trying to work out exactly how I would answer all his questions. The banquet was remarkable. Even Rachel, my cook at home, couldn't have turned out such a feast. Perhaps that was unfair to her, but I was very impressed with the palace kitchen today. Salmon pie was served first, with a peppery parsnip mash. It was followed by poached and baked chicken on a bed of buttery leeks. There were cheeses and crackers with a selection of fruits, some of which were exotic and must have been brought here from abroad. Finally, we were served apple pastries and an enormous honey and almond cake.

Duke Louis was not a greedy man. He ate sparingly, trying most things, but in small or moderate portions. He drank very little wine. At some point between the salmon and the chicken, I mentioned that Lillian was asleep in a chamber in the palace. During the chicken course, Louis discovered that Phoebe was Queen of Mallrovia, and that her husband was indisposed. Phoebe said hardly a word to anyone, but chomped through every course with her customary vacant look. Louis's expression told me he'd met her type before.

By this time I'd worked out a highly plausible story, so while the pastries were passed down the table, I let Louis know that the 'Livonian scoundrel' had abducted Lillian and had, unfortunately, abused her. Reinhard was dead, so Lillian was now safe, but she had not yet recovered from her ordeal.

'I will see her tomorrow,' Louis announced. 'Has the Livonian got her pregnant?'

The directness of the question took me aback, and I

answered cautiously. 'He may have done, your Grace. She was certainly badly treated.' I wanted to ask after Kit and Aggie, but decided to leave that until tomorrow as well.

Louis declined the honey and almond cake, but asked, 'Why is Phoebe crowned Queen? With King Philip and Prince Barney both dead, surely Lillian is next in line?'

'Indeed,' I said, 'but Lillian is married to you, your Grace, and therefore Duchess of Upper Bavaria—'

'Which does not preclude her from also being Queen of Mallrovia.' Louis's tone was icy. 'I am both a duke and a count. Many of the nobility hold more than one title. As you well know.'

'I didn't think your Grace would approve of Lillian spending time in Mallrovia,' I began, and realised too late that I'd blundered into his trap.

'So you thought Lillian would be Queen here while I remain Duke of Upper Bavaria and Count Palatine of the Rhine in the Holy Roman Empire? You did not realise that I, the Queen's husband, would be King of Mallrovia?'

'I apologise, your Grace,' I said at once. 'I did realise it, of course. But we have been fighting the Livonians, as well as rescuing Lillian from captivity. There has been treachery and treason committed here in Hicrown, and we are gradually getting on top of it and dealing with those responsible.'

Louis looked unimpressed. 'As I said, I shall see Lillian tomorrow, and then we will put an end to this charade involving the younger girl. Lillian will be crowned Queen and I shall be crowned King of Mallrovia. A double coronation. There is nothing more to be said about this matter, Lord Rory, since the succession is pre-ordained in your own *Carta Juris Mallrovica*, about which I am extremely well informed, and I am Lillian's legal husband. Whatever happened between my wife and the Livonian is in the past. Neither you nor I will refer to it again.'

But I had to try. 'Your Grace, you will remember the meeting Master Kit and I had with you in Osnabrück. Your wife warned me then about the dangers of Mallrovia being swallowed up by a greater power. I spoke with Lady Rosa, just as Lady Lillian asked me to. She will have exerted her influence on her father—'

'Whatever influence Lady Rosa may have once had on the great Alfonso X of Castile, she has none now. We both know that. We knew it when Lady Lillian spoke to you. There is no need to pretend otherwise.'

'Then why did we meet? Why did you try to warn me of the dangers to my country?'

'It seems you have completely misunderstood. I wanted to meet your minstrel, whose daughter has such gifts. It is the minstrel's daughter who finally enabled Lillian to become pregnant and give birth to a healthy son. One who will inherit my land and my title. I had to have some pretext for the meeting.'

I was shocked, but – much later – realised I shouldn't have been. The games played by those with great power are multi-layered and devious. 'Are Kit and Aggie still at your court in Heidelberg?' I asked, not deferring this question until tomorrow after all.

'Of course. Soon I will have no more use for the minstrel, but I shall keep the girl. There is no one like her in the whole world. She knew Lillian would be violated, so I was unsurprised at your news. The child also predicted that I will have great influence in this part of the world, and now I find she is right again.'

Jonny leant in towards me. 'First the English, then the

Livonians, now the Bavarians. Can Mallrovia survive? And if so, at what cost?'

I'm in my chamber, trying to sort out my jumbled thoughts. Tomorrow Louis will meet Lillian, and we shall find out if she'll speak to him or not. As yet, she's uttered not a single word to anyone, although physically, according to Bethan, Lillian is recovering well. Bruises are fading, no bones are broken, her appetite is reasonable... all that sort of thing. But no speech.

As for Phoebe – *can* you uncrown someone? Clearly Roger Scarning needs to be consulted on that. Between Phoebe and Lillian – Lillian, without question. But between Allan and Louis? Louis is astute, clever and power-mad; Allan is, at least, Mallrovian, but he's bitter and broken, and there's no real intelligence there.

I sit here and wait for Margaret to arrive. She will, of course. Every night, when all have gone to their rooms, she comes running to mine and we devour each other in passionate sex. But tonight feels different. *I* feel different. Jonny's words thunder through my mind: *Can Mallrovia survive?*

35

DOES IT COVER THIS SITUATION AS WELL?

'It is not possible to undo a coronation,' Roger Scarning intoned, frowning heavily at my question. 'I'm not sure why you are asking me this, Lord Rory. Queen Phoebe was the next in line. There is no question of reversing the procedure.'

'*Lillian* is next in line,' I said impatiently, having gone through all this once already. 'She would have been crowned if I'd remembered she could be both Queen of Mallrovia *and* Duchess of Bavaria. Something which you should definitely have advised me about. In any case, you are being paid by Allan, and everything you say is influenced by him. You're a corrupt and greedy man, bishop.'

His face darkened. 'Sir Allan pays me because he has control over the cathedral and those who work here. This is normal practice.'

'Bishop, you were about to crown Allan King of Mallrovia before Phoebe was anointed. Or have you forgotten?'

'I will not readily forget the rage you showed on that day, Lord Rory. Your unpardonable violence before the altar—'

'The only way to stop you.' About my 'unpardonable violence', I was unrepentant. 'Well then. If you can't or won't undo the coronation, the girl will have to abdicate. Begin the procedure for that at once, bishop. There is no time to lose.'

'You would rather have a Bavarian on the throne of this country?'

'Possibly. I don't see Allan doing a very good job.'

'It will take time to prepare the documents for an abdication. This is not something that can be achieved in a day or two.'

'You'd better get on with it then. Make it your most urgent priority, bishop. I want this abdication as soon as possible, and Lillian crowned Queen of Mallrovia. I hope you understand me.'

As I strode away from the bishop's house, I had the unpleasant sensation I was being followed, but when I whirled round to see who it was, there was no one there. A few moments later, I caught a movement and flung out my arm to catch hold of whoever it was. I caught only air, so I darted into the dingy passage which led to the cloisters. Someone was walking rapidly ahead of me, his head and body shrouded in a black Benedictine robe. It took little time to catch up with him, grab him by the shoulder and spin him round to face me. The monstrously scarred face of Sir Allan of Hicrown stared angrily into mine.

'You're a monk now?' I asked him sarcastically, flicking at his black robe.

'I hide my face. Let go of me, Rory. You realise you've laid hands on your king?'

'You're no king,' I growled at him. 'You're the ignorant son of a—'

His fist came out of nowhere, swinging into my face and knocking me to the ground. It was followed by his boot, crashing first into my injured leg and then, viciously, into my groin. Both kicks were disabling, and I lay on the path willing the agony to recede, my face wet with tears of pain. My jaw ached from his punch, but it was torture where he'd kicked me. I tried to move, but I couldn't.

Nobody passed by. Once, monks would have come this way to enter the cathedral for their offices, but the cathedral was all but unusable now and the cloisters remained empty. At some point I heard voices, but could neither make out what they said, nor call for help. I knew I should be able to get up. The kicks had immobilised me temporarily, but – and it was now hours later – I should have been able to stagger to my feet. Yet I did not. I should have been able to shout for help, yet I could not. And I knew why.

The sky eventually darkened overhead but my mind had darkened hours ago. Dragged back into the Darkness, I hadn't even resisted. Recognising this, I began to weep. Tears of self-pity streamed from my eyes, and memories crowded in on me, memories of the worst days last year, when I could not move from the chair in my library.

Kit had looked after me then. Kit had known what I needed, had come and gone without taxing me with too much talk; just enough to rouse me from complete torpor. He'd brought food, but I'd eaten little; ale, which I'd drunk as if I were dying of thirst. No one else had come, and I later found out that Kit had told them not to. Not then, anyway; not during the very darkest days. Later, when I'd felt a little better, Peter had visited me daily with news of the Castle Clock he was constructing, and I'd both hated his visits and hungered for them. It had been the strangest time.

And here I was again. But no Peter, no Castle Clock and

no Kit. The minstrel! What had he said or done in the court of Duke Louis? Had he suggested Louis could claim the Mallrovian throne? I closed my eyes. I didn't know the answers and I didn't care. As I lay on the cold flagstones of the cloisters, I allowed the Darkness to wash over me and I sank deeper and deeper into it.

But when I came to, I wasn't in the cloisters.

'Good, you're awake,' said the Welsh-sounding voice of Doctor Bethan.

I tried to sit up, but hands restrained me, pushing me down again. 'Where am I?'

'You're in the barn in the palace garden,' answered a different voice. Another woman. Who was it? I thought I knew it – but perhaps not.

'Let me get up.'

'Not yet,' Bethan said brusquely. 'I've not finished examining you.'

'Did you find me in the cathedral?'

'Yes, of course.' Bethan sounded irritated. 'You were missed, someone said they'd seen you heading that way, somebody went to look for you, and now you're here.'

It seemed to take a long time. The two women poked and prodded and I yelped from time to time when they touched my injuries.

'I've put a salve on your bruises,' Bethan said eventually, as she pulled me up into a sitting position. 'There's nothing much wrong with you, but the bruising will take time to heal.' Only then did I realise I'd been stripped.

'My clothes?' I asked, but they were folded on the hay

bale next to the pallet I'd been lying on. And I saw that the other woman was Margaret Longsword, whose voice I should have known instantly. I dressed quickly.

'Who did it?' Margaret asked gently.

'Allan.'

'Why?'

But I was not going to talk about the abdication. 'It doesn't matter. I need to speak to Phoebe.' I can't call her the Queen. Not now.

At the back of my mind lurked the knowledge that we already *had* a Queen. Neither Lillian nor Phoebe, but their mother, Julia, Philip's wife, now his widow. She could not rule in her own right, but she could guide whoever did. She had maturity, experience and knowledge, attributes possessed by neither of her daughters. Nobody had found her body – but surely, if she were alive, she would be here? So where was Julia? I should have hunted for her long ago.

I stood up cautiously, but there was only a twinge of discomfort, nothing like the agony I'd felt in the cloisters. Margaret sent someone to fetch Phoebe. I waited in the great hall, and when Phoebe entered, Allan was with her. I noted that Phoebe kept her distance from her husband and steadfastly looked away from his face.

'You wanted to see me, Lord Rory?' Phoebe's childishly high voice matches the rest of her demeanour.

'It's not for anyone to summon the Queen,' Allan said at once. His voice was thick and rough, the slashed lips making it hard for him to speak clearly. 'Anyone seeking an audience with her Majesty needs to clear it first with her secretary.'

'And who is her secretary?'

'Captain Leo is currently appointing someone to the role, but in the meantime, he is acting as secretary to her Majesty.'

'Well, I don't see Captain Leo anywhere, and Phoebe's here now, so I think we'll just go ahead. I've read the *Carta Juris Mallrovica*, in which the status of an hereditary Queen's husband is defined as "Prince Consort". As such, you have little power in Phoebe's court. But even this title will be a temporary one.'

'What the fuck do you mean? Don't try playing games with me, Rory, and don't think you can bamboozle me with the bloody *Carta Juris* either—'

'Article 47,' I continued, 'says that if a woman succeeds to the Mallrovian throne she becomes Queen. If she is married, or marries subsequently, her husband becomes Prince Consort. It's quite clear.'

Allan looked across at his wife. She was folding and unfolding the lacy cuff on her gown. I doubted she'd heard a word either of us had said. Allan jerked his head and indicated we should move off.

When we'd put a couple of yards between us and Phoebe, he said, 'Look. Forget about our differences yesterday. You can see she's not going to cut it as Queen. For the last two years she's be playing pretty games in her chamber all day, or making pictures with coloured chalks, and it'll be the same now. I'll make sure she has a son to carry on the monarchy, but in the meantime, you and I can run the country. Phoebe's Queen, for sure, but you and I can make the decisions. And rake in the taxes too. How about it, Rory?'

'I think Duke Louis has similar ideas. And, perhaps, a better claim than yours.'

To his credit, Allan kept his temper. 'Hardly a better claim. We're talking about a Bavarian on the throne as opposed to a Mallrovian. And I'm offering to work with you. To share the burden. And also the profits.'

'Taxation isn't supposed to yield profits. It's meant to fund defence. Something we're very likely to need, by the looks of things.'

'Defence, certainly. And the royal household. Surely you know King Philip took a good percentage of the levy for himself? Sorry, I mean for his household!'

Did Allan actually wink? I said nothing. I did know, but I'd never thought it worth risking the goodwill that always existed between Philip and me. I was the man he came to for advice when anything went wrong. I was the one who came up with solutions to his problems. Although I often resented his long stays at Castle Rory, I was also flattered that he turned to me first, before his wife, before his other tenant-in-chief, or any of his official advisors. So I'd never challenged him on the high levels of taxation he imposed, nor on what became of the money.

'You're complicit, you see,' Allan whispered. 'If you don't like it, everyone will want to know why you did nothing before. And since no one will know any different, we'll keep the taxes as they are – or perhaps raise them just a fraction – and you'll never have to worry about money again. For myself, it hardly matters. Yesterday you tried to say I was ignorant, and perhaps I am. But I'm wealthy, Rory, and if you fall in with my plan, you'll be the same. Surely you want that? For Lady Rosa? For the Lady Joan? For your children?'

'And what do I say to Duke Louis? And to Lillian?'

'Lillian will know nothing, as you're well aware. She's damaged goods now and Louis won't want her. I hear he's got his eye on the Habsburg girl – Matilda, is it? He'll let Lillian go and marry Matilda. Or he'll execute Lillian for infidelity, as he did Maria of Brabant.'

I feared as much myself. I'd spun Louis a yarn of Lillian having been abducted against her will, Reinhard forcing himself on her, to account for her pregnancy. I hoped she'd come out of it well enough to stay married to Louis. Or at least, to keep her head fixed to her shoulders. But once Lillian began talking again, who knew what she'd say? I didn't know 'the Habsburg girl'. Allan, when asked, confirmed Matilda was younger than Lillian by almost ten years. Louis would like that.

'I've told the bishop to prepare abdication documents,' I said bluntly to Allan. 'Your plan will go nowhere once Phoebe's no longer Queen.'

He took a deep breath. 'Rescind the order. In any case, Scarning's my lap dog. He'll ignore what you've told him.'

'Allan, if you make this a power struggle between the two of us, I shall win. If Scarning ignores my order, I'll have him removed. I can draw up the abdication charter myself with the help of a city lawyer. Phoebe is going to be removed as Queen because Lillian is next in line. I've no doubt it was you who took Lillian to the Navisar Gate, intending, I believe, to have her shipped into slavery in the Baltic states. My next action, if you continue to stand in my way, will be to have you hanged for treason against the Queen. Since you clearly haven't read the *Carta Juris*, you may not have realised that Lillian became Queen of Mallrovia the instant her father died, and has been our legal Queen ever since. Now, get out of my way.'

'You're playing a dangerous game,' Jonny said later, after I'd told him everything. 'Actually, you're playing *two* dangerous games. Allan won't take this lying down. He'll do everything he can to prevent you forcing Phoebe to abdicate the crown.

And, on the way, you might just have some unfortunate "accident", like being trampled on by a horse, or being killed by one of the archers. A terrible mistake, of course, and no doubt there'd be a fitting funeral, but it would clear the way for Allan to do what the hell he liked here. If you oppose him, I guarantee he'll find a way to get rid of you.'

'And what's the other dangerous game?'

'Sleeping with Longsword's granddaughter.'

'How's that dangerous?'

'She's married to an English earl. One who was a ward of court and a favourite of the English king. You're playing with fire, and so's she.'

There was something in the way Jonny said it, and I had a flash of understanding. 'Because she's Longsword's granddaughter? Is that the problem?'

'You take everything, Rory. Here you are, King of Mallrovia in all but name, deciding who does what and who gets to be in power. You trample on those you don't approve of, and you can't stand to be opposed. You take what you want, and you always have done. And now this. You've married the most beautiful Spanish woman, who just happens to be the daughter of the most powerful man in Europe. You have two perfect children, a golden castle and an adoring household. Why do you want Margaret as well?'

'You don't know what you're talking about,' I said, standing up and stretching. These conversations were tiring, and a lot of what Jonny had said was rubbish. My household is far from adoring, and the idyllic situation Jonny had just described simply didn't exist. As for 'you trample on those you don't approve of' – it was expressed with bitterness, and I utterly rejected the idea. But I'd never heard Jonny sound vindictive before, and it shook me badly.

The Darkness had gone back into its lair, but it lapped at

the edges of my soul from time to time, reminding me that it would take very little for it to emerge in full and swamp me. I'd like to think that each time I push the Darkness away, it makes it harder for it to come out again, but I believe the opposite may be true.

As I stood by the high table, with Jonny glaring at me, I knew the Darkness could emerge any moment. I stood completely still, willing it to stay locked away. Willing my eyes to focus properly and stare Jonny out. But I could feel myself losing the battle. My stomach cramped, and bile rose up my gullet into my mouth. The Darkness swirled in front of me.

Desperately trying to keep it at bay, and still shaken by Jonny's venomous speech, I said something unforgivable. 'Jonny. If you want to fuck Margaret Longsword, be my guest. Take her if you want her. See if she prefers your prick or mine.'

Registering Jonny's horrified expression, I turned. Margaret was standing just inside the doorway, her hand to her mouth. As she spun round and swept out of the hall, I groaned and sank to my knees.

'Well done, Rory.' Jonny's sneering tones seemed to come from a long way away. 'You've been reading the famous *Carta Juris Mallrovica*, I believe. Does it cover this situation as well?'

36

ALLAN WAS NEXT ON MY LIST

Master Jenner was the lawyer recommended to me. Having sent for him, I gave him his instructions in the great hall of the palace.

But he frowned and tutted and tapped his foot, sending small showers of ink over the table as his quill shook in his hand. 'Let me get this straight, Lord Rory,' he said, and my heart sank. That sort of preamble tells you at once that the person who needs to 'get this straight' is far from happy to do so. 'You want me to draw up a document invalidating the crowning of the legitimate heir to the throne. Is that right?'

'No.' I tried not to sound irritated. 'The crowning of someone who was *not* the legitimate heir to the throne.'

'Then why was that person crowned in the first place?'

I had no idea why he was talking of 'that person' and 'heir to the throne' when he knew the identities of everyone involved. He'd been at Phoebe's coronation himself, for God's sake!

'Master Jenner. As I explained to begin with, Princess Phoebe was crowned because I thought Princess Lillian ineligible. Now that I know Princess Lillian is really Queen—'

'You'll excuse me if I just interrupt for a moment,' said the exasperating lawyer. 'Your understanding of the Duchess of Bavaria's status is incorrect. The Duchess of Bavaria relinquished all claim to the Mallrovian throne when she married Duke Louis. Perhaps you were unaware?'

I was unaware. And I didn't believe it, either. 'Where do you get this information, Master Jenner?'

'It's common knowledge,' he began, before reversing out of the hole he was digging for himself. 'Common to those in the legal profession, I mean, my lord. I wouldn't expect someone without legal expertise to know the complicated ins and outs of the rules of succession.' He gave a dry little laugh. I remained silent, so he hurried on. 'A woman who marries into nobility in a foreign country cannot also carry a title in the land of her birth.'

'Why not?'

'Well, as I say, Lord Rory, it's a matter of legality—'

'In which case, it'll be written down somewhere. In which document is it written, Master Jenner?'

'I believe the *Carta Juris Mallrovica*—'

'There's no mention of this obscure ruling in the *Carta Juris*. You must have read it somewhere else.' He looked flustered suddenly, and I pressed the point. 'If you can't produce the document in which this law is set out, then we shall go by the *Carta Juris* itself. As you know, having great legal expertise yourself, that instrument was drawn up by King George I and his tenants-in-chief in the Year of our Lord 1101. I think it has sufficient authority for our purposes. So please do as I ask. I require an abdication charter which Queen Phoebe will sign. In so doing, she will relinquish the crown and move down the order of succession. The

Duchess of Bavaria will be crowned Queen of Mallrovia as soon as possible thereafter. You have enough vellum and ink here, I trust, and you will be paid for your time. I will return in three hours, by which time I expect the contract to be ready.'

I couldn't understand why everyone was so determined to thwart me. Phoebe could hardly be seen by anyone as a great monarch, even potentially. The prospect of Sir Allan, whether King or Prince Consort, was equally repellent.

'Perhaps they'd rather have English Henry,' Jonny observed at our next meeting, which we held in the privacy of my chamber.

'Yet he doesn't seem that interested, not now the siege of the cathedral is over and everyone's told him the roof will be repaired. There's plenty of money for that and no need for the fines he wanted us all to pay.'

There was a knock on the door, and I knew from its tentative sound and the nervous cough from the other side that Peter waited for permission to enter. Jonny opened the door to him.

'Lord, I'm so sorry to disturb thee.' The man looked close to tears.

'Come in properly, Master Peter. Has something happened?'

'Aye, lord, it has, in a manner o' speakin'. The Duke of Bavaria has been spendin' time wi' his wife, but she still can't say nowt, an' he's beginnin' to lose patience wi' her, so 'tis said. He were overheard shoutin' at her that he'd have her crowned Queen, even if she were unconscious, like. She in't unconscious, lord, an' they say she heard every word he spoke to her, but she din't respond, an' he's determined now that Bavaria'll rule Mallrovia. What dost tha think o' that, lord?'

'I think it's inevitable, Peter. Phoebe is about to abdicate the throne. Louis and Lillian will rule. We must hope and pray Lillian responds to treatment soon. Bethan is doing everything she can for her, as you know.'

'Oh, aye, lord.' He nodded distractedly. 'But, thing is, lord, not everybody thinks t' way tha does. Most folk d'nt' want a foreign king. T' city supports Sir Allan. An' I'm not sure tha'll get what tha wants wi'out t' support from t' city.'

I looked at him in surprise. 'Whatever do you mean, Peter? I think you'd better explain properly. I have a lawyer drawing up the abdication charter right now. Once Phoebe signs it – and she will – the deed will be done, city or no city.'

'Tha knows what they say about desperate times, lord...' He looked pretty desperate himself, standing in front of Jonny and me and twisting his cap round and round in his hands. And suddenly he began to shake, his cap falling to the floor, tears springing from his eyes. Jonny ushered him to the bed and made him sit down. Concerned, I fetched a pitcher of water from the chest and got him to drink a little.

'I'm so sorry, lord,' Peter stuttered, his teeth chattering on the rim of the jug. 'It's that I can hardly tell thee what tha needs to know...'

'Tell *me,* then,' Jonny invited. 'Look at me, Peter, and talk to me. It'll be easier if you do that.'

'Aye, Sir Jonny, it will, aye. Well, tha knows me son, Leo. I've not seen much o' him over t' years. Very little; very little indeed. I din't know he were growin' up to be such a soldier, an' to feel t' way he does... Sir Allan is payin' him to do it, an' I'm sure he wouldn't *be* doin' it if 'tweren't for his feelin's for Sir Allan...'

'What is Leo doing, Peter?' Jonny asked gently. 'Tell me what Allan's paying him to do.'

'He's marchin' on Hambrig, Sir Jonny. He's taken t' Squad and they're marchin' on Hambrig an' on Castle Rory, an' they'll take it, won't they, because we can't defend ourselves now. My son is goin' to attack my home! I never thought t' day would come...'

Jonny took the pitcher from him, and Peter wept, his head in his hands.

'I'll take my men,' Jonny said softly to me. 'Titus will bring his Wartsbayes as well. We'll catch him and we'll deal with this.'

'Your men are inexperienced—'

'No more so than the Squad. They look pretty, but they don't fight much. We'll sort them out.'

'Why would you do this, Jonny? Castle Rory isn't your home now, and you hate me. You've made that very clear.'

'I think explanations can come later, don't you? I'll mobilise my troops and we'll leave immediately.'

'You may have to kill Leo.'

He nodded and left the room, clattering down the steps to the great hall.

In the afternoon, I went up to Lillian's chamber. Louis wasn't with her, but Bethan sat by her bedside, reading aloud.

'I wondered if Lillian would respond to stories she may have heard when she was a child,' Bethan said, looking up. 'This chamber was her childhood bedroom.'

'What's the story?'

'*Yvain, the Knight of the Lion*. I found the book on the shelf in this room. It's well worn, so I guess this story was much read when Lillian was a girl.'

'And is there any response?'

Bethan sighed. 'Not as yet, but I'm sure she can hear me. And the two of us talking now. We may never know what she suffered, Rory. Having examined her, I can tell you she has been repeatedly raped. Not only has this injured her internally, but it has also altered her mind. She's still pregnant, but this abuse will make the birth much more difficult. I've tried herbal remedies and salves, but while they all help her body recover, there's little I can do for the damage to her mind. Jabir would have been able to help, I'm certain of it.'

Jabir is dead. Or possibly not dead, but alive and living in the south of Spain. Either way, he can't be consulted about Lillian.

'Has the wise woman seen Lillian?'

'I don't trust her. She is more strange than wise, in my opinion.'

'There's nothing to lose, is there. If you've been unable to help...'

'There is a difference between being unable to help and causing harm. I'm not saying she'd cause harm,' Bethan added, seeing my frown. 'But we don't know. And Sir Allan tells me she was burning human hair, which made him feel worse not better after you'd attacked him. I'm sorry, but I don't trust her at all.'

'I'm overriding you.' My voice sounded harsh to my own ears. Allan had also attacked *me*, but there was no reference to that. Nor did I understand the burning of the hair, or the way the wise woman had spoken to me, ever since which I'd kept well out of her way. But now – 'I'll send for her. We will see if she can help Lillian. It's a last resort, Bethan.' Peter's words about 'desperate times' came to my mind. The other half of the saying refers to 'desperate measures', and where Lillian was concerned, I felt the need to resort to them.

I hadn't seen the wise woman for two weeks, and wondered where to start looking for her. Turned out I didn't need to. As I wended my way down the stairs to the hall, I found her sitting demurely on a bench by the wall, hands folded in her lap and a small leather bag beside her on the floor. As I entered the hall, she stood, picked up the bag and walked towards me.

'How is she, sir? Still in her trance?'

'I don't know about a trance. If you mean Lady Lillian, she won't talk or respond to anything anyone says to her.' Still very unsure about this woman, I spoke stiffly. My stance was not friendly.

The wise woman was unperturbed. 'I will go to her, and I would like to be left alone. You must ensure that nobody even climbs the steps to her room, nor lingers on the landing below. I need complete quiet and solitude.'

'To do what?'

'To help the lass, of course. Isn't that what you want?'

'It is what I want. But how will you help her? And when others have failed, even my highly experienced physician.'

'I take nothing from your highly experienced physician, sir. But I am not about to use the type of medicines she will have employed. I have different skills and different methods. I cannot guarantee it will work, but I will do my best.'

Bethan had wanted Jabir. This woman was nothing like him, except that her words were just what he might have said. *Different skills and different methods.* Could be Jabir's epitaph.

Cursing my injured leg, I climbed the stairs again, this time with the wise woman. When we reached the top, I told Bethan to leave Lillian and not return to her bedside until sent for. Bethan looked curiously at the wise woman, but there wasn't the hostility I'd expected to see. And no arguments either, which was a relief. Bethan and I trod carefully down the many spiral steps to the bottom, and then she faced me.

'Do you know that woman?'

'She says I do,' I admitted. 'But I think she's lying.'

Bethan gave me a searching look, turned and walked away.

Master Jenner had prepared the document, and I went to fetch Phoebe myself. I brought her into the great hall and asked Master Jenner to explain it to her. I'd formed an unfavourable impression of him to start with, but now he proved himself to me. Clearly, and without the use of lawyerly gobbledygook, Jenner told Phoebe that her sister must take the throne, and so Phoebe must first relinquish it. To do so, she must sign her name just here. Jenner put his finger on the vellum, where the words *Phoebe Regina* stood out to all of us. Phoebe looked wide-eyed at me, and I nodded.

'It's for the best,' I said to her. 'When the bishop put the crown on your head, we didn't know it should have been Lillian. Now we know she's Queen, she should be crowned properly. Do you understand, Lady Phoebe?'

'Being Queen is very boring,' Phoebe said. 'Where do I write my name again?'

So Lillian is now Queen, but the coronation can't take place until she can utter the words and take part in the ceremonial rituals. Until then, there will have to be a regent to rule in her name. In practice, there's only one person who can do that job.

The sole remaining tenant-in-chief.

Me.

How do I feel about that? Do I *want* to be regent? In all honesty, I don't know. Two days ago Jonny called me 'King of Mallrovia in all but name.' At the time he was being unpleasant, but perhaps he was wiser than he knew. And the more I think about it, the more I feel I could get used to the idea.

Phoebe was asking about her husband, whom she hadn't seen for a week, apparently.

'Your husband was never King,' Master Jenner told her. 'And since you are no longer Queen, he cannot be Prince Consort either.'

Theirs must be the shortest reign in history.

Three days and nights followed. The wise woman did not descend to the hall, and nobody went to the top of the building. No sounds were heard, and, on the landing below, people tiptoed in and out of their chambers as if their lives depended on their silence. I spent each of those three nights alone. Margaret did not come to me, and I was unsurprised. I ached for her, longed for her, but why would she come, having heard my crass words to Jonny? I lay in my bed, wide awake, wondering about Lillian in the room above mine, hoping Jonny and his men would reach Leo before he arrived in Hambrig, and desperately wishing Margaret were lying next to me so I could talk it all over with her.

Very early on the fourth morning, the wise woman

entered my chamber without knocking. I was drowsy, after so many sleepless nights. Not fully awake.

'Margaret?' I murmured, reaching a hand out from under the linen sheet. The woman came to my bed and sat down. She slid her hand under the sheet and touched my naked body. The touch was gentle and seductive. 'Margaret.' I reached up to touch her face. 'I've missed you so much.'

'Of course you have,' answered the wise woman, and I sat up with a jolt, shoving her hand away.

'My God! I thought you were someone else! Why have you sneaked into my room like this? How is Lillian?' I pushed the damp hair out of my eyes, willing them to focus, though they stubbornly would not. My whole body was sweating, my breathing shallow and erratic. This imposter of a woman had touched and caressed me, making me believe she was Margaret...

'Don't worry, sir,' the wise woman said. 'Lady Lillian is doing well, and that's what I came to tell you.'

'You made me think you were Margaret.'

'When in fact, as you now know, I am Karima.'

Jonny and Titus returned, their men bloodied and wounded. They'd caught up with the Squad on the marshes by the River Shamet. The fight had been to the death, soldiers slipping and sliding in the mud. Two had tumbled head first into the river. Leo, Jonny told me, had been a decisive and inspiring commander, leading from the front and making every blow count.

'More of a muddy, bloody skirmish than a battle,' Jonny

reported wearily. 'But they never reached Hambrig, and now they never will.'

Only four of the Squad had survived, and they'd been brought back to the palace in ignominy, their hands tied behind them. One, of course, was Leo himself. Jonny had made sure that young man survived. I was grateful to Titus and the Wartsbayes, and to Jonny and his men from Kettering. But what now?

'English Henry will come back,' Jonny predicted. 'He'll want to know what's going on.'

'He knows already. I've sent messages. The cathedral's being rebuilt; the siege is over; the insurrection is quelled; all is under control. He doesn't need to know anything else.'

'He may want to see for himself. Especially if he hears the Squad is no more.'

'We'll build it up again!' I exclaimed at once, entirely forgetting that Jonny is no longer part of Mallrovia. 'The Squad will rise again!'

'To be commanded by whom? Sir Allan? Duke Louis of Bavaria? The Earl of Warwick? How do you see this going, Rory?'

Ignoring his sarcasm, I expressed my thanks to Jonny for seeing off the threat to my home, and I sent for Peter to tell him what had happened. He was more delighted the Squad had been defeated than he was to hear his son had survived.

'Because it were his idea,' he explained earnestly. 'Leo shouldn't have taken t' Squad down t' Hambrig Road at all. Did Sir Allan give the order, I wonder?'

'More than likely,' I said.

And so Allan was next on my list.

37

YOU WILL FIND OUT EXACTLY WHAT I AM

He was waiting for me. As I walked towards the accommodation blocks, he emerged from behind the palace wall. He must have been pressed up against it, his heart pounding, his dagger slick in his sweating hand, the still-seeping scars inflamed across his face, one eye now permanently out of action. He must have wondered if I'd ever come past, hoping no doubt, but at the same time probably dreading it.

Later, when I was able to put myself in his position, I knew I'd have felt all those things. Killing someone in battle is to be expected. No regrets there. Dealing out death in a hand-to-hand fight, a duel perhaps, is fair play. Murdering someone in cold blood is a lot harder, but you can sometimes justify it. Assassination though – the meticulous planning of the killing of someone with power and influence – that takes real nerve.

I didn't know he was there, and I wasn't watching for him. In my mind, he was in the King's Squad accommodation block, sitting alone in his room, nursing his injuries and his wounded pride. Knowing he'd been deposed as ruler of Mallrovia. And all I wanted to do was talk to him. But he had other ideas, and his dagger was at my throat before I knew what had happened.

Allan's grotesquely mutilated features leered up at me. I'm familiar with scars, wounds and many kinds of deformity, but they're not often thrust so aggressively in my face. Allan is quite a bit shorter than I am. As he held his dagger against my neck, I was forced to tip my head back, but that didn't suit him at all. He'd pinned me against the palace wall. He'd removed my dagger from my belt and had put it through his own.

Now he reached up with his other hand, grabbed a fistful of my hair and hauled hard on it. It was painful, and it jerked my head down and pressed my Adam's apple against the dagger point, puncturing my skin. Blood dripped down my jersey, and its metallic tang assaulted my nostrils. Allan seemed pleased with this outcome. He pulled harder on my hair, lowering my head further, while at the same time his dagger pushed a little further into my neck.

Now I was almost touching his face. This close, I could see that my own blade had almost unseated his right eye. Although the eyelid was closed, the eyeball bulged against it, giving it the look of a freakishly large boil on his face. The long scar that bridged his nose hadn't properly closed up and stinking fluid oozed down his cheeks. I'd gone deeper than I'd realised, though it had been a wild slash, the result of my hot temper rather than any deliberate attempt to disfigure the man. This, now, was very different. Allan intended real damage, no doubt culminating in a kill.

'See. What. You. Did?' he rasped.

'I had to stop the bishop from making you King of Mallrovia. I was only just in time. I didn't mean to cause that much damage, but I had to stop him.'

'Yet you attacked me, not him.'

'Can you let go of my hair please? I'm impaled on your dagger.'

He gave one more vicious tug and then let go. 'I intend to kill you, Rory. I shall get rid of Lillian too. She shouldn't be here, and she wouldn't be if you hadn't interfered. She was due to leave with the next shipment.'

'Tell me about the shipment. You can kill me after that, but I'd like to know how it works.'

'Don't think you'll get the better of me with your slick talking. You're not going to have a clean death, Rory. I've been thinking about this for a long time. I shall mutilate you first. That's fair, isn't it? After what you've done to me?'

His dagger traced its way down my blood-soaked jersey to my hose, where he expertly flicked the blade to cut the leather lacing. I shut my eyes. My mind wandered rapidly through all the many times I'd had men at my mercy, whether on the battlefield or off it. Never once had I sought to deprive them of their dignity. I may have wanted information from them, or I'd kept them prisoner to extract a ransom for their release. Sometimes, I'd had to make awful threats, but I had never tried to unman them. Allan, it seemed, had no such qualms. As my breeches were ripped apart and then my braies were slashed to ribbons, I knew I'd feel the sharp blade next on the sensitive skin of my genitals. Waiting for it was agonising.

'Aren't you scared?' Allan asked. He smacked my face and my eyes snapped open. 'You're about to be cut to pieces.'

'About the shipment,' I said desperately. Cold steel touched my right thigh. I tensed, waiting for the pain of the slash or stab, but forced myself to continue talking. 'The shipment, Allan. Where does it go?'

'Who cares? So long as I get paid.'

'And that's why you're so wealthy? I know you have a great deal of money.'

'Yeah, I do. And I offered much of it to you, if you remember. You scorned me, though. You're a high-born, you wouldn't dream of going into business with someone like me.'

'Someone like you? The commander of the King's Squad? That's a very prestigious position! Your status is almost equal to mine.'

'Don't be stupid.' The dagger flashed round, and its point drew a long line down my leg, a line that quickly turned red and stung like hell. He spat out a question. 'What have you done with Leo?'

'He's under guard. I expect you'll have him released, once you've killed me.'

'I need him released. He's in love with me. Besotted, in fact. He likes to fuck me and I let him do it. It keeps him loyal. What do you think of that, *your lordship*?'

'I don't care who you fuck.'

As I said the words, and they were perfectly true, Allan seemed to fall to the side, his dagger spinning out of his hand. He fell heavily on the path and screamed as his face hit the gravel, tiny stones embedding themselves in his unhealed wounds.

'So first I rescue Lillian and then I rescue you,' said the wise woman. She was standing on Allan's wrist, hobnailed boots grinding into his flesh. 'Find some clothes, sir. You've had a very lucky escape, I think.'

The wise woman allowed Allan to stand, but she quickly relieved him of all weapons and hobbled his elbows with some strong binding she had on her person. How had she done it? She wasn't a young woman, yet she'd overcome this desperate man.

'Not difficult,' she said, seeing my expression. 'The man had his back to me. He didn't know I was there. Neither did you, sir, since you had your eyes closed. Where shall we take him?'

'I want to interrogate him. We'll take him to the great hall.'

'You will get little out of him; he hates you too much. He offered you a partnership and you rejected it. Now you know too much, and that makes this man dangerous. He will not talk to you, and later, if you free him without my help, he will try again to kill you. If this happens, there will be no lucky escape and you will die at his hand. I suggest we put an end to him now.'

Allan turned white. 'I'll talk,' he said quickly. 'I'll tell you everything.'

The wise woman cackled. 'Of course you will! You'll spill the beans, won't you, Master Allan. You'll tell Lord Rory that you've never been knighted and you were never entitled to hold a sword. King Philip rescued you from your dead-end life. He saved you. And look how you've treated his elder daughter. Shame on you, Master Allan.'

'I don't deserve this, though!' Unable to gesture to his mutilated face, he raised his shoulders and shook his head from side to side.

The wise woman considered. 'Perhaps not. But we don't always get what we deserve, Master Allan.'

We don't get what we deserve. Who'd said that? I thought back nearly ten years to a night in Peterborough, when I'd met Martin for the first and only time. A leper from St Leonard's Hospital, he'd befriended me and allowed me to tell him my woes, which were nothing compared to his. How unfair was it that Martin, on the same Crusade as I, should have succumbed to leprosy, while I came home free of disease? So I'd asked my minstrel if we get what we deserve, and he, in his wisdom, told me, 'No, we don't get what we deserve. We get what we get.'

'We get what we get,' I said, picking through the remnants of my torn clothing, but finding nothing that could be worn again.

'Quite so,' agreed the wise woman.

Allan's expression was impossible to discern. The scarring, which looked to me as if it was festering badly, had distorted his face so much, you could no longer read anything from it. His lip was cut, his nose gouged almost in two, and the ear-to-ear line that my blade had scored through his cheeks had opened up like oven spring in a well baked loaf.

'We shall not go to the great hall,' the wise woman said, turning her green eyes on me. 'We shall take Master Allan to my boudoir, and, as he said, he will tell you everything.' She swivelled round to the prisoner. 'This time, Master Allan, there will be nowhere to hide.'

The wise woman's 'boudoir' was, of course, the small room off the white-walled one in the solar, the royal suite. I wondered by what right she had not only commandeered it for herself, but christened it a 'boudoir'.

The three of us entered, and the wise woman turned the key, locking the door from the inside. She threw me a blanket to wrap around my waist, and Allan was made to sit on a chair in the very middle of the room. The woman untied his hands and he immediately covered his face. I wondered why, since we all knew what he looked like.

The wise woman went to stand behind the chair. She put her hands on Allan's shoulders and squeezed them, massaging them beneath her fingers. Something made me look again at her hands. The smallest finger on her left hand had a circular burn mark halfway down, and I caught my breath. Karima had had such a mark. In the desert, she'd told me she'd burnt her finger while cooking vegetables over a flame. My heart began to race.

'Leeks, was it?' I said tentatively. I pointed to the burn mark. 'Leeks – and onions, I think you said?'

'You have a good memory, sir. It was indeed leeks and onions, but it was the hot pan that just caught the side of my hand as I stirred it.'

Which was exactly the story Karima had given me. Twenty-two years ago, that had been – the spring of 1250. Jonny, holed up in the cellar of *our house*, recovering from a severe leg wound, while I spent my days speaking with Eleni and her mother, who cooked food for us and plotted our escape from Mansurah, and my nights in the desert with Karima. *Who could not possibly be this woman!* This woman was too old and looked completely wrong. Even if she'd aged prematurely and had somehow disguised her former beauty, she could not have altered the colour of her eyes. Everything told me this was not my Karima. Everything – except the burn mark, the leeks and onions, her use of 'sir', her knowledge of my past... Confused, I looked away.

'And now, Master Allan,' came the voice of the wise woman, 'it is time. The first thing you are going to talk about are the slaves. Tell us about the slaves.'

Allan looked up, taking his hands away from his face. The scars were weeping more than ever, ghastly yellow-green gunk oozing continuously over the man's face. Why, I wondered? Why weren't they healing as they should? My eyes went to the wise woman's hands, still kneading Allan's shoulders, occasionally rubbing against his neck and feeling under his hair. It gave me the shivers.

'It started in Myrtile,' Allan croaked. 'Myrtile is a strange place. Have you been there?'

The question was directed at me, and I nodded. 'I went to see Sir Patrick, my former steward.'

'Ah yes. Patrick. He built Myrtile himself. How could he afford to build such a place? The roofs are made of solid gold! Even so, there's no crime in Myrtile. Patrick is very particular about who lives there. And who enters or leaves. Did you wonder how he could afford to build a place like that when you visited? Did you ask him? He won't tell you. But there's wealth in slavery, Rory. Vast wealth. Pure, virgin girls, taken from their homes, manacled and brought down the secret paths that run from Myrtile to Hicrown – yes, even to this royal palace! – and to Navisar. Then a ship arrives, and the girls are put on board.'

'Patrick wouldn't have anything to do with such an operation,' I said flatly, knowing I'd already convinced myself of the opposite. Knowing I'd suspected Patrick all along, but hating to hear my suspicions confirmed by this despicable traitor.

Allan laughed, a wild, high-pitched sound. 'He's in charge, Rory! He runs it all! The girls come from his estate. So does the worsted, for that matter. His sheep produce the best wool in the country, perhaps the best in Europe. Since Philip began his tariffs, Patrick's been running a wool smuggling racket as well as the slave trade. All coming from Myrtile, shipped out from Navisar, and it's the Livonian Swordbrothers who take it on from there. I don't know where it goes, and I don't care. I get paid well, although I don't make as much as Patrick does. He has a fortune to his name. He built his crazy city so he could run everything from it. He makes sure no one interferes with the girls because virgins command the highest price. He makes sure his sheep farmers are well rewarded too, so nobody talks.'

Both the wise woman's hands had now disappeared under the greying hair at the back of Allan's neck. The hair curled around his ears, and as those curls moved slightly, I caught the flash of something metallic. A knife? Was she going to cut the man's throat? I was about to spring forwards, when she withdrew her hands. They were empty, and Allan's hair had fallen back into place. So it must have been a trick of the light.

I was wrestling with Allan's testimony. Patrick, the man I'd known since my return from Crusade, the man who'd been my father's trusted steward for twenty years before that – was he really a slave trader? My father had many faults, but he never made errors in his assessment of people. And Patrick, living in Hambrig, surely couldn't have run the Myrtile operation.

But a small voice in the back of my mind was asking: how *did* he afford it then? Patrick had told me he'd used his father's money. Money collected by trafficking girls out of Mallrovia. He said he'd used every last penny to build his city. Yet, thirty years later, his people wanted for nothing. There was *still* plenty of money, it seemed. Perhaps he had, indeed, used his father's filthy earnings to build Myrtile – but how did he fund it now? How had he been buying food and other commodities for the last thirty years?

Stewards are paid a reasonable allowance, but none of them get rich. And look at Myrtile: the city was extraordinary. A city of turquoise and gold, I'd called it. Yet it stands in the middle of nowhere, almost inaccessible, never visited by anyone. Somehow, though, food arrives, craftspeople do their work, buildings are maintained, the church functions and life, for the Myrtilers, is a breeze. All because the shipments of girls are still happening, of course. And our worsted is smuggled, tariff-free, to Livonia.

'Does Patrick have anyone to help him?' the wise woman asked, once more twisting Allan's sinews between her fingers.

'They *all* help him,' Allan replied. 'The Myrtilers. They're all involved, they have to be! It's happening under their noses, isn't it? And there are all these little secret paths that the smugglers use. You found one of them, Rory. You went to Halfway House, didn't you? That's where they rest the girls. Mustn't tire them too much. When they're delivered to the Livonians, their bodies must be plump and their hair's got to shine. They've got to look desirable, so as to get the best price from the whorehouses. Though I imagine they pass through many hands before they reach their new homes.'

In the wise woman's hands was a hank of Allan's hair. No longer attached to his head. I blinked. How had she done that? She must have had a knife after all! She'd cut a swathe of his hair, and, as I edged round the back a little, I saw a long narrow gap where that hair had been, and where now I could clearly see Allan's scalp.

'Witchcraft!' I breathed. 'You, woman, are a witch!' I pointed a shaking finger at the wise woman.

'No, sir, you're wrong. I am not a witch. Surely you found Master Allan's story interesting? Even if you don't believe it. And you don't, do you?'

So I was forced to ask her. 'Is it true? Is Patrick behind this horrendous trade in young girls?'

'Patrick knows all about this,' she said calmly. 'He is the man whose money built the city—'

'And you say you're not a witch?' I broke in, unnerved.

'You know so much about everything, you seem to control what happens—'

'That's your interpretation. All I'm doing is maintaining some sort of order here, just as I did for you in Egypt. Without me, sir, you would have fallen apart. Been no use whatsoever to Jonny, and you would both have died in Mansurah. If you can't accept that, you're lying to yourself.'

'Who are you?' I said, trembling. I was suddenly so frightened, my bowels threatened to empty onto the floor. I clenched my buttocks, knowing from experience this was a battle I was likely to lose.

'I've told you, sir. My name is Karima. I am not a witch, but one day, perhaps soon, perhaps not, you will find out exactly what I am.'

38

I AM YOUR NEMESIS AND YOUR REDEEMER

The wise woman burnt the hank of Allan's hair. She laid it on a piece of slate, and then, with flint, steel and charcloth, she set the hair alight. The same disgusting bitter smell filled the 'boudoir', and Allan began to retch.

'What the hell are you doing?' I shouted. Whatever the wise woman said, this surely had to be witchcraft. 'Why are you burning his hair?'

'This is a spiritual process,' she said calmly. 'I do not burn much. It is symbolic, and it will release Master Allan into his new life.'

'His new life? What's his new life?'

'His new life is one of freedom. I told you not to let him go without my help. But now he will sail away from here and be free.'

Allan raised his head. There were tears in his one usable eye, probably from the smoke and the stink, but perhaps from the woman's words as well. 'Freedom? Sail away?'

If I'd been in Allan's position, I'd have clung to those three words as well, but they could not remain unchallenged. For two weeks this man had thought himself a king. Now he was a prisoner and a wretched one at that. I had every right to hang him. 'Freedom' and 'sail away' were not part of Allan's future.

But the woman came to stand in front of me, and she thrust the slate with its disgusting charred mess under my nose. I didn't retch, but my head began to spin. 'Master Allan is about to tell you his story. And then you will let him go. The ship that was coming for Lillian will be at the beach. Two men must escort Master Allan to Navisar, where he will embark on the ship and sail to distant shores. He will be unarmed, and will take nothing at all with him, just the clothes he is wearing and a salve which I shall give him for his wounds. While he is at sea, the terrible facial scars will heal over and close, but he will always have them. They will remind him of his ill-fated attempt to become king – but Master Allan will never return to Mallrovia.'

White tendrils of smoke float and swirl in front of my face, and in them I seem to see a small Bedouin tent in the sand, inside which waits a beautiful and seductive young woman, her breasts bared and her body ready for mine. The tendrils beckon, inviting me to enter the tent, hot sand between my bare toes. I'm wearing a long white *thob*, which disguises my identity as a Christian Crusader. The Bedouin tent is shadowed but clearly visible, for the desert skies shimmer with starlight. The girl beckons me in, arching her body, holding out one beautiful, long-fingered hand, while the other explores her own sensuousness. She is moaning with desire.

'Now do you believe me?' the wise woman asked. The slate had moved and the tendrils had gone. I was breathing hard. I didn't want to find myself back in this woman's 'boudoir', confronting Allan's disfigured face and the hatred in his single uninjured eye.

'I want her,' I whispered. 'Karima.'

'That much is obvious,' the woman said drily. 'But she was only in your dream—'

'She was real! Twenty-two years ago she was real!'

In a daze, Allan looked from me to the woman. 'Twenty-two years ago?' he said incredulously. 'What the fuck was happening twenty-two years ago?'

The woman put her hands on Allan's shoulders again. As she began to squeeze and manipulate him, he sighed and closed his eyes. 'Twenty-two years ago,' said the woman, 'you, Master Allan, were a mercenary in a troop of English soldiers. You were twenty-nine years old, and had joined the army when you were fifteen, tagging on to a cohort that happened to be passing through Mallrovia at the time. The English soldiers trained you and made you fit and strong. But fourteen years later, you were still just an unimportant, anonymous billman. Nobody took any notice of you. Although you trained hard and took the job seriously, there was little conflict in England at that time and you had no chance to distinguish yourself. But one day in 1260 – and by now you were nearly forty and still unblooded – King Philip of Mallrovia visited King Henry III of England. He wanted men for his garrison. King Henry, a friendly and affable man, agreed to help, and so you, and a good few others, were sent to Hicrown.

'And now Lord Rory is wondering how you became commander of the King's Squad. Well, for a start, you were the oldest man there. Secondly, you boasted outrageously of battles you'd not fought, victories you'd had no hand in, conflicts you had no experience of. In other words, you lied through your teeth. King Philip was not gullible enough to believe you, but he admired your spirit. He told you he would appoint you commander of the garrison, and leader of the prestigious and renowned King's Squad. And you'd only ever been a billman! The lowliest of foot soldiers, the destiny of a peasant!

'King Philip set to work to change all that. He despised your rough, rustic speech, so he taught you to speak properly, like one of those you call "the high-borns". Then you were taught to ride well. You learnt to fight with a sword. Finally, King Philip bestowed the spurious title "Sir Allan" upon you, although, to your shame, he never actually knighted you.'

'I asked him,' Allan whispered. '*Begged* him. He just laughed. Said no one knew the difference, so it didn't matter.'

'But it *did* matter, didn't it, Master Allan? It mattered more and more as the years went by, and as hints were dropped by others. You were terrified of people finding out you were not really a knight at all, that you'd been born an unfree serf in a marshy village. Even worse, there were still no engagements for you and your crack troops to distinguish yourselves in.

'Lord Rory here was fighting off the hostile Swamp-People, or keeping the Dorian rebels at bay. Then he ran off to join the Barons' War against King Henry – or perhaps against de Montfort, it was never too clear whose side Rory was on – and after that there were battles with the Knights Molbenar and strategic games to play with the Teutons… It was all happening for Lord Rory, while you paraded your men in the pretty gardens of the palace and never saw a single enemy. Your sword, which you'd received with such pride, taunted you from within its scabbard. Because it always *was* within its scabbard! You never had to use it in battle.

'Even more humiliating was the fact King Philip would gallop off to Hambrig to seek Lord Rory's advice whenever anything went wrong or threatened the kingdom. He didn't confer with you. He didn't want your opinion on anything, and that was because he knew you for what you were: an imposter. A nobody rigged up to look like a general. He'd put you there of course – and that was the problem.'

'I grew to hate him,' Allan said in a low voice. 'You said I'd tell my story, but you've told it. That's exactly how it was. I'm a good soldier though. I know how to fight.'

'But you hated King Philip. And so you killed him.'

'I didn't kill him.'

'You gave the order to have him killed?'

'Yes.'

'Who did it?'

I wondered why she was asking. She must already know; she'd made it clear she knew everything. She knew me, she knew Allan, she knew our pasts and probably our futures too. This woman had to be a witch, for all she denied it.

Indistinctly, through his thickened, damaged lips, Alan now revealed the killer's name. 'When the royals rode to Nightmolben to inspect the damage, Captain Leo went with them. I told Leo to push Philip, Julia and Barney over the cliff.'

'It was just Leo who went with them?'

'No, there were two others from the Guard. But Leo made sure they were checking Nightmolben Forest when the royals were staring at the ruined castle. Leo said Philip was standing right on the edge, and it was easy to tip him over, almost as if it was an accident. Barney was further back, but when he saw his father disappear, he ran towards Leo.

'Leo hit Barney over the head with something and he went flying. Julia died there too. Leo called his two men out of the forest and made out there'd been a terrible tragedy. They even tried to climb down the cliff to see if anyone was still alive. They gave up, although later, Lord Rory made them go back to fetch the bodies. Julia's body was never found, but Philip's and Barney's were brought home. Leo's guilty of this crime, not me.'

'You're both equally guilty,' I growled, horrified by what I'd just heard.

'So,' the wise woman said calmly, 'I think that brings us up to date. Twenty-two years is a long time, but Master Allan has achieved more in the last year than in the previous twenty-one put together. And now we're almost ready for him to march to the coast and take ship for the continent.'

'We're not ready for that at all,' I said, determined that Allan should face a tribunal and punishment for the King's murder. Leo too, of course. He might well argue that he was only obeying orders, but that wouldn't save him from the noose. 'Look, I know you say you're Karima, which you can't be, but leave that aside for now. You are clearly a very clever and spiritual woman. You may or may not be a witch, but you're not in charge here. This man will face trial for the murder of King Philip, Queen Julia and Prince Barney—' I stopped suddenly.

The wise woman was looking directly at me. Surely it was just in my imagination that she now had the lustrous dark brown eyes of the girl in the Bedouin tent? She held out her left hand, extending the little finger with the circular burn mark. 'We are leaving nothing aside, sir. I am Karima, as you see. I am the girl you fucked in the desert. I am starlight; the past, the present and the future. I am your nemesis and your redeemer. I am Karima, and my name means "generous". Let us, then, be generous, sir. This man has suffered greatly, and the harm he has done cannot be undone. He is no danger to anyone except himself. You will not organise a trial for him, since you do not wish his crime to be made public. Indeed, you yourself are passing the King's death off as a tragic accident. Let it remain so. Give this man his freedom, in the same spirit of generosity that I gave myself to you in the sands of Egypt.'

A week later, when the two Wartsbaye men returned, having escorted Allan to Navisar, they told me a ship named the *Wenno* had been waiting, beached on the sands with an anchor thrown out into deep water. As soon as Allan had climbed aboard, someone had winched the ship off, hauled up the anchor and a sail had been set. The steersman had turned the ship's head to the open sea, and the Wartsbayes had watched her sail into the rising sun, which had blinded them from seeing anything more. When they were finally able to squint out to sea again, they beheld only the rolling waves. There was no ship to be seen.

I'd spent that week making sure Lillian knew her duties as Queen. She was now ruler of a kingdom, and would find it very different from being the wife of the man in charge.

'Where is Louis?' she'd asked on the first morning.

'Gone, your Majesty. He took his fine chariot and travelled back to Hambrig in it. His trading ship will have arrived in Bremen by now and he will be on his way back to Heidelberg.'

'He's going to marry Matilda of Habsburg?'

'I believe so, your Majesty. He has annulled his marriage to you, declaring you to be of unsound mind.'

She'd smiled wanly. 'Better than being beheaded for adultery, I suppose.'

'What happened to you, lady? You did lose your mind for a time. It was the wise woman who helped you recover it, although by then your husband had left Hicrown. Can you talk about it?'

'I will tell you, Lord Rory, but I would rather not mention it again after this. Reinhard's brother had me taken away while everyone was fighting in the gardens. He wasn't cruel to me, but his men were. Their names are Giedrius and Dominykas, and they're in the Osnabrück Guard. Reinhard loved me, and he would never have ordered them to do this. I believe they were bribed by Reinhard's brother, but they were evil anyway. They took me from the palace. They bound my legs and arms and tied a filthy cloth inside my mouth. I fainted, and when I woke I was in a horrible, dark building on my own. Both the men raped me there. They came every day with food and water, and every day they took me again. Both of them, one after the other. They said I was to be sent abroad on a ship, and I would become a prostitute in their own country. They laughed about it. I couldn't wait for the ship to come so that I need never see them again. I know I should thank you for rescuing me, and I do, but you need to know that I will never be with a man again. I will not marry and I will not sleep with a man. Never.'

I would have executed Giedrius and Dominykas, but when Jonny found Lillian at the Navisar Gate there was no sign of them. They did not die on the palace lawn on 4th September, like the rest of Reinhard's Osnabrück Guard. Reinhard had also stayed away from that fight, and now that he's dead, I'll never know why. As for Giedrius and Dominykas, they'll be found one day. And when they are, they will regret they ever set eyes on Lillian, Queen of Mallrovia.

Exhausted, I headed to my chamber. Where I got a shock. Waiting for me was Margaret Longsword. She sat by the window, where the early evening light gave her lovely face an ethereal radiance. I stood in the doorway, my heart thundering in my throat. Ever since my monumental stupidity when talking to Jonny, Margaret had kept well out of my way, and I had not blamed her for doing so.

She looked at me, but didn't move. 'I want to talk to you.'

I came into the room and sat on the bed facing her. 'I want to apologise.'

She waited.

'I was a complete fool, Margaret. I spoke in anger to

Jonny, not knowing you were there. I didn't mean a word I said, and afterwards I was sick with shame. I am so, so sorry. Can you forgive me?'

'I have been speaking to Doctor Bethan,' Margaret said. 'A remarkable woman. She told me things about you, things I hadn't known. Bethan's experiences with men have not been happy ones.'

'I know. She has a rather warped view—'

'I would not say so. She has a realistic view. I told her I'm married to a man who doesn't come near me in bed. I said I'd been sleeping with you, and I described what that was like, what it meant for me. She mentioned the trouble your wife has had in bearing children, but now you have two, a boy and a girl. She told me you were reckless and rude, arrogant and entitled, but you have a heart of gold. I confessed I was in love with you, and she told me to snap out of it.'

I swallowed hard. 'Margaret—'

'I will not sleep with you again, Rory. I would not be able to trust you. I realise I should never have trusted you, for you are married to a beautiful Iberian noblewoman, and your heart is with her.'

'No, Margaret—'

'Don't try to change my mind, please. I wanted only to tell you these things. I am grateful to Bethan for her honesty and her wisdom. I am only eighteen years old. I know little of men, but I am aware my husband is not typical. Before you spoke as you did to Sir Jonny, I had decided to leave Henry, my husband. I thought you might love me and want me. I am pleased you said what you did, for my eyes have been opened, and now I shall leave Mallrovia for good. I should be grateful if you will provide an escort for me to return home, where I intend to be a good wife to my husband, whatever his shortcomings. I am sorry to have been the bearer of bad news for Sir Jonny. I hope he will come back to Salisbury, if only to take possession of his father's goods.'

'When do you want to leave?'

'As soon as it can be arranged.'

She left the next day, Jonny himself providing the required escort.

'Why not?' he'd asked belligerently. 'She needs someone to escort her to Salisbury. Now I know about my father, I also have to go to Salisbury. It makes sense.'

'I need you here, Jonny.'

I *did* need him. Mallrovia was still in great danger. Queen Lillian still required a great deal of coaching in exactly how to carry out her duties, and there was the cathedral to rebuild... I needed Jonny's help. But his mind was made up and I had no authority over Jonny. He would want to talk to Margaret about his father's death, and I could not blame him for that. I watched him ride out through the Palace Gate alongside Margaret Longsword and thought about the irony of it. Jonny had left Salisbury accompanied by William Longsword, and was returning twenty-four years later with the man's granddaughter. Then, a whole week after he'd left, I realised I'd never asked him about Joel Rice.

Would I ever see Jonny again? *Oh yes,* said a soft voice in my head. *You will see him again, sir. Remember what I told you: I am your nemesis and your redeemer.*

39

CUT HIS THROAT

Leo, the murderer, has escaped. After bringing him back from the marshes near the Shamet, Titus and Jonny threw him into the city gaol, as the palace has no dungeon of its own. But the gaol door had not been properly repaired since Master Billinge set fire to it. It was easy for Leo to free himself, and now nobody knows where he is. Peter, Leo's father, is distraught, and goes to enormous lengths to avoid meeting me.

He's not the only one. Margaret has left for Salisbury, and I know I'll never see her again. Patrick, it seems, is a vile criminal who's been exploiting young girls for years, taking over his father's 'business' without a qualm – while Jonny, with whom I would once have shared everything, has gone from my life again. The Earl of Warwick, though no particular friend, has also departed, hopefully to report our new, if fragile, stability to his king.

Titus and the Pevariles are out searching for Leo. So far, no trace of him has been found, and now Peter has also disappeared. Tortoise is gone from the stables, so I can only think Peter has decided to return to Hambrig, although he said no word to me about it. The possibility exists, of course, that Peter is hiding Leo. I've mentioned all this to the searchers, and if it is the case, then Tortoise should be easy to spot, even if the runaways are well hidden. In the meantime, I can only wait here until the reports come in, or a captive Leo is brought to me. He will not escape this time. I was lenient for Peter's sake, and the man did not lose his life for his treacherous crimes. Next time, I shall not show mercy.

I do now think of the wise woman as Karima, though her eyes have turned green again, but I haven't seen her since Allan was marched down to the coast. Had she not turned up in the grounds, though, at the exact moment Allan was about to disembowel me, I'd be dead. Karima saved my life – just as she did in Egypt all those years ago.

Moments like this, on my own with only my precious journal for company, my father's ghost often appears. Usually, it's to chastise and rebuke me for my foolishness, my ignorance or my clumsy actions. Sometimes all three. I know he'll come this morning, if only to tell me how badly I've treated both Margaret and Rosa, and how blind I've been to what happened here in Hicrown. I should have foreseen the rising up of the citizens against the unjust practices of the cathedral officers. King Philip's death left a gaping hole, into which, like molten lava from a volcano, flowed all the decades-old grievances that had been bubbling away below the surface. I should have predicted it. So, of course, should Baron Giles, my fellow tenant-in-chief. But Giles had been ill for months, whereas I…

You, too, were ill, says my father. He's leaning against the wall by the window. There's no light on him, so I can't see his expression.

Not in the same way.

No, it was a different illness. But – the Darkness still counts.

It's just an excuse. Yes, the Darkness is real and it's incapacitating, but that doesn't help Hicrown. And it's my duty to get this city functioning again.

What have you done so far?

I've visited everyone. They're slowly drifting back, now peace has been restored here. The merchants, the farmers, the Jews, the bankers, the craftsmen and women... I've been to see them all. In their own ways, they all said the same thing. They want stability and normality. They don't want to pay higher taxes just because the cathedral owns God's Acre. They want a fair deal.

Can you promise they'll get it?

I don't know. I can't force the bishop's tenants to pay taxes when they've never done so. It's a legacy issue. I've asked that lawyer – Jenner – to find a way round it, but I'm not sure he can.

Sounds like you've done everything possible, boy. But of course, there's still Patrick. Once you've got 'stability', 'normality' and a 'fair deal' in Hicrown – what are you going to do about Myrtile?

Bryce saddled Blue and Trojan. We left Hicrown during the morning of Tuesday 1st November, setting a steady pace down Navisar Road and heading for the grassy track that led north to the city of Myrtile, that strange, shimmering apparition. Who in their right mind would make roofs from solid gold? Who would paint all the spires that translucent in-between colour called turquoise? Even the Romans had not gone for such a degree of uniformity.

'We could've taken the other track,' Bryce observed as

the sun rose ahead of us. 'Straight from the palace to Myrtile.'

'Not so easy on horseback,' I'd answered shortly. I didn't want to tell Bryce my plan. Patrick would undoubtedly keep a watch on the Secret Way to his city of sin, but I intended to surprise him, both with my visit and with my knowledge of his activities. As we rode, I looked for signs of the smugglers. They must come this way, I reasoned. After they'd stored their goods in the warehouses, they must travel along Navisar Road. Today, it was deserted.

'It was a different path they brought the girls down,' Bryce said, continuing some train of thought in his head. 'You remember, lord? You sent me to investigate that day we were on the beach? I didn't get all the way to Myrtile, but I could see I'd've ended up there, and I found tracks made by bare feet, all women's. They bring those girls straight from Myrtile to the beach, they don't go to Hicrown first.'

'Then why do we find traces of human habitation in the warehouses?' I was speaking more to myself than to Bryce. 'And why don't they bring the worsted straight to the beach as well? We know they don't, because my brother spoke of the "stuff" that's stored there. That's what the smugglers call the worsted: *stuff*. Nick heard them talking about it.'

But that had been two years ago. Perhaps they'd changed their operation since then. It seemed the only explanation.

'Look, lord!' Bryce was pointing ahead.

I saw nothing moving on the road, and even, checking behind, could see no cause for alarm.

'Look!' he said again. 'The way's blocked!'

I cursed. We were approaching the track to Myrtile, and Bryce had seen ahead more clearly than I had. At the turning, huge boulders rested firmly, one upon the other, closing the gap between the hedges and the fields and completely blocking the entrance to the lane.

'I'll check what's on the other side,' Bryce called out, moving Trojan forward at pace and dismounting at the same time. I stayed in my saddle and watched him clamber up the rocky obstruction. I wondered where the massive stones had come from. They were taller than I was, even seated on Blue's back, and I could not see over them. It was clear we couldn't take the lane to Myrtile.

Bryce steadied himself on the top of the obstruction, looking down into the lane. Then he turned, showing agility and a good sense of balance, which was a relief. I really didn't want him to come crashing down at my feet. 'Lord, even the path is unusable. It isn't just these rocks blocking us from joining it, it's the lane itself. It's covered with rocks and stones as far as I can see. Someone doesn't want us to visit Myrtile.'

'Someone doesn't want *anyone* to visit Myrtile,' I said. 'Or depart from it, for that matter.'

'Are we going to go back?' Bryce came slithering down to ground level again.

'Either we go back to Hicrown and take the Secret Way after all, or we go on to Navisar and explore the other track, the one you followed before.'

'The Trail of Blood,' Bryce said ghoulishly. 'Which way's quicker, lord?'

'I'm not sure. Can we take the horses up your Trail of Blood?'

'I don't think so. It's too narrow and difficult ...'

'We'll have to leave them on the beach. And then we'll find the path they brought the girls down.'

We rode past the fishermen's cottages and arrived in the dunes at sunset. The fishing fleet was offshore, and we could see their sails on the horizon from time to time. We spent the night in a sheltered, sandy hollow, and soon after dawn we walked the horses along the beach heading north, while the boats surged towards us on the tide, bringing home their catch. The day threatened rain, grey clouds covering the sun.

Bryce pointed out an opening in the dunes where a small stream ran through a gulley down to the sea. 'We have to follow the gulley through the dunes,' he explained. 'It runs north-west, and I'm guessing the slavers use the water to clean the girls up before they deliver them to the traders.'

It seemed probable. I liked the way Bryce thought things through. He was becoming an able young companion. 'Tell me if you have any further thoughts,' I said, in what I hoped was an encouraging tone. Bryce had young eyes, ears and legs, and I was relying on those to succeed in our mission. Having tethered the horses loosely in a patch of shade by the stream, we plunged through the woodland edge into the unknown.

At first it was uphill and difficult. I reminded myself that the girls didn't have to do this; they came the other way, making it downhill and easier for them. It was rocky terrain, with tangled, overgrown vegetation to each side of us. No one would cultivate or prune these bushes, though; they gave cover for the smugglers and deterred any would-be explorers. Bryce and I followed the gulley, dislodging loose stones with our feet and occasionally using our hands to haul us further up the track. As I'd predicted, around midday a drizzly rain began, making it harder to keep our footing and dripping uncomfortably down our necks. We persevered, mostly in silence.

Half a mile later, we came to the end of the gully the little stream had worn for itself. The water bubbled out of the earth at this point, and beyond the spring lay a stony path. This wasn't haphazard terrain. The path had been created by someone, small pebbles and stones laid down to make a trail that would take us to Myrtile. I glanced enquiringly at Bryce.

He answered my unspoken question. 'I didn't need the trail of blood from here; I could see this was an actual path. I followed for a mile or so, and as soon as I knew where it was taking me, I turned round and came back to report to you.'

'Well, you're going to do the whole thing now, Bryce.'

Getting from Navisar up to Myrtile took all day, and it was dusk when we emerged from a copse of trees and found ourselves opposite the turquoise and gold city. Between it and us, though, was the moat.

'Well,' I said, 'they didn't swim the girls across that. Either they walked round from the front, where the bridge is, or there's a boat on this side of the city. Which do you think?'

'Is the bridge guarded?'

'It wasn't when I came here with Master Peter. It was unguarded and lit by tall lamps. A very welcoming sight, in fact.'

'I'll do a quick recce, lord,' Bryce said. Keeping his body

low, he sprinted across the open ground to the moat. I stood at the treeline, watching, and he seemed to disappear when he got to the edge. Dark was falling quite quickly. Although the rain had stopped, the sky was still overcast, and I couldn't see where Bryce had gone. At one point, I thought I saw him at the moat's edge, but then he disappeared again, and a little while later, I heard movement in the rushes. But that might have been an otter...

After what seemed a long time, I sat down, leaning against a large, wet hawthorn tree. I was woken by an owl, which turned out to be Bryce, hooting through his fingers. He plonked himself down next to me.

'I found the way they bring the girls,' he said. 'It's through a tunnel under the moat.'

'*What?* How on earth did you discover that?'

'It's why I've been such a long time. I had to go into the city. I went round to the main entrance, like you said, and walked over the bridge. That was the easy bit. I was challenged as soon as I'd crossed it, but I said I had a message from Sir Allan of Hicrown. The man knew the name, right enough, and he took me to the church. He told the priest I had a message from Sir Allan, so I had to think pretty quickly. It was something close to the truth, although not exactly. I said Allan had double-crossed us, and he'd escaped on a ship.

'At first the priest didn't believe me, but when I told him the name of the ship, *then* he did. So I asked him if there was a new cargo waiting, and what we should do now that Allan had made his getaway. I could see the man was in a quandary. He had no idea what to do with the next batch of girls, so I said, "Let me see them." He took me into the crypt and there they were. Eight sorry-looking females, all around twelve to fifteen years old, I'd say.

'The priest stood with me, and I pretended to inspect the women, and I told the priest there was a back-up plan. I was thinking it out as I went along, and hoping he wouldn't ask what the back-up plan was. But he gave me some crucial information, lord. He said they were due to go out tonight. The sky's cloudy, and that's when they go. The ship will arrive and the girls will meet it. The priest said I should get away quickly, and he showed me the entrance to the tunnel.'

'You've done brilliantly, Bryce.' I'd had no idea my odd-job boy had such a clever, quick-thinking mind.

'I nearly messed up though. I mentioned Sir Patrick, because you'd said he was behind all this. But the priest got angry and told me to mind what I said.'

'So Patrick may not know about this shipment?'

'Looks that way. Or he doesn't know about Sir Allan. There's something being kept secret from him, that's clear.'

'Do you know when the girls will be moved?'

'Sometime tonight, that's all the priest said. He doesn't do it himself; somebody comes for them. He's called "the handler".'

'How are the girls treated in the crypt?'

'They're given food and they're not beaten or abused. They have to be kept in good condition for the market.'

'But they're tied up?'

'No, I don't think so. Do you want me to take you to the tunnel, lord? Are we going in?'

'No, Bryce. We are waiting here, and when this "handler" emerges from the tunnel, we take him out. He won't be expecting anything to happen, so we surprise him.'

'I have my dagger, lord.'

'We know the girls will be brought right here, the start of the trail to the beach. What we don't know is whether the handler follows or leads them. Where he'll be.'

We moved back into the trees a little, and waited in complete silence, one of us each side of the gravel path, both of us grasping our daggers, both of us ready. In my other fist I held a handful of pebbles. It would be easy to know when to strike. We didn't have to wait long. The handler made no attempt to stay quiet. We heard his voice as he swore at the girls, and we heard little high-pitched moans and cries from them. Then came the sound of the handler's boots as they crunched on the gravel, and more cries from the girls, as the sharp stones cut their feet. I had time to think that no one was bothering to look after the women's feet; it was their faces, their breasts and their hymens that must be preserved.

We were, perhaps, fifty yards from the entrance to the trail. The crunching steps came closer. The handler was swearing at the girls for making sounds of distress. Bryce and I were hidden in the trees, and I was confident the handler would not know we were there. The first of the girls came past me, and it was clear the handler was behind them, driving them forward. They were shackled together, and I could smell their fear.

I'd arranged a signal with Bryce, but we'd both thought the handler would lead from the front. The plan was based on that premise. I prayed Bryce would adapt quickly to this new situation. He'd told me there were eight girls, and I counted them as they filed past, one after the other, their ropes stretching back to the handler.

He was a big man. Still swearing and cursing, flicking the ropes as if driving a team of oxen, he came alongside Bryce and me and aimed a heavy-booted kick at the girl nearest him. She screamed and he laughed.

I hurled the pebbles onto the path, the signal to move, and we launched ourselves at the handler. He stood no chance as we brought him down and Bryce grabbed the man's throat while I fleeced him for weapons. We had not decided in advance what to do with him. The options were to kill him or to take him with us. I'd told Bryce it would depend on who he was, how much of a threat he was and my gut instinct.

Even with Bryce's hands around his throat, the handler was able to turn his head, and I realised his face was familiar. I couldn't quite place it though. Then, he spat a great gob of spittle and phlegm straight into my face. With the terrified girls in a huddle by the trees, I made the easiest decision of my life.

'All right, Bryce. Cut his throat.'

40

THE WHOLE THING IS A SHAM

There was only one word for Patrick's expression: stony. I'd never seen him look like that before. He confirmed he knew about the slave trading and the stealing of young Mallrovian girls to be sold abroad, although he'd only found out about it after his father died. Why hadn't he said anything to me before? Two reasons, apparently. One, he didn't think it was still going on; and two, it didn't come under my jurisdiction, Myrtile being its own shire.

I considered both arguments spurious.

We were in the torch-lit hall in Patrick's gold-plated manor house. When I'd been here with Peter, Myrtile's riches had impressed me. Not just the use of gold and other expensive materials, but the intricate and careful design of the buildings, streets and squares; the lit-up bridge welcoming visitors; the grand church that resembled a cathedral in its proportions; and the lack of crime, dirt and stink you find in every other town and city.

Now I saw it for what it really was. The city was a monument to greed and lust, funded from the proceeds of suffering and cruelty. The bright, welcoming bridge on the south side of the city masked the existence of the dank tunnel under the moat on the east side, where girls who'd been snatched from their families were shepherded out into the dark woodland and driven down to the coast like cattle.

I understood why Allan had made himself rich on his income from smuggling and slavery. I knew his type. He'd grown up in poverty and he'd never known a life of chivalry and honour. I understood why the Livonians had been involved, too. Theirs was the market. Shipped far away to the Baltic, the girls would never be traced. Even Lillian would never have been found if Allan's plan had gone ahead. Once Reinhard was dead, Lillian had no defenders. I did not, however, understand why Patrick, a trusted and long-serving member of my father's household, had betrayed us.

'Shall we sit?' he offered.

'This isn't a cosy chat, Patrick. You are likely to lose your head for this, but before you do, I want to know why you did it.'

'I have done nothing wrong. It is true that the gold and the fine tapestries were paid for out of profits from smuggling and slavery. But I never engaged in these activities. Unfortunately, my father did, although I knew nothing of it until after his death. I discovered his wealth then, and decided to use it to make something beautiful out of something dirty. To cleanse it, as it were. So I built Myrtile.'

'Just like that? A golden city rose from the earth, paid for by your father's greed in blood money?'

'There is no need for such spiteful talk. I have made what amends I can. I could not bring back the girls who were enslaved, nor the wool that was trafficked. I could only try to use my father's money for the good.'

'How have you used it for the good?' I cried, suddenly incensed by all this careful, conciliatory talk. 'You've built a city that encourages even more sinful behaviour! From here, girls are marched through dark forests and over stones that rip their feet to shreds. When they reach the coast, they're put on board Baltic ships that take them to Livonia. This happens *here*, in your purified paradise! As for the worsted, the smuggling of which is costing this country a fucking fortune, it comes from *your* sheep, *your* farmers, *your*—'

Bryce burst into the room. 'Lord Rory! I've been talking to the girls, and I know who's behind this! I know how it happens and why, and I know the handler's name! I can tell you everything!'

He stood in the middle of the room, panting, his clothes wringing wet, hair plastered to his scalp. Realising he looked a mess, he came to attention, pushing soaking wet hair out of his face. 'Sorry, lord. It's raining hard out there now.'

'Then I'd trouble you to stand clear of that expensive Indian rug, young man,' Patrick said caustically. Bryce tiptoed to the edge of the room. By now, he was shivering.

'Bryce, I need to hear what you have to say. We will go...' I'd been about to say we'd go to my chamber – but, of course, Patrick would hardly offer me his hospitality now. Not after my accusations.

Patrick guessed why I'd stopped speaking. 'I will light the fire here in the hall, and we will have fresh clothes brought for the boy. I should like to hear his statements. Where are these girls now?'

Bryce looked at me, and I shook my head. We would not reveal their whereabouts to Patrick.

Patrick saw all this and gave a half-smile. He clicked his

fingers, and Rolf, the steward, limped in. Patrick sent him off for dry clothes for Bryce, then bent and lit the kindling in the fireplace. A few logs were added, and soon the flames leapt high up the wall. I told Bryce to strip off his wet clothes.

'I need to tell you right away, lord,' he said through chattering teeth. 'It's him. He runs it all, the girls, the woollen cloth, everything. He's been doing it for years.'

I looked over at Patrick. So the girls were confirming it, were they? Patrick, once loved and trusted in the Castle Rory household, was guilty of these terrible crimes.

Bryce saw my look. 'I didn't mean Sir Patrick! I meant the steward. The girls told me it's the steward. His name's Kaufmann.'

Kaufmann? Was the boy confused? Had he got so drenched in the rain he'd muddled the names up? 'Bryce, it's our steward at home who's Kaufmann. Not Sir Patrick's steward.'

'They said "Kaufmann", lord. "Rolf Kaufmann", that's what they said.'

'And they were quite right,' Patrick put in. 'That is my steward's name.'

And in the man came, right on cue, folded tunic and hose laid over one arm. An elderly man with limited mobility, he didn't look at all like the mastermind behind the smuggling racket. As for the slave trade – how could he be involved in that? His old man's eyes looked rheumily at us in confusion. 'Did someone say my name?'

Patrick took the man's arm and guided him to a chair. 'Sit down, Rolf. I think you need to tell these people your story. It got you into trouble years ago, and looks like doing so again now.'

There was silence for a few moments. Rolf looked at the

floor. Patrick's stern expression was unchanged. Bryce was getting dressed in the borrowed clothes, and I waited – and was prepared to wait all night if necessary. I could not figure out the connection between this man and my own steward. Perhaps, if their names truly were the same, it was just coincidence. But I'm not much of a believer in coincidence.

'Rolf,' Patrick said gently. 'I should like you to explain to me how you've been keeping this business going all these years.'

He looked up then. 'Sir Patrick, you weren't here. You built the city and then you moved away. You were at that castle in Hambrig for years! How were we meant to sustain ourselves?'

'I paid you. I paid everyone. There was no need to raise further funds, especially from such despicable practices.'

'I wanted more,' Rolf said softly. 'We all wanted more. My friend survived the attack, but he died many years ago, leaving four young sons.'

'Meanwhile, you just carried on shipping innocent children out to be sold into prostitution?' I put in. I was sickened by this story.

Rolf shrugged. 'It was a business. It was a business when Sascha and I did it together, and then later I joined up with his son, Carl.'

'Carl?' My heart was beating faster.

'He knows you. He told me he'd been to Bremen with you. Actually, he seems to like you, Lord Rory.'

'So we're talking about Carl von Lutterberg? And his father was Sascha? Sascha von Lutterberg?'

Rolf Kaufmann nodded. He might be in his seventies, but his eyes had regained their clarity, and his mind was sharp. And I was beginning to piece this together.

'You mentioned "four young sons". Would they be Dicky, Otto, Carl and Reinhard, by any chance?'

Patrick narrowed his eyes. 'You know these people, Rory?'

'I knew three of them. Only Carl survives.'

'Reinhard's dead?' Rolf asked, suddenly alert. His back straightened. His 'old man' persona fell away. It had been an act, and a good one. Patrick looked shocked.

I confirmed Reinhard's death. Dicky had been hanged last year. Otto had died in February, but I'd never met Otto. 'Three are dead, Rolf,' I said. 'And I do not know where Carl is now. What does that mean for you?'

'I know what it means for him,' Patrick said, suddenly leaning over and seizing the man by the throat. 'It means he gets to keep all of their money! Isn't that right, you greedy snake in the grass? I offered you freedom, Rolf. The chance to return to your homeland and your family. I was going to let you go. But you chose to stay here. You told me you were ashamed of everything you'd done, and you wanted to make amends. You promised me you would look after my Myrtilers and you would run my city well. But the whole time I was away in Hambrig, you were abusing my people and profiteering from their misery. You had your chance to go home twenty years ago, Rolf. Why should I let you live now?'

Patrick's grip was firm, and his wide hand around Rolf's scrawny throat pinned the steward back against the wall.

But I didn't want the man to die just yet. There were still so many unanswered questions. 'Patrick, ease off a bit. I want to know who this man really is.'

Patrick allowed Rolf to massage his throat for a few moments.

Then I said, 'Who is Inka Kaufmann?'

He looked at me in astonishment. 'How do you know Inka?'

'Just answer.'

'My wife. She was my wife. I don't know if she still lives. We had a house in Bremen. Did you meet her when you were there?'

'I did. And she told me she was a widow.'

'I had intended to return. But Sir Patrick set an ambush. Sascha escaped but I was caught. I never went back.'

'She told me you were a Teutonic Knight.'

'A Livonian Swordbrother, actually. Now we are part of the Teutonic Knights, and we are allowed to call ourselves "the Livonian Order", but we are the Brothers of the Sword! As you are about to discover.'

Before we could blink, Rolf Kaufmann pulled a dagger from his belt and pointed it towards Patrick.

'You see, Lord Rory,' Rolf said, but he was looking at Patrick, 'Sir Patrick thought he was very clever to build this golden city from the money his father had made. Patrick's father was in the slave trade. Patrick discovered this after his father died, but he chose not to tell your father, for whom he worked tirelessly. Nor did he mention it to you, when you became Hambrig's lord. Patrick chose, in fact, to hide this information from everyone.

'He took the money, which he despised, knocked down his father's farm, and built his beautiful city. It took a long time, didn't it, Sir Patrick? And you hated it! You hated the city you built with your father's ill-gotten gains, but you kept building it anyway, adding gold to the rooftops and spending, spending, spending, until all your father's hoard was gone. And then you invited people to live here! Shall I tell Lord Rory who was on the guest list?'

Rolf twisted his dagger and pushed on it at the same

time. It pierced Patrick's padded jerkin. When Rolf withdrew the blade, there was a bright scarlet stain on it. Patrick had not uttered a sound. His eyes bored into Rolf Kaufmann's, as if he were trying to read something there, something that would explain the man's behaviour.

Bryce half stood and looked over at me. In his face was a mute question. *Do we rush Kaufmann? Disable and disarm him? Before he kills Patrick?* I didn't move. I wanted more from Kaufmann. As the Livonian pushed the dagger back through Patrick's jerkin, I felt, rather than heard, Bryce subside again. There would be no attack on the steward until we had all the facts.

Even if Patrick dies? My father asks.

I swallow hard. My father has no right to be here, not at this moment, not when I need to balance the fate of the kingdom against the life of a man I've known and respected all my life. And, in any case, I can't answer because, if I do, everyone will hear me speak.

Well, it's your decision, Father says. *I should tell you, though, that Patrick was the best steward I ever had. Not that there were many. Eddie, the steward I had before Patrick, was rough, tough and good at his job. But I never took to him. Patrick was a man I could like and respect. I could talk to him, man to man. That is a very special and precious thing, boy. Perhaps you should try it?*

I don't know where Father is. I can't see him. And that's because I must not take my eyes off Rolf Kaufmann, Sir Patrick of Myrtile, and the dagger that binds us all together.

But Father's words bounced around my head. *Perhaps you should try it?* Try what? Oh yes. Talking to Patrick, man to man. Or – no! Talking to *Rolf*, man to man! That was what Father meant.

I stood up and moved towards Rolf Kaufmann.

'Don't come close to me,' he growled. 'Any closer, and Patrick gets this blade through his heart, and don't doubt me, Lord Rory. I will do it if I have to. The Livonians need Mallrovia, and nothing will stand in our way. We have money, we have men, and now we have Myrtile.'

During this speech, I'd been motioning to Bryce to stay where he was. Patrick looked very pale, and blood was now seeping through the padded jerkin. I watched the dull stain spreading. There was blood pooling on the floor as well.

Rolf turned his head. 'Don't stand there like a statue. You're giving me the jitters. I could push harder than I mean to if you're not careful.'

'I want to talk to you, Rolf. I want to understand. What will the Swordbrothers do, once you have Mallrovia?'

'It will be our base. From here, we can easily sail to the Baltic and carry out our mission.'

'Which is?'

'To convert the pagans to Christianity, of course.'

'I tried that, Rolf,' I said softly. 'Spent years in the Middle East, attempting to do exactly that, as did King Louis of France and Charles of Anjou, his brother. And do you know what? We did not succeed. We lost a lot of men fighting, and we did not win back Jerusalem nor gain a single soul for Christ.'

'But *we* will. We have a debt to repay. The Lithuanians and the Semigallians murdered us at Karuse, where Otto von Lutterberg lost his life. Sascha's eldest son. We were beaten, dishonoured and forced to retreat. We are building our strength back up again now, and the money from the sale of the virgin girls is our war chest. It is a pity that most of the von Lutterberg brothers are dead, but that will not stop us from being Swordbrothers. We have their deaths to avenge now, as well as our defeat at Karuse. And I will find Carl. Or he will find me. Our partnership is not dead, in spite of your efforts.'

'On a more personal note, Rolf – would you like to see Inka again? Your wife? She's here, in Mallrovia.'

Inka was my secret weapon. Rolf thought her still in Bremen, or perhaps no longer alive.

There was a long pause, during which I was unsure if Kaufmann was digging deeper into Patrick's chest with his dagger. Patrick's eyes were closed, and his face looked ghastly. Blood now soaked the jerkin and his breeches were slick with it. Perhaps I'd made my play too late.

Finally, though, Kaufmann turned and faced me, withdrawing the dagger just an inch.

'Bryce!' I screamed, praying the servant was ready.

Bryce was at Patrick's side in a moment, tugging the dagger free and using his own wet and discarded clothes to bind the wound, staunching further blood loss, while he gently lowered Patrick to the floor. I'd pinioned Kaufmann's arms to his sides, then kneed him in the stomach so that he folded up on himself. He finished up on the floor, of course, and I helped him lean his back against the wall, his hands tied behind him now.

Bryce shouted for Deborah, who must have been asleep in her room. She came flying down the stairs, her long grey hair tumbling from its snood, a hastily donned robe clutched around her, horrified to see her husband so bloodied and wounded. She gave rapid instructions to Bryce, and he ran off to find the physician, who would also have to be roused from his bed.

I turned my attention to Kaufmann. 'You were about to tell me who was on the guest list.'

'He got all the families to come here.'

'The families who'd lost their daughters?'

'Yes. Patrick told them he couldn't bring their girls back, but they could live here, rent free, for the rest of their lives, and their children too, and their grandchildren. No one pays anything. They can work if they want to, but they don't have to. There's always plenty. Plenty of food, plenty of fun, plenty of money... that's Myrtile. The City of Dreams, some call it.'

'It is not the City of Dreams,' Deborah said, as she held her husband's hand and waited for Bryce to return with the doctor. 'It is a City of Nightmares, Lord Rory! This man has been a traitor all along. Knowing what he did all those years ago, what he was capable of, Patrick should never have trusted him.'

And I wondered why Patrick *had* trusted Rolf Kaufmann. When he was at Castle Rory, Patrick used to tell me that Myrtile had been left in the care of a trusted steward. That 'trusted steward' now turned out to be a foreigner who wanted to take over my whole country! And Patrick had *known* of this!

'Not that part,' Deborah corrected me, after I'd stated my thoughts in bitter tones. 'Patrick knew of the slave business, of course, but not the Livonians or their bid for power.'

'And he did not know of the Battle of Saule,' Rolf Kaufmann croaked from his position against the wall. 'It was at that battle, when we were defeated by the Semigallians, that we lost our autonomy. The Teutonic Knights made us a part of their order, and we have been fighting to regain our independence ever since.'

'Mallrovia will also fight for independence,' I said. 'We will not have Livonians ruling our country.'

'What about the English?'

'Nor them. Mallrovians will rule in Mallrovia. And you, Rolf Kaufmann, will hang for your crimes.'

The physician has put Patrick in bed, his wounds salved and bandaged. No fatal damage was done, and Patrick will recover. Deborah sits by his side all the time, the picture of a devoted wife.

I've commended Bryce for his quick actions. That boy has proved his worth more than once now. I'm in my chamber writing my journal, and wondering what to do about Rolf Kaufmann, who is locked up in the cellar. Apparently, there are no law courts and there is no gaol in Myrtile, because everyone is so law-abiding. Even as I write the words, I snort in disgust. Law-abiding! City of Dreams! Yet slave trading and wool smuggling have been going on from here the whole time, with Patrick blind to it all.

King Philip, too, knew nothing, and it was his ignorance that killed him. Carl von Lutterberg, 'Sir' Allan, Rolf Kaufmann and Captain Leo should all have been tried and sentenced to death long ago. If they had been, Philip and Barney would still be alive. *City of Dreams*. I look back at where I wrote that down, and I draw a big, sneering line through the words. The whole thing is a sham.

41

IN TOTAL DARKNESS

Lillian was crowned Queen of Mallrovia, and the very next day we heard that Henry III of England had died. Now the Lord Edward is the English king, but he's an absent king, for he's on Crusade and far away. The letter I've received tells me that a royal council is currently governing England, while awaiting the Lord Edward's return. Except I must not call him 'the Lord Edward', for he is now King Edward. That will be hard to remember, English Henry having been on the throne for so long – longer, even, than I've been alive!

The letter is signed by a man called Robert Burnell, the Archdeacon of York. York is a place I know well, and I've frequently been to the Carmelite priory there. I have never met the archdeacon, though. Burnell implies the council has four members, all of whom have sworn to act in the new king's interests. Well, good for them. And it's also good that they've let me know, but – and I allow the parchment to roll itself up on the desk – I don't see that it's going to make any difference. I doubt very much that any of the four of them will be interested in the goings-on here, or that they'll know much about the fines Henry wanted to impose on the Hicrowners to fund the rebuilding of the cathedral.

Now that we have a monarch on the Mallrovian throne, legitimate and of sound mind, the English are hardly in a position to impose their rulings; after all, it's now the English whose king is absent. This fact, I have decided, must be firmly and decisively pointed out, should any English barons or earls decide to throw their weight about in Mallrovia.

I've authorised the repairs to the cathedral, and somehow the money must be found to pay for them. At the moment, I'm leaving that to providence. There is to be a new St Michael's Church, which Father Wymer is very excited about. This will also be expensive. I could chew my fingers off worrying about money, but that's the one and only good thing about the Darkness: you are so low, you have no feelings at all. So you worry about nothing. It will happen or it won't. It doesn't matter or it does. The outcome may be good or bad, but you don't care. That's what it's like in the Darkness.

'You know, it's a pity you've married,' Patrick said to me late last night.

After attending Lillian's coronation in Hicrown, Bryce and I had returned to Myrtile. Days ago, people from both cities had been despatched to clear the rocks, stones and boulders that had blocked the grassy track, and to level the surface. Travelling between Hicrown and Myrtile is now much more straightforward.

Deborah had gone to bed, and I was with Patrick in his

room. He can sit up now, and his chest hurts a great deal less than it did. I'd lit an oil lamp and several candles, so the room was cosy and bright.

Startled, I asked him why he thought it a pity. Most people had been delighted I'd at last found a wife who didn't die within days of her arrival.

'Because you could have married Lillian.'

'That was the original plan, if you remember, Patrick. It wasn't a good idea in '63, so why would it be one now?'

'With you as Consort, Lillian would have a stable and benign influence. She's level-headed enough, but she's easily taken advantage of.'

I'd told him about Reinhard. And, of course, about Duke Louis, whose tempestuous arrival in, and departure from, Mallrovia had been a lesson in how not to do diplomacy.

'She's definitely free of him now?' Patrick asked.

'He renounced her. So, yes. But *I* am not free, Patrick. I remain married to Lady Rosa, the daughter of Don Alfonso X of Castile, León, etc. etc., whose sister is married to the Lord Edward, I'd remind you. I mean King Edward. We do not want to upset the Castilians *or* the English, so I think I'd better stay with Rosa.'

'Yes, of course. I did not mean to imply you should not do so. My meaning was only that it is a pity you cannot marry Lillian, and ten years is a long time. You did not want her ten years ago, it's true, but she has grown up since then.'

'Well. It's irrelevant now. We must just hope she makes a good Queen.'

'I think we must do a great deal more than hope. We must make sure of it. *You* must make sure of it.'

Patrick has got me thinking. Is there anyone I trust enough to marry the Queen? Someone as yet unmarried, but with good connections. Someone who will put Mallrovia's interests first. Someone I can rely on, talk to in confidence, and with whom I can have a real bond. Someone who can, if need be, help me fight off the Livonians. But he will have to accept that the Queen is expecting someone else's child. Bethan tells me the baby will be born next spring, although it will be a tough birth for Lillian. Still, it will be good to know the line of succession is secure again.

Rolf Kaufmann will not be meeting his wife. In fact, I'm in two minds whether to even tell her of his life, his actions and his fate. Inka believed her husband to be a good man. A good man, who'd joined the Teutonic Order, and who'd drowned at sea. An honourable death.

He'd been young when he'd gone to sea, never to return, and she remembers him as that devil-may-care young man, starry eyed at joining a military order, eager for adventure. She doesn't speak of him often, but when she does, her eyes mist over and I know she's seeing a young Rolf Kaufmann heading off into the unknown, but full of promises to return and take care of his pretty young wife.

Inka regrets there were no children from her marriage. Rolf, she has told me, would have wanted children. They would have had a houseful of noisy, merry boys and girls. I believe she sees it all in her sleep. The husband who never came back; the children she never had. The *life* she never had.

So do I destroy all that? Do I tell her the truth – that her husband never returned, not because he'd drowned, but because he'd been caught selling girls into slavery and had then opted for an easy, and extremely profitable, life in the city of turquoise and gold? Perhaps Rolf had married again and fathered children here in Myrtile. That, I didn't know. Nor can I ask the man, because I've hanged him. The first crime to be punished in Myrtile, but by no means the first to be committed here. The gaudy colours and luxurious buildings have hidden a corrupt, wicked and vile underbelly of abuse, extortion and evil. That will now cease.

Tomorrow, every man, woman and child will parade before me and Patrick. Every one of them will confess their crimes to us, as far back as Patrick's father's day. And with those confessions will come punishment, shame and exile for some; absolution, freedom or redemption for others. Criminals will be rooted out; victims will be compensated.

Patrick, whose horrified expression cannot seem to recover, has been destroyed by this. It is as if he, himself, had driven pitiful little gaggles of eight girls at a time, down to the Navisar beach, for embarkation on a Livonian boat. As if he, himself, had lashed their hands, removed the shoes from their feet and ignored their cries of distress. As if he, himself, had checked their tiny vaginas to make sure they truly were virgins. *Yes, Rolf Kaufmann even did that.*

And it was, of course, the corrupt priest in the church who hid the entrance to the slave-tunnel, who'd secretly married Phoebe and Carl von Lutterberg, in the dead of night, with two witnesses only: Rolf Kaufmann himself, and Captain Leo. Well, much good it did them. Two von Lutterbergs died in the attempt to reinstate the Swordbrothers, and Rolf Kaufmann is gone too. Which leaves Carl von Lutterberg and Captain Leo, both in unknown locations, to be dealt with.

I finished writing, put my journal away and called for my servant.

'Bryce. We'll be leaving Myrtile the day after tomorrow. The parade will take most of tomorrow, together with writing orders and issuing arrest warrants. On Thursday, you're to make sure the horses are ready for a dawn start. You'll be busy helping me tomorrow. Can you write?'

He could neither read nor write. But Deborah, it turned out, could. Patrick had decided he couldn't face the parade, but Deborah, an equable person with a calm, unruffled temperament, was more than happy to be my scribe. I put Bryce to work organising the Myrtilers into groups of eight (yes, there was deliberate irony in that) and sending them through the 'Community Square', as it's called.

'Where shall we hold the parade?' I'd asked Deborah. I wasn't keen on the townsfolk traipsing through the manor house, their feet treading dirt into the sumptuous rugs, their grubby hands fingering Patrick's delicate ornaments.

Deborah thought outdoors would be best. 'There'll be plenty of room in the Community Square, and we can set up a table there. I know it's cold just now, but you and I can cope with that. And Bryce can get people to file past in an orderly manner.'

'What on earth is a community square?' I'd asked.

Deborah had sighed. 'Most towns and cities have a market square. But Myrtile has no market.'

'No market? Then how do people buy what they need? How do the merchants trade goods and conduct their business?'

'They don't. Patrick never wanted anyone to have to worry about buying food. Or buying anything. He didn't want some people to be richer and others poorer. He wanted everyone to have everything they needed, so he used his father's money to provide. No merchants trade here. No goods are bought and sold, except by Patrick, who distributes them. Well, that's what he told me when I first knew him, but it turns out that Rolf was in charge for many years, and the system changed a lot. Sadly, Patrick never realised. He trusted Rolf completely.'

'So what is the Community Square, Deborah?'

'It's in the centre of the city, where the market would be if we had one. Patrick designed it rather like a Roman forum. A place where people could meet and talk and discuss things. The social hub of Myrtile.'

So here we were on Wednesday 23rd November, and the day, although cold, was at least dry. Our table was large, and both Deborah and I sat behind it. Deborah had quill, ink and parchment, while I summoned up my sternest expression. Bryce stood at the entrance to the square and directed his groups with great efficiency.

By the end of the morning, Deborah's head was in her hands, and her tears had washed some of the ink off the parchment. Well, there's only a certain amount of unruffledness anyone can display. Patrick's idyllic vision of Myrtile as a place of equal merit, opportunity and outcome had lasted a couple of years only. Soon after he'd left Myrtile to take up his position as steward to my father, Rolf Kaufmann had begun to play his hand. Patrick had given him complete control of the money and the distribution of food and clothing.

Rolf now made sure people were denied basic goods unless they met his demands and complied with his rules. The wool smuggling had begun in '66, the year King Philip began his greedy tariffs on premium exports from Mallrovia. Worsted wool from the superlative Myrtile sheep was surrendered to Kaufmann, who took it down the Secret Way to Hicrown, where Allan stored it in the Navisar warehouses. Eventually it was taken along the road to Navisar itself and shipped to the continent, tariff-free of course. That road was deliberately kept rough and difficult, and few people used it; only the fishermen who brought their catch to sell in Hicrown, and then – conveniently, and pocketing their pay as they did so – trundled back to Navisar with the bales of worsted. Our fishing fleet was as guilty as Kaufmann and Allan. As far as the wool smuggling was concerned, anyway.

The slave trade was another matter. It had begun before the turn of the century, before Patrick was even born, in fact. Patrick's father, a greedy farmer in a simple agricultural community, was responsible for thirty years of selling Myrtile women abroad. When he died in 1215, Patrick discovered what had been going on. He put an immediate stop to it and built his beautiful city in an attempt to cleanse both the money and his soul.

Fourteen years later, Rolf Kaufmann and Sascha von Lutterberg began their devastating alliance, but once again it was stopped by Patrick, who was so distressed he decided he could no longer live in Myrtile. It was at this point he became my father's steward, moving to Hambrig and leaving the door wide open for Rolf and Sascha to resume operations. After Sascha's death, Rolf made contact with

Carl, and the trading continued. As the men and women who'd sold their daughters and granddaughters paraded past our table, Deborah and I began to grasp the scale of the operation.

'They took both my daughters,' said Master Perry. 'Ten years ago, that was. I don't know where they are, what happened to them.'

'You didn't try to stop them being taken?' I asked, shaken.

'It wasn't like that. You didn't get no choice. They take 'em or they kill 'em.' He shrugged. Moved on. Made way for the next sad person with an even sorrier tale to tell.

'Some men slept with their girls,' sixty-year-old Dickon told us. 'Deliberately fucked their own daughters so as to say they weren't virgins no more. But then Kaufmann found out that was goin' on and he say he kill any men who did that an' he kill their daughters too. So even that dun't work. I lost three girls, and my son lost Eleanor, his only child. She was only eleven. All gone.' He shuffled off too, memories of the lost girls choking his last few words.

And so it went on. Story after story of coercion, threats and enslavement. Mothers spoke to us too, but I can't bring myself to set down all their harrowing stories and their heartache. One had tried to hide her child.

'We knew it was time. Always when it was cloudy, you see. No moon, no stars. My husband and I took Maisie out to our neighbours' cattle barn. We didn't think they'd find her there, as it wasn't our barn, and our neighbours had no daughters. But they knew about Maisie, and they hunted everywhere for her. When they couldn't find her, they killed my husband. My children were screaming. I was screaming too. The men picked up my twin four-year-old boys and started beating them. I had to stop it! I had no choice! God help me, I told them where Maisie was. They dumped the twins and went to fetch her. Then I heard her screaming as they tore her from the barn. That Kaufmann. He's evil. He enjoyed fingering those poor little girls to make sure they were pure. I couldn't bear it. The same thing happened to Mistress Maggie who lived here in the town, and afterwards she couldn't bear it either. She killed herself. I didn't; I had the boys. I had to look after them.'

'When was this?' Deborah asked gently. 'When was Maisie taken?'

'Five years ago. She'll be sixteen now. If she still lives.'

We got to the end of it at last. Every testimony was faithfully written down by Deborah, so I haven't copied them all in my journal. To be honest, by the end I could barely listen, let alone write. I didn't know how Deborah had coped with it.

'I had to,' she said simply. 'I owed it to each and every one of them to write their story. And I've made a list of the girls' names. All of them. Look.'

She'd used a separate roll of parchment, and when I saw the long, long list of names, my breath caught in my throat.

'Don't lose this,' I said hoarsely. 'I want it kept forever. Rolf Kaufmann's dead and Allan is in exile, but there's still Leo to deal with. Bryce and I are going back to Hicrown tomorrow. But we'll be back, Deborah. And things are going to change, here in Myrtile.'

She nodded, tying up her parchments with ribbon and indicating to the boys who hung around that they could take the table back to the house. It was beginning to get dark, and I was hoping for an early night. But Deborah had a question. 'All those people spoke of "they". "They" took Maisie, Eleanor, Beth and the others. So who were "they", Rory? Who else was involved?'

'The priest was involved,' I said at once. 'He looked after the tunnel that they had to walk through to get out of Myrtile.'

'Where is the priest? Have you locked him up, Rory? Though I can hardly believe he was part of this. Patrick and I always trusted him...'

But I'd done nothing about the corrupt clergyman. Cursing, I hurried over to the beautiful church, its turquoise spire rising from golden finials and corbels. Inside, the church was well lit with tall candles every few inches along the long walls. Kneeling in front of the altar was the priest. I tried to remember his name, and when I couldn't, wondered if I'd ever been told it.

'Tell me who you are,' I called, while still only halfway along the nave.

'My name is Father Clarence.' He stood up, but didn't walk towards me.

'And I am Lord Rory of Hambrig.' I took a couple more steps.

'I know who you are, my lord. Have you come to arrest me?'

The direct question took me by surprise. 'Why should I arrest you?'

'You are not here to pray,' he said at once. 'And all day long you have heard about the Myrtile girls. Yes. You're here to arrest me.'

'Who helped you?'

'Well, I have two acolytes. Or I had two. But, sadly, they're no longer here.'

'So the three of you worked together, removing young

girls from their homes? Testing their purity? Is that right, Father Clarence?'

'The three of us took the girls, you are right. We did not touch them sexually.'

'And you brought them here? To this church?'

'To this church, yes. We let them say their prayers—'

'Oh, I don't think you did,' I said. 'They weren't here to pray. What happened to your acolytes, Father Clarence?'

'This.'

He stepped towards me and touched the wall to his right. At once, I felt myself falling. I landed on my hands and knees on a damp and muddy floor, and, above my head, the trapdoor crashed down into place, leaving me in total darkness.

42

HE NEEDS YOU

I knew I was in the tunnel under the moat. In the church, I must have been standing on the trapdoor itself, and there was clearly some mechanism that opened it. The tunnel wasn't that high, so I pushed the trapdoor from below, but it wouldn't budge. Something was keeping it closed or locked from above. Well, no matter. If I just walked through the tunnel, I'd emerge in the long grass beyond the city wall. I'd seen the girls come out. I could do the same.

The moat was about twelve yards wide, but as I walked through the tunnel, my feet kicked against something soft but unyielding. Feeling with my hands, I realised I'd come across the dead bodies of Father Clarence's acolytes. Why they'd died down here, I didn't know, nor did I care. Avoiding the corpses, I continued walking the length of the tunnel, and at the end of it I came to a wooden door. It was padlocked from the inside. I felt for a key, or for a way of scraping the mud from the edges of the door. Anything to help me escape.

After a lot of fruitless pushing, poking, feeling and

scraping, I sat down on the wet tunnel floor and tried to make myself think clearly. Clarence knew I couldn't get out. But he must also be aware I'd be missed pretty quickly, and Deborah knew exactly where I'd gone. Surely it wouldn't take long for Deborah to raise the alarm, and for Bryce and some of the Myrtilers to open up the trapdoor. I'd just have to wait it out.

I slept a little. Then I slept a lot. Nobody came. No one called through from the church – although I'd returned to that end of the tunnel by now. I heard no footsteps, no voices. Nothing at all. Patience became impatience; then irritation; then fury; and finally panic. I leapt up and thumped my fists into the wooden trapdoor. I ran down the tunnel and thundered my shoulder into the wooden door. I acquired sore fists and a strained shoulder, but neither obstruction gave way. After a long time, exhausted, I lay down and went back to sleep. I couldn't even write in my journal, for there was no light to see by.

When I woke, I knew what I had to do. Clearly nobody was coming to the rescue, and there was no way out at either end of the tunnel. My only option was to breach the sides, which were shored up with planks of wood. On the other side of the planks would be the mud and earth which formed the bed of the moat. How thick would that mud be? How long would it take to make a large enough hole in the wood and then dig my way out through the mud? And would I have time to get out before the water rushed in and I drowned?

I still had my dagger. I chose the far end of the tunnel, right next to the wooden door, as I hoped the water would be shallower here. First, I removed my boots. Then I began to cut a large hole through the wooden planks, taking care to avoid damage to the compacted mud wall. Even so, water found its way through, trickling down the muddy barrier onto my feet. Will it sound odd if I say Karima worked with me? I felt her presence, as I had so often in Egypt, Palestine and Cyprus. Karima's spirit flowed through me now, as it had then. For years, she'd strengthened my sword arm, sharpened my eyesight and fired up my energy. Jonny always knew there was something – he'd just never known what.

I felt it now, coursing through my veins, surging down my right arm, tingling my fingers and making the dagger leap in my hand. How many innocent young girls had been made to walk through here? What black misery had they felt? Knowing they were walking to their doom.

In that pitch-black tunnel of despair, and with every inch of my being, I rejected doom. I worked frantically, like a man possessed. Once I'd torn away enough splintered wood, I began on the mud, starting by gouging out a small hole. The small hole became larger, wider and wetter. Water began to pour in now, puddling around my feet at first, then rushing down the mud wall and surging along the tunnel. Soon it was up to my waist. My efforts grew more frenzied. The dagger twisted, gouged and stabbed. The water reached my neck, and, just for a moment, I thought about my journal, ruined now of course. But I didn't stop working at the hole.

And then the tunnel wall gave way. The hole had reached a critical size, and that portion of the wall could no longer hold. As the water closed over my head, I clawed and kicked my way out. I swam upwards, through reeds and waterweed that tried hard to entangle me, but my dagger slashed and sliced its way through, and I emerged, gasping, at the edge of the moat. I threw myself onto the grassy bank, and for a few moments just lay completely still. I thanked God for delivering me.

But not Karima. I had never thanked Karima for anything. It would be a kind of blasphemy. She is not a Christian. I never asked her religion, but I suspect it's not Islam either. A pagan perhaps? It does not matter. Once again, God had protected me, and I was grateful.

I stumbled to my feet, checked where I was and followed the city wall round to the beautiful bridge. I judged the time to be a couple of hours after midnight, so naturally there was no one in sight. Somehow, I dragged myself across the bridge and over to the church by the eastern city wall. Still drenched and filthy, I thundered down the candle-lit nave in my bare feet, calling Father Clarence's name. There was no sign of the man.

I hunted for the way to open the trapdoor, feeling my way along the wall that the priest had leant against. When it sprang open, it took me by surprise. I knelt down and peered into the tunnel. I could see only darkness, but I clearly heard the sloshing of water. I pulled one of the many candles from its holder and threw it into the tunnel, where it made a small splash, confirming that the tunnel was now unusable. It wasn't yet full; the moat's contents were still pouring into it. I closed the trapdoor, but doubted it was waterproof. It had never needed to be. At some point, the water would find its way into the church itself, and perhaps the floating bodies of the two acolytes would beach themselves in their very own church.

In Patrick's house, I shook the man awake and told him about the tunnel.

'I want that priest found,' I hissed in his ear. 'You should have known what was going on here. Even if you didn't know while you served my father in Hambrig, and then as my own steward, you've been living here, in this corrupt and evil city, for the last eight years, and you *still* didn't know. Rolf Kaufmann played you for a fool, Patrick.'

But I cursed myself as well. I'd left the priest to his own devices for over three weeks. In my haste to convict Patrick, I'd forgotten Bryce's words about the priest. Then there had been a gibbet to build, an evil Livonian to hang, a coronation to attend and the news of the death of the King of England. None of which was sufficient excuse for my forgetfulness.

Patrick was barely awake even now. 'Deborah says she has a list,' he mumbled. 'Names of girls who were stolen. What is this, Rory? What have you done?' He sat up in bed, his hand clutched to his bandaged chest, his eyes unfocussed, his white hair wild.

'You created this city where corruption and evil flourished,' I growled. 'The priest you appointed to your church just tried to kill me. He has worked with your former steward to export Mallrovian girls abroad to be sold as slaves! How do you justify building this place, Patrick?'

Climbing carefully out of bed, his torso still tightly bandaged, Patrick answered me slowly. 'I have told you already. I built this city to cleanse the money my father had made from the slave trade. I made it as beautiful and as elegant as I knew how. I used the money well, paying the best builders and craftsmen, and peopling the city with those who'd been exploited and abused, funding every aspect of their lives myself.

'Since then, I have added to the city's funds out of my own pocket, the wages I earned from my stewardship of Castle Rory, first for your father, and then for yourself. Every penny of those earnings was sent to Rolf Kaufmann, whom I left in charge of my perfect city. You know that I offered to let Kaufmann return to Bremen? He did not want to go back. He promised me he would be a good steward here. He convinced me of his repentance and his remorse. He showed me how efficiently he could make and distribute purchases. Rolf Kaufmann was very impressive, Rory.

'Now I learn that he was exploiting our sheep farmers and smuggling our premium wool out of the country, that he restarted the slave trading, some of which has taken place *even while Deborah and I have lived here*! How did he have the impudence to do this? How could he be sure I would not see what was happening? Yet he was right; I noticed nothing.' Shakily, Patrick pulled on his clothes, and I left him to it.

Downstairs, Deborah was lighting the fires. 'He's a broken man,' she said.

'I know. But I'm afraid that's less important than finding Father Clarence. You know the people here. Find enough strong Myrtilers, Deborah, preferably ones who have lost daughters to Livonia, and get them to hunt down the priest. He's either another one of the damned Swordbrothers, or he's a corrupt and greedy Mallrovian. Whichever he is, he must be arrested and sent, under guard, to Hicrown.'

'Under guard? Rory, we have no garrison here. No

military presence at all. It was part of Patrick's dream for Myrtile that there were no weapons, no violence—'

'No violence! There's been nothing *but* violence in Myrtile. Get a small garrison together, Deborah. Use some of the dirty money I keep hearing about, and get your blacksmiths to make weapons, chains and padlocks. They must work through the night if necessary, so pay them well. Send out search parties and find Clarence. Chain his wrists and ankles, put him in a cart and get your most dangerous and most sinned-against men to drive him to Hicrown. Can you do this?'

'I shall do it, Lord Rory. You can depend on me.' Although she stood up straight and sounded strong, I was looking at a Jewish woman in her seventies, not originally from Mallrovia at all. Yet I was putting the saving of Myrtile entirely in her hands. Patrick was crushed by the uncovering of Rolf Kaufmann's treachery. I couldn't ask anything of him at the moment. The whole burden would have to be carried by this dignified, elderly woman. I looked searchingly at her and she did not flinch.

'I'm going back to Hicrown now,' I told her. 'Take care of Patrick, Deborah. He needs you.'

43

AND SO IT GOES ON

Of course, you'll have realised that my journal had not actually been washed away. If it had been, you wouldn't be reading this now, would you – nor could I even have written it! So how did it survive? Well, it is unaccountably strange. Karima told me today that I must have left the journal behind, and that's why it was lying neatly on my bed in my room in Hicrown, ready for me to find it on my return. I'd gaped at her.

Couldn't be the case, I'd argued. I knew I'd had it with me in Myrtile.

And yet, she pointed out, here it is! In Hicrown! So how could it have got here before me?

There was no possible answer to that, other than, of course, witchcraft, and that's Karima's speciality, isn't it? Feeling an onset of the shivers, I decided to shrug, smile and let it go.

But Karima did not want to let it go. 'I haven't read it, sir, so don't worry. I believe you want it kept private. Don't you?'

'For now,' I said cautiously.

'Ah, yes. But one day it will be read, won't it, sir. You'd like that?'

'I'm more concerned with how it got here before I did, and how it wasn't ruined in the moat. These things seem impossible.'

'And what do you know of "impossible", sir? Is it "impossible" that I am Karima, the desert girl? Is it "impossible" that other men also came to the small Bedouin tent in the desert? That you weren't my only lover? And if I told you I'm related to Joel, would you also think that "impossible"?'

'Joel?'

'Your friend's relative. The man who knows *all* about you, sir.'

'You mean – you mean Joel Rice?' My voice was a hoarse whisper, and my body shook with strange tremors. But Pockthorpe was dead. He couldn't threaten me now.

'Keep your journal safe, sir,' Karima said calmly. 'But always remember: *everyone* has secrets.' The green eyes gleamed, and she swung away from me with a provocative toss of her head and a seductive sway of her hips.

Doctor Bethan wanted permission to return to Hambrig. She'd done everything she could in Hicrown, she said, and no one here needed her services now. But had I heard about Phoebe?

Immediately, I thought the girl must have died. Reinhard had been so callous and violent towards her, perhaps she hadn't survived after all. And Margaret was no longer here to look after her...

'She's disappeared,' Bethan informed me brusquely. 'Nobody can find her. She was making a good recovery, so I wasn't spending as much time with her, and the next time I went to check, she'd gone.'

'She was able to walk by then?'

'She could walk just fine. She was almost fully recovered. I can also tell you that Reinhard, the Livonian, did not abuse her sexually, whatever his boast. But where she is now, I do not know.'

So that was a worry. Phoebe, whatever her shortcomings, was still a Mallrovian princess. For her to be missing was not good. I mustered my Pevarile people again and sent them off to hunt for Phoebe. 'Look for Leo again as well,' I told them. 'But Phoebe's the more important. If you find her you can go home, and with extra pay, too. I'll pay a large bounty for Phoebe's return here, and after that, you're free to go.'

They grinned, saluted, and rode out through the gatehouse, kicking up the dust in their haste. It wasn't until the next day that I realised they'd never find Phoebe. Carl had taken her of course. Slipping out of my grasp when I'd nearly had him on Navisar Road, he'd disappeared. No one saw where he went, and I'd given him little thought, assuming he'd run down to the beach with the other surviving Livonians, and they were all back in Bremen by now.

But something told me Carl had not done that. Doubling back to the palace, he'd lain in wait for the injured Phoebe to be brought in. Waited some more, several days in fact, while Bethan tended to the princess and the slow recovery took place. Where had he hidden himself? I'll probably never know. No matter.

When Bethan's visits became less and less frequent, Carl

knew the girl was well enough. He'd have crept into the palace in the middle of the night, scooped her up, and made his escape. In my mind's eye, I could see exactly what had happened and how he'd done it. What I couldn't understand was *why* he'd done it. He'd married Phoebe in Myrtile in order to gain control of Mallrovia. He must know now that the plan had failed dismally. He would never rule this country. So why go back for Phoebe?

As I chewed it over, eventually I found myself concluding that, however implausibly, Carl actually loved Phoebe, and at that thought, I didn't know whether to laugh or cry. Though we'd been enemies, I'd had a sneaking admiration for Carl von Lutterberg. And he, I knew, had seen something in me, too. Phoebe, though? Half-witted, gormless, childlike in manner, speech and behaviour – surely Carl could do better than that? I shook my head in disbelief.

I checked Queen Lillian was managing, although as yet she had little enough to do. I told her I would write back to Robert Burnell and his royal council in England. Until Edward returned from the Holy Land, these people were ruling the country. Henry might have left them instructions about Mallrovia, and I needed to make sure they were aware we now had a ruling monarch and a stable government.

Then, three days after I'd seen the Queen, Patrick rode into Hicrown.

'Deborah has done as you asked,' he told me in the great hall of the palace. 'Clarence is secured and will be brought to you. She has raised a militia, a veritable army. She had more volunteers than she knew what to do with. She's chosen the best of them, and our blacksmiths, carpenters and craftsmen have made bows, arrows, spears and swords. Deborah has appointed a commander of her militia, a woman named Marieke. Marieke's three daughters were all taken from her in the recent abductions. Marieke is full of hate, but Deborah has schooled her in self-control and iron discipline.' Patrick sighed. 'My wife should have been in charge of Myrtile all along. Not me.'

Despite my previous rants, I tried now to lessen the disgrace. 'Patrick, you are an honest, decent man. You didn't see the wrongdoing because you are above such things. You were ashamed of your father and of his wealth. You did your best to find absolution.'

'I should have known! I should have seen it, and you told me that yourself, Rory!' Patrick, in a rage such as I'd never seen before, screamed out the words. 'I was *blind*. Blind to the destruction of my dream, even as it happened all around me! Rolf, and Clarence and his cronies. How did I not know what they were doing? And don't tell me it's because I'm "an honest, decent man". An honest man would have acknowledged Myrtile was too good to be true. And a decent man would have smelt the indecency of human trafficking a mile off. Yet I did not. I went about my days oblivious to it all. I lived an illusion of light and purity, when, in reality, Myrtile was dark, dirty and polluted.'

'Why are you here, Patrick? Why come to Hicrown?'

'To explain to you. To apologise to you, and to Queen Lillian. To seek forgiveness from God, which, since Myrtile's church is contaminated and foul, I cannot do there. I would pray, if you will allow it, in Hicrown Cathedral.'

So Patrick had his audience with the Queen, and then, in sackcloth and ashes, made his way *on his knees* from the palace to what's left of the cathedral. The Hicrowners lined the Palace Road and watched the slow, painful progress of this seventy-year-old man.

But I could not watch. Instead, I waited for Deborah's prison cart to arrive, and when it did, I saw Father Clarence laid out on a hurdle, his arms and legs spread wide, secured with chains to the hurdle's slats. In front and behind the prison cart, rode two columns of men-at-arms, equipped with shining newly forged swords, and behind *them* marched a phalanx of pikemen and bowmen, all with spanking new armour and weapons.

At the head of this impressive array, rode the new commander. Marieke was probably in her mid-thirties. Below her gleaming new helmet, long blond hair fell onto her shoulders and spread itself over her breasts. She wore a chain mail tunic, belted around her waist, with men's boots on her feet. At her hip hung a bright sword, and on her arm was a shield with a blazon I had never seen before.

Clarence did not receive a fair trial, or, in fact, any trial at all. The gibbet I'd had rapidly constructed for Kaufmann had been dismantled, and brought to Hicrown in the prison cart. Indeed, Clarence's hurdle rested on the thing. It took little time for the gibbet to be reassembled. An hour later Clarence was dangling from it.

'I'm sorry we were so late arriving,' Marieke said to me, watching the spectacle. 'Lady Deborah wanted it done properly. We kept Father Clarence in the strong room at the manor house, and Lady Deborah had the blazon created and the shield decorated with it, while the smiths made the armour and the weaponry, and the carpenters fashioned the longbows. And the arrows, too, of course.'

'Tell me about the blazon.'

'Lady Deborah said Sir Patrick's favourite story from the *Lives of the Saints* was the one about Saint Martin giving half his cloak to a beggar. Sir Patrick is a bit like Saint Martin. He only wanted to do good, and when he'd built the city of Myrtile, he wanted to root out poverty and allow everyone to have what they needed. Exactly like Saint Martin. Our blazon is based on the story. Red for the cloak, and the gold indented bend shows it was rent in two.'

'And the silver trident?'

'Saint Martin was a Roman soldier. The trident symbolises the Roman army.'

'Deborah chose all this herself?'

'I think so, lord.'

'It's a striking blazon, Commander Marieke. And you do it justice.'

She was proud of it, I could see that. And proud to have been chosen to lead the Myrtile Saint Martins, as they are now, apparently, called. The four remaining members of the King's Squad, demoralised and leaderless, mustered in the palace garden. And I immediately put Marieke in charge of the lot of them.

'Sort 'em out,' I told her brusquely. 'Bring these men into your unit and give them your new blazon. When they've integrated well, and when the whole unit is working as one, I'll let you take your Saint Martins home.'

Into my mind came a picture of Jonny, in the lead up to the Battle of Baudry Hill, beating the whole of Hambrig into a force that could defend the castle. I doubted Marieke could do the same, since she, too, hadn't served in anyone's war. But I thought she had vision, drive and leadership. And you can do far worse than that.

I wrote those words a week ago, and – reading them back now – I'm struck by how great the need for those three things is. Our new Queen needs vision, drive and leadership like never before, but shows little sign of any of those qualities.

'I never thought I'd be on the throne!' she wails. 'It was supposed to be Barney, my brother!'

Yes, indeed. I grit my teeth and remind her that Barney died on the cliff at Nightmolben and she is next in line. She should always have been prepared for this possibility.

And then, her hands raised to ward off argument, 'You can't make me marry, Lord Rory. I won't marry any man. I want nothing to do with them. I hate them all.'

Which will not work, since it's her duty to provide an heir to the throne. She is already pregnant, and we must hope for a live birth and a healthy child. But marry she must, and more children must follow. *Legitimate* children, with a Mallrovian father. This is not optional; it is her duty.

Finally, and inevitably, 'Haven't you found my mother yet? I'm sure she's alive, perhaps imprisoned in some horrible place. You *must* find her, Lord Rory!'

I don't tell her that, on Allan's orders, Leo killed Julia. But I also know that when I travelled to Nightmolben, and I saw the broken bodies of my King and his heir on the rocks, there was no sign of Queen Julia. So something is wrong, and Lillian is right: now that all the fighting is done, I must at least search for Queen Julia. But I warn Lillian that, even if her mother is found alive, she, Lillian, will still be Queen.

'But why?' she moans again. 'It shouldn't be me! I won't be any good as Queen!'

And so it goes on.

44

FAC FIAT

As I predicted, Titus and the Pevariles did not find Phoebe. But, hiding in the wilds of the Hambrig Hills, they found Peter, and with him, Leo, who was taken into custody again. Into the gaol went Leo, and it was pointed out to him that the door had been mended and had a secure new lock. There would be no more escapes. Meanwhile, Peter made no attempt to defend his son's actions. Nor did he ask for mercy on Leo's behalf.

Wanting to understand, I visited Leo. The twenty-nine-year-old soldier stood in front of me in chains, and I interrogated him about his march on Hambrig, his treachery against Mallrovia, and the murders he'd committed.

'You've told me you're not Mallrovian,' I said, 'and you do not care who sits on the throne here. But you were appointed to the garrison in Hicrown, and that makes you a defender of this country. You were hired, and *paid*, to defend Mallrovia. You were the commander of the Palace Guard, yet you slaughtered your comrades while they walked, unarmed, to the hall for dinner. You murdered the King, the

Queen and the heir to the throne, again in cold blood, pushing them to their deaths in an act of monumental cowardice. You are now going to explain all this to me, so that I can at least try to understand your motives.'

I would not have offered any other murderer such an opportunity, but Leo was Peter's son, his only child, and the only thing he has left of the woman he loved so much. Peter had told me more about his wife, Gabriella, her father, Leonardo, and their life in Pisa.

I'd discovered that Peter, Gabriella, Leonardo and little Leo had been a family like none I'd ever known, mutual respect being afforded to everyone, whether man or woman, child or adult. A family where love was not only felt, but expressed daily, both in words and in deeds. Where science and mathematics were the obsession of all three adults, resulting in intellectually stimulating conversation at every mealtime. All these things were foreign to me, but, as Peter's Yorkshire voice described the little family he'd once belonged to, I found I could picture it vividly.

I've known Peter since I got back from Crusade. Nine years ago, Peter's skills as codebreaker saved Mallrovia from invasion and conquest by the notorious Swamp-People. Then, a year later, Peter was the *only* person in my household who did not believe me guilty of rape and murder. He organised a defence which he set before King Philip, masterfully presenting incontrovertible evidence to prove I was innocent, without which I would have been found guilty and executed. I owed my life to Peter. And so I offered Leo the opportunity to defend himself, in private, *before* he came to trial.

'I know you won't understand,' Leo told me. 'I did it all for Allan. Allan told me what he wanted, and I had to do it, even if I didn't want to.'

'Because he was your commander? You didn't think to go to the King and tell him what was happening? If a general is corrupt or wicked, his soldiers do not have to obey. It is their duty to let the King or Queen know what is happening. How did you not think of this, Leo?'

'You don't understand, Lord Rory. I did it for Allan, not because he was my commander, but because I loved him. We slept together. But only if I followed his orders—'

Grimly, I interrupted him. 'Let me get this straight, Leo. You murdered my King, Queen and Prince and marched across the country to attack my home, so that your commanding officer would allow you to fuck him. Is that right?'

Disgusted, I nodded to the warden to let me out and lock up again.

In the great hall, I told Peter everything his son had done. I did not hold back, and so this gentle Yorkshireman heard of sodomy, bribery, betrayal, treason and murder.

After a few moments' silence, Peter asked, 'Wilt tha hang him, lord?'

'I will not hang him. But only because he's your son, and you are the man who saved Hambrig by cracking Anthony Merry's code. You are also the only person who believed me innocent of rape and murder eight years ago. You organised a defence which worked, and which saved my life. I have not forgotten those things. But you are not Leo, and it's Leo who murdered Philip, Julia and Barney, fought against me in Hicrown, and marched his men on Hambrig. He'd have taken the castle, had it not been for Titus, Jonny and their brave warriors.'

'I believe Sir Jonny told thee Leo fought well, lord,' Peter said desperately. 'He's brave and he's strong, so I were wonderin'...'

'What were you wondering?'

'We need a commander in Hambrig, lord. An' a garrison to command! Leo could recruit and train soldiers, an' he'd be that good, lord.' Peter stared at me, his round face shining with sweat, spectacles encrusted with it.

'I'm sorry, Peter. I couldn't appoint Leo to that position.'

'He's a good fighter, lord, and his men like him and follow him—'

'That is not the point. Leo switched sides without warning because he saw his lover on the palace steps. That was all it took. One sight of Allan, and your son's heart did a flip – and so did he. Do you think I can take the risk of that happening again? Remember, he murdered King Philip, Queen Julia and Prince Barney out of love for Allan. Allan was evil, but Leo was weak. I'll not have him anywhere near Castle Rory, Peter. I'm sorry.'

'What will happen to him then, lord? He can't stay in gaol for the rest of his life!'

'When I've decided, Peter, I'll let you know.'

'In't it for t' Queen to decide, lord?'

It's unheard of for Peter to question my judgement or push back against my authority. I didn't answer, and he slunk away, ashamed and distressed.

Meanwhile, I'm reunited with my journal, God knows how, and have finally caught up with everything that's happened. Time to take stock, in fact.

So, in no particular order: Patrick has made his confessional statement to Roger Scarning in the cathedral. He has received absolution with various penances, the details of which I have already forgotten.

All knights of the realm have been summoned to Hicrown, and a ceremony is organised for them to pay homage to our new Queen. Naturally, banquets are to be prepared. Lillian wants a tournament. I hate tournaments, but I've agreed to this one in order to bolster her status as Queen and make her feel better about it. This should all have happened at the coronation, but that was a hastily conducted affair, with little of the normal pomp and fancy stuff.

Finally, I've written two letters, which have been sent off with a couple of Marieke's Saint Martins. One is to Robert Burnell, informing him of developments here in Mallrovia, and wishing the Royal Council of England a peaceful and productive time in office. The second letter is to Anno von Sangershausen in Bremen, *Hochmeister* of the Teutonic Knights. Again, I described the events of the past four months, the fate of the Livonian Swordbrothers who'd made their power play here, and a few details of my plans for the future of my country – plans which involve no Teutons, Livonians, Bavarians or Englishmen.

And yes, you may be thinking that these letters should have been written – or at the very least *signed* – by Queen Lillian, but she shows no interest in politics, government or diplomacy. Instead, she's pretty wrapped up in preparations for the Grand Ceremony of Vassalage, which she clearly envisages as an enormous party in her honour.

'Isn't it a party?' Bryce asked, as I grumbled and laid out my grievances after Mass this morning. 'I've never seen it done.'

'You've seen vassals pay homage,' I told him at once.

'Yes, lord. But not a ceremony for the whole country.'

I grunted. I'd never seen that either; it would only be done at a coronation. But I continued writing lists and ticking off completed jobs, while staring angrily at those still waiting to be done. A pity, I thought sourly, that Bryce was the illiterate son of a stonemason. He could have scribbled this down for me instead of asking inane questions. And suddenly I'd had enough of the whole business.

'Get Blue ready,' I cried, startling Bryce out of some reverie.

'Are we going somewhere, lord?'

'That was an order, Bryce. Get my warhorse.'

I rode for a couple of hours, venturing part of the way into the King's Forest, which is actually too dense for riding, but allowed me to disappear from the constant questions, objections and pudding-headed bewilderment. In the back of my mind, I hoped Karima would join me. Making love on the forest floor under the tall, swaying trees would be – would have been – incredible. But no, it didn't happen. Perhaps Karima had gone from my life again. In the Egyptian desert, where I knew her intensely, I'd thought her mine. But she refused to come with me when Jonny and I left Mansurah, and after that, I didn't see her for more than twenty years. I wondered if I'd have to wait another twenty years before I could once again put my hands on her breasts, kiss her arching neck and experience the soft wetness between her legs.

So I waited. I sat on Blue's broad back in the King's Forest, surrounded by oaks and beech trees, and, in my heart, I called to Karima. The same way I'd always done in Mansurah. The way she'd taught me.

Birds sang and the leaves on the trees swished and rustled in the breeze. Blue stood quietly, shifting her weight from side to side every so often. In many ways, I understood Lillian's reluctance. I was in her position right now, making decisions and judgements that would affect the fate of the kingdom. It was the reason I'd come into the forest, the reason I was calling for Karima. The burden was too great.

How had King Philip born it? He'd had advisors of course. Counsellors. And he'd had Baron Giles of Wartsbaye and me. We'd been his tenants-in-chief, his sounding board for new ideas and his refuge when they went wrong. I had none of that, although I could have managed if I'd had Margaret Longsword by my side. I'd hated it when she left Mallrovia, but my life was with Rosa, not with Margaret.

But Lillian would not struggle. The cathedral would have to work with the palace, not against it. The citizens would have to accept their new Queen and make obeisance to her. I would appoint advisors to the Queen, and she would learn to depend on them; probably for everything to begin with, until gradually she became used to the reins of power and took them over herself. These were all things for the future, and there would be plenty of small problems to solve along the way. They would easily be dealt with, now that the kingdom was safe again.

For a few moments I allowed success to wash over me. I, Lord Rory of Hambrig, saved Mallrovia. Not single-handed, for Jonny and Titus helped, and others had also played their part. But it was to me that Pockthorpe, Wymer, Conesford and Mancroft had come, all those months ago, and I'd done it. I'd saved my country from invasion and conquest.

As I sat in my saddle in the middle of the King's Forest, I felt the Darkness finally ebb away. How did I know it was 'finally'? I felt it. That's all I can say. I turned Blue round and walked her back to the road. To my right was the capital city of Mallrovia. To my left, if I rode far enough, was home. I bent down and whispered in Blue's ear, then lightly flicked the reins. Blue began to canter back to Hicrown. We would never be in such mortal peril again. I would make sure of that. *Fac Fiat*.

EPILOGUE

It's important to look the part, even if you don't feel it. My clothes have been washed for the occasion, and I will be wearing my surcoat with our family's red-and-gold blazon across the chest. It's a proud blazon, created by my great-grandfather when he was made Lord of Hambrig in the Year of our Lord 1160, over a hundred years ago.

'What does it actually mean, Lord Rory?' Bryce asks. He's helping me dress, a practice run. He's already polished my sword, and now he's buffing up my shield, which of course shows exactly the same design as my surcoat. For some reason, Bryce has chosen this particular inauspicious moment to ask me to explain it to him.

'It's the arms of my family,' I say shortly. I'm not looking forward to the ceremony, and I've always hated wearing the surcoat. Not that I have to wear any of it yet. It will travel with me to Hicrown, and next week we shall all be resplendent in our colourful symbolic garb. 'It's symbolic,' I add, that word having just occurred to me.

'Symbolic of what, lord?'

If there's one thing I've learnt about Bryce, it's that he's tenacious. He keeps at it until either it buckles under the pressure, or he understands it enough to let go.

'My great-grandfather was made Lord of Hambrig when he built this castle.' I am the one to buckle this time. 'It was after the Great Flood. You know about that?'

'A little,' Bryce says cautiously. 'Was that when the Nahvitch ran away?'

'The Toosanik, not the Nahvitch. And not even, really, the Toosanik...' My mind drifts off into thoughts about the people we'd thought were a tribe of Celts who lived, at one time, on the other side of the River Hurogol, but who eventually settled on the Great Plain here in Hambrig. We'd called them the Swamp-People, which was an insult. My attention wanders again, remembering Joy, who was a Toosanik servant, but also Kit's mother, and so I think about Kit, now living in Heidelberg, of all places.

But Bryce has been speaking, and I didn't hear a word of it. 'What did you say, Bryce?'

'I'm really sorry, lord.' He sounds worried, which increases my irritation. 'It's just that there's a great big hole in your surcoat. I'll have to get it mended for you.'

'I have to leave in half an hour. There isn't time for mending. Let's just leave the horrible thing behind.'

He looks shocked. 'Can I – can I fetch someone, please, lord?'

'Oh, for God's sake.' No longer irritated, I'm furious. I should never have appointed Inka Kaufmann as my steward. She's a woman! Which doesn't matter at all most of the time, but it's now that I need a good steward, who knows what he's doing, to help me prepare for this grand event, and Inka bloody Kaufmann can't help me dress, can she? I mean, it's obvious, isn't it?

It wasn't obvious to her, though. 'Why not, lord?' she

asked last week, standing about three inches in front of me, her neck craned back, her bosom actually, *physically*, in contact with my stomach.

I recoiled. 'Because you're a woman.'

'A *married* woman,' she said, as if that changed everything.

'Yes, for about five minutes,' I bit back at her, which was grossly unchivalrous. Kaufmann had, in fact, been married for precisely two weeks before Rolf had gone to sea and ended up captured by Patrick. And I couldn't say any of that, because Inka still doesn't know anything about Rolf's fate. Nor will she, as I've made up my mind not to tell her, and I've sworn Bryce to secrecy as well.

The woman was unfazed by my sarcasm, though, maintaining that at her age it hardly mattered, and why was I so concerned? This, of course, is the other problem: Inka has no idea how she should speak to a Mallrovian lord.

Now, though, I'm wondering how she'd have coped today. Would she have discovered this 'great big hole' at the last moment? Or would it, as in Patrick's day, have been found, repaired and made presentable long ago, so I wouldn't even have known about it?

Bryce scampers away before I can shout at him again, so now, only half-dressed, I'm forced to wait in this freezing cold chamber until he comes back with whoever he feels can cope better with my mood. My best breeches are folded on top of the cupboard, and the offending surcoat lies on the bed. Bryce will have gone to seek help from Rosa, of course.

But the woman who enters is not Rosa. When Bryce opens the door, it's Inka Kaufmann who steps inside my chamber, and I snatch up the surcoat from the bed to cover my lower half. This is the wrong thing to do, because Bryce wants to show Inka the hole in the garment, and she, without a word to me, simply pulls it away, spots the hole at once, and confronts me.

'I shall have this ready for you in shortish time. I will do my damnedest best work, so you will have no complaining.' And off she goes with the surcoat.

Bryce grins at me, but I am not in the mood for humour.

'Get my wife,' I snap at him, and his grin disappears immediately. As does he.

Alone again, I pull on my hunting breeches, leaving the clean, best pair folded on the chest. When Rosa enters, I'm more or less dressed. There's no sign of Bryce, and I guess Rosa has told him to stay out of the room.

'I need help,' I say.

Rosa is gentle. She neither hurries nor chastises me. Together, we put the ceremonial clothing into a drawstring bag, and collect up sword, dagger and shield. I explain about the surcoat, and Rosa merely nods. My wife does the folding, collecting and packing.

'Are you ready for the journey, lady?' I say at last.

'Yes, lord, I am ready. And now, so are you. I will go and get your surcoat from Inka.'

'She won't have done it yet. She's only just taken it! You didn't see the size of the hole! You don't understand—'

'Hush now,' Rosa says calmly. 'Inka will have it ready before we have to leave.'

I say nothing. Rosa can't possibly know that Kaufmann will get the job done in time. I try to breathe slowly, something Stephen once taught me to do. And it helps a lot.

Rosa sits on the bed and pulls me down next to her. 'It will be all right,' she says softly.

'What about the children?'

'They are with Jenny.'

'And with Geoffrey, I suppose? I don't like it, Rosa.'

'It is good for all of them,' Rosa says. Her compassion always takes me by surprise, but it shouldn't. When I remember how she was with poor Guido, I realise that my wife has a soft spot for all the underdogs of this world. The losers, I suppose. But, though I'm still a bit shaky, I'm not a loser, and I won't be one of Rosa's projects.

'No,' I say firmly. 'I won't have my children living with that imbecile. Find somewhere else for them.'

'If that is your wish, lord,' Rosa says compliantly.

Hicrown is colourful and vibrant. Flags fly from every pillar, rooftop and shop front awning. People are wearing their best outfits, and the bells are pealing out from Hicrown Cathedral. The city is stuffed with people! They have come from all over Mallrovia, since every knight must bow the knee and pay homage, but there are even barons, earls and knights and their ladies from England, Wales, France and the Low Countries. There is no representation from Bavaria, but then, you wouldn't expect that.

The Earls of Surrey, Warwick, Oxford, Hereford, Pembroke and Lincoln have returned, but with their wives and retinues this time. Gaudy pavilions have been set up on the Cathedral Green, and in God's Acre behind Wharf Street, which is – or was – the contested land for the paying of taxes. That quarrel seems to have gone away in this new excitement, thank goodness.

I wrote to invite Jonny, but he declined to attend. I also invited Margaret Longsword, who is here, of course, with her husband. Though I long to see her, I'm very aware of

Rosa's presence. I'd thought this would be an unwelcome restriction, certainly as far as being with Margaret was concerned, but I actually find it liberating. With Rosa here, I don't have to prove myself, either in bed or in battle. With Rosa here, I breathe more easily and deal with problems more calmly.

But even Rosa can't protect me against Karima.

Karima is the reason I wanted Jonny to come. How many times, all those years ago in *our house*, did he ask what I did? How many times did he guess I was meeting someone, but I told him nothing? How many times did I deceive him and lie to him? And does he know? Does he know, also, about Joel Rice, supposedly Jonny's relative? Jonny never once mentioned a relative on Crusade with us. These questions, the unknown answers, the memories of that time are the legacy of Mansurah. Karima is my fate, but it's too late now; I should have accepted her offer in the desert. I have to tell Jonny about Karima. But how can I, when he has refused to come?

And now it's time. Rosa helps me dress in my ceremonial outfit, declaring that I look commanding, strong and handsome. I thank her for the compliments, knowing she's trying her best. Arm in arm, we walk to the cathedral, ahead of the golden coach in which rides our new monarch.

The cathedral is thronged with people, although these are the nobility only. I spot Margaret Longsword across the nave and I give her a quick smile. Seeing Rosa, she lowers her eyes. As tenant-in-chief, and the only one, I have a place of honour at the front of the cathedral, and I lead Rosa there. The English and the other foreigners are at the back, although Margaret isn't with them. I wonder why.

The bishop steps in front of the altar. Roger Scarning has a solemn duty to perform today, and oddly, it's the third time he's done it in the space of a year. He should be well versed in the procedure, I think grimly. The first occasion was a farce, quickly and necessarily overturned ten days later. The second was genuine, but secretive and hasty. That reign lasted four months. This reign, however, must be both real and lasting. After all, monarchs are crowned in the sight of God. And yet – there will be no actual crowning today. Today we shall witness, and be part of, a religious ceremony of huge significance. But the crowning itself – well, that is years away.

And so the Queen takes her place beside the bishop, the babe in her arms. Everyone expects the baby to cry, but he doesn't. He is perfectly behaved for the occasion. And now the silent cathedral hears the Queen declare that she will be faithful and bear allegiance to King Harold III of Mallrovia. She will faithfully execute the office of regent and govern according to law. She will promote the welfare of King Harold's people, and she will be obedient to God and the Church.

Scarning draws a cross on the child's forehead, and blesses him. Then he blesses the Queen Regent, and commends both of them to us, and one by one we file up to the altar and pay homage to King Harold, swearing our oaths of allegiance in the time-honoured way.

Harold was King from the moment his mother died while delivering him on 13th March this year. From the moment of his birth he was my King. Now his grandmother has been proclaimed regent, and the Kingdom of Mallrovia is in her hands.

But was it always? I think back to Philip's reign. Philip always had some new project, something to excite him. He was a great warrior king and a good ambassador for our country. But he was not good at domestic affairs, here in his own land. Had Julia, behind the scenes, been running the country all along?

'Not really,' she says, wearily.

We're in the palace solar. I've described this great suite of royal quarters before, and it even includes Karima's so-called 'boudoir', which is now to be a room for Baby Harold and his nurse. The baby sleeps peacefully on, but I have to get the truth from Julia, and it is not the same as Allan's account.

In Nightmolben, Julia saw her husband and son pushed over the cliff to their deaths. Fearful and frantic, she ran into the forest, chased by two of the Palace Guard. Desperation gave her mind the acuity it needed to outwit her pursuers. She knew she couldn't outrun them, but she also knew the forest's reputation for being haunted. More importantly, she knew the Mallrovians chasing her would be well aware of it too. Hiding behind a tree, Julia howled and shrieked in a ghostly, unearthly tone. Far from giving her position away, the eerie sounds made the soldiers run in the opposite direction. She picked up two stones and threw one as far as she could in one direction. As the soldiers shivered and huddled together in fright, she threw the other stone in the opposite direction. Then she watched as they ran, terrified, out of the forest. I imagine they told Captain Leo that the missing queen was nowhere to be found.

'But why didn't you come back to Hicrown after Leo left?' I ask.

'Rory, I could not move. The soldiers ran away and I waited and waited. I had no idea how long they would stay in Nightmolben. I stayed exactly where I was, wide awake and petrified, for a night and a day. Then, when I tried to move, my limbs would not work. I could not even stand, let alone walk. I couldn't bear the thought of walking past the place where my husband and my son had been murdered, but even if I'd found the courage to do so, my body would not let me. So I lay on the ground in the forest and gave myself up to death.'

Two days later, Julia was found by a farmer who lived a few miles north of Nightmolben. She was lucky; even in normal times, hardly anyone enters Nightmolben Forest. After the landslide, who would go there? There was no reason for anyone to go into the ruined woodland, where trees had been uprooted and everything was dark, dismal and doomed. But, for whatever reason, the farmer went into the forest, and it was Julia's further good fortune that he heard her moans of despair. He took her to his farmhouse, but he didn't know she was his queen.

'I couldn't speak at all,' Julia says. 'He asked who I was, why I was in the forest, was I hurt, what had happened, so many, many questions. But I could say nothing at all. My mind was blank. I could not remember who I was, nor what had happened, nor why I'd been hiding. All these things returned to me gradually, but it took a long, long time.'

'Did the farmer have a wife or a family?'

'No, it was just him.'

Every day Julia lay on a rough straw mattress on the farmhouse floor, while the farmer tried to coax her to eat and drink a little. The rustic care she received did more for her than all the expensive physicians in Hicrown could have done, but it took many months. In fact, Julia was in the farmhouse for just over two years, receiving care from the lonely farmer, a man named Nathan.

Eventually, Julia remembered her own identity. But she still couldn't come to terms with the death of her son. Philip's death was hard enough to bear, but Barney's was too much, and for a long, long time she could not speak. Like mother, like daughter, I think. Violence, abuse and grief sending them both into a silent world.

I have one last question. 'I'm sorry to have to ask you this, Julia – but do you know who the guardsmen were? The ones who followed you into the forest?'

'Why does that matter? You told me the Palace Guard are all dead, anyway!'

I hear her voice rising in pitch, the hysteria not far away, and I call softly for Rosa. She's just outside the door, waiting to see if I need her. This is how we planned it. I'd thought Julia might not speak if Rosa were there, but now I need her help. Rosa comes in and hurries to Julia's side. Tears are streaming down the older woman's face.

I get up and walk to the window. The Darkness. Julia is in the throes of it, and I know the suffocation of it far too well. Julia asked why my question mattered, and the truth is, I don't even know why I asked it. I think I want to know more about the Palace Guard's behaviour. Leo murdered them all, and I know it was because of Julia, yet Julia was chased into the forest two years before the Guard met their deaths. That puzzles me.

I turn back and I see Rosa rocking Julia in her arms. She motions to me to come over.

'Do not distance yourself from grief, lord,' Rosa

admonishes me. 'Grief for a son. This is something you know well.'

I am knocked sideways by this remark and the perception it shows. Grief for a son. Yes, Julia and I have both outlived our first-born sons. And Julia has also lost her daughters, Lillian and Phoebe. What is left for her now?

I'm home. Finally, I'm back in my own castle. I've written down everything that has happened in the official Hambrig record book. Most of it is fact, but a little is conjecture. Since hearing Julia's testimony, I've spoken again to Leo, and I now know why Leo murdered the entire Palace Guard.

The men he sent to find Julia in the forest came out again with a story that they'd killed her. Leo was satisfied, and so was Allan when Leo reported back. But it gradually emerged that Julia had not been killed after all, and that her pursuers had left her somewhere in Nightmolben Forest. Word got around among the Guard, and Leo was terrified Allan would find out he'd failed to get rid of the Queen. Leo's instructions had been to dispose of all three of them: King, Queen and Prince. Allan must never find out that his fawning admirer had failed, so the entire Guard had to die. Leo's love for Allan knew no bounds, it seems.

It's Rosa's opinion that Julia will make a good regent for her grandson, who will never know either of his parents. I agree. Gone is the haughty, patronising woman she once was.

Having lived the life of a peasant for two years, Julia will now understand what ordinary people go through. She will bring Harold up to be a good king. I find I have faith in Julia, and this faith is confirmed and bolstered when I receive a letter from her, three weeks after the ceremony in Hicrown Cathedral.

Lord Rory,

Thank you for your wise counsel when you spoke to me here in Hicrown. Everything has been very hard recently, but I know now there is a future – and that future is Harry.

But Harry would have no kingdom to rule had it not been for you. You saved Mallrovia from invasion by the Bavarians and by the Livonians. You placated the English king too. Your diplomatic and fighting skills have saved our nation again and again, and we all owe you a great debt. I should be delighted if you will continue to be King Harold's tenant-in-chief, and act also as my advisor whenever I need the advice of an experienced man. I don't doubt this will be more often than not!

I mourn the loss of Barney, Lillian, Phoebe and Philip every day. But they must live on in Harry.

I have taken some important decisions already. To protect the kingdom, I have appointed Marieke of Myrtile as commander-in-chief here in Hicrown. I have stood the King's Squad down and disbanded it. Loyal soldiers are now in the Palace Guard, and the elite troops will join the Saint Martins, who will now be housed and trained at the palace. Sir Patrick is taking his beautiful city apart, stone by stone. There is no future for the Saint Martins there.

I have surrounded myself with loyal men and women, with faithful servants, and with a stalwart army of well-trained troops. I am appalled at the corruption which was allowed to grow unchecked, both here in Hicrown and also in Myrtile. The smuggling of our best wool, the stealing of our young women and the murder of innocent people will be things of the past from now on. Thanks to you, and to those who gave their lives for our country, we are now able to move forward as a sovereign state, with integrity and honour.

Please convey my thanks to your beautiful and gentle wife for comforting me in my time of need. I will never forget the help she gave me that day.

Julia, Queen Regent to King Harold III.

Stone by stone. Patrick cannot abide the thought of his city of turquoise and gold remaining standing, now that his vision of protection, tranquillity and healing has turned to dust. Everything, he tells me, will be destroyed. Only not quite everything, because I asked him for the rug I'd admired so much, the one which reminded me of my stay in the house of Shajar al-Durr in Mansurah. I want to give that rug to Joan. Patrick agreed, and the rug will be brought to Hambrig.

The rest of it has been, or is being, sold. An enormous quantity of gold, precious tapestries, valuable ornaments and those striking turquoise roofs. Everything will be sold, and the vast sum of money raised is to be donated by Patrick to fund the repairs to Hicrown Cathedral and the rebuilding of St Michael's Church. Father Wymer is delighted, of course, and he'll resume his post at St Michael's once the building is finished. Minus his curate.

Conesford, the cathedral cantor, will no doubt sing praises to God for it all, although really he should be praising Patrick. The funding of such major works is a grand gesture, but one Patrick is determined to make.

'My atonement,' he tells me, his voice devoid of emotion.

For now, I'm happy to continue as King Harold's tenant-in-chief, but there should be two of us. When I was in Hicrown, Julia made it clear she didn't think Amie a suitable person for that role, and so I told Amie to come back to Castle Rory. Well over a year ago, Inka Kaufmann complained at the lack of music. My journal from July last year confirms the conversation we had, although I took little notice at the time. Now Amie's back, and we have singing and music at our hearth again, so I hope Inka's delighted. Amie has regained her true place in life. She is a servant again, but a well-regarded and highly talented one. She is comfortable in this role.

Young Davy is here too, a playmate for my son. His nurse, Rosalind, has joined my household as well. So who's in charge at Wartsbaye? For now, it's Titus, who has orders to rebuild the garrison and make it strong again. We do urgently need a second tenant-in-chief, though. I shall give Julia a little longer, but I will have to raise the matter again with her soon. She mentioned 'those who gave their lives for our country', and one of those was Gael, who would, by now, be Baron Gael of Wartsbaye, if he hadn't forfeited his young life fighting the Livonians. And what *of* the Livonians? Carl is out there somewhere. Carl and Princess Phoebe. Where have they gone, and what are they doing?

The horn blows for supper. Slowly, I descend the south-west tower and make my way across the courtyard. In the great hall, Rosa sits at the high table. My children are still too young to join us here. One day, though. One day, Baby Rory and little Maya will sit between Rosa and me, and we shall look out from the dais at the people who make up my household, which will, eventually, be Baby Rory's household. I shiver at the thought. My son will succeed me when I die. He will be Lord of Hambrig. He'd better be a good one, I think fiercely, and for some reason my eyes have filled with tears.

'Do not worry about anything,' says Karima softly. 'You must know I will look after it all.'

'Even after my death?'

'Especially after your death. Have you forgotten what I told you in Mansurah?'

'Tell me again.'

'Only if you make love to me. Rosa can't have you all to herself, you know. That wouldn't be fair.'

'And afterwards? You'll remind me what you said in Mansurah?'

'I promise you I will.'

Four months later, a letter arrives from Jonny. On my instructions, he organised the envoy to go to the pope with a letter signed by me, as tenant-in-chief to King Harold, and by Julia, the Queen Regent. The pope is informed that Mallrovia is now a stable sovereign state again, and that Hicrown Cathedral is being rebuilt – bigger and better than before. The pope is pleased, apparently, and there is no more talk of excommunication. The letter tells me all this, but nothing more. I have written back to ask Jonny how things were in Salisbury. Whether he found out more about his father's death. I also asked if he had any idea who Joel Rice was, and how this man, Jonny's relative and Master Pockthorpe's uncle, could possibly have been in Mansurah. If, indeed, he was. So far, Jonny has not written again, so I have no answers to these questions.

While I'm still thinking about Jonny's letter, I get the

message that Rosa is asking for me. This is a worry, since she normally comes to my library when she wants a word. If I must now descend the tower to talk to her, then something must be wrong.

'There is no doubt, lord,' Rosa says, as we stand in the chilly courtyard. 'I am pregnant. We are going to have another child.'

My heart sinks, knowing that *The Empress* is still missing, and that Rosa, as always, will pin her hopes on this little scrap of parchment. There's no Kit, no Aggie and no *Empress*, so Rosa will of course predict nothing but disaster. Or so I assume. But while Jenny wrings her hands in despair, Rosa strolls down to the *Egg* and spends a long time talking to Joan, after which the two of them walk arm in arm up the bailey, and Joan calmly informs me that Rosa will be staying with her in the *Egg* until the baby is born.

'I have no objection to that,' I tell Joan pompously, catching her expression which tells me that any objection I might have had would have been ignored by both women anyway. Neither Joan nor Rosa was asking my permission; they were merely informing me of the arrangements.

But Jenny hovers on the edge of my vision. 'Lord Rory, we must hunt everywhere for *The Empress*! We must search again!'

I tell her sternly that we did exactly that two years ago, and nothing was found. It's highly unlikely the little parchment square will turn up now.

'Then what shall we do, lord?' The poor woman is distraught.

'We shall trust in God,' I say heavily. 'And in Joan, too. Jenny, women all over the world give birth successfully without a ridiculous picture of a pregnant woman secreted under their pillows for nine months. Lady Rosa will do so too.' And I hope and pray I'm right.

Meanwhile, Inka is quite definitely finding her feet. She mended the hole in my surcoat so well it can hardly be seen, and so quickly I was able to use it at the ceremony. Now, my entire household delights in telling her she's become the 'damnedest best steward' we've ever had!

Thank you for reading
***The City of Turquoise and Gold*,**
Book Eight in *Tales of Castle Rory*,
An Epic Medieval Fantasy Saga
Of
Love, Legacy and Heroic Sacrifice!

Did you enjoy *The City of Turquoise and Gold*?
Please leave a review and let everyone know!

You'll find all the books in the series at
https://mybook.to/TalesOfCastleRory

Want to know what happened to Rory before he became Lord of Hambrig?

Rory and Jonny, barely out of their teens, join King Louis IX of France on Crusade.

This Crusade is a disaster for the Christians, but it forges a tremendous and lasting friendship between Jonny and Rory, who go to war as boys and return as men.

Read about their adventures in Egypt, the women they fell in love with and their miraculous escapes from the Saracens!

This story is told in
Mansurah: Jonny's Tale,
a free ebook only available to members of The Household!

Joining is free and also gives you access to fortnightly newsletters with behind the scenes action, giveaways, backstories, fun competitions and much more!

Go to www.talesofcastlerory.co.uk
to find out more about The Household and get your free copy of
Mansurah: Jonny's Tale

Go to www.talesofcastlerory.co.uk to find out more about
Tales of Castle Rory

AUTHOR'S NOTE

***The City of Turquoise and Gold* is Epic Medieval Fantasy. But how much is Medieval? And how much is Fantasy?**

Lord Rory's latest journal chronicles the events of the summer and autumn of 1272, the year of the famous Norwich Riots.

Civil unrest broke out between the monks of the Cathedral and the people who lived in the City of Norwich. I decided to use and adapt this event in my story.

The area near Norwich Cathedral is called Tombland, and the Norwich citizens who paid taxes were incensed that people living in Tombland didn't need to do so, on account of it being cathedral land. Their grievances festered for twenty years.

The trigger-point for the real-life full-scale rioting occurred when the citizens put up a quintain, a target for lance practice on Tombland, the location deliberately chosen to annoy the monks. By August, a state of siege had been reached, and the cathedral was closed down. The citizens' actions caused serious damage to the cathedral, and they also burnt down St Ethelbert's church. Eventually, King Henry arrived to take control, and excommunication by the pope was threatened.

In *The City of Turquoise and Gold*, I've made use of the Norwich riots. Had you spotted that the capital city of Mallrovia – Hicrown – is actually Norwich? In fact, the two names are anagrams of each other.

So I decided we would have riots in Hicrown too, more or less mirroring what happened in Norwich in the same year. I renamed Tombland, calling it God's Acre, but kept almost all the details the same.

Roger Scarning was actually the Bishop of Norwich from 1266 to 1278, although I've had to invent his appearance and his character. The other clergymen are my own creations: Father Wymer, Master Pockthorpe, Master Conesford and Master Mancroft. However, if you're familiar with Norwich, and especially medieval Norwich, you'll recognise their names: Mancroft is an area west of Norwich Castle, and now houses Norwich's famous covered market. Conesford was the south-east part of the city. Pockthorpe was a small settlement to the east, close by the city wall, and Wymer was also in the east. My fictitious city of Hicrown has no areas with those names, so my clerics have used them instead.

Of these four, only Father Wymer and Master Conesford survive. Mancroft has his throat cut by Captain Leo, and

Pockthorpe succumbs to disease. Although not much was known of diabetes in the Middle Ages, the bishop at least knew that he needed to give Pockthorpe bread when the man started shaking. Unfortunately, nobody cared enough to do this during the riots, and Pockthorpe's diabetes killed him.

St Michael's church in Hicrown has taken the place of St Ethelbert's church in Norwich, but the burning down is the same in each, and they occupied roughly the same part of each city. When St Michael's is rebuilt, using the money from the sale of the wrecked city of Myrtile, Father Wymer will take up his position there again. As for Conesford, no doubt he will resume his role as cantor in the newly-rebuilt cathedral.

Early on, I decided to tie the Norwich Riots to my previous story involving the Livonian Swordbrothers and their bid for separation from the Teutonic Knights. As explained in a previous Author's Note, the von Lutterberg family existed, and Otto von Lutterberg did indeed die at the Battle of Karuse. I've given him three brothers, two of whom vie for control of Mallrovia by each marrying one of the princesses. I also gave the brothers a fictional father, Sascha von Lutterberg, and had him involved in the slave trade from Myrtile.

I wanted to build a credible story for the Livonians' takeover of Mallrovia, for which a substantial amount of money would be needed. Slavery was extremely lucrative, and the worsted smuggling was another way to add to the war chest. As Livonia was outside the Hanseatic League at the time, the imposition of tariffs would have been a problem, and – then as now – unscrupulous people try to make a profit out of everyone else.

This linking up of the slave trade, the wool smuggling and the Norwich Riots allowed me to give Sir Patrick a difficult time. In Books 1 and 2 of my series, Sir Patrick of Myrtile has been more upright and honourable than anyone else. He is honest and dignified, the soul of discretion and the epitome of decency. He is courteous to everyone and appears to have no flaws (other than that of being perfect!)

So I gave him an evil father who profited from selling young virgin girls into prostitution abroad. So now, of course, it's obvious *why* Patrick is so squeaky clean. He found out about his father when he was seventeen. He discovered the riches his father had accumulated from the illegal wool trade and the people trafficking. Patrick, shocked and horrified, set about building the purest, loveliest place on earth. It was supposed to atone for his father's sins. It was supposed to turn 'dirty money' into fresh, wholesome virtue. When Myrtile turned out to be more contaminated and deadly than anything that preceded it, Patrick found genuine atonement only in dismantling the whole thing, 'stone by stone', as Queen Regent Julia poignantly puts it.

Master Peter the alchemist has been a long-time resident of the Castle Rory household, and has appeared in almost all the *Tales* so far. Yet, as Lord Rory notes with astonishment, there has never been any mention of a wife or son. Readers may wonder why I have suddenly introduced a family for Peter. The truth is, I have had enormous fun crafting backstories for many of my characters and writing them up as short stories. At some point, there will be a published collection of these. One of the short stories is called *Master Peter's Christmas*. It was made available in digital form to subscribers to my newsletter last year. Anyone who hasn't read it but would like to just needs to get in touch via my website, and I'll send you a link to the story, in which Peter, a young and destitute mathematician from Yorkshire, meets the love of his life.

Margaret Longsword, normally called Margaret Longespée in the history books, is an historical person, as is her grandfather, who really did die at Mansurah. Margaret, married in childhood to Henry de Lacy, was the fourth Countess of Salisbury.

I've kept to the known dates of the births and deaths of every historical person in these *Tales*, and therefore their ages are accurate too.

The Battle of Mansurah – the city is now called Al-Mansoura – took place in 1250 and was a bloodbath of the

Crusaders. Baibars, the Saracen leader, set a clever trap, which no one in the Crusader command foresaw. Most of the Crusaders died, without even having the chance to fight back.

This story is told in my free prequel, *Mansurah: Jonny's Tale*, which is written from Jonny's point of view and makes no mention of Karima, since he knew nothing about her until many years later. But it's a murky bit of Rory's past, and one he doesn't want to talk about. Incidentally, when I wrote *Mansurah: Jonny's Tale*, I had no idea the events of that time would inform Rory's and Jonny's behaviour all these years later. But the more I think about it, and the more I research PTSD in modern-day service men and women, the more I realise the Crusaders would never forget their experiences. Jonny and Rory will never be free of 'survivor's guilt'.

Wenno von Rohrbach and Walther von Nortecken led the Livonian Swordbrothers during different periods in their history, and Anno von Sangershausen was Grand Master of the Teutonic Knights. Von Nortecken actually survived until 1273, but in *The City of Turquoise and Gold* he dies at the burning barricade in Hicrown. I apologise to any von Nortecken fans that I've cut his life short by a year!

While it's true that the Livonians were incorporated into the Teutonic Knights, losing the name "Swordbrothers" and becoming the "Livonian Order" instead, there's no record of them trying to break free from the Teutons. Which doesn't mean some of them didn't want to. There's a parallel between the subsuming of the Swordbrothers into the larger and more powerful organisation of the Teutonic Knights, and the (potential) subsuming of Mallrovia into a larger and more powerful country. The Livonians don't appreciate the comparison, but Rory is completely alive to it.

Rolf and Inka Kaufmann are my own invention, and I've used them to bridge the gap between the Livonians, Sir Patrick of Myrtile and Lord Rory of Hambrig. In my opinion, Rory's decision to let Inka remain in ignorance of her husband's life and death was uncharacteristically sensitive of him! But undoubtedly the right thing to do.

A note about the name of William's new ship: *Yakuza*. William's previous ship was the *Senjo*, a Japanese word meaning "battlefield". Elsewhere, I've explained why William chooses Japanese words for his ships (and embraces their philosophy, too, although he's never actually admitted to this). "Yakuza" means a warrior. It stands for strength and aggression. My source for this is the *Book of Five Rings*, written in 1645 by Miyamoto Musashi. William decorates his ships with a proud dragon figurehead, painting the dragon red, blue and yellow. These are the colours of the three pivotal warriors in the Senjo: Hatamoto (mind), Yakuza (body) and Yamabushi (spirit). It's a complex diagram, which you can see here and here if you want to know more.

The problem, of course, is that Musashi was born three hundred years after the events in Lord Rory's journals.

William could not have known of the Samurai Creed or the Senjo Battlefield Strategy. So perhaps William's moral code and conduct foreshadowed these things in some way, or perhaps his Japanese friend had more insight than we now know of. Either way, I thought I should make it clear I'm well aware of the discrepancy in the dates!

I've kept Henry III of England much as he's reputed to have been: intensely pious, but a weak king, and unable to keep order in his own country. Both the first and the second Barons' Wars were fought against him because of his inability to make sound decisions and keep control. King Edward I, who succeeds him, will be a different matter entirely, but that's another story, as they say.

R. Marsden, August 2025

ACKNOWLEDGMENTS

I'm grateful as always to my family and friends for their encouragement and support.

In particular, I'd like to mention Will, my son-in-law, who has been a tremendous source of good ideas in so many ways. I very much value the friendship I have with Will.

Readers of *Tales of Castle Rory* will know that I have written and published the series in honour of my mum, Joan Marsden. And so she must be mentioned in the acknowledgments to every book I write. Joan was an inspirational person, and I miss her terribly.

I'm very grateful to Sharon Rutland, my editor, and to Peter O'Connor who designs all my book covers. They both do a magnificent job, and I'm always happy to leave these aspects of my books in their capable hands.

Many grateful thanks also to Ian Ward, whose maps have guided my thinking on how long it takes to get from A to B and what obstacles might lie in the way. Ian works from the extremely rough sketches I send him, and somehow produces amazing drawings, floor plans and three-dimensional maps from my unpromising efforts.

My children, Kit and Kerry, are fantastic supporters, and, as always, I thank them both.

Thanks also to Debbie and Stephanie for keeping in touch and being so interested in these *Tales.* Their encouragement makes the world of difference to me.

Finally, I must mention my friend, Patrick. In *The City of*

Turquoise and Gold, Patrick takes a lead role, and, for the first time, is found wanting. I must point out that in real life, Patrick is every bit as decent, honourable and generous as his namesake, but without the moral blindness that caused all the trouble in Myrtile!

Printed in Dunstable, United Kingdom

66703631R00275